THE SI

ANDREY BELY (pseudonym of Boris _____ w in 1880, son of a world-famous mathematician. He entered literature in 1902 with the publication of his experimental prose work *Second (Dramatic) Symphony*. During the next six years he published three further prose *Symphonies*, in which he continued the attempt to apply principles of musical composition to prose fiction. *The Silver Dove*, his first novel, was written and published in 1909. It was followed by the work for which he is best known, the novel *Petersburg* (published 1913–14), in which he took up and transformed the myth of that city as it had developed through the nineteenth century. He wrote five further novels, including the quasi-autobiographical *Kotik Letaev* (published 1917–18), which records the earliest childhood recollections as the recapitulation of ancient myths. His last novel, *Masks* (1932), takes to their ultimate development the linguistic innovations that had first appeared in his early fiction, and for which he has sometimes been compared with James Joyce.

Bely spent most of his life in Moscow. In 1910–11 he travelled to Italy, North Africa and the Holy Land with Asya Turgeneva, his first wife. In 1912 they joined the travelling entourage of Rudolf Steiner, and in 1914 settled at the anthroposophical colony he was establishing in Dornach, near Basel. In 1916 Bely was recalled to Russia for military service, though never called up. He experienced the period of revolution and civil war mainly in Moscow. Like his friend and rival Aleksandr Blok, he at first perceived the October Revolution as the realization of the Symbolists' hopes for spiritual liberation and the total renewal of culture, but soon understood that the Bolsheviks had merely replaced one form of coercive power with a worse one. After Blok's death in 1921 he sought and received permission to leave the country. But his relations with Asya Turgeneva, who had stayed in Switzerland, were not restored, and he spent two unhappy years in Berlin. Returning to Russia in 1923, he married another fellow anthroposophist, Klavdia Vasilyeva. He lived in straitened circumstances in and near Moscow, continuing to publish in a variety of genres. He died in 1934.

Bely was also a poet, one of the main theorists of the Symbolist movement in Russia, a literary scholar and the author of invaluable memoirs. These developed from the *Memoirs of Blok* which he wrote immediately after Blok's death into three volumes published shortly before his own. Since the fall of the Soviet regime previously unpublished memoirs and letters have begun to appear.

JOHN ELSWORTH is Professor of Russian Studies at the University of Manchester. From 1964 to 1987 he taught at the University of East Anglia, Norwich, and has also held visiting posts at the universities of Virginia and of California at Berkeley. His publications include a short biographical study of Bely (1972) and *Andrey Bely. A Critical Study of the Novels* (Cambridge University Press, 1983).

ANDREY BELY

The Silver Dove

Translated from the Russian by
JOHN ELSWORTH
with an introduction and notes

NORTHWESTERN UNIVERSITY PRESS
Evanston, Illinois

Northwestern University Press
Evanston, Illinois 60208-4210

ISBN 0-8101-1757-6

This book is printed on acid free paper conforming to the British Library
recommendations and to the full American standard

∞

Typeset in Great Britain by Ray Perry
Printed and bound by Redwood Books Ltd, Trowbridge, Wiltshire

Contents

Introduction

By the early 1880s the great period of the Russian realist novel had come to an end. Dostoevsky died in 1881, Turgenev in 1883, while Tolstoy's work took a different direction. For the rest of the nineteenth century short fiction was the most active genre: this is the period of Tolstoy's 'The Death of Ivan Ilyich' and 'Master and Man', and of the greater part of Chekhov's output, to say nothing of such lesser writers as Garshin or Korolenko. The turn of the century witnessed a resurgence of poetry, but also a blurring of hitherto accepted genre boundaries, as experimental prose forms appeared in the interstices, as it were, between the traditional short story and verse. Of course novels in the established realistic mode continued to appear, as they have done ever since, but the modern novel which surfaced in the first decade of the twentieth century was very different from its nineteenth-century predecessors.

Literary genres change because sensibilities change, and even if there is nothing new under the sun, the impression of newness is created by the fresh recuperation of the old. In the last years of the nineteenth century a substantial 'transvaluation of values' took place in Russia.[1] The ideological subordination of the individual to the community, an almost undisputed article of faith since the 1840s, gave way to a rediscovered fascination with individual experience. The pursuit of individual uniqueness led to a preoccupation with the intensity, rather than the continuity, of experience, and thus to a predilection for shorter forms and lyric poetry in particular. It was in 1894 and 1895 that a series of three slim volumes appeared with the title *The Russian Symbolists*. They contained both translations from French (Verlaine, Maeterlinck, Rimbaud, Mallarmé) and original poems that struck readers by their daring use of metaphor and paradox, and also by their sometimes daring subject-matter. The assertion implicit in the title of these volumes, that there now existed a Russian Symbolist school just like the French one, hardly corresponded to fact. The bulk of the poems were written, under his own name and a variety of pseudonyms, by Valery Bryusov (1873–1924), who thereby established himself as impresario to the new literature, a role he maintained for fifteen years. However, even if the *Russian Symbolists* volumes were not the proof, there did exist by this time a group of poets who were genuinely linked by shared attitudes to poetic form and content that were markedly distinct from the utilitarian orientation of earlier decades: Konstantin Balmont (1867–1942), Zinaïda Gippius (1869–1945) and Fyodor Sologub (1863–1927). They were all in sympathy with Bryusov's dictum that the poet's task was above all to express experiences that had not previously been expressed; and value, clearly, lay for them in the success of the expression, not in the nature of the experience itself. Aesthetic judgements took precedence over ethical ones. The historicism of the nineteenth century and the ideal of progress naturally withered in this atmosphere, and by the early years of the twentieth century a sensibility held sway that privileged subjectivity and intuition. This was the particular contribution of the group that came to be known as the 'older generation' of Russian Symbolists.

Boris Nikolaevich Bugaev (1880–1934) was born in Moscow and his early years coincided with these developments in Russian culture, which he readily absorbed. He made his own literary debut in 1902 with an experimental prose work entitled *Second (Dramatic) Symphony*.[2] It was for the appearance of this mildly scandalous piece that the pseudonym Andrey Bely was invented, to save the public face of his father, Professor Nikolay Vasilyevich Bugaev, a world-famous mathematician and Dean of the Science Faculty at Moscow University. The title points to Bely's understanding of music as the supreme art form, an idea for which he is indebted both to Schopenhauer and to Nietzsche. Music's supremacy lies in its ability to express fundamental levels of experience which cannot be expressed through language. If verbal art can be made to function more like music, then it will come closer to the successful expression of these most valuable experiences. Bely already differs from his 'older generation' predecessors in seeing such experience as not merely personal, but as potentially mystical and religious. As a literary form, the *Symphony* was designed to reveal the intuited world of transcendent reality that lies behind everyday life. The work depicts a fully recognizable Moscow, populated by intellectuals and mystics who are awaiting the Second Coming. This world is, however, deliberately fragmented, so that it ceases to cohere as a mimetic reproduction of space and time.

1. At that hour, as he left for the hospital, the pale, bilious-looking hunchback tied a bandage over his cheek: his teeth ached.

2. He did not tie it very well. Two little ears stuck up over his head.

3. And once again someone who *knew* said impassively: 'Pigsty', and the cockerel in the paved courtyard seized its opponent by the comb.

4. Then everything slipped out of place, everything broke away, and there remained the . . . *fathomless*.

1. And the moments passed. Pedestrians succeeded each other like moments...
And every passer-by had his moment of walking along over every place.
2. Everyone did everything at a certain time. There was not one capable of
doing without time.
3. And time passed unceasingly, and the passing of time carried the reflection of
misty Eternity.[3]

Bely argued that the work of art had its own principles of coherence, which
need not coincide with those of the world depicted. The *Symphony*'s aesthetic coherence is established through a kaleidoscopic pattern of vari-
ously recurring images, motifs, themes and rhythms – in short, by devices
of an essentially musical nature. The reader is invited to perceive this level
of the text as representing a superordinate reality.

During the following decade Andrey Bely established himself as a poet,
and published a number of further prose works (three of which were also
entitled *Symphony*), but became best known as a tireless participant in the
literary and philosophical debates of the time, contributing literally hundreds of essays, large and small, to the various periodicals that appeared in
Moscow and St Petersburg, such as *Libra* (*Vesy*, 1904–09) and *The Golden
Fleece* (*Zolotoe runo*, 1906–09). In the process of this activity he came to be
recognized, along with the poets Ivanov and Blok, as one of the leaders of
the 'younger generation' of Symbolists, a group who were concerned –
without losing their immediate predecessors' insights into the importance
of the individual and the value of the aesthetic – to restore to cultural discourse a concern with the nature of community.

They derived their understanding of community from the Slavophile
tradition of the mid-nineteenth century, and the subsequent developments of those ideas in the late work of Dostoevsky and the philosophy of
Vladimir Solovyov. Where the Russian Westernizers had emphasized the
need for legal structures that defined the rights and obligations of individuals and groups in relation to each other, the Slavophiles saw such legalism
as emptying human community of spiritual content and replacing it with
a system of functional relations. In *The Brothers Karamazov* Dostoevsky
formulated the opposition of *church* and *state* in similar terms. True community, the Symbolists believed, must rest upon a shared religious awareness, upon a common intuition that all individuals relate to each other as
children of the same father, rather than citizens of the same state. The
achievement of such a community, an 'organic culture', as they called it,
was the ultimate aim of the Symbolist movement in the 1900s.

The question then arises of how such intuitions can be expressed and
shared. This is not to be achieved by the mere observation of existing reli-

gious doctrines and rituals. The Orthodox Church – except, importantly, in its monastic variant – had been perceived throughout the nineteenth century as an arm of the state, and therefore as part and parcel of the mechanical culture that the Symbolists sought to transcend. True religious experience inhabits a region of the soul that is not accessible to traditional ritual, nor indeed to language when understood as a referential system. But the practice of the new art showed that language could be employed in such a way as to communicate previously inexpressible areas of experience, those inner recesses of the psyche where the transcendent is at home. This is what Bely set out to achieve in his *Second (Dramatic) Symphony*. Thus the younger generation of Symbolists took over the older generation's aesthetic insights, but turned them to a purpose more in keeping with the perennial concerns of earlier Russian culture. They saw art neither as self-sufficient nor as that vehicle of conscious social comment that nineteenth-century positivists believed it to be; to them it was the harbinger and instrument of religious transformation. Art would attain its purpose when it was itself transcended.

Religious revival was very much in the air. Vladimir Solovyov (1853–1900), perhaps the most important single influence upon the writers of Bely's generation, had developed an overarching vision of a fallen world that could be reunited with God through the activity of mankind. His philosophy rested upon the cornerstones of love and art: love is transcendent, the only sign of divinity in the material world, while art is destined to become 'theurgy', to act as a force for the sanctification of reality. D. S. Merezhkovsky (1865–1941) initiated in 1901–03 a series of Religious-Philosophical Meetings, at which representatives of the intelligentsia and the church, groups utterly disparate in culture, met to seek common ground.[4] Many people at this time experienced the attraction of theosophy, that eclectic revival of ancient and oriental occultism which had been propagated in the latter decades of the nineteenth century by Helena Blavatsky (1831–91) and her successors, notably Annie Besant (1847–1933). Its attempt to fuse the mystical and the rational seemed to provide a new religion for the scientific age.[5] Among the uneducated masses, particularly in the countryside and far from the cultural centres, religious sects, many with roots going back to the Schism of the seventeenth century, flourished afresh. These held a profound fascination for the intelligentsia, many of whom saw them as a possible route to the overcoming of that gulf between the ordinary people of Russia and the Western-educated intelligentsia which had long been identified as the cardinal problem of Russian culture and national identity.

No other text in Russian literature embodies these issues as fully as *The Silver Dove*. The hero, Daryalsky, is a poet who abandons – he would say, transcends – poetry, in order to participate in the creation of a new religious community by attempting to father the offspring of a sectarian *bogoroditsa* ('Mother of God'). Success in this – it is thought – will bring about the Second Coming and the world's redemption. Love is explored both in the form of the passionate physical attraction that draws him to the peasant woman Matryona and in that of his gentler but no less sterile love for his aristocratic fiancée, Katya. The gulf between intelligentsia and people is signalled in the novel's locations, as Daryalsky moves from West to East, from the aristocratic estate of Gugolevo to the nearby village of Tselebeyevo and finally to the town of Likhov.

The novel was written in 1909, and reflects not only the apocalyptic enthusiasm of the younger generation of Symbolists in the early years of the century, but also a distanced judgement on it by a sadder and wiser man. The intervening years witnessed both defeat in the Russo-Japanese War of 1904–05 and the Revolution of 1905–06, events which left a deep imprint upon the national consciousness. The viewpoint of 1909 is also crucially affected by developments of a biographical nature. It is self-evident that the aesthetic philosophy of the younger Symbolists was not a matter merely for the library and the writing desk. Such beliefs demanded the test of experience. The Symbolists tried in their own lives to create the kind of community of which they dreamed, to fuse art and life into a single text, and that attempt is itself part of the subtext to *The Silver Dove*.

* *

In 1903 the poet and classical scholar Vyacheslav Ivanov (1866–1949) returned to Russia after a long period of residence in Western Europe. Bely made his acquaintance in the following year, and a strong friendship developed between them, with Ivanov becoming the oldest member of the 'younger generation' of Symbolists. One of his first acts on returning to Russia was to publish his lengthy study of the Dionysian religion of ancient Greece, to which many years of research had been devoted.[6] He saw the Dionysian religion not only as a precursor of Christianity, because of its worship of a sacrificial god, but also as a unique revelation of the fundamental nature of the religious impulse. His study of it was an attempt to delve beyond the particular forms of religious practice that he found recorded in his sources, and to reach an understanding of this fundamental impulse. His theoretical writings in the years following publication of the study constitute an attempt to apply that understanding to general questions of aesthetics and to particular questions of contemporary culture and the destiny of Russia.

The religion of Dionysus is distinguished from other Greek cults in two ways. All other Greek gods and their attendant myths are names and narratives associated with particular states of mind: in Euripides's *Hippolytus*, for example, the inner conflict between chastity and passion is symbolized as a conflict between Artemis and Aphrodite. The worship of Dionysus, however, is associated with an ecstatic state that precedes all myth and is the source of all religion. It expresses the fundamental quality that distinguishes the human race from all other species: its quality as the *animal ecstaticum*. Secondly, the Dionysian religion was distinguished from all other Greek religions by the fact that all its participants were actively involved in the ritual. The state of ecstasy is of necessity collective; it can only be experienced by men as a group. As Nietzsche had already pointed out in *The Birth of Tragedy*, Dionysian intoxication entails the overcoming of the *principio individuationis* and the surrender of the self to the inchoate forces of nature.

In his poetry Ivanov explores the Dionysian theme through the vehicle of sexual love, experienced as a means of overcoming the limits of the individual and attaining the loss of self that is the hallmark of Dionysian ecstasy. But the community of two that arises this way is not sufficient, and in his aesthetic theory Ivanov develops his ideas of how the artist can employ his art to generate a shared religious culture. He sees the modern poet as tragically isolated from the people, but able to overcome that isolation by retrieving the symbols that lie dormant in the people's soul. A symbol is understood as an image which intuitively links the real world with the transcendent. Out of symbols there develop myths, the shared narratives by which a community recognizes its common relation to the transcendent, its common identity.

Ivanov's ideas about the Dionysian religion had a profound influence upon Bely in the early years of their acquaintance. In an essay dedicated to Ivanov as 'preacher of Dionysianism',[7] he picks up the idea of the preverbal substratum of experience from which Ivanov's poet has the task of summoning symbols. Although words cannot penetrate it, Bely says, the collective 'identity of intoxications' can be expressed through rites, dances, songs. He uses the same word for 'round-dance' (*khorovod*) that appears in some of Ivanov's essays, and invokes the image of the 'green meadow' on which these dances are to be performed, an image which goes back to ancient Greek literature and which was common currency among the Symbolists.[8]

The legacy of Dionysus is evident in *The Silver Dove* in a number of ways. The novel's climactic scene in Chapter 6, in which the members of the sect enact a secret ritual culminating in a vision of the 'dove-child', very closely follows Ivanov's description of Dionysian ritual, in which ecstasy is followed by visions that resolve themselves into an epiphany of the god. Ivanov reminds us that in Euripides's *The Bacchae* the figure of Dionysus appears in the flames of Cadmus's house, which has miraculously caught fire.[9] In Bely's novel it is Ivan Stepanov the shopkeeper's barn that catches fire, shortly after the epiphany scene, and by means that are far from miraculous. But the juxtaposition invites a parallel with Euripides's version of the Dionysus myth. The immediately preceding scene, depicting a drunken crowd in the teahouse, can well be read as a parodic reflection of the sectarians' ecstasy; the fire is several times mentioned as lighting up the meadow of Tselebeyevo, which is a clear descendant of the 'green meadow' of the Greeks.[10]

Certainly the figure of Daryalsky, Bely's hero, has many features in common with Dionysus, the sacrificial, reborn god.[11] The mythic references are never singular; pagan and Christian motifs intertwine in many details. As Daryalsky sits in the hollow oak tree waiting for Matryona, wearing a wreath of fir branches, he can be likened not only to Dionysus Dendritis, 'the horned Dionysus in the ark of wood', but also to Osiris of Egyptian mythology and to Christ, willingly donning the crown of thorns in anticipation of crucifixion. His cane, for which a grotesque battle is fought during the final journey to Likhov, can be identified with another traditional attribute of Dionysus, the *thyrsus*, the rod, or wand, tipped with a pine cone, which was borne by initiates of the Dionysian cult. In this instance, too, the associations are plural in nature, as the image also carries a reference to the cross, so that here too Dionysus and Christ are invoked simultaneously. Such an affinity is in keeping with Ivanov's conception of the Dionysian religion as a forerunner of Christianity and of its capacity to embody essential qualities of all religious experience. All these features, and others, can be found in Ivanov's account of the Dionysian rites.[12]

It was with the third principal member of the younger Symbolists' group, the poet Aleksandr Blok (1880–1921), that Bely had the most complete spiritual affinity and the most painful personal conflict.[13] The two began a correspondence at the beginning of 1903, and became personally acquainted a year later. Even before they met, they were both struck by the astounding similarity in their perception of Russia, religion and poetry, and later, in the years of their alienation, deep affinities still continued to appear in their work.

Blok's early poetry, written before his acquaintance with Bely, bore the title 'Verses about the Beautiful Lady'. It was an open secret that the beautiful lady to whom this blend of eschatological and erotic longing was addressed was Lyubov Dmitrievna Mendeleyeva, to whom Blok became engaged in the autumn of 1902, and whom he married in August 1903. Blok cast her as the earthly embodiment of St Sophia, Divine Wisdom, who, in Solovyov's philosophy, will appear as the herald of the world's redemption. Bely was at first perturbed by what he saw as a confusion of the spiritual and the erotic, and by the idea that Blok could think of *marrying* Sophia. However, on meeting her, Bely was enchanted and reconciled to the situation. By the summer of 1905 it became apparent that Blok himself was losing faith in the idea of poetry as mystical service, and also that he and his wife were not really living together. Blok appeared to acknowledge his own responsibility for this state of affairs, and to be magnanimously standing aside in order not to infringe his wife's freedom, leaving Bely to assume the mantle of knight. He believed he might succeed where Blok had failed, and create with her the transcendent love which Blok had evidently renounced, and sanctify the physical through its combination with the spiritual. Through the latter part of 1905 and much of 1906 an intense but indeterminate relationship continued between them, with Bely repeatedly travelling to St Petersburg in order to set off abroad for their new life together, and Lyubov Dmitrievna repeatedly sending him back to Moscow while she made up her mind. In the end they never became intimate and never set off anywhere, and she decided not to leave her husband after all. Bely was left with a deep sense of injury at her vacillation and her ultimate curt dismissal of him.

The two strands of Bely's infatuation with Lyubov Dmitrievna and his involvement with Ivanov's ideas about the Dionysian origin of religious community merge in an essay which carries the title 'The Green Meadow', and is perhaps the most important background text to *The Silver Dove*. He wrote it in August 1905, and later described it as a coded love-letter to Lyubov Dmitrievna.[14] Much of the imagery is derived from Gogol's story 'A Terrible Vengeance', in which the heroine, Pani Katerina, is in thrall to a wicked sorcerer who has possession of her soul. The personal implication is clear: Blok exercises a baneful hold upon his wife, whom Bely seeks to liberate.[15] Pani Katerina is evoked by Bely not only as an image of Lyubov Dmitrievna, but also as an image of Russia, entrapped in a mechanistic conception of culture. Organic culture will be generated by those whose souls converse beyond ordinary discourse: 'There is a secret link between all those who have stepped beyond the borders of that which is already formed.'[16] This is addressed not only to Lyubov Dmitrievna as an individual, asserting that she and the author share an intuitive understanding beyond ordinary communication, but also to the greater organic community that Russia, following their example, is to become. The essay includes references to the events of 'Bloody Sunday', 9 January 1905, when some two hundred peaceful demonstrators were shot and killed on Palace Square in St Petersburg by panicking troops. This happened to be the day on which Bely arrived on one of his visits to St Petersburg, and the event inevitably coloured his entire sojourn there and his relations, at that time still untroubled, with the Bloks. It marked perhaps the high-point of the intelligentsia's self-identification with the masses, which was understood by Bely in a Dionysian rather than a practical political manner. Thus the image of the 'green meadow' carries intimations of liberation, and of the new culture of religious community and transcendent love at the levels of personal biography, cultural creation, and national history. The images of the green meadow and the round-dance became central to the depiction of the village community in *The Silver Dove*, but between 1905 and 1909 they acquired an ambivalence not present in the earlier formulations.[17]

The ambiguous appeal of the peasant woman Matryona, and the ultimately destructive nature of the erotic hold she exercises upon Daryalsky, reflect Bely's sense of betrayal at the way his relations with Lyubov Dmitrievna ended. It is in this connection that the hero's name can best be understood, as a reference to Lermontov's poem of 1840, 'Tamara', a version of the legend of the beautiful princess whose unresisting lovers are found after a single night of bliss, floating dead in the river Daryal.[18] There is, however, a further biographical element to the novel's central plot.

The hero is an amalgam of features derived from various contemporaries and from the author himself, but based most directly upon the experience of his lifelong friend Sergey Solovyov (1885–1942), always known as Seryozha. Seryozha was the nephew of the philosopher, and from 1895 had lived in the same house as Bely, in a flat one floor below. His mother was a relative of Blok's mother, and it was through this connection that Bely had learnt about Blok's poetry long before they met. In 1906 Seryozha was a student of classics and infatuated with all things Greek. In August of that year, just when relations with the Bloks were in such a state of crisis that Bely challenged Blok to a duel (which never took place), he and Seryozha were staying at the country house of Seryozha's grandmother; in his memoirs Bely describes how the two of them occupied a separate guest wing, a stone's throw from the main house, but culturally at a vast distance from it: 'two cultures, two ways of life; there the eighteenth century was still alive; here was the twentieth; there was the "paradise" of enlightened absolutism; here were the "horrors" of anarchism: the bomb and the red cockerel . . .'[19] (The 'red cockerel' is a standard metaphor for an act of arson, such as frequently occurred in the Russian countryside in the aftermath of the 1905 Revolution.) The estate of Gugolevo and Baroness Todrabe-

Graaben's household have their origin here. Seryozha thought himself in love with a peasant girl from a neighbouring village, to whom he had not at that point even ventured to speak; he would drag his friend over to admire her from a distance, and created a mythology in which she was no longer Yelenka the cook, but Helen of Troy. By the end of the summer Seryozha had overcome his shyness, made a formal proposal to the girl's family, and introduced her to his own. In a letter to Bely he declared his intention of marrying her on 1 October. Yet his letters also reveal a duality of emotion that is reflected in the novel: an anxiety that he is yielding to a spell, from which he must at all costs escape. Unlike Daryalsky's, Seryozha Solovyov's relations with his peasant sweetheart evidently remained chaste, and neither tragedy nor marriage ensued.[20]

But if Solovyov ultimately held back from realizing his dream of fusion with the people, there were those who took such ideas to their logical conclusion. It was not uncommon in these years for educated Russians to abandon the privileges of their station and go to live among the common people. Such a movement can be traced back to the populists of the 1870s, and owed much to that belief in the virtue of simple, self-sufficient life which is central to Tolstoyanism. For the generation of the Symbolists, however, this idea had a particular religious and apocalyptic resonance, reflecting their conviction that the culture of the intelligentsia was doomed and that redemption could come only from reunification with the ordinary people. Two names recur in the memoirs of the period when this theme is raised: that of Aleksandr Dobrolyubov (1876–1944?), a poet who abandoned civilization and became a wanderer around distant parts of the Russian Empire, living as a simple labourer and consorting with religious sectarians;[21] and that of Leonid Semyonov (1880–1917), who underwent a development from decadent poet via revolutionary activity to a simple rural life and eventually the church (only to be brutally murdered by marauding peasants after the February Revolution of 1917).[22] Bely had long talks with both of them, and the theme of the abandonment of civilization also figured in his conversations with Blok. Daryalsky's actions in the novel, therefore, enact a central tendency in the culture of the period. In 'The Green Meadow' Bely asserts that the same religious quest informs the lives of both educated and uneducated Russians, and his evocation of the revolutionary days of January 1905 carries the belief that the chaotic struggle for basic human rights on the part of the urban workers and the peasantry, which later descended into simple brigandage, was entirely compatible with the striving for a new, organic culture on the part of the intelligentsia, a culture which must include those groups if it was to exist at all. The revolutionary turmoil had by no means subsided by the summer of 1906, and formed the background for Bely's and Solovyov's response to the peasantry at that time.

* *

The bulk of the material for the novel was thus collected by the late summer of 1906, and the first idea of the novel began to take shape in 1907.[23] The writing of it only began, however, two years later, and by that time important changes had come about in the way Bely perceived his material.

The years between 1906 and 1909 witnessed substantial realignments in Russian intellectual life. Among the Symbolists themselves it was a period of internecine warfare, as the Moscow group, led by Bryusov, Bely and Seryozha Solovyov, mounted a critical attack upon the St Petersburg group for what they saw as the vulgarization of their shared ideals. The most prominent members of the St Petersburg group were Blok and Ivanov, and Bely's personal conflict with his former friend spilled over into the literary polemic. A particular bone of contention was the appearance in 1906 of a brochure proclaiming the doctrine of 'Mystical Anarchism', with which Ivanov had rather unwisely aligned himself. The relaxation of censorship following the Revolution of 1905 made possible an expansion of more lowbrow literature that aped some of the now fashionable attitudes of the Symbolists. The development of the 'God-builders' around Gorky and Lunacharsky, proponents of a secular faith in natural goodness, appeared to many as a simple-minded deification of the common people, and a dangerously self-denying approach to the perennial problem of the intelligentsia's relations with them. And for much of this time senseless civil unrest continued, meeting ruthless suppression from the government which provoked the ageing Tolstoy to write his condemnatory essay 'I Cannot be Silent' at the wave of retaliatory executions.

The question of whether the intelligentsia could make common cause with the ordinary people in their shared rejection of the status quo, which had been answered in the affirmative in 1905, received a very different reply in the essay-volume *Landmarks*, which appeared in 1909. Its contributors were philosophers and critics, rather than poets; some had belonged to the group of 'legal Marxists' in the previous decade, and none of them was directly associated with the Symbolist movement, but the views they expressed constituted a weighty attack on the traditional populist attitudes of the Russian intelligentsia, and the volume's appearance marked a swing in public opinion with which many of the Symbolists were in sympathy. Bely wrote a supportive review in *Libra*.[24] There is ample evidence of Bely's shift of opinion away from 'social democracy'[25] during

1908, as he lost sympathy with Merezhkovsky (who he later claimed provided part of the basis for the character of the carpenter Kudeyarov, the
sectarian leader[26]) and came increasingly under the influence of Mikhail
Gershenzon, one of the contributors to *Landmarks*.[27]

Despite their lack of personal contact in these years, Bely and Blok perceived and expressed the spiritual problems besetting Russia in strikingly
similar ways. Blok's play of 1908, *The Song of Fate*, shows considerable
similarities in its plot with Bely's novel,[28] while his poem-cycle 'On
Kulikovo Field' and the associated essay 'The People and the Intelligentsia' evoke the battle in which the Russians finally turned the tide
against the Mongols in 1380. Blok sees this battle as one of the symbolic
events of Russian history which are bound to be repeated. The laconic
Preface which Bely wrote for the first volume edition of *The Silver Dove* in
1910 (page 33 of the present edition), in which he describes it as the first
volume of a planned trilogy entitled 'East or West', makes clear the extent
to which he regarded his novel as touching upon those same deep-seated
and endemic issues of Russian history: notably the conflict between the
Christian West and the forces of chaos and barbarism associated with the
Mongol East. At the same time it has to be noted that the West in Bely's
novel, represented as it is by the denizens of Gugolevo, offers little in the
way of positive alternative to the religious distortions of the sectarians.
Even the evidently positive character of Katya, who was based in part
upon Asya Turgeneva, Bely's first wife, with whom his close friendship
was developing during the writing of the novel, is represented as a potential, rather than an actual, source of enlightenment. In this respect she has
evidently taken over the role of Pani Katerina, the Sleeping Beauty, the
image of a future Russia, previously attributed to Lyubov Dmitrievna.

Another important change that came about between 1906 and 1909 was
Bely's increasing absorption in theosophy. He had some familiarity with it
from the early years of the century, but it was only in 1908 that he returned
to it and began a serious study of its doctrine. The influence of theosophy
upon the novel is easy enough to detect in the character of Daryalsky's
friend Schmidt, who is immersed in occult learning. It has been shown
that the horoscope which Schmidt works out for the hero in Chapter 5 is
very similar to one that Bely worked out for himself during the writing of
the novel. Maria Carlson has in fact suggested a reading of *The Silver Dove*
in which the theosophical aspect comes very much to the fore, and much of
the work's imagery, even some of its sound-patterning, can be interpreted
in this light.[29] If the novel is approached from this angle, its ending can
then also be read as allegorical of a mystical initiation. In many occult sys-
tems the act of initiation imitates not merely death and rebirth, but quite

specifically crucifixion and resurrection; the image of crucifixion is clearly invoked a number of times in the passages leading up to Daryalsky's death. The theosophical doctrine of evolutionary cycles in which all past parallels are eternally present then provides a paradigmatic model for the identification Dionysus-Daryalsky-Christ and the many lesser mythic prototypes that the novel reveals.[30]

By 1909 the internal conflicts within the younger generation of Symbolists had subsided. Bely was completely reconciled with Ivanov, following their quarrel over 'Mystical Anarchism', by the beginning of that year, and reconciliation with Blok followed soon afterwards. However, having dominated cultural life for some fifteen years, Symbolism as a movement was now disintegrating. In the following year many of the major Symbolists (of both generations) contributed to a debate in the press about the path they had traversed in the previous decade and the lessons they had learnt. As far as Bely, Blok and Ivanov were concerned, this was the occasion for a re-examination of the religious demands they had made of art in earlier years. Unlike Bryusov, who insisted that the Symbolists had always seen poetry as a self-sufficient activity, they maintained their view that art had a further dimension, and gave access to a world beyond the ordinary. They nevertheless agreed that, as their apocalyptic fervour had waned, and they had become worse mystics, they had become better artists. They had become more aware of the necessary limitations of art as it exists in the real world, of the distance between an artistic vision and its realization in life. It is noticeable that all three turned, at about the end of the decade, to forms of a more epic nature, in which the contingencies of real life and the historical context of individual experience have to be fully represented. In the cases of Blok and Ivanov this meant narrative poetry – Blok's *Retribution* and Ivanov's *Childhood*. Bely turned to the novel, and this reappraisal of the relations between artistic and religious creation lies at the very heart of *The Silver Dove*.

*   *

What, then, are the literary characteristics of the novel that embodies this sensibility? As noted above, Bely insisted that the principle of coherence governing a literary work is not the same as any principle of coherence that may be discerned in the external world depicted. The prose of his experimental *Symphonies* was characterized by a studied dislocation and fragmentation of the external world. Images would be juxtaposed in such a way as to disrupt their expected relations in space and time, events would be narrated in a manner that disregarded any question of their causal connectedness. In other words, the literary work, while depicting people, places and events in the real world, did not reproduce their empirical coherence. The coherence of the *Symphony* had to be perceived through its internal patterns, its imitation of musical structures. These structures then established a different system of coherence between the elements, as, for instance, a structural echo (a repeated metaphor, a rhythmic repetition) drew together two elements that were not connected at the representational level. Governing the whole was a contrast of time and eternity, the dislocated events in the world constantly juxtaposed with a recurrent image of the 'eternal tedium' of the sky.

The possibilities of such writing were relatively quickly exhausted. The 'symphonic' form is essentially lyrical rather than epic in nature, as the work's meaning is traceable back to the single, authoritative consciousness of the implied author. Bely never repeated the success of the *Second (Dramatic) Symphony*, and his other works by this title have dated badly; his last attempt at the genre, the *Fourth Symphony: A Goblet of Blizzards* (1908), is virtually unreadable in the complexity and elusiveness of its imagery. Once Bely conceived of a more truly epic work, concerned with destinies that are acted out not only in the mind, but in the real, historically determined world itself, he had to reinstate some of the standard features of epic writing, in this case, of the traditional novel. He had to depict a historically recognizable environment; he had to create credible and consistent characters; he had to construct a coherent plot. He had, that is to say, to restore the external coherence of the depicted world that had been removed in the *Symphonies*. All these features are present in *The Silver Dove*. They are combined, however, with structural and stylistic features that owe a great deal to the 'symphonic' principle. These can be seen in the recurrent patterns of imagery which link the fate of the hero (and, to a smaller extent, the fates of other characters) to mythic archetypes, thus asserting – as in the *Symphonies* – the subordination of experience here-and-now to eternal patterns. They can be seen also in networks of imagery that serve to convey to the reader experiences of the characters which lie below their conscious awareness. Much of Daryalsky's experience in the first chapter, as he gradually succumbs to the mysterious attraction of the 'doves', is rendered in this manner. In ways such as these, despite its greater similarity to the realistic tradition of the nineteenth century, *The Silver Dove* firmly maintains the Symbolist practice of expressing the deepest discernible layers of experience and relating them to extra-temporal archetypes.

Where this novel differs most radically from most of Bely's earlier prose is in the narrative voice, or, more correctly, voices. There is no longer any single authorial consciousness, no dominant voice. It is in fact impossible to trace with absolute assurance the gradations from one narrative voice to another, or, indeed, to say with any certainty how many there are. For the most part the narrative voice is implied by the linguistic register employed in a given passage. Much of the novel is narrated in an essentially unmarked literary style, but it may change without notice to a voice that is clearly identifiable by its rustic vocabulary or by its urban affectation, or one which is marked by its evidently limited understanding of what it describes. This can be seen on the very first page of the text. The first paragraph evokes the village scene in a style that betrays nothing of the narrator (except perhaps a touch of irony in the description of the sweating bell-ringer), but the second switches abruptly to the colloquial voice of a villager, addressing the reader on intimate terms, and referring to the authority of the priest on the scantiest of evidence. This voice, or a similar one, recurs in later passages where reference is made to events outside the novel's plot or time-scale, which are ostensibly presented as the common knowledge of narrator and reader. In Chapter 2, for instance, the narrator reflects: 'for two years now – no, by your leave: when was it that Konovalov's pigsty burned down? Why, it must be three years ago that the pigsty burned down . . . So it's three years, then, since Fyokla Matveyevna joined the brotherhood of the Dove . . .' On occasion the register of the heroic folk-tale makes an appearance, notably in descriptions of Daryalsky as the 'dashing stranger' and of Katya as the 'fair maiden' (for example, in the second section of Chapter 1). Here and there the text is interspersed with totally unironized lyrical digressions, particularly in the paeans to the Russian fields in Chapter 5. In a few sections the narratorial voice is almost completely absent, as snatches of uncommented dialogue stand by themselves. The complexity is increased by the way in which the voices merge imperceptibly and 'contaminate' each other.[31]

A particular feature of the narration is the use of snatches of song as external comment upon the action. Many are real quotations from songs that were popular at the time in which the novel is set, others may well be inventions of Bely's that are nevertheless clearly marked by features of one or another traditional genre. They amount to a separate subset of narrative voices, providing a further range of perspectives. This is a technique which anticipates in important respects the method by which Blok later composed his famous poem of the Revolution, *The Twelve*.

The model that Bely adopted in his recourse to nineteenth-century traditions was first and foremost Gogol, and the connections between Bely and Gogol have been extensively researched. Gogol held a crucial importance for Bely not only during 1905 and 1906, when the material for the novel was taking shape in his mind, but also in the year of its writing, 1909, which was the centenary of Gogol's birth. In the summer of 1906 Bely and Seryozha Solovyov interpreted their experience of Russia through the prism of Gogol, seeing the expropriations, assassinations and murders in terms of images from Gogol's 'A Terrible Vengeance' and other stories. The red shirt which Solovyov affected at the time, and which was inherited by Daryalsky, was a deliberate reference to the similar garment worn by Gogol's sorcerer, who holds Pani Katerina, the image of the ideal Russia, in thrall.[32] The Gogol centenary was the occasion of widescale celebration and commemoration, including the erection of a new statue to him in Moscow. It is clear from reports of the celebrations and the messages attached to wreaths laid on the new monument that the perception of Gogol as uniquely embodying features of 'our Russian Russia', as distinct from versions of official patriotism, was shared by many besides Bely.[33] Bely wrote a long essay about Gogol while working on the novel, emphasizing the impossibility of fitting him neatly into any established literary category, and declaring him and Nietzsche to be 'the greatest stylists in the whole of European art, if by style we understand not merely verbal style, but the reflection in form of the living rhythm of the soul.'[34] This 'living rhythm of the soul' was exactly what Bely was seeking to reflect in *The Silver Dove*.

*   *

Partly, no doubt, because it was originally presented as the first part of a trilogy, and was followed quite quickly by Bely's better known second novel, *Petersburg*, to which it was then perceived as a kind of prologue, *The Silver Dove* has always been overshadowed by the later work.[35] But the trilogy never came into being, since in the course of composition *Petersburg* turned into a completely independent work, and *The Silver Dove* would remain a fascinating and important work in its own right, even if Bely had written no more. Its final chapter was published in the last issue of *Libra*, the most influential of the Symbolist journals, and it provides the most compelling summary of the strivings, the hopes and the disasters of this generation of Russians. It was immediately appreciated by a wide spectrum of opinion, not only by the contributors to *Landmarks*, whose sympathy was perhaps assured, but by critics of other persuasions and none. It was perceived, above all, as having successfully captured the chaotic, eastern aspect of the Russian people. One of the *Landmarks* contributors wrote to Bely that he had been 'granted such penetration into the soul of the people as we have not had since the time of Dostoevsky'.[36] The novel had a direct influence upon such writers as Pilnyak,[37] Khlebnikov[38] and Pasternak[39], even though Bely's great influence on the prose of the 1920s is usually attributed to *Petersburg*. It was not without reason that Bely later claimed to have anticipated, in the figure of Kudeyarov, something of Rasputin.[40] *The Silver Dove* depicts a culture on the brink: aware that it can no longer survive without incorporating the formless strivings and undisciplined imaginings of the common people, which it has hitherto repressed, but simultaneously aware that the attempt to do so may spell disaster.

NOTES

[1] This topic is explored in Edith Clowes, *The Revolution of Moral Consciousness: Nietzsche in Russian Literature, 1890–1914*, Northern Illinois University Press, De Kalb, Ill., 1988.

[2] His *First Symphony*, though written earlier, was not published until 1904.

[3] Andrey Bely, *The Dramatic Symphony and The Forms of Art*, translated by R. J. Keys, A. M. Keys and J. D. Elsworth, Polygon, Edinburgh, 1986, p.28.

[4] Avril Pyman, *A History of Russian Symbolism*, Cambridge University Press, 1994, pp.150ff.

[5] See Maria Carlson, '*No Religion Higher than Truth*': *A History of the Theosophical Movement in Russia, 1875–1922*, Princeton University Press, 1993.

[6] V. Ivanov, 'Ellinskaya religiya stradayushchego boga: Opyt religiozno-istoricheskoi kharakteristiki' (The Hellenic religion of the suffering god . . .), *Novyi put'*, 1904 no.1 (January), pp.110–34; no.2 (February), pp.48–78; no.3 (March), pp. 38–61; no.5 (May), pp.28–40; no.8 (August), pp.17–26; no.9 (September), pp.47–70.

[7] A. Bely, 'Maska' (The mask), *Vesy*, 1904 no. 6, pp.6–15.

[8] The image occurs, for instance, in Euripides's *The Bacchae*. Ivanov used it in his essay 'Nitshe i Dionis' (Nietzsche and Dionysus), *Vesy*, 1904 no.6, p.9. It also occurs in Bryusov's poem 'Orfei i Evridika' (Orpheus and Euridyce) of 1904.

[9] *Novyi put'*, 1904 no.3, p.53.

[10] There is probably also an intertextual reference here to the ending of Sologub's *Melkii bes* (*The Petty Demon*), which has been convincingly shown to be deeply indebted to *The Bacchae*. See G. J. Thurston, 'Sologub's *Melkiy bes*', *Slavonic and East European Review*, 1977 no.55, pp.30–44.

[11] This aspect of the novel was first noted by S. Cioran, *The Apocalyptic Symbolism of Andrej Belyj*, Mouton, The Hague, 1973, pp.123–4, and has since been developed particularly by M. Carlson, 'The Silver Dove', in *Andrey Bely: Spirit of Symbolism*, ed. J. Malmstad, Cornell University Press, 1987, pp.60–95, and by Gudrun Langer, *Kunst-Wissenschaft-Utopie: Die 'Überwindung der Kulturkrise' bei V. Ivanov, A. Blok, A. Belyj und V. Chlebnikov*, Vittorio Klostermann, Frankfurt am Main, 1990.

[12] *Novyi put'*, 1904 no.1, pp.124–6. See also M. Carlson, 'The Silver Dove'.

[13] These relations have been fully described in Avril Pyman, *The Life of Aleksandr Blok*, vol.1: *The Distant Thunder, 1880–1908*, vol.2: *The Release of Harmony, 1909–1921*, Oxford University Press, 1979, 1980.

[14] A. Bely, *Mezhdu dvukh revolyutsii* (Between two revolutions), Moscow, 1990, p.183.

[15] The relationship is also expressed, in a reflection of Bryusov's poem (see note 8 above), as that of Orpheus and Euridyce.

[16] A. Bely, *Lug zelyonyi* (The green meadow), Moscow, 1910, p.14.

[17] The same imagery derived from 'A Terrible Vengeance' appears also in the short story 'The Bush', written in May 1906, in which the hero enters into a triangular relationship with a gardener's daughter and her lover, a quasi-human bush, who exercises a tyrannical hold over her. The story was immediately understood as a transparent and tactless allegory of the Blok–Bely triangle. Perhaps the bush that stands as a permanent threat to the village of Tselebeyevo in the novel has its origin in this image. See R. E. Peterson, *Andrey Bely's Short Prose*, Birmingham Slavonic Monographs no.11, 1980, p.37. The relation between this story and the novel is further explored in V. N. Toporov, ' "Kust" ' i "Serebryanyi golub' " Andreya Belogo: k svyazi tekstov i o predpolagaemoi "vneliteraturnoi" osnove ikh' (Andrey Bely's 'The Bush' and 'The Silver Dove': the connection between the texts and their possible extra-literary basis), *Blokovskii sbornik*, XII, Tartu, 1993, pp.91–109.

[18] A. V. Lavrov, *Andrey Bely v 1900-e gody* (Andrey Bely in the 1900s), Moscow, 1995, p.292. The name 'Daryal' is Persian in origin, and other interpretations of the hero's name have been based upon its meaning of 'gateway'.

[19] A. Bely, *Mezhdu dvukh revolyutsii*, p.82.

[20] A. V. Lavrov, 'Daryal'sky i Sergey Solov'yov', *Novoe literaturnoe obozrenie*, 1994 no.9, pp.93–110.

[21] Bely describes his meetings with him in *Nachalo veka* (The beginning of the century), Moscow, 1990, pp.398–402; a full account of his life is given in K. M. Azadovsky, 'Put' Aleksandra Dobrolyubova' (The path of Aleksandr Dobrolyubov), in *Tvorchestvo A. A. Bloka i russkaya kul'tura XX veka. Blokovskii sbornik III* (The work of A. A. Blok and Russian twentieth-century culture. Blok anthology III), Tartu, 1979, pp.121–46.

[22] Bely's meeting with him is described in *Nachalo veka*, pp.277–81. Further information is to be found in V. Baevsky, 'Leonid Semyonov – zhiznestroitel' i poet' (Leonid Semyonov – life-builder and poet), *Voprosy literatury* (Problems of literature), 1994 no.5, and V. Baevsky, 'Kto doshol do optinskikh vrat' (He who reached the gates of Optina), *Izvestiya A. N. Seriya literatury i yazyka* (Bulletin of the Academy of Sciences. Literature and language series), 1998, vol.57 no.1, pp.49–59.

[23] See K. Bugaeva, A. Petrovsky, 'Literaturnoe nasledstvo Andreya Belogo' (The literary heritage of Andrey Bely), *Literaturnoe nasledstvo*, 27–8, Moscow, 1937, p.599.

[24] A. Bely, 'Pravda o russkoi intelligentsii. Po povodu sbornika *Vekhi*' (The truth about the Russian intelligentsia. Concerning the anthology *Landmarks*), *Vesy*, 1909 no.5, pp.65–8.

[25] It is worth remembering that 'Social Democrat' was the official name of the Bolshevik Party.

[26] A. Bely, *Mezhdu dvukh revolyutsii*, p.316.

[27] A. V. Lavrov, *Andrei Bely v 1900-e gody*, pp.251–300; A. Etkind, *Khlyst* (Flagellant), Moscow, 1998, pp.406ff.

[28] This has been pointed out by Gudrun Langer, op. cit., p.248.

[29] Theosophy took over ancient Indian ideas about the creation of the world through sound. In the esoteric tradition to which reference is made in Chapter 5, mystical significance is attributed to specific sounds which can be seen to recur in some names and images in the novel, such as the g–l combination that appears in the name Gugolevo and in the Russian words for 'dove' and 'depth' (see also 'A Note on the Text and the Translation', page 27). M. Carlson, 'The Silver Dove', pp.68–73.

[30] Further details are given in the endnotes.

[31] R. J. Keys, *The Reluctant Modernist: Andrei Belyi and the Development of Russian Fiction 1902–1914*, Clarendon Press, Oxford, 1996, ch.19, pp.199–222.

[32] A. V. Lavrov, 'Daryal'sky i Sergei Solov'yov', p.100.

[33] *Zolotoe runo*, 1909 no.4, pp.88–9, 93–4, 95.

[34] A. Bely, *Lug zelyonyi*, Moscow, 1910, p.121.

[35] M. Koz'menko, 'Avtor i geroi povesti *Serebryanyi golub*'' (Author and hero of the novel *The Silver Dove*), introduction to Andrey Bely, *Serebryanyi golub*', Moscow, 1989, pp.5–28.

[36] S. N. Bulgakov in a letter to Bely of December 1910, *Novyi mir*, 1989 no.10, p.238, published by I. B. Rodnyanskaya. (Cited after A. V. Lavrov, *Andrei Bely v 1900-e gody*, p.297.)

[37] V. E. Alexandrov, 'Belyj Subtexts in Pil'njak's *Golyj god*', *Slavic and East European Journal*, 1983 vol.27 no.1, pp.81–90.

[38] G. Langer, op. cit., p.451.

[39] K. M. Polivanov, 'Boris Pasternak i Andrey Bely. "Sestra moya – zhizn'" i "Serebryanyi golub'"' (Boris Pasternak and Andrey Bely. 'My sister – life' and 'The Silver Dove'), *Literaturnoe obozrenie*, 1995 no.4/5, pp.156–7.

[40] A. Bely, *Mezhdu dvukh revolyutsii*, p.315.

A Note on the Text and the Translation

WRITTEN in 1909, *The Silver Dove* was published in serial form during that year in the flagship journal of the Moscow Symbolists, *Libra* (*Vesy*). It was republished in book form in the following year.[1] It was to have been republished as part of a collected edition of Bely's fictional works in 1917, but only the first four chapters appeared before political events supervened.[2] A second edition did, however, appear in Berlin during Bely's two-year sojourn there in 1921–3.[3] No other editions appeared during Bely's lifetime, and apart from facsimile reprints of the 1922 edition produced in Germany and America in the 1960s and 1970s, no further editions appeared before the Gorbachev reforms of the mid-1980s. Since then the novel has been reprinted a number of times. There are hardly any significant intentional differences between the two lifetime editions, though each contains a small number of typographical errors which can be corrected from the other. The present translation is based upon the original book-form edition of 1910, but account has also been taken of every subsequent edition of the novel in Russian. The titles of Chapters 3 and 5, which are missing in both complete lifetime editions, have been reinstated from the text of the original journal publication. They have never been included in any complete Russian volume edition. In many recent editions confusion has arisen between the missing chapter titles and the headings of sections within the chapters.[4]

The Silver Dove has been translated into many languages. An English translation appeared in the United States in 1974,[5] the only one before the present edition to have been published in the English-speaking world. It contains numerous inaccuracies and omissions. The present translation sets out to be as accurate as possible, while providing, as an absolute priority, a readable and enjoyable English text. Bely's Russian presents some considerable difficulties, and it would seem appropriate here to give a brief explanation of the approach that has been adopted towards their resolution.

In the first place, the acoustic properties of Bely's prose are foregrounded, as though the text were designed to be read aloud. The rhythm is a prominent feature. Patterns of assonance and alliteration are much in evidence. These aspects cannot always be reproduced locally, but the attempt has been made to create similar effects in English where an appropriate opportunity arises. Furthermore, the text contains many examples of what can be called acoustic-semantic parallelism. The complex internal connections are carried not only by synonyms, or by images that evoke one another by a similarity of sensory referent, but also by phonetic similarities and echoes. This exploitation of relationships that are clearly specific to the language of original composition creates especial problems for the translator, which at best can only be resolved in part. Two examples must suffice. The Russian for 'dove' is *golub'*, which is phonetically similar to *glubina*, meaning 'depth'; it is also related to the adjective *goluboi*, meaning 'light blue'. Readers will notice the frequency with which the image of depth appears in the text, often with a suggestion of inversion, based on a reflecting water-surface or a 'bottomless' sky. Although 'dove' and 'deep' have the natural advantage of alliteration, there is no sense in which this pattern can be systematically rendered into English, and the only recourse is to rely on the semantic, rather than the acoustic parallel. Thus the word *goluboi* has for the most part been translated as 'dove-blue'. On occasion the acoustic aspect can be rescued. The Russian for 'ripple' is *ryab'*, which is related to an adjective used recurrently – as a leitmotif – to describe the 'pock-marked peasant woman', Matryona – *ryabaya baba*. In the first chapter the hero's spiritual confusion is expressed in the image of a blurred reflection on the surface of the pond, where the ripples are likened to 'silver doves', obscuring the depths: *golub'* has a distorting effect upon *glubina*. The ripples are related to Matryona only on the acoustic level. If the ripples are said to 'pucker' the water-surface, then an acoustic affinity with 'pock-marked' is recreated. However, it has to be admitted that in the absence of a systematic reproduction of this aspect of the text, the occasional such instance is unlikely to impinge upon the reader's awareness.

The word *ryabaya* generates problems of its own. The Russian word has associations which do not naturally attach to any of the equivalents that could be chosen in English. The usual dictionary translation, 'pock-marked', is not incorrect, but is limited to that pitted texture of the skin which we associate with a previous infection by smallpox. When Dickens's heroine Esther in *Bleak House* recovers from smallpox she is marked in this way, creating a contrast between her unchanged inner purity and her outward blemishes. But the Russian adjective may signify quite a different kind of blemish and moreover carries other associations in addition. The marks may be more like what in English are known as 'strawberry marks', a kind of birthmark not associated specifically with disease, and since those marks are red in colour, there is an association with red hair, which is traditionally linked in Russian to the idea of evil. In fact, if all the descriptions of Matryona are considered, both interpretations are found to be confirmed: she must have a face which is both pitted and blotchy. She also has red hair, which is separately described; the English association of hot-tempered, temperamental, is not inappropriate and may be left to stand, but the Russian association of the original adjective with evil is in danger of getting lost. Numerous alternative translations of this word have been considered with a view to rendering the associations of the Russian word more effectively, but all have been rejected, since none of them could be used in all the instances where the Russian adjective appears, and in the end the fact of repetition is too important in itself to change the English according to context.

A somewhat similar problem arises with the Russian word *zarya*, which denotes the red coloration of the skyline at either dusk or dawn. It is an important recurrent image in the novel, and ought, ideally, always to be rendered by the same word. However, there is no English word that fully corresponds, and according to context it has had to be translated as either 'dawn' or 'sunset'.

The Silver Dove contains much regional and substandard usage, but it does not carry any consistent regional character, and there was never any question of attempting to translate it into a specific regional English. Nevertheless, it is necessary to reproduce this characteristic in a general sense. It is at this point that the vexed question of the difference between British and American usage becomes most acute. I know as I write that this translation will have readers on both sides of the Atlantic, but as a speaker of British English, I cannot produce anything other than a version that sounds right to a British ear. However, the attempt has been made to avoid vocabulary which is not, and never has been, part either of the American language or of the common language before their differentiation. For example, the word 'codswallop', which is evidently unknown in America, and is in fact of quite recent provenance in Britain, has been removed and replaced by 'balderdash', which is equally comprehensible in both countries. As a general principle words have been avoided that are peculiar to the present-day slang of one or other version of English; however, where a word belongs to the common stock of the language, even if its recent history on either side of the ocean may be different, it has been regarded as permissible. A particular example is the word 'bap', a reasonably common regionalism in Britain, apparently quite unknown in modern America, but a word that has existed in the language since the late sixteenth century. Of course, British and American usage differ in more ways than such easily identified matters of vocabulary, but it is hoped that the worst misunderstandings and irritations will have been avoided in this way.

I have picked many people's brains in the course of this project, and wish to express my particular gratitude for the help and advice I have received from Philip Alexander, Maria Carlson, Catherine Elsworth, Nikolay Kotrelyov, Aleksandr Lavrov, John Malmstad, Kenneth Parry, Avril Pyman, Doreen Rayner, Vladimir Skorodenko, Gerry Smith and Katya Young. The Introduction is fully annotated, but for reasons of economy bibliographical references have been largely omitted from the endnotes. My apologies to those whose published contributions to the study of this novel have thus gone unmentioned.

NOTES

[1] Andrey Bely, *Serebryanyi golub'. Povest' v semi glavakh*, Knigoizdatel'stvo Skorpion, Moscow, 1910. This edition is identical with the journal publication except for the titles of Chapters 3 and 5 (see page 26 and note 4) and the pagination.

[2] Andrey Bely, *Sobranie epicheskikh poem. Kniga 4-aya. Serebryanyi golub'. Povest'*, Izdanie V. V. Pashukanisa, Moscow, 1917.

[3] Andrey Bely, *Serebryanyi golub'. Roman*, Epokha, Berlin, 1922. The change of designation from *povest'* (tale) to *roman* (novel) has no particular significance.

[4] The title of Chapter 3 was reinstated in the incomplete 1917 edition, which indicates that the omission of the chapter titles in the other lifetime volume editions was an oversight.

[5] Andrey Biely, *The Silver Dove*, translated from the Russian and with an introduction by George Reavey, Grove Press, New York, 1974.

THE SILVER DOVE

In Place of a Preface

The present tale is the first part of a planned trilogy 'East or West'; all it tells is an episode from sectarian life; but this episode has an independent significance. In view of the fact that the reader will meet the majority of the characters again in the second part, 'Wayfarers', I thought it possible to end this part without mentioning what became of the characters in the tale – Katya, Matryona, Kudeyarov – after the principal character, Daryalsky, had left the sectarians.

Many have taken the sect of the Doves to be flagellants; I agree, there are features in this sect that show an affinity with the flagellants: but flagellantism, as one of the agents of religious ferment, is not adequately embodied in the crystallized forms currently practised by the flagellants; it is in a process of development; and in this sense the Doves, as I have depicted them, do not exist; but they are possible with all their insane deviations; in this sense my Doves are entirely real.

1910. 12 April. Bobrovka *A. Bely*

CHAPTER ONE

The Village of Tselebeyevo

Our village

A gain and again, into the blue abyss of the day, hot and cruel in its brilliance, the Tselebeyevo bell-tower cast its plangent cries. In the air above it the martins fretted about. And heavy-scented Whitsuntide sprinkled the bushes with frail pink dogroses. The heat was stifling; dragonfly wings hung glassy in the heat above the pond, or soared into the heat of the day's blue abyss, up into the blue serenity of the void. A perspiring villager assiduously smeared dust over his face with his sweat-soaked sleeve, as he dragged himself along to the bell-tower to swing the bell's bronze clapper and sweat and toil to the glory of God. And again and again the Tselebeyevo bell-tower pealed out into the blue abyss of the day; and above it the martins darted with shrill cries, tracing figures of eight.

It's a fine village, Tselebeyevo, not far from the town, surrounded by hills and meadows; its scruffy cottages, scattered here and there, are richly decorated, one with a carved frieze like a real lady of fashion with curls all over, another with a painted tin cockerel, others with crudely painted flowers and angels; it's finely adorned with wattle fences, hutches and pens, the odd currant bush, and a whole host of starling-cotes that stand out against the twilit sky on their crooked broomsticks: a fine village! You ask the priest's wife. When the priest used to get back from Voronyo (his father-in-law has been a dean there these last ten years), this is how it would be: back he comes from Voronyo, takes off his over-cassock, greets his buxom wife with a kiss, adjusts his cassock and straight away it's: 'See to the samovar, my love.' And then he gets up a sweat, sitting by the samovar and, sure as eggs is eggs, gives voice to his emotion: 'Ours is a fine village!' And he ought to know, the priest; besides, he's not the sort to tell lies.

In the village of Tselebeyevo the houses are here, there and everywhere; a one-eyed hovel gives the day a sidelong glance with its bright pupil, or peers with an evil gaze from behind gaunt bushes. Another displays its tin roof – not a roof, but a green headdress shown off by a proud young wife; and over there a timid hut peeps out of the ravine – one peep, and then by evening it's coldly veiled in mist and dew.

From cottage to cottage, from hill to hill, from hill to hollow, into the bushes, the further the thicker; and before you know it the whispering forest has cast its drowsy spell on you, and there's no way out.

In the middle of the village is a big, big meadow, green as green; there's plenty of space there for carousing, and dancing, and pouring out your sorrow in a maiden's lament; there's room for an accordion too, not like merry-making in towns – the grass doesn't get trampled down or covered in spat-out sunflower husks. And when the round-dance starts to twist and turn, pomaded girls in silks and beads let out wild cries, and as their feet step out the dance, a wave runs through the grass and the evening wind halloos – it's weird and merry: you can't quite make it out, how weird it is, or what it is that's merry . . . The waves keep running, they chase in fear along the road and break with a splash as they topple. Then a bush by the roadside sobs, and the tousled dust springs up. Put your ear to the road in the evening and you will hear the grass growing and the big yellow moon rising over Tselebeyevo, and the hollow rumbling of a belated farmer's cart.

White road, dusty road – on and on it runs in a malevolent grin. It ought to be dug up, but that's not allowed; the priest himself was explaining about that only the other day . . . 'I wouldn't mind at all,' he said, 'but the authorities . . .' And so the road runs past and no one digs it up. There was trouble once though, when the peasants came out with spades . . .

Those in the know will tell you, as they stare quietly into their beards, that folk have been living here since God alone knows when, but since that road was built people's feet just up and walk off along it of their own accord; young lads hang about, just hang about, cracking sunflower seeds – nothing out of the ordinary, it seems at first – but let them once take off along that road, why, there's no returning; that's how it is.

The road slices through the big green meadow of Tselebeyevo in a malevolent grin. An unknown power drives all manner of folk along it – waggons and carts and drays laden with cases of vodka for the liquoropoly; waggons, carts, itinerant folk are driven along: a worker from the city, a pilgrim, a slocialist with a knapsack on his back, a village constable, a squire in his troika – the road is teeming with them. The cottages of Tselebeyevo are huddled together beside the road, the meaner and scruffier ones, their roofs askew like a bunch of drunken lads with their caps over one ear; the inn's here too, and the teahouse is over there, where a ferocious scarecrow spreads out its arms like a clown and shows its filthy broomstick through its rags – right over there: there's a rook on it, cawing. Further on stands a pole, and beyond it the wide empty field. And the white, dusty road runs on and on across the field, grinning at the expanses on either side – runs on to other fields, to other villages, to the fine town of Likhov, from where all sorts of people turn up, sometimes such a merry bunch as you've never seen the like of: in motor-cars they come, some smart alec with a city miss in a fancy hat, or drunken icon-painters in fantastic shirts along with a stew-dent (the devil only knows what that is!). They make straight for the teahouse and then the fun begins; the Tselebeyevo lads get in on the action and oh, how they bawl out:

> 'The yea-ears have pa-a-assed,
> The yea-ears go by-y-y;
> I'm lo-o-ost, poor youth,
> For ever and a-a-aye.'

Daryalsky

On the golden morning of Whit Sunday Daryalsky was walking along the road to the village. Daryalsky was spending the summer as the guest of the young Gugoleva lady's grandmother; the young lady herself was of the most pleasing appearance and of manners more pleasing still; the young lady was engaged to be married to Daryalsky. Daryalsky walked along, bathed in heat and light, musing on the previous day, which he had spent so delightfully in the company of the young lady and her grandmother. Yesterday he had entertained the old lady with sweet words about olden times, about unforgettable hussars and all the other things old ladies take pleasure in recalling. He had entertained himself with a stroll through the leafy groves of Gugolevo in the company of his betrothed; picking flowers had given him even greater delight. But neither the old lady nor the hussars of her unfailing memory, nor yet the leafy groves that he loved and the young lady whom he loved still more, could arouse sweet memories today: the heat of Whitsun stifled and oppressed his soul. Today he was not even drawn to Martial, lying open on the desk, slightly fly-stained.

Daryalsky – surely you notice something about my hero's name? Look here, it's Daryalsky – you know, that same Daryalsky who two summers running rented Fyodorov's cottage with his friend. Wounded by a maiden's heart, two summers running he sought the surest means of meeting the young lady he loved here – in the meadows of Tselebeyevo and the leafy groves of Gugolevo. And he made such a good job of it that for the third summer he moved completely into Gugolevo, her grandmother Baroness Todrabe-Graaben's estate. This wizened lady was of firm opinions about her granddaughter's marriage to a man who was young, and who, in her opinion, had a gale blowing not only through his head, but (most important of all) through his pockets as well. Since youth Daryalsky had been regarded as a simpleton; he had lost his parents early and his parents' means earlier still: 'poor as a church mouse!' respectable people would snort into their moustaches. But the maiden herself was of a different opinion; and so, after a lengthy interview with her grandmother, in the course of which the canny old lady in her armchair pulled many a wry face as she sipped her water, the fair Katya went and blurted straight out to the late priest's daughters that she was engaged, while Daryalsky removed to the opulent estate with its park, its conservatories, its roses and its marble cupids coated with mildew. So it was that the fair maiden succeeded in persuading the wizened old lady of the dashing stranger's pleasing qualities.

Since youth Daryalsky had been regarded as a misfit, but rumour had it that he attended a place of learning where some dozen of the wisest men deign to spend their time, year in year out, deciphering the most indecent verses in heaven only knows what languages – and this passes for studying – honestly! And Daryalsky had quite a liking for verses of that sort, and was something of an expert at them; he wrote about everything – about the lily-white heel, about the myrrh of the lips, and even . . . about the unction of the nostrils. Just imagine: he had published a book himself, a fat one, with a fig-leaf drawn on the cover; and in it the youthful bard went on about the lily-white heel and the Gugoleva girl in the guise of a young goddess, naked as the day she was born. The late priest's daughters praised it to spite the priest; the priest swore that Daryalsky only ever wrote about naked peasant women; his friend spoke up for him (his friend was still renting a cottage in Tselebeyevo) – he spoke up and said that the fruits of the bard's inspiration weren't naked peasant women but goddesses . . . But, I ask you, what is the difference between a goddess and a woman? They're all the same. Who were the goddesses of antiquity if they weren't women? Women they were, and pretty loose ones at that.

Daryalsky's friend was extremely modest: his surname wasn't Russian and he spent his days and nights reading philosophical books; although he denied the existence of God he still used to visit the priest; and the priest didn't mind; and the authorities didn't mind; and altogether he was just like an Orthodox Christian, only his name was Schmidt and he didn't believe in God . . .

Daryalsky roused himself from his thoughts again as he was approaching the church; he was passing the pond, reflected in its deep blue water; he roused himself and then sank back into his reverie.

When there are no clouds the lofty sky is fresh and seems to be hoisted higher than ever, so high, so deep; the meadow enfolds like a rampart this crystal-clear, pure, mirrorlike pond, and sad little ducks swim about in it – they have a swim, then come out on to dry land to nibble the grasses a bit, waggle their tail-feathers, and waddle off in strict formation after the quacking drake, carrying on their incomprehensible conversation; a hollow birch tree overhangs the pond, for years and years it has hung there, stretching out its shaggy arms, and what it has seen – it will not tell. Daryalsky felt an urge to throw himself down beneath it and gaze and gaze into the depths through its branches, through the spider's glistening filament stretched taut up there – while the voracious spider, having sucked its fill of flies, sat motionless, spreadeagled in the air, and seemed to be in the sky. And what of the sky? What of its pale air, pale at first, but at a closer look, quite black? Daryalsky shuddered, as though some secret danger were threatening him there, as it had threatened him more than once, as though some terrible secret, kept in the sky since time began, were secretly summoning him, and he said to himself, 'Don't be afraid, you're not in the air – look how sadly the water splashes against the jetty.'

On the little jetty a pair of sturdy legs protruded from the tucked-up hem of a red skirt, and a pair of arms were rinsing out washing; but who it was doing the rinsing – an old woman, a young woman, or a girl – could not be seen. The jetty seemed so sad as Daryalsky looked at it, even though it was daytime, even though the festive bell was calling in the clear sky. Clear sunlit day, clear sunlit water: so blue that looking into it you couldn't tell whether it was water or sky. Beware, young man, your head will spin, go away!

And Daryalsky went away; he walked off from the pond towards the village, towards the bright church, at a loss to understand where the sorrow in his soul had come from, that sorrow which arrives, as in childhood, from no one knows where, and seizes you and carries you away; and everyone calls you a misfit and, without noticing it at all, you speak out of turn, so that people smile at your words and shake their heads.

Daryalsky walked along, wondering: 'What the devil is it that I want? Isn't my fiancée beautiful? Doesn't she love me? Haven't I been in quest of her these last two years: I've found her, and . . . be off, weird thoughts, be off . . .' It was only three days since he had become engaged to his beloved; he thought how lucky he had been at that stupid gathering where he had smiled a cutting witticism at the lovely young lady, how he had then paid

court to her; but the fair lady was not quick to yield; at last, though, he had
won her white hand, and here was her gold ring on his finger, its pressure
yet unaccustomed . . . 'Dear, radiant Katya,' he whispered, and caught
himself in contemplation not of a tender girlish image, but of something
else – a kind of blur.

With these thoughts he went into the church; the smell of incense,
mixed with the smell of fresh birch branches, of a crowd of perspiring
peasants, of their blacked boots, of candle-wax and ubiquitous red calico,
struck his nose with a pleasant sensation; he had settled down to listen to
Aleksandr Nikolaevich, the sexton, whose voice, from the choir on the left,
was beating out a drum-roll – when suddenly from a distant corner of the
church his eye was caught by the movement of a red shawl with white dapples over a red cotton bodice; a peasant woman gave him a penetrating
glance; he was about to say to himself: 'There's a woman for you!', to clear
his throat and assume a dignified air, in order to forget everything and start
bowing in prayer to the Queen of Heaven, but . . . he did not clear his
throat, he did not assume a dignified air, and he made no bow at all. His
breast was seared by a sweet surge of unutterable dread, and he was
unaware that the colour had left his face, that, pale as death, he could barely
keep his feet. Her browless face, covered in large pock-marks, had glanced
at him with cruel and avid agitation. What it was telling him, this face, and
what in his soul had responded to it, he did not know; there was just the
movement of a red shawl with white dapples on it. When Daryalsky came
to his senses again, Aleksandr Nikolaevich, the sexton, had finished his
drum-roll from the left choir; Father Vukol had mounted the ambo more
than once, and a ray of sunlight had played in his ginger hair and over his
silver chasuble, embroidered with dark blue flowers: now the priest was
genuflecting beyond the open altar gates; 'Borne on high by angels' had
been sung; and five of the landowner Utkin's daughters – one here, one
there – one after another turned their faces, round as turnips, towards
Daryalsky and then stood primly, pouting flirtatiously to the point of inde-
cency, while the sixth, an old maid, with a cluster of ripe cherries on her
hat, bit her lip in irritation.

The service ended; the priest came out with the cross and started distributing plump communion wafers to Utkina and her six ripe daughters,
to the richer and more eminent peasants, those with the newer smocks and
the boots that creaked, who by wile and native wit had contrived to build
resplendent huts and amass money by the secret sale of spirits or by
shrewd dealings – those, in short, who were more ruthless and tight-fisted
than the others; they came up to the holy cross with due decorum and
solemnity, gravely bowing their bearded faces with pudding-basin haircuts

that reeked of lamp-oil; when the village notables had stepped back from the ambo, the priest began to wave the cross with a certain determination along the noses of the peasants who crowded forwards (it wasn't for nothing that Miss Shkurenkova, the 'schoolmarm', hissed that the priest had caught her so hard in the teeth with his cross that she had had toothache for a long time afterwards). Daryalsky was just coming up to the cross, and the priest was holding it out to him with one hand and with the other reaching for the communion bread, when suddenly the wondrous woman's gaze scorched him again; her red lips, faintly smiling, quivered slightly, as though freely quaffing of his soul; he had no recollection of kissing the holy cross, nor of the priest's invitation to partake of pie, nor of his own reply; all he remembered was that the pock-marked peasant woman had laid claim to his soul. In vain he tried to summon in his soul the image of Katya, and kept repeating to himself, 'My lovely bride, my gentle bride!' – the beloved image was as though drawn in chalk on a blackboard; the cruel teacher had wiped it off with his sponge and not a trace of it was left.

A pock-marked peasant woman with browless eyes, a hawk: this was no tender flower, burgeoning in the depths of his soul, no daydream, morning light, or honey-scented meadow-grass; a stormcloud, a tempest, a tigress, a werewolf, had entered his soul in a trice and was calling him; the faint smile of her soft lips aroused in him a gentle, drunken, dull sweet sadness, laughter and lasciviousness: so it is that the recesses of a millennial past, opened for a moment, restore the memory of that which never happened in your life, call forth an unknown face, so terrifyingly familiar from your dreams; and that face rises up as the image of a childhood that never was but nonetheless took place; that is the sort of face you have, pock-marked peasant woman!

Such were Daryalsky's thoughts – but it was not he who thought them, for the thoughts occurred in his soul without his volition; she had already left the church, and Kudeyarov the carpenter shuffled off behind her with his sickly face and his fist enmeshed in the yellow bast of his beard; he bumped into Daryalsky, looked at him – for an instant: a glance from his face, and there passed across Daryalsky's soul something incoherent – a kind of blur. Daryalsky didn't remember going out into the church porch; he didn't hear the Tselebeyevo bell-tower cast its plangent cries, nor the martins crying shrilly as they fretted about above it. Whitsuntide sprinkled frail pink dogroses and flies settled in swarms of ringing emeralds on the sun-scorched backs of the peasants' faded smocks.

A young fellow passed by, squeezing an accordion and pressing it to his stomach, while dust in noiseless bursts rose softly from his footfalls; along the road he went, bawling out some sort of song; carts trundled along the road; their ungreased wheels creaked and screeched; the tin roofs of the cottages and the heat-enraged windows (those that hadn't been stopped up with pillows) threw back the sun's glare. In the distance portly girls were walking out in pairs, with green, blue, canary-yellow or even golden bodices over their ample waists; they had coaxed their feet into blunt-nosed shoes that looked like logs of wood, and strutted out like pea-hens. The delicate branches of the weeping birches stirred now and then above the cemetery. Someone was whistling, and the bushes vibrated with the sound. Domna Yakovlevna, daughter of the late priest of Tselebeyevo and an old maid, was bent over her parent's grave; the caretaker emerged from the currant bushes and, shading his eyes with his hand, observed the old maid from a distance; he was at loggerheads with her and growled loudly, as though into space, but so that Domna Yakovlevna would hear his words: 'Ought to dig up the bones and clear the place; there's little enough room as it is, without keeping old bones . . .' Then, coming closer, he amiably doffed his cap and humorously remarked: 'Come to visit your old dad, have you? Not much to visit, really: his remains have all rotted, I'll be bound . . .'

'The old devil!' thought Daryalsky, and began to rub his eyes: had he been asleep there in the church, or not, had he imagined it all? Nonsense; he must have dozed off – it's not good to dream in the daytime; not for nothing is it written in the Scriptures: 'Save us from the devil of noon-day . . .'

And, twirling his moustache, Daryalsky set off towards the priest's house, trying to evoke by force the image of Katya in his soul, and in the end he began to recite from memory his favourite verses from Martial; but the Katya he saw was not Katya, and instead of lines from Martial, he began, to his own surprise, to whistle: 'The years have passed, the years go by, I'm lost, poor youth, for ever and aye . . .'

In such an unexpected way did this day begin for Daryalsky. It is with this day that we shall commence our story.

Cabbage pie

'Pfa!' grunted the priest, as he and the sexton, Aleksandr Nikolaevich, downed another glass of vodka, following it with pickled mushrooms, gathered in the autumn by the priest's virtuous wife and their multitudinous offspring, each one smaller than the next.

The priest's wife had completed three years at the secondary school in Likhov, of which fact she liked to remind her guests; on her battered upright piano she still played now and then the waltz 'Times Gone By'; she was buxom, portly, with crimson lips and eyes the deep brown of ripe cherries in a delicate, almost icing-sugar face, sprinkled with yellow freckles, but already with a double chin. Here she was, making one joke after another about clerical life, the rough-hewn yokels and the town of Likhov, while bustling around a steaming pie and cutting slices of immense proportions, each a boundless expanse of crust with the thinnest layer of cabbage inside. 'Anna Yermolaevna, do have some more pie! . . .Varvara Yermolaevna, why so little?' She addressed in turn Utkin the landowner's six ripe daughters, who formed a pleasant herbaceous border round the neatly laid table; the room was filled with a twittering, emanating from six open pink mouths, and a chirrupping about all the news of the neighbourhood; the priest's deft wife could hardly keep the plates filled, time and again administering clouts to one of her offspring who turned up inopportunely, munching a crust and dribbling from mouth and nose; at the same time she chattered more than anyone.

'Have you heard, good lady – the constable was saying those Slocialists have appeared not far from Likhov, distributing their foul leaflets; he says they want to rise up against the Tsar, so as to take control of the "Monopoly" and get all the people tight together; and he says the Tsar has sent out writs everywhere, printed in golden letters, calling on the Orthodox people to fight for the holy church: "Proletarians unite!" it says on them. They say the archpriest at Likhov is expecting one of these epistles from the Tsar any day, to send round the district . . .' Aleksandr Nikolaevich, the sexton, suddenly blurted all this out and then, with a twitch of his rowanberry nose, fell into an embarrassed silence as six maidenly heads fastened their gaze upon him with an expression of open and utter contempt.

'Pfa!' grunted the priest, pouring Aleksandr Nikolaevich another glass. 'Do you know, my friend, what a proletarian is?' And seeing that the part of the sexton's forehead where his eyebrows should have been (the sexton had no eyebrows) formed an arch, the priest added graphically, 'It's like this, my friend: a proletarian is someone who's in favour of letters, but can't write . . .'

'Now then, you stop that, Father Vukol!' whispered his wife as she passed, addressing her words not to the pleasant and humorous meaning of the priest's elucidation, but to the rowanberry vodka, to which her better half had already extended his hand more than once; whereupon the priest snorted: 'Pfa!' and downed another one with Aleksandr Nikolaevich, the sexton; then they each followed it with a pickled mushroom. At one corner of the table Daryalsky puffed in silence at a cigarette, now and then applying himself to the rowanberry vodka, and he was already tipsy, but his inebriation did not dispel his strange thoughts; although he had accepted the invitation to partake of pie, because he had no desire whatsoever to go back to Gugolevo, nevertheless he was so sullen that willy-nilly everyone gave up their attempts to talk to him; in vain the young Utkin ladies tried twittering to him; in vain they turned their languid eyes upon him, using their lace handkerchieves as fans with manifest coquetry; with manifest coquetry they adjusted their décolletage; or made somewhat transparent hints at Daryalsky's heart and the rascal Cupid who had pierced it; Daryalsky either made no answer, or mumbled something irrelevant, or else agreed openly with the girls' hints at the state of his heart, leaving all joking aside; and he paid no attention at all to the girls' glittering eyes, and even less to their décolletage, that shimmered an enticing pink through diaphanous muslin. For two years Daryalsky had been loitering in these parts, and no one could say with what purpose; people with their heads screwed on assumed at first that he had a purpose, he must have a purpose, and that that purpose was seditious; there were some inquisitive snoopers, too, who loved whispering and, if they got the chance, loved making denunciations (Daryalsky attracted most interest from the deaf-mute Sidor, biggest gossip in the district, who couldn't pronounce a single word except an unintelligible 'Apa, apa' – but could express himself intelligibly by sign-language) – well, anyway: neither Sidor nor anyone else could find anything harmful in Daryalsky's behaviour; then they came to the conclusion that his appearance in these parts had another meaning, and that that meaning had to do with matrimony; then every young lady in the district took it into her head that she was the object of his amorous yearnings; all six Utkin daughters took it into their heads too; and although each of them, out loud, named one of her sisters as the object of Daryalsky's affections, in their own hearts they concluded differently; and so they were all thunderstruck by his betrothal to Katya Gugoleva, the baroness's wealthy granddaughter; nobody had imagined that, to put it bluntly, this common mug, this johnny-come-lately would manage to worm his way into quality. I have to explain that the expression 'common mug' was used in respect of my hero only as a turn of phrase, for that part of his anatomy which is known in vulgar parlance as, if you will pardon the expression, a 'mug' was, to put it plainly, not common at all, but decidedly uncommon: the velvet sheen of his dark eyes, his sunburnt face with the prominent nose, his thin, crimson lips, adorned by the down of a moustache, and his shock of wavy, ash-blond curls constituted an object of secret desires for more than one young lady, peasant girl or youthful widow, indeed for married women too, or, begging your pardon, let's put it like this . . . well, not to mince words . . . even for the priest's wife herself. They did a bit of wondering and gasping, but they soon got used to it; Daryalsky's sojourn in our parts was taken for granted; he was no longer followed, and indeed following him wasn't easy: not everyone was admitted to the baroness's estate. To be sure, there were other people here who understood better what it was my hero wanted (just love, or something else as well), on what the languishing gaze of his velvet eyes was fixed, with what passion and lust he stared in front of him when neither in front of him nor anywhere else was there a girl to be seen, and while all around the evening twilight blazed and glowed; they understood much else in Daryalsky, too, and encircled him, so to speak, with an invisible net of glances for some purpose no one knew; they were simple people, not educated at all: well, we'll talk about them later – let's just say: *there were such people*; and let's say too that if they had understood the subtleties of poetic beauty, if they had read what was concealed beneath the fig-leaf drawn on the cover of Daryalsky's book – oh yes, they would have smiled, and what a smile! They would have said: 'He's one of us' . . . Well, anyway, it isn't at all the right time for that now; it's just the time to introduce the illustrious inhabitants of Tselebeyevo themselves.

So here goes.

The villagers of Tselebeyevo

Illustrious people, don't you disdain our village; we've had visits from the likes of you often enough and we're not easily impressed by anyone any more. Don't turn up your noses, there's no point: it's you who'll be the laughing-stock, the peasants will make fun of you and walk off in a crowd, blowing their noses with their fingers; they'll leave you all on your own in the meadow, with the ducks for company, as if to say, you walk about by yourself, pick some flowers, impress the ducks; maybe you'll meet the schoolmarm: but what's the schoolmarm – a real fright.

The people here aren't impressed by anything. If you come, you'll be made welcome and treated to all manner of pies – they won't let you go hungry: your horses will get their oats and your driver his dram: you can live here in peace and comfort and grow fat: if you don't want to, God's your judge: the people of Tselebeyevo will manage to live out their days without you.

When some garrulous woman starts counting up the illustrious visitors on her fingers, why, it's a wonder how many she finds: Yeropegin the merchant, who's a miller in Likhov and rich as rich can be, the rural dean from Voronyo, and Baron Todrabe-Graaben, an important general (and son of the old Graaben lady who lives at Gugolevo), and guests from Moscow: they kept coming to see the daughters of the late priest, fine upstanding young ladies, about whom there are quite a few odd things to tell: they got themselves a little house after their father died – Agrafena Yakovlevna, Domna Yakovlevna and Varvara Yakovlevna; well then, they often had students visiting them, and writers, and once even a man who collected songs turned up: he had them all singing and did a round-dance with the village girls, and wrote everything down in his notebook. 'That songster, a stew-dent is he, or a striker?' good people said, 'a striker, most likely, because afterwards the lads were bawling out "Stand up, arise, working people!" for an awful long time. What's he mean, anyway, "arise"? Everyone here gets up to go to work at the crack of dawn without him telling us!' So when this vigorous woman starts counting on her fingers you will get the impression that the whole Russian nation has nothing else to do but live in Tselebeyevo or come to Tselebeyevo; she'd count them all up, only she hasn't got enough fingers: she'll stare at the ground with a look of such dignified indifference, as if to say: 'We've seen a thing or two, we have . . .'

So just you try turning up your nose!

There are people of substance living in Tselebeyevo: in the first place there's Ivan Stepanov, who's been keeping a shop here for many years, selling haberdashery; he's not a man to cross: he'll fleece you in the twinkling of an eye, he'll have your trousers off you and send you begging, and ruin your wife's reputation; you needn't be surprised if your house burns down; none of your kith and kin will come away unscathed; your cousins and your in-laws and your in-laws' cousins will all have something to remember him by and no mistake: he's a godfearing man, stands there in church at the candle table jingling coppers; he's an imposing figure with his full beard and his hair cut level all round, high boots gathered at the top, with studs and a creak, always blacked with tar, and sporting a brass watch.

Then secondly there's the priest, Father Vukol Golokrestovsky, and his wife – a fine priest, you won't find another like him anywhere in the neighbourhood, even if you drive forty versts, a hard-working priest he is, strict, keen on prayers.

But when he's had a couple of glasses, then straightaway he makes his wife sit down and strum the guitar (they've got a real guitar: the priest's wife brought the guitar with her when they moved to the village about eight years ago; it does have a broken string, it's true, but what's the point of being a priest's wife if you can't pluck away on a three-stringed guitar without being embarrassed; after all, she did have three years at secondary school in Likhov!) – so the priest makes his wife sit down and play the guitar: 'Masha, play the Persian march!' His face is all aglow and comes out in yellow freckles, and his eyes keep glinting in the direction of the front garden: 'Play, Masha, cast aside all worldly care.' But his wife bursts into tears, 'You ought to go to bed, Father Vukol.' And the reverend Golokrestovsky would go to bed, if it weren't for the sexton: it's the sexton who eggs him on. And so he digs his heels in: go on, go on, keep playing! His wife weeps and strums the guitar, while the priest takes up his position: rolls up his sleeves and enacts, for his own consolation and the edification of the sexton, the storming of the mighty fortress of Kars; the make-believe lasts as long as the priest's energy, until the shrill martins start their crying above the church cross, until cold dew-drops hang, like clusters of transparent berries, on the currant bushes in the priest's garden, until the fiery sunset spreads its crimson velvet over the edge of the house; then Father Golokrestovsky jerks his ginger beard towards the evening glow, shakes his locks, taps his feet, and smoothly swings his arms, palms forward, from left to right, from right to left: 'Listen – the drum is beating: the enemy forces are crossing the bridge: the machine-guns are rattling . . . Aha, we'll take note of that !'

And in the sunset, against the evening glow, the guitar twangs away plaintively; plaintively the priest's wife sobs, bent over the guitar, swallowing her salty tears, but she dare not stop playing: Aleksandr Nikolaevich, the sexton, sees to that; the priest wouldn't notice, but Aleksandr Nikolaevich would denounce her straight away; the sexton may be drunk, but he remembers everything: he sits by the bottle of rowanberry vodka, twitching his rowan-coloured nose, and marvels at the priest; the priest goes on with his game of make-believe: he hunches himself up so that his head disappears into his shoulders, and shuffles off into the bushes: heaven alone knows what he does there, but when he comes out of the bushes he shouts, 'Hurrah, our men have won the day!' (The priest has quite an imagination.) As soon as he shouts 'won the day', the priest's wife lays the guitar aside: she knows that Father Vukol won't be doing any more make-believe: he'll go and sleep till morning; the sexton will calm down too, and, intoning a verse of King David the Psalmist, will totter unsteadily home to his wife, where a sound pummelling awaits him. The priest, when he wakes up in the morning, will run off like a lamb to Ivan Stepanov's shop, all of his own accord, and buy some peppermint cakes (at fifteen kopecks a pound) to treat his buxom better half; and that will be an end to the matter.

Everyone knows by now: when the guitar starts twanging in the priest's currant bushes, it means the priest is tipsy and is enacting the storming of the fortress of Kars by a valiant warrior and the utter rout of the Turks; people gather in the bushes; the priest is a good actor; they stare, crack sunflower-seeds, giggle and pinch the girls; the girls squeal – and everyone scatters. The priest is a good actor: but he wouldn't dream of doing anything like this at any other time: he's conscientious, demanding and thrifty: and he's often had to tell the sexton off.

Such is the priest in Tselebeyevo: a fine priest, you won't find another like him, no one else is up to all that, you can be sure. That's what our village is like, and those are the kind of people that live in it: a fine village, fine people!

But it has never been heard of anywhere for fine neighbours to live together in harmony and show each other equal respect and kindness with presents and other marks of goodwill; one will doff his cap and bow low before his neighbour's wealth, his shining, squeaky boots, not because he's short of a decent suit himself, but out of courtesy – but his neighbour sticks his nose in the air and his hands in his pockets; it hurts: the first man nurses his grievance and plans to get his own back: who does he think he is, that neighbour? Other people are masters in their own homes too and have their own icons in the corner; they don't need charity; and so one neighbour starts to injure the other to protect his honour: he scrawls an obscenity on his neighbour's fence, or throws his neighbour's dog a piece of meat with a nail stuck in it; the dog dies – and there you are, the neighbours are at loggerheads, laying booby-traps for each other and setting each other's houses on fire, tormenting each other with denunciations: given half a chance they'd scatter each other's ashes to the winds.

Whatever for!

It surprised people that Father Golokrestovsky stood up for Ivan Stepanov so firmly; but then Ivan Stepanov wouldn't let the priest down either, he became mild-mannered in his presence, and when he looked at the priest his eyes lost their lightning-bolts and turned quite different, dull and fishlike . . . They kept on the right side of each other.

When the priest's wife baked a cabbage pie, the priest would send round to invite Ivan Stepanov to come and try it while it was hot, or he might start fussing around himself, applying his nose to the crust while the pie was baking, testing to see if the dough was baked through; then he would choose a nice juicy piece and send a workman round to Stepanov's shop with it. But Ivan Stepanov wouldn't be outdone: he would send the priest's wife some musty calico for a bodice, would regale her with stale fruit-drops in twisted paper wrappings, or dry spice-cakes and diverse other delicacies; there was never a shortage of sweets in the priest's house, and the flies consequently multiplied in abundance.

The shopkeeper had made no mean contribution to the repair of the church. It was an ancient church, and the icons were old too – dark, sombre, austere countenances: Bishop Mikola, and the wisest of pagans – Plato was his name – and the Ethiopian saint with the head of a dog, a negro (evidently in the old days they painted by the calendar of saints) – sombre, sombre faces: no fun to look at at all; so when some third-rate icon-painters arrived from the city they first of all set about scraping these faces off; when they'd scraped them off they replastered the wall and on this fresh surface they painted happy, smiling saints (nice fashionable ones with social graces) after the pattern of Likhov Cathedral; it became much more inviting! But then something funny happened.

I have to tell you that the icon-painters had got it firmly into their heads that they could touch the tight-fisted shopkeeper for some victuals, but he wasn't having any: he wasn't a shopkeeper for nothing; so the canny painters upped and painted a certain man in the likeness of Ivan Stepanov: in his left hand he holds a five-domed church like a communion wafer, while in his chastening right he deigns to brandish a heavy, sharp sword – Ivan Stepanov to a T . . . only in brocade with an omophorion and a halo of gold leaf round his head with Church Slavonic lettering; his eyes flash thunderbolts as he keeps watch – just like the shopkeeper (particularly when the shopkeeper has a mind to put a match under his enemy and adversary!). Well I'm blowed: did you take it into your head to smile? If you come into the church I'll show you the man straight away: that righteous man is still there to this day, painted to the right of the iconostasis (you can see for yourselves). Well, you can believe me anyway!

Since then Ivan Stepanov has taken to standing through the service beside that icon in full view of the congregation, as if to say: look, and compare; crossing himself fervently, and at the same time peeping round in all directions to see if they were comparing, and everyone whispering . . . Tyurina, the landowner's wife, went into Stepanov's shop (she had some business there) and smiled; just before Whitsuntide Utkin came and gave Ivan Stepanov such a look, up and down, and then down and up, and asked him straight: 'Well, then?' And Stepanov gave him a straight reply: 'Quite well, thank you. We get by.' The lame carpenter, though, kept going into the church and in the end he couldn't stand it and went straight to the priest: 'People say this and that, father; it's a disgrace.' But the priest didn't bat an eyelid: 'You will have to prove,' he said, 'that it's a deliberate resemblance and not just a coincidence they look alike: Stepanov is a god-fearing man; maybe he prays to that saint and so he bears his imprint on his face; I'm afraid, my friend, that these, how shall I put it, emblematic outlines are altogether a bit beyond you; but there's no blasphemy in it. And if there were, it would be the painters who had sinned; and they'd be the ones to answer; I can't forbid Stepanov to stand under the icon, can I? Judge for youself, I've no business doing that: the Lord's temple is for everyone . . . So you should hold your tongue and calm down; you'd do better to think of your own transgressions' . . . The carpenter spat and turned away from the priest.

The schoolteacher grumbled too: 'It's an outrage, they've defiled the church.' But who's going to take any notice of the schoolteacher's words? What sort of authority is she? It would be all right if the district clerk, or the volost chairman, or someone else, if, say, General Todrabe-Graaben himself were to express an opinion on the issue, then it would be a different matter; but the volost chairman is godfather to one of Stepanov's children and fell into his clutches long ago; the district clerk says nothing, and nobody has ever seen General Todrabe-Graaben in our church. And then, would you believe it, you're expected to take account of some Shkurenkova woman, a schoolteacher; just see what she looks like: her face is greener than green, always shiny, full of freckles – she's mutton dressed up as lamb in pink and mauve blouses.

Her blouses are dirt-cheap! Cotton or calico at 12 kopecks a yard; as soon as they're washed they come out in stains all over (the girls are always poking fun at her); if she sees a good-looking lad, or if a holiday-maker turns up, she'll lift her skirts (showing her laddered stocking) and twirl her toe, with her eyes full of the joys of spring.

Who's going to take any notice of the schoolteacher's words? Who was it who kept tripping the priest up, who was it the long-suffering priest gave way to? It was her, it was her, because you can't pin anything onto her: giggling right and left, as though it was all a joke; but what sort of joke is that, always trying to sting where it hurts most: 'Why hasn't your wife played the Persian march for so long? I have a vivid imagination and I'm passionately fond of music! You ought to ask her to play more often.' She rolls her eyes and her lips twitch with laughter. Once she made a jibe at the priest in the presence of the landowner Utkin and his six ripe daughters, Katerina, Stepanida, Varvara, Anna, Valentina and Raisa. The priest keeps his peace, but sometimes it galls him so that he calls for the sexton, sends out for vodka – and before you know it the guitar is twanging away in the currant bushes, while the schoolteacher gloats.

Just once the priest lost his patience: as soon as he got home he sat down to dash off a denunciation; he scribbled and scribbled – and finally got it down: that this nuisance of a woman professed some unheard-of faith and intended to establish relations with the Caucasian Molokans for the purpose of overthrowing the powers-that-be; that was why she was a socialist; and she didn't teach the children anything, but spent all her time on this mischief, to which he, the priest in charge of the church of Tselebeyevo, was a witness. He set everything out elegantly and tied it all up cleverly, naming Ivan Stepanov as witness; you could tell straight away that the priest had an imagination, and had enacted the capture of the fortress of Kars more than once. Ivan Stepanov testified on his own account that for nigh-on two years the said schoolmarm, Shkurenkova, had been trying to seduce him, Stepanov, and threatening at the first convenient opportunity to commit an act of indecent assault against him.

They signed the paper and sealed it in an envelope, but at the last minute they had second thoughts and didn't send it; the authorities wouldn't believe them, and they might get into trouble. To tell the truth, the teacher was an Orthodox believer, and anybody could see that she taught the children to read and write; well, there's no objecting to literacy; both the district clerk and the village constable in our parts were very much in favour of literacy in those days.

But then she went and found out about the priest's design and lay in wait for him when he was going round his parish. You know how it is, everyone put some eggs into his cart, or some flour, or bread, or onions (priests used to live by what they collected from their parishioners); he was on his way home with his cart full of flour, bread and eggs, and stopped by the school to have a drink of water at the well: out comes this sprightly spinster and natters on, giggling right and left; then up she jumps into the cart as though by chance and sits down on the eggs and squashes them – about four dozen of them she squashed. Take that, she seemed to say, now how are you going to get your own back?

Ever since then they've kept their distance; but what's that to us? It's their quarrel, we'll keep well out of it; they can call each other names, we'll just stay mum.

Another notable inhabitant of our village is the carpenter, Mitry Kudeyarov. He lives in that little cottage over there that peeps out of the sloping hollow; if you stand up on the hillock, then . . . there's its roof – over there: there's a puff of smoke coming from it.

The carpenter made furniture and received orders not only from Likhov, but even from Moscow; he was lame, and sickly and pale, he had a nose like a woodpecker's and coughed all the time, but he supplied the furniture shops; people passing on the road often called in to see him: an invisible power drove all manner of folk along the road: gypsies, slocialists, workers from the city, pilgrims would all have walked straight past, but for the fact that we happened to have Kudeyarov in our midst; he was the one they turned off to see. That was why the path from the road to his hollow became more and more clearly defined. Whenever a small dark figure on the road started hobbling this way or yellow dust rose up, and there in the dust a cart rumbled by, Mitry would climb up onto the hillock, shade his eyes with his hand, and wait . . . And what was it he kept waiting for? Waiting – while an invisible power drove all manner of folk past: a cart rumbles by, not stopping in the village; one person walks past, another, bawling out a song; now and then one turns off onto the path, going to visit Mitry. The carpenter didn't like answering when people asked him, 'Who's been drinking tea with you?' 'Ordinary decent folk.' He'd frown and fall silent.

He's a decent person himself, hospitable; when you come to see him, he sends his woman (he's buried his wife) to the well to fetch water for the samovar; straight away he cleans the bench of shavings and starts to chat away about his furniture business. 'Do you make furniture?' – 'That we do indeed, we make period furniture and ordinary furniture; if it's to Moscow you're sending it they always want period: there's steady styles that pay well because there's a lot of carving in them, you know: like rococo, for example, or Russian style. And then there's ordinary rubbish, what we knock together any old how: that sort of work doesn't fetch much nowadays, but we get plenty of orders for it; you can't make much money on that sort of style, it's very tricky.' As he says it, he winks with his whole face; and what a face, I ask you! It's not a face, it's a gnawed mutton bone; and what's more it's not a whole face, but only half a face; that's to say, it's a face like any other, but it always seems to be only half a face; one side of it gives you a crafty wink, but the other is always on the lookout for something, afraid of something or other; the two halves conduct a conversation with each other: one half says, 'I've got what it takes,' while the other replies, 'Come on, what are you hiding?', but if you stand straight in front of his nose, there's no face at all to be seen, but something else . . . a kind of blur.

After a day's work, with the collar of his red shirt unbuttoned and the back of it soaked in sweat, when the cool of evening floods the distant copses with transparent, sparkling turquoise, and everything starts to gloom – when the darkness spreads and shadows multiply, while on the other side the weary sun spills the last of its rays – then Mitry lays aside his planes and chisels and drills, the thin bast of his yellow beard dangling over them, leans pensively on his saw, and then wends his way quietly through the meadow in his worn bast shoes. The children shy away from him, because he has a hard, unfriendly way of looking at them, only he wouldn't hurt a fly, he's a decent person; everyone knows where the carpenter is trudging off to at this time of day, and why: he's off to see the priest, to argue about texts; he's very well-read in the Holy Scriptures and has his own opinions – no one quite fathoms what they are, though he seems to make no secret of them: there isn't time to worry what the carpenter Kudeyarov understands by 'one substance', or what opinion he holds about the schoolmarm's outrageous behaviour.

So there he'd be, wiping his sweaty face with his sleeve, he'd turn towards the priest the half of his face that said, 'I've got what it takes', and pose his question; there they'd stand, he and the priest, debating in the grass in the quiet of the evening, while a faint mist rose up over the meadow. The priest would sweat and sweat, as Kudeyarov rattled off the texts, and get angry when Kudeyarov, as if by chance, turned the other half of his face to him ('Come on, what are you hiding?'); the priest would get angry, remember his wife's samovar, and wave Kudeyarov away: 'Go on with you, do you think I've got time to argue the toss with everybody: there are too many of you around, all kinds of folk!' Only the priest wouldn't really mean it; it would just be that he wanted some tea, or that he'd caught sight of his wife's sweet white neck in the window: he really liked showing Kudeyarov how clever he was. He'd spit, and look at the carpenter, but the carpenter's face wouldn't be there: just a kind of blur. So the priest would walk away, and Kudeyarov would wink after him, and trudge off over the meadow to his sloping hollow, where it was cool in the dew. And the stars would begin to shine.

What could you say about Kudeyarov the carpenter? But people did say things. They said that at night Kudeyarov closed the shutters in his hut very tight (only he and the priest had shutters), and a weird light blazed out through the shutters, and the murmur of voices could be heard: some of the gossip had it that he was saying special prayers of his own with his pock-marked woman; other people thought differently – that the devil's work was being done there. However, all these things were said cautiously and vaguely, and even those who said them didn't believe them; it was the deaf-mute who first spread the rumour; he came into Ivan Stepanov's shop one day and pointed in the direction of Kudeyarov's hut muttering his 'Apa, apa' and making the sign of horns over his dishevelled head. To tell the truth, Stepanov didn't believe him, because he knew what kind of news you could get from a deaf-mute: it was with good reason that at confession the priest only tried to make him understand that it was forbidden to eat meat or eggs or drink milk on fast days, for which purpose he shaped the palms of his hands into a herring-tail and put his whole hands together to make a head of cabbage. The deaf-mute understood that all right, but about Kudeyarov he might have got it all mixed up.

As for the woman – she was quite a different matter. A strange woman he had, with a pock-marked face. Whether she shared his bed or not, no one knew; she probably did. Only the villagers didn't like the woman, and she kept herself to herself. A bit silly, she was, kept gazing at the stars; as soon as the stars came out, she'd go outside and sing away in her plaintive voice – you couldn't tell whether it was a devotional hymn she was singing or a salacious love-song. She was often to be seen on the jetty: she'd sit on the jetty not washing her linen, but gazing at the stars shining in the water.

The Dove

In the heat of the day, when even the girls sought shelter, although it was a holiday, when their green, red, canary-coloured bodices disappeared from view, and the most that could be seen was a sparrow hopping out of the dust into the bushes, when there was only the wind, the hot wind, rocking the melancholy pines, and swirls of dust from the road winding across the field – there were no waggons trundling along the road, no villager passing by: it was as though the village had died – such was the peace, the emptiness, the drowsiness that hung in the glaring sunlight and the grasshoppers' chirping.

Only where the houses cluster beside the road, the meaner and scruffier ones, shouting and singing could be heard from the teahouse: the roadside folk of Tselebeyevo have taken to unclean living. More respectable people frowned firmly at this part of our village; the priest frowned, the schoolteacher, Ivan Stepanov (wealthy peasant that he was) and the lame carpenter.

There the road ran – on and on – beyond the village and into the fields – ran away up the gentle incline of the plain to lose itself at the very sky, for here the sky bent low to the village (there, over the border and, it seemed, beyond the sky, was the fine town of Likhov). And a gnarled bush could be seen there, but from the village it looked like the dark figure of a traveller, wandering in solitude towards the village; the years passed, and the traveller walked and walked: he could not reach human habitation, but kept on threatening the village from afar.

At this oppressive hour only the carpenter would clamber from the sloping hollow where his hut stood and up the hillock; shading his sickly face with his hand, he kept peering out along the road to see if dust was rising, if a traveller was approaching, if the Lord was sending him a visitor; the carpenter stood a while – the distance was clear, everything shimmering. Nobody. The carpenter would slip back to his lair: he'd sit a while in the corner under the icons; and then the waiting would get too much for him again and out he'd go on to the hillock, though it was time for tea; the pock-marked woman who worked for him, barefooted Matryona, had already laid the table; the white tablecloth with the edging of red cockerels, the cups with their design of roses, bread and eggs were already on the table; the samovar was steaming: time for tea; but how could they sit down to tea without their visitor, and still he wasn't there; and once again Kudeyarov the carpenter went out on to the hillock; the road ran far into the distance; the distance was clear, and there was no one there; no, there was someone, surely someone was approaching the village; that was not the bush – its dark figure was over there; and beside it was another figure, a dark one too; soon it would be down here – 'Hey, Matryona, make ready for our guest!' And Matryona bustled about, shuffling from stove to table on her sturdy white legs; a smile appeared on her pock-marked, browless face, with the dark reddened eyes and slightly quivering scarlet lips, as though she had long been waiting for tidings from afar; she kept glancing at the carpenter, but he just sat there in silence, not responding to the silly woman's glances, waiting for his guest. And the guest appeared.

A strange guest he was too: Abram the beggar, well-known in the district; he would turn up in our parts every now and then, going barefoot around the villages and estates, and everywhere people would give him something: a hunk of bread, some eggs, a kopeck (it was mainly the gentry who gave him money), some people would just give him a meal or somewhere to sleep, and some would threaten to set the dog on him; and then he just disappeared from view and wouldn't be seen for months; you might come across him far beyond Likhov, he'd even been seen the other side of Moscow: tall, broad-shouldered, with a shaggy mane of dark hair, streaked with grey, that fell down to his shoulders, with a large nose and narrow, slanting, crafty eyes, he knew for certain who could be touched for what; he had a way of coming up under the window and singing a psalm in his deep, bass voice, beating out the time with his stick. It was a strange stick he had, a cross between a walking-stick, a club and a crook. He was a giant of a man: if you met him in the forest you'd take fright, thinking he might get you with that club of his; but the strangest thing of all was that on his club there glinted the image of a dove, made of tin, but bright as silver. But since people knew the beggar, knew his character and his ways, knew how he used to play with the children, and sometimes even guard the forest, since everyone knew him, even the authorities, they wouldn't have been scared to meet him in the forest: it's only strangers that would have been. There was just one sin he was known for: he often used to sit in the teahouse, where he traded eggs and bread for tea and a bite to eat; he'd sit in the ale-house in the town, too, sit there in silence, listening to people's talk: it was said he knew the low-down about everybody – the peasants, the priests and the gentry, who'd been where, and who was planning what, Abram knew it all; but heaven only knows why that was said of him: himself, he didn't say much, hardly talked to anyone, and when he was asked about anything, he wouldn't tell: said he didn't know.

On entering the cottage Abram crossed himself before the icons and took off his leather rucksack and the white felt hat which some people of quality had given him, the sort the gentry call a 'toadstool'; he and Kudeyarov embraced and kissed three times, Abram made a low bow to Matryona as though she was the lady of the house, and she held her hand out to him with her work-worn fingers tightly squeezed together. He took off his belt without ceremony and sat down to tea with Matryona and the carpenter, as though he wasn't a beggar, but some invited guest, and from the way they looked after the wanderer at table there was no telling he was a beggar. They drank their tea in silence. But when the tea was drunk and the cups turned upside down, and the samovar was giving out a high-pitched hiss as if to drive someone away, then Kudeyarov the carpenter raised the thin bast of his beard and fixed the beggar with the side of his face that seemed to say, 'I've got what it takes', whereupon the beggar, understanding the carpenter without words, winked at Matryona: 'We know what we know: why keep secrets from friends!'

Matryona stood a little way off in her red bodice, resting her pale face on her hand; only her lips quivered, and her eyes flashed mysteriously. Putting her finger to her lips she bent it thrice, deliberately, beside them; her lips began to mutter something; and again her eyes flashed wondrously. Then the carpenter, sitting in the icon-corner, turned his whole face to the beggar, and his whole face expressed something like – a kind of blur, while his hand rapped thrice, deliberately, upon the table and drew crosses on the tablecloth.

The beggar bowed his head low, as though assenting to what he had seen, and whispered, rather than spoke, the words: 'In the likeness of the Dove . . .'

And all the heads bowed lower still, in silence. Then the carpenter said deliberately: 'We see, friend, that you too are one of us; tell us what you have seen, what you have heard, what people are saying . . .'

'Let's talk, by all means,' the beggar winked, and slid his hand inside his shirt; soon he produced a grubby sheet of paper, folded in four, opened it out and began to read:

'From a humble woman to our father and teacher, Mitry. Our brothers and sisters greet you; do not abandon us, father and benefactor, in your prayers. Also we are sending you, father, our brother Abram, son of Ivan, known as the True Pillar. And we beg you, our gracious master, to trust this brother in everything; as you have trusted us, your faithful wives and widows, trust him likewise, your pillar. Dovecote Annushka also sends greetings, and Yelena, Frol, Karp and Ivan the Fire. My clod of a husband still knows nothing; I am giving him the herb you sent with much benefit; to what end, father, you yourself know best; we pray to the Holy Ghost in our new chapel, to wit in the bath-house, on those days when my better half is away travelling round the district. One of our brethren, a painter, is painting the image of the Dove. And do you not abandon us, gracious master, in your devout prayers. Also to your spouse in the Spirit,' the beggar went on, with a bow to Matryona, 'my humble greetings. Your faithful slave and beloved in the Dove, Fyokla Yeropegina . . .'

'That's the way of it then, brother Abram,' Kudeyarov broke the silence. 'So the boss isn't in town just now . . .'

'Of course he isn't: out on business all the time, travelling from one mill to another; our Fyokla Matveyevna is always on her own' – the beggar winked – 'that's to say, she's with the brothers and sisters all the time; she doesn't get the chance to give him much of the herb, though.'

'Well, there'll be time . . .'

They were talking about the wife of the richest miller in Likhov, Fyokla Matveyevna Yeropegina, who had joined a certain secret community. They spoke of how the true brotherhood had already made its appearance in the surrounding villages, and there were now circles meeting for prayer here and there, and nobody had the slightest inkling of it; not as it had been before, when all they could muster had been a mere two parishes of brethren in the whole district; and one parish met secretly in Fyokla Matveyevna's house, with the help of Annushka and her mother, an old woman of a hundred who was born a peasant in Voronyo. From their further conversation it transpired that Mitry Mironych Kudeyarov was the secret head of the entire holy cause: so it was for good reason, evidently, that for years he and the pock-marked woman Matryona had locked themselves in at night and chanted their strange prayers in secret; evidently the Lord had blessed them to stand up for righteousness with a new faith, the faith of the Dove, that is, of the Spirit, which was why their community was called the Community of the Dove. What the community itself consisted of could not be told from this conversation. One thing was clear: that the brotherhood had set their hopes on certain mysteries; Kudeyarov was expecting their revelation, but what was lacking was a man with the daring to take it upon himself to be the instrument of their enactment, and without this Kudeyarov and Matryona could not rely upon the mysteries that were known to them alone among the brethren, and therefore had to conceal themselves from the brotherhood until the time was ripe; the brethren heard only that there were among them certain holy people who were dwelling in silence until the hour was come, that they might do battle with the enemy of humankind in the days when fratricidal strife broke out in Russia; who Kudeyarov was in reality only a few select people knew, among them Fyokla Matveyevna Yeropegina. Abram the beggar was the tongue for all tidings among the brethren of the Dove community, he it was who carried messages; but even Abram until lately had not seen the head of the community and it was only now for the first time that Mitry had been revealed to his eyes.

'Well then, has the man been found?' Abram bent forward and whispered to Kudeyarov. 'Hush,' the other turned pale, 'nowadays even walls have ears.' He glanced round, stood up and stepped out of the door; reassured that there was no one outside the cottage, he closed the door more firmly, and motioned to Matryona with his eyes. 'Ask her, she's my spouse in the Spirit; she's been looking for the man, and seems to have found him: only will he take the bait?' The carpenter gave an ugly laugh. 'She won't do it with me: I'm too old for her . . .'

And when the beggar turned to look at Matryona she was no longer there: blushing deeply, she had run out of the cottage: she was standing on the hill, all flushed, with a sullen expression on her reddened face, chewing a grass stalk, and a stubborn thought was imprinted on her face.

The carpenter and the beggar talked a little longer, and took leave of each other; the beggar took his staff, belted on his bag, and went on his way, raising the dust with his bare feet. Soon his staff was heard tapping at the windows of the huts; now here, now there the tin dove gleamed briefly in the sunlight of the stifling day, and the words of the holy psalms rang out in the sultry air.

All was quiet.

Only where the houses clustered beside the road, the meaner and scruffier ones, could shouting and singing be heard; for the rest it was as though the village had died – such was the peace, the drowsiness that hung in the glaring sunlight and the grasshoppers' chirping.

Times gone by

The sun stood high in the sky; the sun was already descending; the heat was stifling; the day was cruel; in the afternoon the lustreless sun was misted over with a lustreless haze; it went on shining, but it seemed to suffocate you, to make your head spin, to invade your nostrils with a smell of burning that spread out perhaps from the huts, perhaps from the scorched, parched earth: it was a cruel day, the heat so stifling as to make your dry throat contract in convulsions: you would drink water in unutterable agitation, seeking a meaning in everything, while a languid, lustreless shroud languidly, lustrelessly smothered the neighbourhood, and the neighbourhood – here a sheep, there a silly peasant woman – without rhyme or reason took possession of your soul, and, enraged, you would no longer look for meaning, but roll your eyes and sigh. And what of the cruel flies? You would swallow a cruel fly as you sighed: cruel flies would ring in your nose, your ears, your eyes! As you killed one, the air would throw them at you in hundreds; in the swarms of flies longing itself turned languidly lustreless.

The sun stood high in the sky, and already it was descending, and the light burst rudely through the muslin curtains of the priest's house, so that every speck of dust stood out and every notch on the white deal floor, and every stain stood out on the wallpaper, dotted with crudely drawn roses alternating with cornflowers, while the uncleared table, stained with wine and littered with remnants of cabbage and the unkempt head of Aleksandr Nikolaevich the sexton, who had let it fall there, befuddled with rowanberry vodka, was smothered in a black legion of flies; they gathered around the wine stains in myriapod swarms, in myriapod swarms they crawled across the face of the inebriated sexton, while the priest (he had just sworn an oath before the icon of the Queen of Heaven that he would not get drunk, so was still sober), his face dripping from the heat and the vodka he had downed nevertheless, with a soaring movement of his bony hand crushed in his fist the black, crawling swarms and threw them frenziedly into scalding water. 'Twenty-five, twenty-six, twenty-seven', he drowned the flies, and in the boiling water the flies floundered, wriggling their legs, but new swarms crawled across to the wine stains or flew to join their fellows, and again the priest captured them, drowned them, smothered them; and new swarms came flying to join in and the whole room seemed filled with a black, buzzing mass; and the air seemed to grow dense with a multitude of stinging barbs, with a multitude of ringing voices. Over on the other side of a thin partition was a little room with one window and two sorry-looking armchairs in loose covers, and a settee of the same ilk from which a broken spring protruded, so that an unwary guest might impale himself upon it; the floor in this room was painted and washed with kvas and your foot stuck to the floor, which was why the priest's wife had stretched out narrow pieces of canvas here and there in this room. The room was adorned by a yellow card-table with a knitted tablecloth and the fourth leg only attached for the sake of appearances, a wicker basket with the remains of a once resplendent palm-tree in the shape of a withered leaf covered in greenfly, a copy of the *Cornfield* supplement depicting a gypsy girl with a tambourine, hanging on the wall, and a portrait of Skobelev, fly-stained and with a hole made by someone's walking stick; but most of all it was adorned with an old upright piano. Here was the priest's wife's realm; here, once in a blue moon, she would sit alone by the window with

her knitting; here, once in a blue moon, she would forget both the priest
and her offspring; here the remnants of a certain feeling, not yet wholly
done to death by quarrels with the cook, by gossip, and by the wiping of
noses and other parts of her scrofulous brood, would flicker into life; here
she would sometimes sit down at the piano, or take up the guitar, and play
her favourite waltz 'Times Gone By', without noticing that half the keys
tinkled pathetically or emitted no sound at all. And so it was now, the waltz
'Times Gone By' tinkled out feebly, pathetically, as though in the last
stages of consumption, and the sounds flowed, and Aleksandr Nikolaevich, the sexton, gave a drunken sob, and the priest's fist, full of flies, froze
in the air, then dropped, became unclenched, when times gone by began to
tinkle pathetically behind the thin partition; and the priest, too, remembered his own times gone by, when, as a young seminarist, he used to ride
in the spring to Voronyo, where the pink face of a priest's daughter
bloomed amongst the pink cherry blossom, not yet a plump, cantankerous
and vulgar woman, but a tender girl; and like a broken string they jangled,
the times gone by, in the sexton's soul, when the sexton raised his head to
the feeble sounds and tried to join in, singing to the wrong tune: 'Burn out,
my smouldering ember, I shall burn out with you . . .' And at once the
smouldering ember of the past burned out, and the sexton's head collapsed once more into the crawling mass of flies.

Daryalsky, too, was lost in thought; here he was at the priest's, still sitting smoking by himself, when he ought to have been back at Gugolevo,
where no doubt they had already missed him, where dinner had gone cold
and Katya was gazing out from the green acacias of the garden on to the
dull dusty road, which grinned malevolently at her from the green
rye-fields and ran off to Tselebeyevo; and where, leaning on her crutch,
the lace-trimmed old lady trembled in the flower-bed, all in black silk with
a white tulle cap and lilac ribbons, trembled and grumbled amongst the
nasturtiums. Why was Daryalsky, too, seized by times gone by, why did he
too remember his life? Young in years but old in experience – he'd experienced enough for a dozen ordinary lives – Daryalsky remembered his
father, a Treasury official, a simple and honest man; he had striven for all
he was worth to give his son a proper education; Daryalsky had been sent
to an educational establishment, and he ought to have attended it, but no –
he had gone off to libraries and museums and spent days poring over
books, and then, after a month's truancy, had entreated his mother to write
a note to the headmaster, without his father's knowledge, to say he had
been suffering from an illness. Still a child, he had declared to his father
that he did not believe in God, in proof of which he removed the icon from
his room and tossed it into a corner; his father and mother had been sad-

dened, while he, the youthful heathen, prayed to the crimson sunsets and all manner of things that descended with the sunset into his soul; he wrote verses, read Comte and worshipped, young heathen, the red flag, transferring to this material sign his cherished secret, unguessed by anyone, that the future would come to pass. Times gone by!

His father had died, then his mother; he became a student: he was the first among his comrades – in their discussion groups, their disputes with the authorities, leader, not led: immersed in fat folios, studying Boehme, Eckhart, Swedenborg just as he had studied Marx, Lassalle and Comte, seeking the secret of his sunset, and failing to find it anywhere, anywhere at all; and then he had turned unsociable, no longer leading anyone; and here he was now, a wanderer, alone amidst the fields with his strange, disordered thoughts, but always with his sunset, its play of crimson hues, its ardent, avid kisses; the sunset presaged his secret's proximity, promised its approach; here he was now in church; he visited holy places, Diveyevo and Optina, and at the same time he was in pagan antiquity with Tibullus and Flaccus; and he no longer had words to express his thoughts; outwardly he had turned unsociable, uncouth, coarse – while his feelings grew ever more ardent, his thoughts more subtle and ever greater in number, and his soul was bursting from its fullness, craving caresses and love; and Katya, gentle and serene, had come to him and come to love him: there she was, loving. But why did Daryalsky sigh? 'Times Gone By' . . . Why, that time was no more than yesterday; yesterday he had still thought that his secret would be revealed in Katya, in her love, her kisses: that she was his new path and the sure support of true life. But why was this yesterday already a time gone by: was it that the secret glance of the pock-marked peasant woman had filled his soul with frenzy? The pock-marked peasant woman: it was not love in her gaze, but an avidity; no, neither avidity nor love, not only love: but it was not only love that he wanted; what did he want, if in love was the way, in love the affirmation of truth? . . . Oh, you flies, you avid, cruel flies, stop buzzing, stinging and crawling into my mouth! Oh, doleful sounds, pitiful notes, stop tinkling! Away with you too, priest: you go and drown in the swarms of flies! . . .

He bade the priest good-bye and left; the lustreless sun gleamed dully, rumbling with light, and with thousands of insects from the fields; it was setting already, and behind Daryalsky vibrant sounds were borne; they shattered the pond into thousands of sparkling splinters: flashes and splashes, like silver doves – in the water or in the sky? – skipped by, as the breeze puckered the pond and green air soughed by. In the foreground a puff of smoke rose from the sloping hollow: a red headdress flashed by there, a shawl with white dapples, flashed by, to be hidden in the sloping hollow by Mitry Mironovich the carpenter's hut. Daryalsky shuddered.

He walked away from the church, and without his realizing, his feet brought him to a bare stone that stuck out above the pond; the cool lapping of the water lulled him strangely: drowsy now, he could hear his nanny's lullaby in its ripples, and here, in broad daylight, everything turned towards him a face that was unfamiliar, indistinct; with his eyes he sought a passing villager, but no villager passed by; only the wind wafted by and rocked the bushes; it rocked his thoughts, and he was lulled to sleep.

Listen – the water babbles and the martins swarm: the martins' cries are indistinct above the bell-tower that stands over the village with its carved golden cross; the martins wheel around it. Black martins bathe all day, morning, noon and night, in the waves of air above the cross, they bustle and dart about, they soar and plunge, cutting the sky: they cut and scorch the air, they cleave and drill the air with their scorching cries, branding the soul for ever with unquenchable desire; only at nightfall do they calm down; not altogether – even at night, at the hour of humble rest, when dogs bark in the distance and cockerels answer one another, a sudden screech will come from beneath the bell-tower: they're well-known throughout the district, the martins of Tselebeyevo. But don't you listen to the martins, my friend, don't gaze at them too long: they'll tear your heart apart and, as though you had a red-hot drill driven into your breast, you'll want to run, to shake the dew-laden bushes, to fall in the dew-soaked grass, pressing it to your breast. Your life for a brass farthing – you'll wither away.

See how they bustle about, scything the air with their wings – completely obscuring the cross.

Daryalsky looked at the cross, at the bell-tower: beyond the bell-tower were bushes and a small ravine; beyond the ravine more bushes: more and more, the further you look: and as you look, the whispering forest pours out its drowsiness, while in the forest a silly bird cries out; it cries so plaintively.

What does it want?

And so he loitered around the village all day, strolling beside the meadow and glancing into the sloping hollow (where Kudeyarov the carpenter's cottage stood).

The village girls made their way to the pond, singing in chorus; they threw off their scarlet skirts and bodices, and rushed, a crowd of white bodies, into the pond; what a giggling there was! For a long time they chased each other along the bank – just as nature had made them, plump and white. And the village girls went away from the pond, singing in chorus. The men came too, threw off their foot-cloths and shirts and rushed, a crowd of tanned bodies, into the pond; and there was even more shouting, more snorts of laughter. They came without singing, and without singing they left. And there was no one at the pond; only the black silhouette of a gull in the cool air.

And a pock-marked peasant woman walked to the little jetty with a quiet, plaintive song; she did not throw off her scarlet clothes: she sat a while on the jetty, splashing her feet in the water; she combed her russet plaits over the water. And when Daryalsky walked past her, her lips just quivered and her eyes gleamed mysteriously – oh, how they lit up! When he turned, she turned too; oh, how those eyes stared at him again! He made to approach, but the pock-marked woman had already made off from the pond with a quiet plaintive song. And the first star began to shine, and the timid cottage peeped out from the sloping hollow with its two windows, yellow in the damp.

The limpid evening hovered and hung over the village, joyfully kissing bushes, grass or shoes with summer tear-drops, as the sky of day, not blue at all, nor grey, set firm in indigo, and as the jaws of the west opened wide and into them drifted the flame and smoke of day. From there the air cast its red sunset patches, patterned like carpets, to cover the door-jambs and beams of the huts, the fretwork angels and the bushes, to thread priceless rubies on to the bell-tower's cross, while the tin cockerel seemed carved on the evening sky with its eager crimson wing; a patch of the patterned red air fell upon the priest's currant bushes, landing right on Father Vukol; the priest was sitting on a birch stump in his white cassock and a straw hat; he was flushed, smoking his meershaum pipe, and seemed so small against the sunset.

The patterned air laid a strip of red across the road, cutting it in two, and making off towards the huddles of smaller and meaner cottages, and for some reason there was a bawling of songs there and an accordion was tearing the air to tatters in clouds of dust, and for some reason a triangle had appeared from somewhere to tinkle in accompaniment, while from the darkening east a current issued forth, and into that dark current's flow the road receded; and into the indigo murk of the indigo night, someone was approaching the village, a small black figure walked and walked, but seemed to be far, far away and unable ever to reach our village.

In the teahouse

'Just use yer gumption, you blockhead – use yer gumption: who is it works the land? The peasant – me, right? So it's the peasant what should have the land, full fleehold possession. Other than land we don't want no fleedom;

it's just a bind, fleedom is. What d'we want fleedom for?'

'You're all a bunch of Jews, you strikers!' a bedraggled little peasant showed off his knowledge.

'What'ya gawping at me like that for with your ugly mug? You'll win your rights in battle!' – a worker from the Prokhorov factory spat on the floor, a young lad with a disintegrating nose.

A high-pitched nasal voice resounded loudly from across the room.

'There was a great storm and it bore me to the tavern; and the tavern-keeper quoth unto me: "What is it, man, that you desire?" And I made answer unto him: "the water of life". And he did close his five fingers together; and did strike me in the teeth. And, struck down, I did expire . . .'

'Have you seen that there forest echo, lads?' a goggle-eyed youth from Tselebeyevo, soaked in sweat, turned to a couple of simpletons gulping tea from the saucer.

But everything was drowned by the rasping noise of a huge accordion, played by a lad in a dark blue silk shirt, with his cap over one ear, and with a fixed, provocative expression on his coarse face, while the drunken voices of other lads, lounging around him, quietly sang along:

> 'Transvaa-aal, Transvaa-aal, my country fair,
> You're all afla-a-ame, I see . . .'

The teahouse was full of visitors from the surrounding villages; clouds of steam filled the air; here and there vodka was being served in the teapots; some people were wolfing down stinking sausages with their fingers, straight from the dish.

In one corner the worker with the rotten nose and hoarse voice was already defending himself against the onslaughts of the bedraggled peasant; at the next table a Likhov resident, passing through, a seminarist expelled from the seminary, was tugging at his goatee beard and singing in the manner of a church sexton, while in the other corner the young lads were talking about the 'forest echo'.

'Hey, what are you up to? Is it a fight you want? Here are we, going into battle for you sons of the devil, and you haven't a clue. Look, lads, he's going to break my skull open like this!'

'And as I went, I cried out: driver, driver, what recompense wilst thou demand to take me to the temple? And he answered, saying: "A coin, which is known as 20 kopecks," and he mounted his chariot, and his mare did kick and did bear me off . . .'

'We were walking through Kobylya Luzha, mate, and we called for that there echo: "Old Nick", we called, and it shouted back: "Nick" – "Come out", and out it came from the bushes, all in white, like, and we skedaddled.' – And the accordion rasped on, and the voices droned:

> 'The bo-o-oy came to the ba-a-attery,
> A ca-a-artridge in his ha-a-and . . .'

They talked about the Japanese stirring the people up, about spies living near Likhov; they said that the railway workers had marched along the track with a red flag, and that they'd been led by General Skobelev, who had been in hiding, but had now revealed himself to the people; that a witch in the village of Kobylya Luzha had given up her soul to the devil, and before she died she'd been looking for someone to pass her powers on to: she hadn't found anyone, so her powers had slipped away into a reed; and that some devilishly crafty leaflets were passing round, telling people not to rise up to work for the landowners; folk read them and shook their heads: tempting stuff: but they just smiled . . .

Away to one side Abram the beggar sat silent and the tin dove on his stick was dull and lustreless; now and again the Likhov resident went up to him, exchanged a whisper and returned to his seat, where he went on intoning his nonsense. – 'And I cried out in a great voice: "Driver, driver! Curb this nag!" And there was another great voice: "Whoa, you devil's daughter!" And the horses did stop, as though rooted to the ground . . .'

'Hey, you there, flee-dumb!', he called suddenly to the worker, who had just had a beating and was totally drunk. 'That's as may be: it's all very well how it's written, but have you got your own Slocialist god?'

'We'll leave the heavens to the sparrows and plant the red banner . . .,' the other mumbled, totally drunk, 'of the proletariat.'

'Don't you mean the red coffin?' The Likhov resident suddenly raised his voice so that the accordion fell silent, the lads stopped marvelling over the 'forest echo', and all heads turned in the same direction; but how the Likhov resident's eyes gleamed: 'Listen, Christian people, the Kingdom of the Beast is at hand, and only the fire of the Spirit can burn that Beast; brethren, red death will walk among us, and the only salvation is the fire of the Spirit, that makes ready for us the Kingdom of the Dove . . .'

The Likhov resident went on talking for a long time, and vanished.

The villagers wondered at these wondrous words; some were making their way home, others had long since gone, while others again, having drunk themselves silly with vodka straight from the teapot, were lying under the benches, and amongst them was the worker with the rotten nose.

A bright, clear, quiet, cool night. In the distance a dog barks and a watchman's rattle can be heard; in the distance the lads' song resounds as they wander home:

> 'For tru-uth the Lo-ord has mer-ercy,
> For fa-a-alsehood He conde-e-emns . . .'

A cart trundles by; the Likhov resident is taking Abram the beggar somewhere: 'Well, then, have they found the man? – 'They've got their eye on one . . .' – 'Who is it, tell me?' – 'Just a layabout from the gentry, only he's one of us, all the same . . .' – 'Is he taking the bait?' – 'He will . . .' A bright, clear, quiet, cool night.

CHAPTER TWO

The Town of Likhov

The road

The road led through woodlands, past bushes and bogs, it crossed the slanting slopes of the plains against the hasting, hostile wind, it passed fields of green oats that whispered liquidly, streams and ravines – it passed them all as it ran away, hazy, to where the sky was shrouded utterly in sackcloth. The rain spread from there over woodlands and bushes and bogs, over the slanting slopes of the plains, and a church stretched out its silver spire from the mist, although it seemed there was no village within a dozen versts of here. The road skirted the church at a distance, and the village hid itself between two gently sloping hillocks covered in rye, which puckered in the wind. If you were to climb up the hollow willow-tree which has survived, Lord alone knows how, by the roadside (in ancient times great willow-trees were planted along all our roads), you might pick out the village, if it weren't for the rain, because the village is only a stone's throw away if you stand by the willow. On such a grey and rainy day, though, the poor grey houses clung so forlornly to the poor grey earth that there was no way of distinguishing them through the rain. The humps of earth broke off steeply over a gully, which cut through the plain at just this point, splitting the village in two, its vegetable gardens slipping down to the spring at the bottom of the gully: the spring was called Serebryanyi Klyuch, while in the old days the villagers had called the gully Myortvyi Verkh. At least a verst it stretched, turning into a gully of sand, crossing many other gullies, breaking off here and there at ravines; it spread and spread, devouring vast areas of ploughland; in the old days it was a haunt of highwaymen; the gully lay in wait on the road from Tselebeyevo to Likhov, and the village down in the gully was called Grachikha. It was a poor village, not like Tselebeyevo, and the huts weren't roofed with tin, but with straw; it had its own sort of life, a different one, not like Tselebeyevo, and the peasants here were different too, both men and women; there weren't any of the better-off householders, and the traders had died out altogether: there were only two families occupying the whole village, the Fokins and the Alyokhins. They had multiplied so fruitfully in Grachikha that all the rest had gone and died out – become extinct, you might say; the Fokins were what you'd call beanpoles: one beanpole after another – a shifty lot they were, too, and drinkers to boot. The Alyokhins didn't drink as much, and although they weren't entirely on the straight, they were at any rate straighter than the Fokins. Only it seems the clap ran in the family. However, they lived the way people do, had a priest of their own, and everything else of their own, too, different.

There's a lot that could be told about the village, but there's no point in telling it really, because the road to Likhov skirted past the village. If no one told the traveller that the nearby village really was a village he'd pass the gully without noticing anything, wouldn't turn a hair. The Alyokhins are nothing to do with him, and neither is the priest. There's just a silver spire stretching up into the mist, over the plain between two gently sloping humps; it stretches up – and it's gone; no sooner glimpsed than vanished: vanished into the mist.

Where the road to Myortvyi Verkh broke off in lumps of yellow loess, and where the spire made a vague patch of deeper murk in the mist, Kude-yarov the carpenter was descending the rain-washed road; he was wearing a new homespun coat but his feet were bare; the sticky mud oozed and squelched between his toes like a mixture of pease pudding and oatmeal gruel, or like pigswill; he had taken off his boots and hung them on a staff over his shoulder (his boots were new), on which his travelling bundle dangled too. The carpenter made his laborious way through the woodlands, the bushes and glades; he was making his way to the town of Likhov; the drizzle breathed its dust all over him: the drizzle swirled all round – and the whole expanse of space from Likhov to Tselebeyevo seemed to be dancing in a gale of tears; the bushes sobbed as they danced; the wearisome weed-stalks were dancing too; the rye was dancing; and a brisk, light ripple fuss-ily puckered the surface of the cold, calm, mud-brown puddles. On the carpenter trudged through puddles and bushes, through bearded rye, and his sickly, doleful face drooped dolefully with its woodpecker's nose over the road. His eyes were obscured by his cap, so that his face seemed blind: did he see what was going on around him, or didn't he? Around him was mud and mire, the drizzle danced, bubbles burst on puddles – quite a sight. The carpenter trudged through the mire.

The carpenter looked up – and there was Abram waiting for him in Myortvyi Verkh; his rust-coloured knapsack over his shoulders, his toad-stool hat pulled down over his unkempt head against the rain, the beggar sat and sat on a stone, whistling into the wind, waiting for the carpenter. He didn't mind the rain, it was Whit Monday and his heart was at peace, so what if the rain sprayed down and all about was drenched in dew; let the mists swirl and the rains gurgle. Where should the heart find peace, if not on Whit Monday? Abram hummed hoarsely into the wind, beating with his stick in a puddle:

> 'Maidens fair, the chamber's bright,
> Your guest will come, drink beer and mead,
> The longed-for traveller is nigh . . .'

Water dripped from the beak of the tin dove on his staff. Around him wet rooks cawed fulsomely.

Abram the beggar looked up, and there was the carpenter coming down the gully; Mitry lost his hang-dog look – there was a companion waiting for him at the bottom of the gully, they'd be walking to Likhov together – one road, one care, one business, one life – and life immortal and eternal; they smiled to one another, and as soon as Kudeyarov came abreast they set off together, up the other side. Myortvyi Verkh is steep and slippery, if you fall you'll get covered in mud: but never mind, it's all God's – the sky, the earth, the stars, the distant clouds, the people – and the mud; it's God's too. They were not like some people, whose ways are open for all to see, whose actions are unstained, who do their business simply and openly; like footpads, wolves, the two of them, for days and weeks and months, had made their way by roundabout paths, so that no one should see how their ways met; now, too, they had left human habitation in secret: the beggar had left Grachikha along the ravine, while the carpenter had made a big detour, so that no malicious neighbour's eye should see what road he took.

'You must have got soaked, sitting there, my friend. Had a long wait, have you?'

'Never mind, Mitry Mironych, it don't matter; you had to go a long way round, I'll be bound; no doubt you were up at cock-crow?'

'For the work of the Spirit I'd go further round than that; it's no hardship to walk the spaces of the earth,' Mitry drawled nasally, as he emerged from the ravine, to see the open spaces stretched out again for dozens of versts on all sides; he gave a twitch of his nose as he gazed around. It was as though the wind took umbrage at that gaze; in its anger it struck more fiercely still at the oats and the puddles; the rainy pestilence began to swirl more wildly still; the clouds sank lower and a bush bent down; another bent down, then a third; they came to a patch of young forest; the road wriggled through it; then open spaces again; and there again the spire thrust out to puncture the leaden murk; one thrust, and it was gone.

The beggar tapped his staff as he walked; it was good to walk like that – not knowing what you had left behind you, not knowing what lay in store for you ahead; behind you – a huddle of huts, and before you – a huddle of huts; behind you – towns, rivers, provinces, the icy sea, Solovki; and in front – identical towns, identical rivers, and the city of Kiev; there you sat in a hut, between four walls (if they'd let you in for the night), amongst benches, women, children, hens, cockroaches and bedbugs; you sat and hid, or else you begged under windows; you might go on sitting there, just as before, by the peasant's kindness: and the same woman would bustle about, and the same children would swarm all over you, the same bedbugs. But here there were no children or bugs – just the free, cold spirit that breathes upon you: it bloweth where it listeth, and where it comes from, where it goes, people do not know; it is only in the open fields that you can breathe your fill of the spirit, and you can wander, like the spirit, where you will; and there will be nothing else: you will go across the seas, across the earth that lies beneath the sun – you will go off into the world: that is to say, you will become of the spirit; that's why wandering is the spirit's work, a sacred idleness; if everyone wandered the fields as you do they would all breathe one spirit and become one soul: the one spirit has clothed the earth in its raiment. Only it isn't like that, evidently: from the breath of the fields alone no sacraments have been received: Kudeyarov the carpenter seems to know what mysteries are needed to transform the brethren: a feat of the spirit is needed, a great act of daring; people shall not rejoice, nor beasts of the field, nor shall the birds of the heavens rejoice until that selfsame spirit assumes a human countenance.

Here Abram took a sidelong glance at the carpenter: sickly, with his woodpecker's nose, and coughing all the time, but he knew secrets, every-thing was revealed to the carpenter: the fates of men, why nations rise up, and why people have the nag of hunger in their bellies from birth.

And Abram glanced into the carpenter's face, and, bending his fingers three times at his lips, intoned: 'In the likeness of the Dove . . .' All spiritual discussions began like that among the members of the brotherhood . . .

'In the likeness of the Dove,' Abram repeated. 'We believe, father, that any man can take on the likeness of a Dove, if he gives up his belongings, his bit of land, his woman, and sets off to wander across Russia and breathe the free air: spiritual verses, or prayers, you might say, are the fruit of the spirit, the very breath of lips that have received that air; this is a mystery, which drives people forth from the place where they were born; but our land, our mother, has been fenced around with turnpikes and wire, to make us sit still with our rags: no open spaces for you! You keep your property, and I'll keep mine, that means – but how can you live by property? All

that's mine is rags, just dirt, that is; there's no such thing as property;
you'll grow a fat belly from your riches, and little demons will grab you by
it and off you'll go tumbling neck and crop into the bottomless pit: belly-
first into the ground, and they'll heap some earth over you – just you lie
there and rot; that's what we believe, isn't it? But the people can't wait to
rot alive; nowadays it's strikes that make people go on a diet of fresh air;
they sit around a bit, and then they're up and off with banners; and new
sacraments are appearing, new prayers . . .'

'Now, brother Abram, you've got that wrong: Faithful Pillar you may be,
but your tongue's got the faith wrong; your heart's pure gold, but your
tongue's a brass farthing.' The carpenter stared hard at him, winked with
his whole face and twitched his nose.

'Well, I'm just, sort of . . . So that's how . . . I didn't, I mean . . . you're
the one who knows, you're the head . . . we're just, you might say, not quite
. . . and all the rest of it, that's how it . . .' The beggar got lost in confusion,
puffed into his beard and made an embarrassed squelch in the mud with
his bare foot. (He was the Faithful Pillar, sang verses well, was as cunning
as they come, but as regards the destinies and secrets he was, compared
with some of the other brethren, a real simpleton: somehow he got everything wrong, couldn't get things into his head properly: that was why he
got involved with the Slocialists, and prattled away with the Stundists, and
went to visit the shakers in the summer, but as for betraying anyone of his
own, on that score you could rely on Abram completely; he was a Pillar all
right, and he'd put a padlock on his tongue when he needed.)

'What day is it today?' Mitry asked him, pulling his cap down even further, so that only the tip of his nose and his scraggy beard protruded out of
his coat; you might think there was no man there at all: a coat, on top of the
coat a cap, and coming out of the cap, a nose. The carpenter walked on,
bending lower and lower under the fine lashing rain. 'What's the day
today?'

'Whit Monday . . .'

'That's right, Whit Monday. And where are we going? Think now . . .'

'To our chapel, on a journey.'

'Think now, who are we going to see?'

'Ivan the Fire and Dovecote Annushka . . .'

'That's it, Fire, and whose is the Fire?'

'It's the Fire of the Spirit.'

'And whose are the Doves?'

'They're God's.'

'There you are then. You think it through. We're going to our own property, our own possessions, our church – and there's a mystery in that. Our

spiritual path turns into a dwelling-place: the wind blows and it is gone; but how the holiness of spiritual deeds turns into the substance of the flesh, that, my dear friend, is a mystery. Our substance is the spirit; and our property is from no one but the Holy Ghost . . . Substance is like rough timber: you shape the timber, saw it here, plane it there, and, hey presto, you've made a chapel.

'It's the same with furniture,' the carpenter went on after a pause, and his face took on a strict concern to find the right expression, it turned doleful, pitiful, all over blurred and blotchy. 'The s-s-same with f-f-f-f . . .' (the carpenter started to stutter when he wanted to reveal in words the feelings that possessed him; no doubt it was his sickness that made him stutter).

'F-f-furniture!' he finally blurted out like an exploding shell, and turned from pallid to beetroot, even broke out in a sweat. 'It's imp . . . imp . . . impo-po . . . portant, too,' he raised a finger, 'it isn't just that I supply f-f-furniture; it's done with meaning, with prayers, all the sawing and planing, my friend' (now he had regained control of his thoughts), 'you sing the right songs, and the furniture – where does it go? To all sorts of people, and if you've made it with a prayer, it will do you a service: when some merchant or master sits on it he'll start to think about the truth; that's how prayers help . . . So it's the same with furniture . . .' But he didn't succeed in expressing anything, and again his whole face disappeared; there was nothing left but his cap and coat and his bare feet, squelching through the mud . . .

'We have to build, my friend, to form and fashion the house of God; that's what, it's all the same, furniture, women: the resurrection of the dead, first of all it's in memory, in the spirit: the dead will come and sit down to table with us, they will, especially if you put some property of theirs, some clothes, a portrait, on the table, and call them in the spirit, in the spirit, mind you. That's how our spirit becomes incarnate, like, in a man; it'll be born a little man, like us; and you go on about the air: the wind blows, and it's gone . . . That's what . . . And as for furniture, just you leave it alone . . . With furniture it's the sa-a-ame!'; he dragged the last word out.

Quietly his face emerged from his coat, and it had become quite different: it was white now, luminous – not pale or red – the carpenter had become white. The fine rain lashed harder and harder; ragged clouds rushed busily from one horizon to the other: there was neither end nor beginning to their legion; a bush snorted merrily in the rain and wind, bending a twig over the hollow where its branches forked; the grass rustled even when there was no rain; it was both raining and not raining – raining here, not raining there: but the open spaces were everywhere; and in the spaces other spaces were concealed – they hid, and then revealed themselves; and every spot in the distance, as the travellers approached it, turned into space. Russia herself was a multitude of such spaces, with a hundred thousand Grachikhas, millions of Fokins and Alyokhins, with their priests and their rooks; Likhov rose up, just the odd paraffin lamp winking into the night here and there. The travellers came closer and closer to Likhov, and still there was no trace of Likhov on the horizon, and no one could say where Likhov was; but it was there. Or maybe there was no Likhov at all, and it was all illusion, and there was nothing more than burdock and briar: just look, there's the open field, and here and there a gaunt, solitary broomstick standing in it; pass on into the mist and look again, and you'd say there was some wicked person chasing after you across the field; there's a willow, go by and look again, and it will holler at you.

'And the enemy of human kind – there's him too,' the carpenter went on, 'you get it into your head, my friend: the enemy breathes on every material sign, on all fleshly being, that is; and it's gone, fleshly life is: the enemy makes himself out to be spirit, him too, but (you get this into your head), you never mind about that, you just go on making creatures of the flesh, because that's the only way the human spirit takes on a countenance, from a woman, that is, a child is born: there's spirits and spirits, Abram, my friend, this one's the spirit, but that one's the enemy; and we understand about the air, what you were thinking about the air; but think some more – is air with a stink in it the same air? There you are, then . . .'

'I see what you mean, Mitry Mironych, I can understand that all right, I'm not saying anything against . . .'

'Wait and see: the man's been found: my woman, Matryona, she's an artful one, she is! When sh-sh-she g-g-gets him hitched,' here the carpenter started choking again, 'then the mystery will be fulfilled: but until that time, not a word.'

'A layabout, you were saying the other day, you said the man was a layabout from the gentry'; Abram became alert, and his little eyes seemed to twinkle with cunning. 'It's not that fellow who's staying in Gugolevo, is it? You won't catch him with a peasant woman; he's well on the way to getting a woman of his own, and it's the baroness's granddaughter, what's more . . .'

'That's all right, let him get her; the baroness's money isn't to be sniffed at. The Doves wouldn't mind some grains of gold to peck. Of course he'll marry her; he's only got to s-s-sleep with my woman, and when she conceives, that's an end to it!'

'Why should it be him, and not someone else, like you, say, Mitry Mironych? What's wrong with you, you've got the face for it, and the

spirit!' Abram fibbed, because although the carpenter had the spirit for it
in abundance, you couldn't say the same about his face; what sort of face
did the carpenter have, I ask you? Where have you seen its like? It wasn't a
face, but a gnawed mutton-bone, and, moreover, it was only half a face. A
face like any other, granted, but all the same it seemed to be only half.

'M-m-me, I'm too old; you see, friend, I came to the faith late in life; I
used to defile the flesh terribly before – woman's substance is harmful to
me now, not to my taste: praying helps; preserving insight about the substance, that's another matter, but doing it myself, no: the offspring of the
Dove,' Kudeyarov gave a bitter sigh, 'won't come from my seed, but from
another's, a stranger's . . . And that one, that layabout, Daryalsky, or whatever his name is' – the carpenter hissed with grim jealousy – 'his flesh is of
the spirit. When I was mending the furniture last summer at old
Graaben's, I spotted him in the garden; I could tell, whatever he looked at,
he sent out rays of spirit – at the grass, at that Katka of his, everything; I
could tell by his eyes he was one of us: his talk is all about mysteries, but
he's from the gentry: he can't really grasp what the mystery is: because he's
studied too much, he can't see the wood for the trees; but nowadays the
secrets are with us, the ordinary people; he's sensed it with his heart, but
it's beyond his brain evidently. But there's spirit a-plenty in him . . . So I
thought, Matryona and I can't do it, so why shouldn't I let her, I mean, go
with him . . . (she looks at everything with the spirit, too, the woman does,
she's got a very spiritual body . . .). At first she was too shy, but then she
really got thinking about it, and that was when the idea properly took hold
of her; we started praying, and that was when the Spirit came down upon
us (it came to her while she was praying, and I had a vision in my sleep); so
I said to her, through you, woman, I said, a great joy will come, I said, to the
world. And then I started informing the brethren about it: soon, I told
them, be patient, it won't be long; and then all sorts of portents began to
appear; Slocialists all over the place, folk took to prattling on about liberty,
strange clouds appeared in the sky. Pugachov was on everyone's lips.
That's just the flowers, friend, but what berries there'll be . . . I've got what
it takes!

'And with Katka's money we'll build lots of chapels, make new congre-
gations – with Katka's money and Yeropegin's. It's odd, how sick the old
merchant's become; I keep sending herbs to his missus – doesn't help: the
illness just seems to get a firmer hold: and when he dies, who will his
money trickle down to, if not to us; so you see, that's what we turn the air
into, the spirit, I mean: hard cash here and furniture there . . . That's it . . .'

And then they were silent, there was just the light rain drifting down,
the swirl of the light wind; the lisp of a gaunt bush – and nothing else.

They passed a farmstead: a well-heeled man had settled there beside an oak copse; he'd planted an apple orchard and surrounded it with a wall of rough-hewn stone, just at the point where the country track came down to the highway; the highway stretched away, cutting through the fields of oats and other crops like a white stone, marching away with its telegraph poles, flying off with its dark network of wires, and tumbling with a striped stone marked with a number, tumbling in a heap of roadside flints; the stones had crosses on them, vainly drawn in lime (the stones got stolen); the rumble of carts was heard, the screech of wagons, people on foot began appearing, and dancing to meet them came carts laden with crates of vodka, covered in tarpaulins; beside the road farms appeared more frequently, hamlets passed by, now a village loomed out of the mist on a hill, and among its cottages emerged a lone house with a tin roof: that was the government shop; in front of it, on a post, was a wooden lantern; the shop sank back again, the village sank back, veiled by the mist. And then, from the other side, Likhov emerged from the murk, just when our travellers had started to think there was no Likhov there at all: just then the shapes of its cathedral and its many huddled houses were outlined in the mist; and a little to one side there gleamed the points of the railway station, from where an engine gave a dull, plaintive bellow.

The Dollop

'Your wife, old man, is quite a dumpling . . .'

'Oh, no, she's more than that; it wouldn't be too bad living with a dumpling, she's not a dumpling, she's a . . . a . . . dollop!'

That was how Yeropegin the miller christened his wife, sitting one day in drunken company with a chorus-girl on his knee on a drinking bout in the provincial capital. And as he called Fyokla Matveyevna a 'dollop' in the presence of the Marshal of the Nobility himself, so the nickname stuck: dollop this, dollop that; soon in Likhov Fyokla Matveyevna was known only as the Dollop, and not just among her friends and acquaintances, but among smaller shopkeepers, the farm manager, the workers in the flour-mill and other people in service.

It wasn't that she was all that plump: but she seemed to šag everywhere; it made no difference whether she put on her mauve silk dress, and squeezed herself into her corsets, or whether she wore the chocolate one – her stomach and her breasts stuck out all over the place: her chin would swell, her whole head would be thrown back; you couldn't say she had a fat face, rather it was flabby and pale; 'an unhealthy plenitude', Pavel

Ivanovich the doctor said: Fyokla Matveyevna hadn't filled out, she'd grown bloated; it was more than a year since she'd been able to get her wedding ring off: her fingers were bloated too. Her lips had seen better days as well: her lower lip had taken leave of her upper one by a full half-inch; and on the very corner of her lip was a wart; that wouldn't be too bad, except for the curly bristling hairs that protruded from it, which many people, particularly those of masculine gender, and tender damsels, couldn't stand at all; one Easter Sunday Fyokla Matveyevna paid a visit to the marshal of the nobility's wife, and the marshal's son – a fair-haired little boy – went and said: 'Why have you got a strawberry growing on your face, auntie?' His mother sent the little chap to stand in the corner straight away, but the face of the miller's wife became sad, and her eyes became sad; she had calm, grey eyes, a docile humility shone out of them. It doesn't need saying that on the very next day all the gentlemen paying calls in Likhov talked about the strawberry as much as about the weather, as they exchanged Easter greetings with the young ladies. But there was really no call for such an insult (to Fyokla Matveyevna, of course, not the strawberry), for no one had suffered any ill at her hands, and she had done a lot of good for widows and old women: there was a home for old women just nearby on Panshin Street. And whenever the hooves of the Yeropegin horses were heard clattering along Panshin Street, and Fyodor sailed past the windows, followed by waving taffeta flowers, foulard and fruit on Mrs Yeropegin's hat, the face of an old woman would appear in the windows of the home and splutter something nice: on holidays the old women would sometimes flood over to Fyokla Matveyevna's, from Panshin Street to Ganshin Street, where the Yeropegins had a two-storeyed wooden house with an orchard, stables, storesheds, a barn, and even a bath-house. She was a kind soul, was Fyokla Matveyevna, and her husband, Luka Silych, should have been ashamed of making fun of her like that, he really should. What kind of a dollop was she? Dollops don't have hearts like that, one look at her eyes was enough to tell you!

But Luka Silych never saw his helpmate's eyes; he saw everything else and that was why he called her a dollop and went out womanizing on the side, and even, shame to say, arranged a little spooning with the servants in his own house. (Their children, a student son and a daughter still at school, were safely studying away from home and even spent the summers staying with friends. Their children were young people with convictions, and so they stayed away from home.) You couldn't tell by looking at Silych that he was such a ladies' man; he was tall and skinny, with thin, compressed lips and grey hair cut short in a fringe, and with a small grey beard; he wore a long-tailed black caftan and walked with a stick (he suffered from gout), and with a modest cap on his head; his brown eyes glinted sternly from behind his glasses: you'd be hard put to it to guess that those sternly compressed, dead lips could joke so freely, or that those eyes, primly concealed behind his glasses, had such a way of twinkling and glinting. You might say that the modest and decorous appearance of Luka Silych expressed his wife's beautiful soul, while Fyokla Matveyevna's unprepossessing aspect was nothing other than the noisome entelechy of her wealthy husband. In short, if you could turn the master inside out (with his soul outside) – he would become Fyokla Matveyevna; and if it were the other way round then Fyokla Matveyevna would indubitably turn into Luka Silych; the two of them were the split halves of a single countenance, but the fact that this countenance was of two heads and four legs, and that each half led, so to speak, an independent life – this fact casts doubt upon the aptness of the comparison.

The two halves had long since split off from one another, and now they looked in completely different directions: one half kept a sharp eye on the work of more than ten mills, scattered around the district, bred horses and didn't miss a single halfway beguiling skirt; the other was completely enclosed in herself: strangely so, with anxiety, fear, and bitterness; it was ages since she had looked her husband in the eye, and, sinful as it may be to say so, it could well appear to others that she was pleased at her husband's incessant absences at mills and fairs, and in the district capital, although the Dollop knew full well that it was not only official contracts that drew him to Ovchinnikov, but that chorus girls drew him there too. And every time her husband returned the Dollop lowered her eyes – and her eyes were bright, sparkling, pure eyes, and she shouldn't have been the one to drop her gaze, indeed she shouldn't; but such circumstances had arisen in Fyokla Matveyevna's life that she had to lower her eyes even before a husband like Luka Silych; it would be strange to suppose that so ample a merchant's wife (and moreover a dollop, and not simply a dollop, but a dollop with a strawberry on her lip) should indulge in pleasures of the flesh, if only with the coachman: no, the reasons for Fyokla Matveyevna's discomfiture were quite other; for two years now – no, by your leave: when was it that Konovalov's pig-sty burned down? Why, it must be three years ago that the pig-sty burned down . . . So it's three years, then, since Fyokla Matveyevna joined the brotherhood of the Dove, and joined in such a way that she became its support and benefactor; she supplied the sisters and brothers with money, she sent them on pilgrimages to holy places or to religious teachers if they needed them; moreover, this year, since Kakurinsky, the former seminarist, had joined the brotherhood with his entire household, the merchant's wife had donated a very substantial sum for the acquisition of a machine that could print proclamations to Brother-Russians; these proclamations incited the people to rise up against the priests, and while they were at it, against the authorities too; the seminarist installed the machine in his own house and now and then tapped something out on it: bundles of leaflets were then dispatched to some distant place (they were still afraid to spread the leaflets in our district); on the leaflets was a cross: in short – off you go, do your darnedest! Fyokla Matveyevna didn't understand the first thing about this, but the seminarist insisted, and even the head of the brotherhood, Mitry Mironych Kudeyarov, who lived in Tselebeyevo, tacitly connived, so that it could be considered that Kakurinsky had printed these leaflets with his consent. But how had it come about that this Likhov millionairess had been converted to a sect whose beliefs were so indeterminate and strange that they were impossible to understand in full, while what could be understood of them seemed wild and terrifying? It had happened very simply; about four years ago a girl had come to work for them in the poultry-yard, called Annushka; she was still young (she'd been working for some landowners nearby), pale as pale, and not beautiful: but there was something about her face, because one day Luka Silych paid a visit to the poultry-yard, and, well – it goes without saying what came of that: Dovecote Annushka wept bitterly (I forgot to say that before he visited Annushka, Luka Silych kept teasing her about the dovecote in the poultry-yard; and if the master gives anyone a nickname, then that nickname will go with them to the grave) – anyway: she wept and wept, until the Dollop herself came to the poultry-yard to try and console her: and console her she did; and ever since then they became friends, so that before long Annushka confessed to the Dollop about the brotherhood she'd joined: her own tedious life and Dovecote Annushka's marvellous talk about the carpenter of Tselebeyevo, and about how sweet it was to pray in the brotherhood, how free from shame, all of this had its effect: under the pretext of repairing furniture the carpenter appeared before the Dollop, and once the carpenter has cast his gaze on someone, that person will never escape from his power; to cut a long story short, from that time on Fyokla Matveyevna not only ceased to be her husband's wife, but became the carpenter's worshipper; started collecting books: she copied out some prayers herself; then, at night, she would get up to embroider vestments, she acquired some special vessels – and, oh, not to forget: shortly after that the Yeropegins dismissed their nightwatchman, and in his place appeared Ivan, a giant with a red beard, with red freckles and very nearly red eyes: 'he's not a man, he's a fire' was what Luka Silych said about him – and so the great oaf got his nickname: Ivan the Fire. It turned out that the Fire had been sent by Kudeyarov the carpenter; and so, little by little, the previous servants disappeared and in their place came sectarians from the nearby villages; the Yeropegin house became a House of Doves (by that time the carpenter had spawned over two hundred Doves, although he kept himself hidden from many of them, and in Tselebeyevo he hadn't corrupted anyone at all, but kept hidden, except that the pock-marked woman was thought to be his she-dove). That was how the new faith was brought to Likhov, and it began to spread around Likhov like a pestilence, here, there and everywhere: sectarians turned up in Likhov – not many, for sure, but their numbers grew: some families of local traders joined, Kakurinsky joined, the Doves whispered among themselves that two young ladies had also taken to praying after their fashion; but who the young ladies were, that they didn't know; honest to God, you'd gasp – and I daresay you'd denounce them – if I told you straight that every single one of the old women in the home had started mumbling the words of the new prayers, had renounced the true faith, and trudged off to pray in Fyokla Matveyevna's bath-house on the days when the master went to Ovchinnikov to enjoy himself; and in secret the Dollop received them all, passing on to them all little messages from the carpenter, because the whole household, with the exception of Fyodor, belonged, were members of the brotherhood; and Fyodor – well, what was he likely to see apart from his vodka bottle? No sooner was the master gone, than he was at the bottle, so Fyodor didn't see anything; among the servants there were Doves of many sorts, old ones, young ones, bearded ones, bright-eyed cooing ones; but a wave of terror swept through them when Luka Silych came home; he would wear a frown, and the mistress would go all limp and flabby and her lips would sag: she was always afraid that a rumour would reach him – oh, how afraid she was; but he didn't know anything; true, he realized sometimes that his house had undergone a great change: the walls seemed the same, but they weren't; the same absurdly rotund, gilded furniture – but the furniture wasn't the same either: it seemed to be grinning at him; if he chanced to go into one of the rooms, the room would behave like a woman bather caught unawares, and try to hide something from his proprietorial gaze, just as Fyokla Matveyevna for ages had been trying to hide her gaze from her husband's: he realized sometimes – and would feel cold and frightened, he would take a look at the walls – they were all right, nice walls, with opulent wallpaper and portraits; but still he would frown, look at his wife and see just a dollop: he'd realize something and go away again. And that was just what the Dollop wanted; she was fond of the walls, as she was of the whole house, which day by day was being transformed by her prayers. And if Luka Silych had been able to talk to her, and had told her that at night in the corners there was a rasping, a whickering, a shushing, Fyokla Matveyevna wouldn't have believed any of it, but would have said, 'We've got cockroaches.'

That wasn't what worried her about her husband, but rather the fact that he kept losing weight and had started to cough – that seriously worried her: she secretly laced his tea with a herbal infusion that the carpenter sent; but, as though in mockery of the healing herb, in mockery of her, Fyokla Matveyevna, Yeropegin quickly began to get thinner and thinner; and something kept pulling him away from home; it was as though he didn't live in Likhov any more; he went away for a bit and came back hale and hearty, but a day or two living at home and his face was drawn again. Fyokla kept wondering why it was she couldn't help her husband with that herb.

Likhov

The dry dust of Likhov seared the eyes of passers-by till they could see no more; but on Whit Monday morning a grey sieve, full of water, hung low over the town, and through the sieve seeped rain; soon the streets of Likhov turned to porridge, where cabriolets and carts, tumbrils and troikas, and pedestrians most of all, floundered helplessly; if out in the country it was still just possible to make your way, through the streets of Likhov there was no possibility at all; it was as though all the mud from the region had been collected to spite the inhabitants and splattered all round the town; but what was most surprising was that in summer this mud was in the habit of drying out in two hours at most; and then every last scrap of it turned to dust; thus the inhabitants of this thrice-blessed town conducted their manner of existence, as it were, between the devil and the deep brown sea: the devil of dust and the deep brown sea of mud; and they were all divided, all without exception, into those who liked mud and those who liked dust; the former category comprised married people, shopkeepers and tradesmen, who produced a welter of chickens, rags, children, straw, jamjars and upturned boxes, and threw this produce of theirs out on to the surface, so to speak, of Likhov life, for how on earth, I ask you, was such a welter to be accommodated in a single-storey house with two or three windows and a fence on Ganshin, Panshin or Galoshin Street? The chickens foraged in the town's dust, or in the town's straw, or even in the town's thistles and burdock, which grew in plenty under the fences and gave the town, if I may be permitted the expression, a flirtatious air; the children, how shall I put it . . . The straw, however, was scattered round the town quite simply and clearly, simply to the point of obviousness, so that at muddy, that is, rainy times certain parts of the thrice-blessed town resembled a farmyard (the expression 'thrice-blessed' is applicable to the town of Likhov rather as a form of rhetorical ornament; to tell the truth, Likhov was a town that had never been blessed by anything or anybody, not even once; it was, on the contrary, cursed with stomach ailments, fires, drunkenness, debauchery and boredom). It remains only to tell the reader about three products of the mud party among Likhov's population: rags, jamjars and boxes; the first of these, it goes without saying, covered the fences, and lent a pleasing variety of colour to the view; the second could be broken in large numbers as you climbed the steps to any house, for they blocked the entrance very irksomely; only the upturned boxes sheltered humbly in the Likhov gardens; the upturned boxes served no purpose at all. Such were the vital products of the town's most vital part – the mud party; I say 'vital part' for very understandable reasons; this part of the town's population multiplied very readily, was engaged in trade, even the sale of grain, and was fatter than the other, the dust party; all of which went eloquently to show that it was from here and nowhere else that the salvation of the fine town of Likhov, and its incorporation into the annals of history, would issue.

As regards the other, very meagre party, the dust party, it consisted of minor civil servants (from the offices of post and telegraph, the Metelkino branch railway and the savings bank), municipal officials, the vet, two agronomists, two midwives, the doctors, the regional insurance agent, and one or two other people; this part of the population sighed and languished openly; in the summer they opened wide all the windows of the accommodation they occupied, whereupon yellow dust burst in through the windows in clouds and covered all the objects most necessary and essential to them (brushes, combs, toothpicks, books) with a thick layer of sand that could easily be wiped away, but reappeared more easily still; this part of the population was openly covered in dust; so that it could appropriately be called the dust party; it could also be called the dust party because, to use a metaphorical expression, it was good at throwing dust in people's eyes, though mainly in the form of tobacco smoke; if some wise hand were to wipe off all the dust in the rooms of this populace, the rooms would still be dusted with cigarette ash, and the tables, floors and cushions would be covered in squashed cigarette butts and patches of ash; there is no need to add that the mud party was most content with its situation and looked forward to the future with hope, while the latter party regarded itself as belonging to the discontented, to the innocently suffering; however, the basic feature distinguishing them was not that one, but another, and indeed it was this: the courageous mud party wrote denunciations of the dust party; but the dust party wrote no denunciations at all; its membership in Likhov was therefore always quickly changing; the first party related to the second as evil to good, and vice versa; there were some people who held themselves proudly and freely aloof from all the life of Likhov, thus standing, as it were, beyond good and evil, and though they lived here summer and winter alike, they did not live on Ganshin, Panshin or Galoshin Street, but on Dvoryanskaya and Tsarskaya, raised above both mud and dust parties in two- and sometimes even three-storeyed mansions; they included a few landowners who had moved into Likhov (for them the Likhov hotel could always find fresh fruit, French wines, cheeses and sweets), and a few millionaires who had risen into high society from the mud of Likhov; the exception was Yeropegin, who had indeed risen into high society, made his million and added a second storey to his wooden outbuilding, but had stayed in the place of his muddy residence – on Ganshin Street. Just as the world of the human soul, invisible in space, has, as they say, an immense striving to leave a visible impression with the aid of the signs of its perishable substance, so likewise this class of Likhov residents who were elevated and transformed left its mark upon the outward aspect of said town with the civic pleasure garden, where a brass band zealously thundered marches of a Sunday, and also left its mark with an asphalt pavement that possessed – truly it did – no fewer than five electric lamps; both pavement and lamps fringed the huge building of the government distillery, from where carts laden with crates of vodka trundled off to all the villages in the Likhov district. The Liquor Monopoly, transfiguring Likhov with its bright illumination, gathered to itself in the evenings all the aristocracy of Likhov; while the dust party set off on quiet summer evenings for the civic garden, as from afar a yellow twilight smiled joyfully into the darkness, from beyond the splendid, dusty lamp-bulbs, the best families of the mud party sent out on to the asphalt of the government distillery their grown-up sons and pallid daughters in silk shawls, or even hats, to stroll in the light of 'the electric', and spit out sunflower husks on to the asphalt; these two Edens worthily encapsulated the enlightenment of this fine little Russian town.

On the day in question the brass band trumpeted its marches in the garden in solitude, and the asphalt beside the government distillery was entirely empty; no one relished the prospect of getting drenched by the rain, even in the civic garden or on the asphalt, or of getting stuck in the viscous mud on the way there, sinking in it up to the knees, and leaving their galoshes in it. Everyone, with the exception of the pigs and some hapless wayfarers, those veritable martyrs, had stayed at home; some, on the occasion of the holiday, had collapsed into sleep at four in the afternoon, others sat by the window, with their arms folded on their laps, twiddling the thumb of their right hand round the thumb of their left; they sat and sighed, and glanced now and then out at the wet sky, which looked as though it were hung about with dirty rags, watching the rain drumming against the panes, or a crow flying by, or a pig, its snout buried in the mud, transfixed in ecstasy beneath the window: only its tail wiggled, then it raised its grimy snout for a breath of air, only to plunge it back into the mud. There were many who sat like that beside their windows, silent, drumming with their fingers, hiccupping, sighing, dozing, and sitting, sitting – interminably.

But Fyokla Matveyevna did not sit still on that day; she did not crack nuts, she did not scratch her back with a stick especially designed for such an occasion; it was Whit Monday, and her better half had been away travelling round the district for two days; and so she had a mass of things to do: in the first place, she had to make sure Fyodor got drunk (and Fyodor was drunk already); secondly, everything had to be prepared for the reception of guests in the bath-house; she and Dovecote Annushka had been busy – they went to morning service, not just for appearance's sake; then they dragged a heavy trunk out from under the bed; they pulled out of it vessels, long, floor-length shirts of white linen, a huge piece of light-blue silk, with a human heart embroidered on it in red velvet and a tiny white dove tearing at the heart (the dove in that handiwork had been given the beak of a hawk); out of the trunk they also pulled salvers, two tin lamps, a chalice, a red silk altar-cloth, and a communion spoon and spear, while Ivan the Fire broke off birch branches in Yeropegin's garden and took them to the bath-house.

Lamps were lit in the family rooms; only the formal rooms languished in solitude away from all the palaver; the reception room languished with its rotund gilded green furniture and its rotund mahogany mirror, with its parquet floor that gleamed like a mirror too; the drawing-room languished, bedecked in pink silk, bestrewn and behung with soft carpets on which naked youths represented a boar-hunt; and the dining-room languished as well; it was empty and joyless here; only occasionally could the rustle of silk be heard: and then Fyokla Matveyevna herself sailed by in a graceless chocolate-coloured dress, her stomach and breasts and chin and lips all protruding; swiftly her dress soughed by across the carpets and swished across the parquet, surfacing and sinking in the mirror as she glided away, her hands folded on her stomach, to her own rooms where life, in contrast, billowed and brimmed; two ancient women from the home, with, it may be observed, grey faces and pale, drooping mob-caps, shuffled their feet, blethered and babbled; and Dovecote Annushka flew by along the corridor, pale, dressed all in white, like a bloodless bat; her bare white feet flew by, her loosened red braids; at three in the afternoon the old women and widows from the home began to ply their course from Panshin Street to Ganshin Street, through ditches and puddles and mud, sinking in the ruts: only their grey backs heaved above their heads, and their shawls floated in the puddles, crows' wings, fluttering in the wind. Soon this coven of crones set up a lively grunting at the gates of the Yeropegin house, using their sticks and umbrellas to threaten a pig that raised its snout from a puddle to point it at them; but the gates were opened by a pock-marked peasant, covered in hair, with freckles a horrendous red; he hissed at them sullenly, where did they think they were going at such an early hour; after which the gates slammed to again, and the flock of dowagers, pursued by the pig, shuffled discontentedly back from Ganshin Street to Panshin Street.

Oh, what earthly need was there to send the old women packing – after all, Kakurinsky had been ensconced there in Luka Silych's study since two in the afternoon – he and two of the local tradespeople; all three were immersed in the leaflets that had been brought in, their voices barked in a businesslike way, the pages whispered (on the leaflets was a black cross); they slurped their tea amid peals of brazen laughter; the seminarist's goatee beard danced in the air as, raising a bent finger in the air, he held council about the immediate aims of the brotherhood, and the two trades-men, a cobbler and a tinsmith (whose sign, without any indication of the trade he practised, but simply 'Sukhorukov', adorned the market-place, but everyone knew that Sukhorukov mended pans) – the two tradesmen, rolling their cigarettes, concurred with Kakurinsky: their words revolved around the idea that it was high time for the Dove-brethren to join with the strikers, to make common cause with the Slocialists, without revealing themselves to the Slocialists until the time was right, but, on the contrary, steering the Slocialists themselves, where necessary, yes, indeed, because these Slocialists could see the truth all right, but only when it was right under their noses; and everything else of theirs was rubbish. This was how the Likhov tradesmen discussed what you might call their political plat-form for Likhov, planning to keep both the Slocialists and the carpenter sweet; they were in no doubt that the carpenter knew about it all, even though he might appear simple, just as they were certain that both were 'for fleedom'.

Dusk was setting in. In a little room, where stood a bed of unlikely pro-portions, with feather mattresses and downy pillows of more unlikely pro-portions still, Fyokla Matveyevna lowered her unwieldy bulk on to her knees, under an ancient lamp-lit countenance, with a book in her hands; the bulky, perspiring merchant's wife whispered the wondrous words of new prayers, which seize the heart like old songs and are borne over the broad expanse of the Russian land. And there's no knowing where such words have come from – for it surely wasn't Fokin or Alyokhin who composed them: the words of these sweet-scented prayers sprang up by themselves, from the cool and joyous breathing of the spirit, from the sobbing of the human heart, from the scars of the crippled soul – so breathe these prayers then, merchant's wife! And with all your aspirations you will float away: and Fyokla Matveyevna did breathe those prayers, and the room began to float before her; more and more fervently she mumbled and intoned, beating her forehead ponderously against the floor amongst the featherbeds and pillows.

It was completely dark, and the rain was beating on the walls, the window-panes, the fence of Yeropegin's house; a yellow mass of buttercups strained in desperation by the fence, and a burdock beat in desperation against the wooden steps of Yeropegin's porch; down at the far end of Ganshin Street a lantern seemed to light up by itself, and faint lights poured out of the windows into the mud; the sky above the fences turned duller, darker, bluer with night, ever more ominously; it came down and crept stealthily towards the houses, perniciously permeating the Likhov air, clinging to the windows, tearing down the shutters.

Then, when this dripping darkness had poisoned all the air, two men stood under the porch of Yeropegin's house; they were outlined in the darkness, drenched, dirty, dismal; Mitry and Abram; they stood there a little while longer, blew their noses with their fingers, took a deep breath, mumbled something and finally climbed up on to the porch.

Then inside the house the doorbell tinkled plaintively and barely audibly: but everyone began to bustle about for all they were worth; Annushka sailed through the formal rooms with a candle in her hand; slipping across the cold, unfruitful mirror-surface of the unlit formal rooms, she was engulfed in the entrance-hall.

The Countenance of the Dove

Annushka peeped out, keeping the door on the chain: she saw the rain-dust raging: but she was struck by a blinding flash of light from a silver dove, reflecting her candle-flame, and above the bird a human visage bowed its dripping locks; a familiar voice pierced her heart with its languid velvet tones:

> 'Maidens fair, the chamber's bright!
> My sweethearts, loves, drink beer and mead!

Await your guest, he is not far –
From distant lands he comes in sight.'

From the entrance-hall doors led into the reception room and into Fyokla Matveyevna's chambers; from the reception room the flabby face of 'herself' peeped out, a candle in her hand; from the door opposite two old women obtruded (the tradesmen were whispering on the other side of the doors); all the faces had an apprehensive look: the spirit of Luka Silych writhed invisibly in the shreds of darkness, ripped by candlelight, and threatened disaster; then Annushka opened the door slightly, the crones in the door's dark orifice twittered more anxiously; the tradesmen on the other side set up a wilder whispering, like yellow leaves, drawn by the darkness, when the wind tears them off and torments them in the sighing air – there, on the other side of the doors, their rapt faces melted in a smile; everyone bowed before the open door as the beggar crossed the threshold, with an imperious knock of his heavy staff; his dark locks spattered moisture from under his white toadstool hat, his dark eyes sparkled from under their swollen lids, the dove-bird flashed with light on the threshold of the house: grace descended into the house . . .

And as Abram stretched out his calloused hand to the brothers and sisters, drenched in the darkness, rejoicing that rest and peace awaited him after so many frigid versts, so many unfruitful spaces – there behind Abram, behind the dove-bird – there in primeval darkness nothing could be discerned, but there was something: its footfalls echoed on the steps of the porch – like primeval darkness, like primeval peace; and then it manifested itself in the entrance-hall: something sickly and pathetic lumbered after the beggar; it entered sullenly, as though concealing in a gloomy guise the sweetness that it brought – the carpenter himself took shape from out of darkness; he stretched out his sickly hand – his face loomed close, but they dreamed there was no face there, just wrinkles and vague lines – and from beyond the face, as though from deathless distances beyond the stars, there burst into their sweetly aching breasts – not eyes, but a warm rush of light . . .

Mitry Mironych had arrived in his new boots (he'd been struggling to pull them on: that was why he hadn't come in immediately after the beggar), he addressed them with a general bow; and the old women greedily dragged him off away from the others, so that he should not be distracted, but might gather his prayers for the evening – jealously they led him through the garden, through squelching puddles of mud: a lantern blinked unseeingly in the yard, then behind the apple-trees: the light stood still in the distance, at the bottom of the garden by the bath-house; and the light went out: the carpenter and the crones vanished in darkness. On the carpenter's arrival they all dispersed: it was time to concentrate; to start with solitary prayer, to cleanse their souls of everyday vanity. Once more the merchant's wife rustled by in the formal rooms, her candle gleamed – and all was darkness, sightless, soundless; the world receded and the walls dissolved in darkness.

Again the bell tinkled; a candle glimmered in the dark rooms; the walls arose, took shape in its light; Luka Silych's shade writhed mournfully in the corners; in the entrance-hall stood tradesmen, townspeople and their wives; they stood a little and disappeared, led off by someone's hand to someone's room. And the flood of crones from Panshin Street to Ganshin Street began again – they pushed at the gates, hammering with their umbrellas.

In the separate building by the gates, where the watchman's room was situated, in that room a samovar was boiling; the beggar, scrubbed and steamed, was sitting at the table where it stood; he winked craftily at the darkness as he sucked the Chinese liquid from a saucer – and talked to Ivan the Fire, who sat before him sullenly picking his large nose and snuffling anxiously: 'So you'll be clattering away round the bath-house with your rattle again today, will you, driving off the demons and doing battle with the dragon, will you, when we stand up in the bath-house to pray – you might say,' he added, meaning by this 'you might say' heaven only knew what.

The rattle was lying on a bench; Ivan the Fire bent over it with his lupine, permanently terror-struck face; what was most unpleasant about this face was not the fact that it was lupine, but that, lupine as it was, this face ended with a tuft of horrifying red hair below and a shock of horrifying red hair above; he wore a white shirt with a red patch under the arm; by what was not clear, but Ivan the Fire had been terror-struck by something once and for all; most likely the carpenter had put the fear of God into him when once he had pointed out the darkness and the wicked wind's laughter in the dark; on that day it had been revealed to the Fire that the devil existed; Ivan gave up his soul to the destruction of that ghastliness wherever it might show itself; like a consuming fire, Ivan strode fiercely round the world, wrestling with Gehenna; and it was not for nothing, evidently, that the carpenter had set him up as night watchman here, in this house. Ivan the Fire could see the powers of evil even in the dark; as soon as he caught sight of them he would wield his rattle, and its sound would carol forth – the demons were scared stiff of that rattle; not long back, though, the dragon himself had paid a visit to Ivan the Fire, just as day was dawning – Ivan couldn't remember what had happened, only he nearly set the lodge on fire; and that was how Ivan the Fire narrowly missed turning Yeropegin's house, and all his barns and stables, into the flames of Gehenna.

Just lately – maybe someone whispered it to him, maybe he got there by himself – the night watchman had started having deep thoughts about what his stern master, Luka Silych, really was: might he not be a creature of the dragon? He sank into thought, but stayed silent and frowned more deeply with his already furrowed face (evidently it is not for nothing that he who looks upon the horror of Gehenna bears a slight reflection of Gehenna on his face; such a reflection had come to rest on Ivan's face).

Everything aroused in him only fear and wrath; and when the brethren were praying, and their dulcet cries resounded from the bath-house, their sighs and laughter, full of bliss, and the reverberating roar of the carpenter at his prophecy – then Ivan seethed with mighty wrath at the enemy of humankind, and, as though calling hell and darkness out to battle, his rattle throbbed and danced, choking on its wooden trill, and strained from his grasp to assail the darkness, while Ivan himself clattered through the bushes, and danced and choked on his own whispering, and strained into the darkness to assail it; the brethren thought Ivan a great zealot: some whispered that the flames of Gehenna would swallow him, that he would fall into the flames, defending the brothers and sisters; they did not let Ivan into the bath-house: without him who would chase away the fiends and demons who winged down into the night, jeopardizing prayer and vigil?

Today was Whit Monday, and Ivan was already collecting himself for the battle, anticipating the demon, selecting imprecations in advance, and spitting on the floor, while Abram the beggar sipped his tea without concern and it seemed no power on earth could tear him from this mundane occupation: only Abram was allowed to take tea and break his fast before the midnight meal, for Abram was a man of the fields and his whole mien, to tell the truth, was of a different kind, not like the brethren's.

So Abram drank his tea, merry at heart, while Ivan, sunk in wrath, put on his short fur coat and set out into the darkness; and in the darkness of the orchard that divided the bath-house from the stables a bush crackled, a branch bent; something snorted sullenly beside a stump: it was Ivan, the night watchman, wandering around and keeping guard, but he made no noise with his rattle; the hostile darkness was still only rustling its wings in the distance: the demons had not yet come down to earth: the battle still lay ahead – and what a battle!

There was silence in the bath-house; in the bath-house it was cool; the bath-house was not heated; but the whole of it, with its shutters tightly closed from inside, gleamed, shone, floated in light; in the middle stood a table covered with a satin cloth, turquoise as the sky, at its centre a red velvet heart, at which a tiny dove was tearing; in the middle of the table stood an empty chalice, covered with a cloth; on the chalice lay a communion spoon and spear; fruits, flowers, communion bread adorned the table; green birch branches adorned the damp walls; in front of the table tin lamps already flickered; aloft above the tin lamps there shone a heavy silver dove (when the spirit alighted on the brothers and sisters, the dove would leave its staff and fly about, cooing, flutter its wings and play in the bathhouse); in the smaller adjacent room stood a solitary lectern, with no embellishment; on the lectern lay a book; dressed all in white, his feet bare, with a wax candle burning above the book, the carpenter, now, while the room was still empty, was – no, not praying! – frenziedly prostrating himself, prostrating himself and rising up again from the floor, rising and falling – with arms outstretched, a white-hot pallor on his face, enraptured to the point of horror – but was this a face at all? No, it was not a face: like a pale morning mist that, dense as lead, weighs down on the surrounding land, then coils in the sun in wisps of vapour, to vanish altogether in the blinding morning light, so his face became translucent as vapour, turned quite insubstantial and finally disappeared: so these sickly and pathetic features were first suffused, then outlined, drenched, dissolved in light – by another, living sun, another, living prayer, another Countenance, not yet descended into the world, but on its way into the world – the Countenance of the Spirit. And those eyes? There were no eyes: there was something that could not be looked upon without yielding, gasping with rapture, crying out in horror; the light that emanated from his eyes melted his face, spilled over on to the white raiment of the solitary supplicant, who fell and rose again, stretching out his frenzied arms for the brethren, for Russia, that Russia's secret joy might come to pass, that the incarnation of the Spirit into human flesh might come about not as the world desired, but as he, the carpenter, wished it; he groaned and called and begged for that one thing: there was nothing else he wanted . . .

This blinding vision in the empty bath-house was beyond bearing, beyond words; but soon his lonely prayer must stop; near the bath-house, among the apple-trees, by the house, feet were already squelching through the mud; both where a lantern floated through the darkness, and where no lantern could be seen, feet were squelching towards the bath-house: the brothers and sisters were processing to their prayers; in the attentive darkness a rattle clattered awesomely; in the awesome attentive darkness the sentinel proclaimed: the enemy is nigh; and they all hurried – hurried to their prayers.

Quietly they entered the anteroom, one after another, men and women:

in the anteroom they took off their shoes and donned white garments. One by one they passed through into the bath-house itself: they prayed around the table, but none set foot in the adjacent room where the carpenter was standing at the lectern; he was no longer the same, anyway: the carpenter's face was no longer shining: his face was now white again, it had taken on the appearance of a white cloud again – there was the long bast of his beard, and his nose, and all the rest of the carpenter's face, unmistakable, only it all seemed translucent; his eyes were closed; there he stood, reciting prayers.

Then the old crones came tumbling into the bath-house; little old ladies, repulsive, stooping, covered in warts – death-spawn, but all in white; they stood along the walls, mumbling prayers to themselves; Kakurinsky had arrived, and Sukhorukov the tinsmith, the other tradesmen, several wives, and the mistress herself, and various others: at first you couldn't tell who they all were, you couldn't recognize them: the candles had so lit up their faces and the white garments had so transformed them: they prayed away, and the bath-house filled up; it was full of people now, brightly lit, and locked, as though now quite cut off from the world: here was a new world, everything here was different, their own, of the Doves; raised aloft among bright lamps the dove had spread its wings of shining silver over everything; a piece of dove-blue, rich, thrown silk was spread beneath it and in that silk the dove seemed to be reflected.

The carpenter finished his recitation and turned to spread his arms over the festive table, over the satin, flowers, fruits and communion bread; he spread his arms over the chalice: it was empty, to be filled only on the day the Lord of Doves was born – the shining infant; but as long as there was no sanctity, there would be no wine in the empty chalice. The carpenter spread his two arms over the brethren: the people bowed, fell to the floor; on the day that their joy came to them they would not fall, but would see with brightly opened eyes into each other's brightly opened eyes with a beauteous smile. Over the birch branches, too, the carpenter spread both arms: the birches did not move; they did not rustle, did not bow; it would not be so on the day that the dove flew down from the staff where it now hung flat: it would descend on silvered plumage, coo contentedly and settle on those birch branches. To the white walls the carpenter stretched out his now tired arms: when the hour came the white walls would become a white expanse with neither end nor limit; on that day the walls of that city would move apart; and the people would start to live freely and easily in the new kingdom, the land of silver, under dove-blue skies. And in that kingdom, in that land of silver who would shine upon the land? – The Spirit. And in that sweet sky, on dove-blue air, who would fly by? A giant dove-bird would fly by with its beak; and it would peck the scarlet heart of the world and from that heart would gush blood as purple as the dawn. And the supplicant, exhausted, stretched out his palms towards the ceiling – and lo, there was no ceiling, the ceiling had turned into an icon: the sky was painted in blue pigment and the stars were picked out in tinsel. Why was it so high: it was an altogether new sky, and it was the carpenter who could see it; the brethren did not see it: the carpenter had strictly forbidden them to look around, and they saw neither walls nor ceiling – as though there were no bath-house; they circled, taking one another by the hand, around the carpenter in a round; they stepped calmly, solemnly, demurely: they did not dance – dancing was not permitted to them; great calamity might come from dancing: – they did not dance, but walked, processed, and quietly chanted a song:

> 'Bright, oh bright, is the dove-blue air,
> Bright in that air is the spirit dear.'

They just sang away.

And their faces? Heavenly powers, what faces! No one has ever seen such faces before: these were not faces, but suns; an hour before they had ugly, dirty, beastly faces, but now from these faces there streamed forth peace, pure as snow and clear as sunlight: their eyes were lowered; the air was not air, but quite simply a rainbow; their prayers were cascades of aerial rainbows.

They sang away and circled in procession:

> 'Bright, O bright, is the dove-blue air!
> Bright in that air is the spirit dear.'

In that dove-blue, golden air, the supplicant quietly wove among them with a cup of oil: now and then he dipped two fingers into the oil and drew a sign on someone's forehead; the anointed might raise his eyes to him, or glance at him from under lowered brows – and he would bathe them both – not in warmth or cold, but in strength and light; then both of them – and that most radiant face – were sitting at table; all of them were now seated at table in a seven-hued rainbow, in the pure white land of paradise, amidst pine-needles and green woods under the skies of Mount Tabor; a radiant man broke the communion bread and passed it round; and they swallowed from a goblet (not from the chalice) the red wine of Cana of Galilee; and it seemed there was neither time nor space, but wine, blood, the dove-blue air, and sweetness; they did not hear, beyond the walls, the rattle rolling out its trills, the fiery sentinel protecting their door from the dragon – for them, what was not with them did not exist. With them were blessed dormition and eternal peace. The silver dove came to life on its staff, gurgled, caressed them, cooed: it flew down from its staff to the table: scratched the silk with its claws and pecked the raisins . . .

Ivan, the night watchman, exhausted by the struggle, his beard dishevelled, made a din with his rattle at the door of the bath-house: he was afraid, 'Let me in, hey, the struggle is beyond my strength.' He hammered on the door. And received no reply: on the other side of the door there was a deathly silence; did he not know, Ivan, that there was no one there? If you broke the door down now and went into the bath-house, all you would see would be grimy walls and benches, and maybe you would hear a cricket: but the people, the candles, the flowers and lamps – tell me, where were they all? They must have slipped out of the bath-house by some secret passage and now were strolling in heaven, plucking the flowers of paradise, conversing with the angels.

Ivan snuffled and snorted outside the bath-house door; and went away from the bath-house; went away to sleep in the lodge . . .

In the morning everything was blue, the sky, the air, the dew: just as it grew light, the gates of Yeropegin's house creaked; out of the gates emerged green-faced, frowning people, and silently, lifelessly, went their separate ways; later still a red dawn appeared above Likhov, reflected in the morning puddles, and the pig, inadvertently left at liberty, grunted and rooted around in the damp undergrowth; and then Fyodor, returning home drunk as a lord, hammered on the gates, and then calmly, submissively, smoothly lay down in the mud. And when it was quite light, some woman or other, her skirt hitched high, strode bravely through the knee-deep water; and across from Yeropegin's, where a sign hung – 'Tsizik-Aizik: Tailor', a sleepy Jewish face appeared in the window of a little crooked house.

Likhov life

Next day the weather was close; a sweaty sun scorched the earth gloriously; glorious clouds scudded over Likhov; and the clinging quagmire of mud was, in some manner, drying; with God's help; and the town itself was, in some manner, drying; and a despairing Likhov resident, his cap at a jaunty angle, ran hurriedly from shop to shop: at the market he bought himself a herring, a jar of something, and for some reason poked his finger into a mouldering head of pickled cabbage and made a rude gesture at someone with his dirty fist; and various men of Likhov – and women of Likhov in particular – would have given him a good jostling at the market, if it weren't that he was out to jostle everyone else half to death. In the market-place carts creaked; the Likhov tradesmen's wives exchanged abuse with the peasant women from nearby villages; as the popular expression has it, both priest and beast were there, that is to say, all sorts of people were at the market: from Likhov, from Bryukhatov, from Saratov, and swarthy folk from Chmar (in Chmar and all around Chmar there lived a swarthy tribe, though Chmar wasn't any more than seventy versts from Likhov); a swarthy Chmarian was setting out cart-wheels, one beside another – and the priest from Tselebeyevo, Father Vukol, who heaven only knows why happened to be in Likhov, felt those wheels with his hands, trying to strike a deal with the man from Chmar; but the Chmar man wouldn't budge, and Father Vukol, hitching up his cassock, moved off from the Chmar man into the crush of the market, sweating and sighing, 'Oh, Lord, forgive them: truly they have no respect for either age or station . . .' And the man from Chmar, without turning a hair, swapped curses with another man from Bryukhatov about his wheel, and a man from Kozliki nearly ran over them both with his cart.

In the Likhov hotel the rural bigwigs had been drinking since early morning; they had arrived from the country the previous evening to settle their own business between them: and in the morning they started drinking: there they were, drinking, in the two-storeyed building that stared out at the market with its fiery eyes, while to the side, directly above the market and next to the hotel, there blazed a red sign with fat blue letters: 'Sukhorukov' was all it said: don't look for more – what more is there to say?

That day burned up with feverish speed, with feverish speed night descended on Likhov; and in the night Yeropegin, Luka Silych, came back to his house; he had a drink of tea in the dining-room and again felt ill: he looked – and it wasn't his wife washing up the cups, but some dollop; he went out into the garden – the trees were whispering: something sinister had taken hold in his house; Fyokla Matveyevna waited on him in fear: something sinister glinted behind her husband's glasses, in his eyes, that is: she looked – and it wasn't her husband there: but just a grey, desiccated stranger, and what's more a sick one, gouty.

Together they felt oppressed, suffocated, stale.

The June night was stale, suffocating, oppressive; rattles resounded in the gardens; there were flashes and flickerings from the horizons; now and then a cart rumbled by and once, somewhere beyond the sky, there came a sound of lead weights being rolled along: must have been thunder.

Red, blue, grey, close, thundery, windy days were inflicted on Likhov, and after them airy nights were rendered now sightless, now full of ominous fire; and the carpenter went on staying there, not leaving Likhov; he slipped secretly in to see Fyokla Matveyevna, to bring her some herbs, he crossed swords with Sukhorukov the tinsmith over the meaning of some texts; he gathered the townspeople together at Kakurinsky's, to read out some papers (yes: – once a notice with a black cross on it appeared, hanging on a fence, telling people to stop work in the name of the Spirit and not to obey the masters; the constable took it down – he read it and shoved it in his pocket; so the notice never reached the people); great events were approaching: and the brethren knew already that the Spirit of the Dove would assume human form, would be born, that is, of a woman . . . There had been no sign of Abram in Likhov for a long time; a week ago he had set off across the fields; but the carpenter went on staying there, not leaving: at last he got ready to go, deciding it was time: left to her own devices Matryona must long since have got herself hitched up with her fancy-man. 'I bet he's spending the nights with her!' Kudeyarov thought to himself, and grinned into his beard: he's a crafty one, he left her behind in Tselebeyevo on purpose; the workmen would do their planing and go home: and in the evening Matryona would be on her own, and under her windows he'd be there, Daryalsky, or whatever his name was . . .

'They'll have got down to the job by now, I'll be bound: time to go home.'

Likhov was behind him; if you had turned round all you'd have seen would be dusty darkness on the spot where Likhov used to be: as though there had never been any Likhov at all.

'That's Likhov for you!' chuckled the carpenter; he turned off the highway and skirted round the farmstead of the well-heeled man: from hill to hill, from hollow to hump; further and further. And he passed Myortvyi Verkh.

The Fokins and Alyokhins had ploughed up Myortvyi Verkh; now there were ploughed fields all around; the last Alyokhin was just finishing the last strip.

And the last Alyokhin was behind him. There, in the dark-blue gloom, from the east, a dark figure appeared over Tselebeyevo, but it seemed it was far away, it seemed it would take a long time to reach the village.

CHAPTER THREE

Gugolevo

He remembered Gugolevo

'Yes, yes, yes!' (rust-coloured water glinted in a moonbeam ahead of him) . . . 'It's night already, quickly back to Gugolevo . . .' (he jumped over a ditch; morning, noon and night the water lay there putrid). 'Anything might happen . . . stop confounding me, you dark, accursed thoughts of mine!' (a green eye watched him from behind, unblinking: it was a glow-worm).

'I won't go to the village, I won't go into the church any more, and I'll stop looking into the eyes of the peasant women I meet . . .' (pine-trees pressed in ominously from one side: a cluster of hazels rustled on the other, from the left) . . . 'I know that only you, Katya, are my life, and "may God be resurrected" . . .' (damp, angry ferns soaked his knee) . . . 'Drive away the devil: chase out the devil' (he strode off beside the ditch, merging with the shadows, then catching the bright tatters of the moon's white haze between the tree-trunks) . . . 'Katya, my love!'

So Daryalsky whispered, and under his feet a stunted bush whispered back, fending off his anguished, crazed exhalations . . . It was a steamy night as Daryalsky returned from Tselebeyevo after Whit Sunday along the forest track, beside the forest ditch.

'Once again you have stolen a glance into my soul, hateful secret! Again you are looking at me from the darkness of the past . . .' (all around him glow-worms pierced the darkness) . . . 'Ever since I was a child, right from my cradle, you have been after me with your rustling . . .' (the endless, drowsy forest crept close to Tselebeyevo itself, embracing the village with two wings; and on it stretched, further and further) . . .

'Since the first moments of my life I've been afraid; my gaze was fixed on the darkness in my earliest childhood days; since those earliest days I have heard you, sweet song, mocking song, at dawn, and in the darkness . . .' (was that a flash of light somewhere in the forest – no – there was nothing:

Lord alone knew where the forest ended on the other side of Gugolevo: it
belonged to the state) . . .

'I waited and waited: and now people have taken shape out of the darkness; I kept expecting someone terrible but wistful to come to me from the
darkness and call me away . . .'

A twig crackled, a clearing passed by: it was said that here once upon a
time, in a ray of moonlight, the villagers had seen the dead face of a shaven
convict, on a stump; the forest was a sure sanctuary for convicts.

'I waited, I called: but no one came; I grew into a man: and no one came;
I called, I listened – to the rustling of the trees: and understood: but when
I talked about that rustling, no one understood me; and the rustling called
me, just as I called someone – and someone sobbed their heart out over my
life, in sweet, unfathomed weeping – what could that weeping have been
about? The same weeping is in the trees now: and hark, that sounds like
distant songs . . .' (away in the distance the mournful song of midnight
revellers resounded, and was swallowed by the night) . . .

'Quickly back to Gugolevo: forest upon forest: how many times the she-
wolf has howled in the forest . . . Katya, my love – safe in your warm bed,
Katya, think of me . . .' (how many times the she-wolf had howled in the
forest, and in the winter a bear had crept up to the village along with the
frost, killed some horses and retreated into its thicket) . . .

And like a snake in the grass an involuntary fear built up in Daryalsky's
breast at all the events of the day, now immersed in night – entered his
heart like a snake's venom, and now his heart was stopping in his breast: his
heart.

Like a traveller surrounded by a mass of tree-trunks, bushes, forests and
forest swamps that envelop him in the icy breath of their mist, to enter his
breast and consume his blood with fever, so that, stumbling, he seeks in
vain the forest track that he has long since lost – like such a traveller,
Daryalsky had given his life and his light and his soul's nobility to Katya,
his fiancée, for she had become the compass of his life; but now his path
with her was a path no longer: in a day, an hour, in one brief soul-caressing
moment his path had become a path of mists, which raised aloft, now here,
now there, a cold, forbidding hand: a day, a glance, a moment of the pock-
marked peasant woman – and his light, his way, his soul's nobility, had
turned to forest, night, to marsh and putrid swamp.

'Stop! I've lost my way!' Daryalsky whispered; he stood still, alone in the
middle of the forest; no track to be seen, no ditch: stumps, mosses, tree-
trunks, twitter of birds, the ringing of the Tselebeyevo bell-tower, the far-
off, spherical moon, sinking into the bushes. Nobody, nothing. A bell,
perhaps? Again nothing. A dream, perhaps? The distant, muffled note of

midnight winging through the thicket. Daryalsky noticed that he was standing above an unwholesome spot: the very spot where the forest reared up in a bristling row of pines and broke off abruptly into a mass of soggy undergrowth on putrid ground; the very spot where a man had vanished last summer into a hole in the swamp; it was just above that very spot that Daryalsky was standing now and straining to listen: 'Katya, my love: I love you . . . – ah, I remember!' As he stood there, another face shone out at him: from behind a bush he was struck by the light of that face: that pock-marked peasant woman's face, but it wasn't a face at all: it was the big, yellow moon that peeped between the bushes and disappeared again.

'Katya, my love: you are the only one I love, Katya, the only one!'

A strange recollection arose in his soul, illuminating his life with a terrible light: he remembered a night: he was sitting at his desk, surrounded by books; he had an exam the next day, but his head was full of childhood memories, and already it was drooping sleepily over his book (from tuft to tuft he ran through bushes, put his boot in a puddle, into fir needles, into a soft, mossy ant-hill – and he ran); he remembered: he had read everything, but nothing had taken shape yet in his mind; behind the partition his aged mother clicked now and then with her scissors or scratched with her needle against the satin she was working, and a shiver ran down his spine and his thoughts fell apart: his poor, dear mother – how she used to chide him for his sleepless nights and his smoking; he sometimes got cross with her for disturbing him in his work, or for scratching her needle on the satin at an inopportune moment – anyway, he remembered, that night . . . (the trees strained in the wind, in the wind a bush set upon him; bush after bush; and now the swamp was sucking him in) . . .

He remembered that night, the ticking of the clock, the irritating rustle of the satin: he remembered raising his head from his book and memorizing the phrase: '*Wolf* in Slavonic is *vl"k.*' He saw the open window and a patch of moonlight on the floor – and suddenly he remembered . . . (he emerged onto the road: Katya, save me – it's not far to Gugolevo now: he started running beside the clearing, through the rye) . . . Back to Daryalsky's mind came the fateful moment on that fateful night when, his attention wandering from his book, he saw the open window – he remembered that he had drawn the curtains: and he went up to the window; and leaned out of it – and . . . and in that fateful moment he remembered nothing . . . (here is Gugolevo: he was past the stone gates: there were lions over the gates; the wrought-iron wicket was not closed) . . .

And when he came to he saw his mother bent over him: with trembling hands she was giving him some drops, she was whispering over him, sighing: 'I'm with you, my little boy, I've closed the window: God be with you!'

His poor mother: she had found eternal rest now in her quiet grave; her needle no longer scratched and her scissors did not snip! In that terrible moment his mother was standing over him: and Daryalsky had no recollection of why that minute of oblivion had come over him when he went up to the window: he remembered that his mother had heard his wild, heart-rending cry, he remembered that after the swoon it had seemed to him that there, outside the window, some woman was standing: yes, her face was pock-marked and without eyebrows – yes: all that had happened then: but that pock-marked face was twisted in such a horrid smile, and such vileness distorted that face, which gazed at him without a trace of shame, and hauntingly invited him to wantonness. But why did that face contain his secret? Could it be that his soul's secret held a foul and unchaste meaning, when his soul smiled at the bright rays of the dawn? Yes, the dawn had both lit and sullied the face he had thought he'd seen outside the window . . . (he was in the avenues of the old park) . . .

But now Daryalsky had recalled the face of the ghost, because it was the face of the pock-marked peasant woman that he had met in the church . . . (My soul, don't glance into the abysses; you're here, inside the wrought-iron gate – in the middle of the Gugolevo oak-groves) . . .

Then he remembered – the gates weren't closed; he went back and locked them; as he pushed the bolt he thought that the caretaker ought to be ticked off, and told to lock the gates at night, or anybody might come wandering in through the fence; try finding him in the bushes then; he could even get into the house and strangle you in your bed, robbing the baroness into the bargain.

'I've remembered – and away with you, begone, vanish, chimera!' (His feet crunched on a path choked with greenery; and day was breaking) . . . 'Sleep peacefully, Katya, beloved: my soul will never forget you, Katya' (the meadow was shrouded in mist, the columns of the house loomed white) . . . 'Over there is your window, covered with lace curtains; I will stand guard here, under your windows; I will protect you from disasters, from chimeras!'

Daryalsky turned sharply as he came to an outbuilding drowning in flowers: white and pink campanulae nodded by his feet; the key turned, and yesterday's stale noisome air enveloped him in the sealed walls of the building.

'Sleep, Katya, sleep; I won't surrender you to evil fate.'

And he fell asleep: he dreamed of a girl's tender kisses, a sigh, and silver tears: it seemed to be the dew on his mother's grave; it seemed to be his mother herself: then it seemed she was a sister, friend, bride . . .

Outside a tearful day had dawned.

Katya

The hall, with its two rows of windows, gleamed in the morning light; the morning light was a grey and gloomy light; the plump stalks of castor-oil plants waved in the rain outside the window; they were showered in crystal and silver; clouded streams outside the window were carrying red sand from the paths.

That was how Gugolevo greeted a frowning Whit Monday.

In the hall, with its two rows of windows, the butler walked about grumbling as he laid the table between two white pillars with peeling plaster; the pillars divided the hall, as it were, into two rooms: one half served as a dining-room; there was nothing remarkable about it: bentwood chairs stood around the table; the butler Yevseich came and spread a clean tablecloth on it; muttering to himself, he laid the breakfast table and, muttering to himself, he opened the door to the terrace hung with creepers that formed an awning, from under which the lawn opened out and a flower-bed with a headless naked youth, reclining on a stone plinth and raising aloft his yellow, mildewed elbow.

In the other half of the hall, the drawing-room, stood Katya Gugoleva, the baroness's granddaughter, leaning on the grand piano, and absent-mindedly inspecting the old furniture, upholstered in red morocco, with here and there some faded gilt.

There were portraits hanging here; for years a general with a tricorn hat in his hand had been prancing on a big, dark canvas with cracks in it; and for years a bomb had been exploding at his feet, and for years it had been belching out flames that were no longer very bright; for years the general had been smiling in the gunpowder smoke while the green plume on his tricorn danced in the wind: the Battle of Leipzig was in full swing and the courageous horseman, hastening into battle, smiled as he watched the bomb that belched out yellow flames: that was how an unflattering artist in a flight of creative freedom had depicted Katya's forebear, General Gugolev.

There were other portraits here too: a lady-in-waiting of Catherine's time with a lap-dog on a cushion and a diamond monogram on her shoulder, a landscape with a declaration of love and a shallow-arched rainbow, over which Cupid had spilt a garland of pink flowers; there were mountains, too, the like of which could not be found in Gugolevo, and ruined castles, and a beautifully copied still-life fruit – itself the fruit of the endeavours of a certain blue-eyed person, prim and languid, whose seductive visage also gazed down in melancholy from the wall, and whose impressionable diary was preserved in a cupboard, along with cupids,

shepherdesses, porcelain chinamen and a dandy; there was a carved book-
case of uncertain provenance; from behind its dusty glass volumes of
Florian, Pope, Diderot and the damp-stained spines of Eckarthausen's
Key to the Mysteries of Nature dimly lowered.

Katya stood leaning against the piano with a slim volume of Racine in
her hands; she had been brought up on the French classics.

Look at her: there she is imprinted, leaning against the piano, in a
slightly short, blue dress, tight-fitting at the waist, leaning slightly forward, a little hunched – and she seems to be just a little girl. Her face is
strained; blue rings are clearly visible under her eyes; her thoughts have
flown away to him, her lord and master; to him she has surrendered her
childish heart, her childish heart! There is no crime that cannot be forgiven! But how to forgive a crime that wounds a child's heart? Be careful
with a child's heart – if a child's heart stops there is nothing that will make
it beat again, nothing. And it is hardly beating as it is, Katya's childish
heart; the invisible worm has found it out: the worm of heavy anguish that
creeps unnoticed into the breast; since the time – all has stayed the same
since the time she fell in love with him; she still feeds the doves as before,
smiles impishly at the swallows; her gaze is just as innocent and pure;
Katenka is just the same silly little girl she always was; she walks in just the
same way, stealthily, timidly, or maybe mischievously: but when she sits
down at the piano – what a wave of thunder pours out from her waxen
hands! Thunder, sadness, passion have shaken these walls more than once
when she has sat down at the piano since she became betrothed: but she's
still a child; woe to him who disturbs her peace!

Her old granny had grumbled endlessly about her sweetheart yesterday.
She cavilled and inveighed against him, impeaching her beloved for his
lack of noble ancestry, and complaining that Katya should not have joined
her fate to his; and how the little girl had jumped up from the table, thrown
her napkin down like a crazed panther, rounded on her granny and
reproached her to Yevseich's astonishment; the silly girl found such an
angry, hawk-like glance to cast at the old woman; and then she sat forlornly
in the summer-house all day, and cried forlornly, and didn't laugh at the
wayward swallow, took no admiring interest in its nest, and didn't smile;
she went to bed early, but did she sleep?

Now she had blue rings under her eyes; to look at her, you might say
there was nothing but listless grace and girlish coquetry in her posture as
she leaned against the piano; her waxen hand unclenched, as soft as wax,
and the slim volume of Racine slipped onto the carpet.

Katya was always like that: when she was looking it seemed as though
she wasn't, when she was listening she seemed not to hear, and if she knew

anything it always seemed she knew nothing at all: she was equable – always calm, and smiling: she would steal through the rooms with a smile, she would curl up in her armchair with a smile; she'd been abroad and met a lot of people: you'd think she had things to talk about, and things to think about; but did Katya do any talking?

It was hard to decide whether she ever did any thinking; if you came up to her and talked to her for a while, you would see she had an acute feeling for nature, that she understood and loved all forms of art; but if you tried to expound your ideas to her, or tried to display how talented you were, how knowledgeable and clever: she would not be impressed by cleverness – cleverness was like water off a duck's back to her, and talent she took to be something essential, something that goes without saying, that you cannot live without; but at knowledge she merely shrugged her shoulders, merely laughed – and with whom? With Yevseich, the butler.

Was Katya clever? Hard to say – and what need is there to know? Either she's the cleverest of people, or she's a proper little dunce. Does she know a lot of subjects? Not one. Is she good at any of the arts? Not in the slightest. So why does she ignore learned and famous people, and lavish her attention on Yevseich, on the swallows, and her silly friend Lyolya? I ask you, who can make head or tail of a young girl's soul?

Oh, what a storm was brewing today! Grandma would be frowning this morning – frowning at everything: at Yevseich, even more at her, worthless girl that she was, and more still she would be frowning at her fiancé; she would disdainfully scrutinize his not always dirt-free boots, would keep glancing at his angular movements; and if he chanced to burst into song in his hoarse, loud voice that missed all the right notes – oh, my goodness, what would happen then! With what a penetrating stare grandmama would fix Pyotr through her lorgnette!

He was blind, somehow, Pyotr, he didn't notice anything. What about her, silly girl? Her silly heart would start beating fast, then stop, then she would flare up, and then she would again say something biting, hurtful, caustic to grandmama: then Pyotr would understand, then he would notice everything: if he was in high spirits Pyotr didn't see anything, he became rowdy, even a little indecent; if he was in high spirits, he would get some abstruse line of poetry on his brain and respond to everything with a snatch of verse, and knowing grandma's views on snatches of verse and the proper way for young people to behave, how could he be so remiss?

Pyotr thought a great deal – there was no one cleverer than Pyotr; but neither with her nor with grandma did he talk about clever things; only he and his friend talked together about things no one could understand, about Aristophanes's beetle, and on and on about some Wilamowitz-Moellen-

dorff; to listen to them, you'd think they were deranged or had some
speech defect; but they weren't deranged and they hadn't any speech
defect, they were philologists and poets: they kept on talking about Wilamowitz-Moellendorff and some Brugmann or other. The worthless girl
knew very well that if every exclamation that Pyotr exchanged with his
friend about Wilamowitz-Moellendorff was properly explained, you'd get
a clever book about Wilamowitz; even if she was a silly chit of a girl, even
so she knew that Pyotr was the cleverest of men when he talked about
Wilamowitz-Moellendorff, and she and grandma had no hope of understanding; but Katya didn't know who Wilamowitz was.

Anyway, when Pyotr noticed how her proud grandmama took every
opportunity of humiliating him – and Wilamovitz-Moellendorff – referring to her wealth and noble ancestry, or dropping hints about Pyotr's mer-
cenary intentions, his wish to get rich, and how if it wasn't for him, a mere
priest's son, Katya would be marrying Prince Chirkizilari, then Pyotr
would tap his heel, become dejected, fall silent, and would stay dejected for
days on end – he'd turn to stone, become quite still; when he had a con-
tretemps with the old lady it was Katya who had to bear the brunt of everything – both Pyotr's sullenness and her grandma's hurtful hints.

The same today: her heart could sense: a storm was surely brewing; and
what a storm! How could Pyotr fail to understand that her grandma had
her own ideas about propriety, and that she lived wholly in a past that was
drifting away from life, and that she set Prince Chirkizilari above all Wil-
amowitzes and Brugmanns? Why, oh why, had he gone away so thought-
lessly in the morning, and stayed away all day, without a word to anyone?
After all, it was only two days since their engagement: how much trouble
she had had, how many unseen ruses she had devised to make the engagement happen; and even now Pyotr hadn't given her a thought.

Pyotr did think about her, a lot, but evidently he thought about
Brugmann a lot more; well, why didn't he sit there in his room with his
Brugmann, then, but he had gone off to Tselebeyevo to look for company,
and what company? He went off to make merry with the priest and crack
jokes with his wife; so perhaps he did have clergy blood in his veins? No,
she couldn't believe that, she wouldn't; no, these were all her grandmama's
bad thoughts coming to her: she knew, of course she did, that Pyotr was
quite special. No, she wouldn't let herself believe that he could have been
drinking at the priest's, although she knew quite well that Pyotr had been
drunk more than once before, as on that fateful evening in town.

As she was passing the inn in her sleigh one day in the winter, she had
seen the inn-door open and a drunken crowd of artists come tumbling out
of the lighted entrance with indecent shouts; one of them had caught sight

of her and had started chasing her sleigh, laughing, and had fallen over in the snow; but what was most terrible for her was that (though only for a moment) his gaze, Pyotr's, had rested on her; he was there among them, he too, Pyotr, and was drunk – his collar was unbuttoned and his fur hat on the back of his head; he looked at her, but didn't recognize her: that's how drunk he was; her heart sank in fear at that moment, as though someone had shouted at her, shouted the kind of horrid thing they shout at painted women with feathers in their hats – at her, his Katya!

But it wasn't her he had been looking at so silently, when he looked at her; he was gazing into space, into the blizzard, into the howling storm; and he vanished again into the blizzard, the storm, but in her soul there remained the gaze of his glazed, horror-struck, but horribly calm and utterly drunken eyes. She had forgotten – or seemed to; but she would never forget that all men, without exception, drink; that even he, Pyotr, her Pyotr, drank, like every other man, like the lowest debauchee: oh, a child's heart is a silly heart: if he drinks like the rest, then everything else in him is like the rest, like those who spend the day saying clever things about Wilamowitz-Moellendorff or even Brugmann, and in the evening sit in taverns drinking, and then, without exception, all set off for . . .

Here Katya tossed her head, and her thick curls fell over her shoulder; but the furrow between her fine eyebrows, her momentarily compressed lips, begging to be kissed, her head, thrown high, and her whole figure – which seemed taller, light, but severe in its lightness – all expressed a strange tenacity, not of childish years: as a white birch-tree, suddenly seized by a gust of wind, breaks out of silence irresistibly, spreads out its fine web of foliage imploringly, and bursts for a moment into tears – but only for a moment: and once again it is barely trembling, the birch-tree; no one could say that a fierce gust had passed through it and died down, not without trace: leaves from it are whirling along the road impetuously, but the tree itself? Green it stands, as though it had not lost those wind-snatched leaves; those prematurely shrivelled leaves will rustle idly under the feet of a chance passer-by; and the chance passer-by will not realize that death has been here, if only the death of a single feeling, but death all the same; the young soul is like that; the young soul's feelings murmur like the leaves of a tree; there are many such feelings, but many storms too; do not trample the wayside leaf, never touch the youthful soul! Never, never will you know where, when and why a death occurs in a young soul!

Katya shuddered momentarily, and at once it seemed it was not she who had shuddered; her oval face, framed by curls, inclined forward on her swan-like neck, her eyelashes closed – and she stole timidly towards the breakfast table past the porcelain shepherdess, past the porcelain dandy, past the general, prancing merrily regardless of the bomb, and her whole face lit up with a smile – but not an easy smile – with a glance towards the baroness's bedroom, from where the splash of water and the scent of eau-de-cologne could be clearly detected; seemingly quite cheerful she watched with eyes that were nevertheless quite green, as the decrepit butler Yevseich, all in grey, sucking his toothless gums, set out the silver for breakfast, all the while reflecting on the trickery and cunning of the housekeeper, whom he had all the same outsmarted; Yevseich muttered threats of what he would do if she ever again appeared in the mistress's apartments; and outside the windows was dampness, outside the windows was rain; outside the windows was Lord alone knew what, or why.

Yevseich

Yevseich! . . . Where is there a butler like him: the very essence of a butler!

Picture to yourself a butler: times have changed; and the butler, it may be said, has long since been facing extinction; the butler has dwindled to nothing; and if there is one still living somewhere, he must be very old; the butler in modern times has become decrepit, and if the desire takes you to employ a real butler, then be sure to look for an old one; anyone on the young side will not be a butler, but a thief or a boor; and even if he isn't a boor, do you know who he is? – he's an independent person: he'll grow a natty little moustache or some kind of beard, or else he'll have his moustache cut in a yankee style and dignify himself with the title 'comrade', or even 'citizen', no less; and, mark my words, a butler like that won't be with you even a year: he'll run off to work in a restaurant, or some cheap and cheerful drinking place . . .

That Yevseich was neither a boor nor a thief was something anyone could swear to with no risk; and, well, as regards his citizenship, then . . . 'Yevseich, are you a citizen?' – 'Tee-hee-hee, sir!' So you can judge what sort of citizen he is: well, just take a look at this citizen, consider his citizenship: he's no citizen, he's a subject. The baroness's subject and there's nothing more to say.

Hm, hm . . . Yevseich is very old: he's well past seventy; and he's genuine, through and through: a butler to end all butlers. A genuine butler has grey sideburns: I dare say you will choose to contradict me here, pointing to clean-shaven specimens (we won't argue about butlers with moustaches, for a moustachioed butler is likewise no butler at all); but for a butler to appear clean-shaven is a liberty on his part: a clean-shaven butler is a second-class butler: the cassock becomes the priest, the epaulette becomes the general, just as the paunch becomes the merchant. And in just the same way, only more so, most of all, the sideburns become the butler, and I don't mean big ones or thick ones, just ordinary, modest ones: and that was the kind of sideburns Yevseich had.

Furthermore, it becomes the butler to shave – not all that often – to wear a not entirely clean tie, but a white one; and above all it becomes him to wear white knitted gloves, moderately stained with yellow; taking snuff, it has to be admitted, is fitting for a butler, just as talking roughly is for the housekeeper, and in the absence of such a person then it becomes a butler to strum a guitar in his pantry or play draughts with the coachman. And Yevseich didn't shave very often; he wore a not entirely clean tie, his gloves were always stained with the yellow of dust and even more with the yellow of snuff; he made life intolerable for one housekeeper after another and relaxed only when the final housekeeper lost her final shred of patience and was transferred to the poultry-yard; then in the butler's pantry Yevseich started with especial fervour to play draughts with the coachman, a man of dignified appearance and the most rascally character imaginable.

Then there's the question of dress: butlers wear all kinds of clothes – black frock-coats, blue frock-coats; but only grey clothes do a butler honour, distinguishing him equally from boor and citizen; Yevseich dressed entirely in grey.

In short, whoever were to summon up a butler in his imagination would be confronted by Yevseich with a tray, or with a feather duster in his hands.

A distinctive feature of Yevseich's was the extraordinary timidity he displayed towards the baroness; it was not so much the tremulousness of the slave that was manifested here as pure adoration; the old lady had but to cast a single haughty glance at him, and he drew himself up to his full height, smoothed down his sideburns and sucked his toothless gums; if she turned away – he was at his snuff: a quick sniff, and a bashful sneeze into his sleeve; but when the young lady started talking to him – about her joys or her sorrows – no matter, Yevseich nearly died laughing . . . 'Pfff . . . Pfff . . .' was all you heard; the butler grumbled at everyone else: patrician or pleb, no one escaped his grumbling: Yevseich went around grumbling like a persistent fly: he grumbled at his draughts: after a day's grumbling came the night: but even at night Yevseich didn't sleep; he tossed and turned – and muttered.

Such was Yevseich: and as such he lived his life – as such he went to his grave: peace to your dust, you last of butlers!

'Will grandmama be long, Yevseich?'

'Tee-hee-hee, miss!' Yevseich didn't draw himself up to his full height in front of Katya – now he was Yevseich, not the butler: he noticed the

young lady, still quite a child, and laughed; in Yevseich's view Katya was
still just the child of the manor, and it wasn't proper for a self-respecting
butler to listen to childish prattle: everyone knows what childish prattle is
– just like the warbling of birds, no more.

'Tee-hee-hee, miss . . .'

'Come on, tell me, Yevseich, when will grandma come out for her
morning tea?'

'Tee-hee-hee . . .' Again Yevseich didn't catch the question: what point
was there in listening to a blue-tit, or a bagpipe, or a child of the manor; he
took out his snuffbox, took a sniff of aromatic snuff and sneezed deco-
rously into his sleeve. All the while he was laughing slyly to himself – he
couldn't see Katya without laughing, but kept darting mocking glances at
her, as though he was making fun of her and teasing her; Katya knew why
it was like this, she knew how this game had come about between them; it
had started the previous summer.

The previous summer, before she was engaged, Katya had got absorbed
in a game with the tawny dog, Barbos, and she became quite carried away:
she pretended to be a cat, climbed up onto the balustrade of the terrace,
arched her back, all flushed, and set up such a hissing: there she sat on the
balustrade with her hair falling over her face: she made such a good cat that
Barbos got hoarse with barking; when she looked round she saw Yevseich
in the window, peeping out at her, chortling away fit to burst . . .

Katya had given Yevseich quite a surprise, indeed you might say she'd
tickled him to death: in all his life he'd never roared with laughter the way
he did then, standing at the window; well, wouldn't you? A grown-up
young lady, of aristocratic birth, seventeen years of age, and the way she
threw herself into it in front of Barbos, arched her back and hissed, and
seriously, mind you, absolutely seriously! As soon as the young lady caught
him watching, Yevseich was overcome with confusion, like a thief caught
in the act; for modesty's sake he quickly hobbled away, muttering to himself, and set about the carpets with a special brush butlers have; all the same
he really thought he was the one who had caught the young lady in the act,
and a disgraceful act at that.

A year had passed, and still he went on winking at her craftily, as if to say,
I know you, you may be the young mistress, but all the same you're just a
little kiddy really, a real little kiddy. And so a special secret of their own had
been established between them since that time; and when the two of them
were left alone together, Yevseich and Katya, the old butler let her know in
all sorts of ways that, well, he too, as it were, wouldn't mind having a go at
some such funny games: and this was how it started, with Yevseich playing
at being a goat for the child, or a dog, and once he even started running

around like a rabbit, or sometimes he would make a shadow image of a pig with his hands – no harm meant in saying it; but one cough from the baroness in a distant room, and Yevseich drew himself up to his full height by the wall with a feather duster in his hands; and if anyone passed they wouldn't see Yevseich – just a butler like any other!

Katya knew all this, but on the morning in question Yevseich's chuckles aroused nothing but anxiety in her: she had no time for his chuckles when a storm was brewing in her soul; she drew her brows together in a frown and tossed her curls in irritation; and as he brought in the samovar Yevseich realized that today the kiddy had no time for jokes, and he pursed his lips with all his proper butler's dignity; but to his own surpise he suddenly chuckled out loud, turned his back on Katya and, like a thief caught in his felony, quickly hobbled off with his uneven gait.

No, Katya did not laugh to see him go, but neither did her face flash any anger after him; she slumped forward on the table in her flowered shawl, with her ash-blond curls; her blue-black lashes veiled her dark-blue eyes, her rosy lips pressed together anxiously and passionately; the little girl in her had died: in this pose she seemed ready to receive the storm, she seemed a woman, thirsting for caresses.

Morning tea

But it only seemed so: the tap of a stick echoed through the rooms; somewhere a floorboard creaked under the baroness's heavy tread, and the dull sound of the old woman's laboured breathing came from the next room; a branch quivered outside the window, a floorboard trembled; Katya gave a shudder, and flashed a sharp, sideways glance at the door from under her eyelashes; all this lasted less than a moment.

And there she was again – a limp, listless girl, barely inquisitive – and so, so little: she blinked her eyes, stood up with her shoulders hunched and went to meet the baroness as was her childhood habit, in her dress too short for her years, with her soft, stealthy gait, while the stocky old lady was already puffing in the doorway, leaning on her ungainly stick with its cut-glass knob, swathed in silks and flowered lace, her grey hair touched with yellow.

The baroness's plump face swayed proudly, haughtily, sternly – unnaturally white from creams and powder: in her youth the baroness had been a raven-haired beauty, and now the dark bags under her eyes, which seemed singed and scorched, the swarthy skin showing through the powder, her full scarlet mouth and upturned nose, the birthmark on her cheek,

all wordlessly expressed obstinacy and incivility, as she extended to
Katiche her soft, plump, clammy hand, and caused her silk matinée robe,
edged with fine lace from Lyons, to rustle; her smoky hair tickled Katya's
hand; Katya kissed her soft, plump, clammy hand: 'Good morning, grandmama'; with unfailing obstinacy, as though throwing down a challenge to
fate, her own fate, the baroness's, she did not lower her gaze to the bowed
girl, and her lips did not smile at her, but strangely formed into a kind of
funnel above the child's bent head, which made the wrinkles at the corners
of her mouth and the whiskers on her upper lip, already outlined as though
in charcoal, stand out more sharply still, and all the while Yevseich stood
stock-still and silent, rooted to the spot, as still and silent as a grey wax
statue; dressed all in grey he stood with a tray in his outstretched hands,
and his eyes, the same pigmentless grey colour as himself, contemplated a
fly, stock-still and sleepy on the wall; this moment seemed to last for all
eternity, and then the stroke of time hoarsely announced that it was twelve
o'clock.

As though challenging fate to a battle, her large emerald ring glittering,
the baroness heavily crossed the room and quickly took her seat at the
breakfast table – just as heavily and quickly as her proud life had passed;
and the solid morocco and mahogany chair creaked and groaned under the
heavy old woman, while her ungainly stick tapped insistently on the faded
carpet by her velvet slippers; without surprise, with a calm smile, Katya
poured the coffee, while the reverent Yevseich helped the old lady into her
chair, winked at Katya behind her back and sniffed his snuff-permeated
gloves.

All this was enacted in total silence, and the profound taciturnity of the
daily ritual evoked a mood of reflection, summoning in the soul majestic,
limitlessly melancholy sounds.

You, too, old and dying Russia, proud and petrified in your majesty, do
you not likewise, every day, every hour, in thousands of chanceries, offices,
palaces and estates, perform these rituals – the rituals of ancient times?
But, O sublime one – look around you and drop your gaze: you will realize
that beneath your feet an abyss is opening: you have but to look, and you
will tumble into the abyss!

'Will you take coffee, grandmama, or tea?'

Silence; the old lady's outstretched fingers drum on the tablecloth, and
the look with which she stares at her cup is black enough to smash it into a
thousand pieces . . .

'Er-er-er . . . if I may make so bold . . . your grandmother . . . yesterday
and the day before was pleased to take . . . er-er-er . . . tea . . .' Yevseich
unexpectedly interjected, but, suddenly overcome by timidity, at once fell

silent, pressed against the wall for fear, and his indirect, imploring glance quickly slipped from Katya to settle on the baroness, then drifted to the ceiling and came to rest on the toe of his own shoe; but grandmama's outstretched hand went on drumming; it stopped a moment and then it started its drumming again; and in her other hand her stick jumped up and down convulsively, and tapped convulsively on the floor.

'Will you take coffee, grandmama, or tea?'

Silence.

'Well, I'll pour you some tea.'

Silence.

'Er-er-er ... yes, ma'am ... er-er! Her ladyship ... with your permission ... er-er-er ... is pleased ... er-er ... tea ... beg pardon, ma'am?'

Silence.

'Well, here's your tea, grandmama – will you take it with cream or without?'

Silence.

'Without cream?'

Silence.

'Yevseich, pass grandmama her tea.'

Yevseich, trembling, peeled himself from the wall like a piece of tracing paper, grasped the cup, and, tripping on the baroness's white lapdog which yelped in feigned injury, spilt the tea on the carpet, scalding his hand – but the old lady's soft, puffy, scented fingers rejected the proffered tea with disgust; and Yevseich, mistaking her ladyship's tastes, hastened to correct himself:

'Er-er-er . . . coffee, ma'am, coffee, Katerina Vasilyevna . . . Indeed, ma'am! . . . Her ladyship is always pleased . . . er-er-er . . . to take coffee . . .'

But hardly had he uttered this than grandmama's deep throaty voice rang out:

'You dolt! Give me the cup.'

The old lady's puffy fingers received the cup, and Yevseich retired in shame and confusion to a dark corner, from where he emitted a slight yawn of relief.

Silence.

'Perhaps you're not comfortable like that, grandmama? . . .

'Would you like me to give you a cushion? . . . I'm sure you'll be more comfortable with a cushion! . . .

'Mimi, Mimi, little white Mimi! Let me give you a nice piece of sugar; grandmama, Mimi's ribbon has got twisted . . . Come on, little Mimi, let me straighten your ribbon . . .'

'Grrr – bow, wow!' resounded from under the baroness's skirt, from where a small creature – not recognizable as a dog – poked out its nose.

'Oh, you nasty little dog: grandmama, she's bitten my finger again!'

'Grrr – bow, wow!' resounded from under the baroness's skirt.

'Mimi!'

'Grrr – bow, wow!'

......

'Don't be cross with me, granny . . .

'It hurts me when you say bad things about Pyotr for no reason . . .

'I won't do it again, grandmama . . .'

......

'We ought to send the coachman into town, grandmama: the coachman says we're running short of paraffin; and I don't think you've enough eau-de-Cologne, either . . .

'The weather's bad today, grandmama, but yesterday the sun was shining . . .

'There's more sunshine in the summer, grandmama, and less in the winter: but I like both summer and winter, grandmama . . .

'Lyolya likes both summer and winter, too, but Prince Chirkizilari, grandmama, now he doesn't like either winter or summer. He lives in Biarritz winter and summer.

'Would you like some more tea?'

Silence . . . Katya was the only one to speak: and silence greeted her every utterance; her grandmother was taking revenge for her little performance of yesterday, though it required an effort not to speak: grandmama was always like that; but Katya wasn't afraid, only Yevseich was quaking with fear; she had exhausted her stock of words: Katya talked so little, so little – the thoughts of silly little girls are not formed into words; remembering that more than anything her grandmama feared the lack of eau-de-Cologne, Katya tried a subterfuge, though she knew there was plenty of eau-de-Cologne; but the old lady knew all the naughty girl's ruses inside out, and didn't answer; finally Katya mentioned the cherished name Chirkizilari, in order to wrest from her grandmother at least a grumble about her Pyotr being no match for Prince Chirkizilari; but the old lady still stayed silent; if her silence could not be pierced by Prince Chirkizilari, then what indeed could pierce it!

'Prince Chirkizilari, grandmama!'

Silence: the old lady's puffy fingers stretched out tenderly towards her Mimochka, her lap-dog, and rested dotingly on the horrid little creature, and Katya became cross, her brow furrowed in vexation; from under her eyelashes an angry emerald stung her grandmother jealously, although Katya pretended not to care about this move of her grandmama's: but angry she was – and any moment she would arch her back and pounce on grandmama: ugh, what a beastly little dog Mimi was! And not a word for her, her granddaughter!

'Er-er-er . . . indeed, ma'am . . . young Prince Chirkizilari . . . er-er . . . I knew his lordship . . . er . . . when he was so high . . . Chirkizilari, the young prince,' again Yevseich butted in, but, informed that he was a dolt, retired to the corner with woefully downcast gaze.

Of course, how should Katya not remember Chirkizilari: she arched her back – ugh: receding hair, a lisp, a gammy leg and bad breath. Mimi's horrid, Chirkizilari's an idiot, it's a stupid day – they're all idiots! She'd show them!

Grandmama cast a sideways glance at her granddaughter and was already on the point of stretching out her puffy fingers, so as to kiss that forehead, those eyes, that hair, when – dong! – half past twelve.

Thus was performed, in profound taciturnity, the daily but lofty ritual of a life that was already disappearing into the past, while from the open terrace could be heard the new sounds of the new Russia, and the song of the lads passing in the distance was bawled out, and the golden squealing of the tiger-striped accordion: 'A band of fresh warriors will come in your stead . . .' Then everything fell silent in the distance.

But those sitting here did not know the new Russia, neither the songs of the new Russia, nor the words that stir the soul behind the linden-trees; the lads, and the song, and the words of the song – why, distant they sounded, those words and those songs, in the distance the lads were singing; and never would those words and those songs reach this quiet haven, never would those lads find their way into this garden; but that was an illusion: both the words and the song itself were here, and the lads were here: for a long time already the song had been poisoning this air, filled with the sounds of old, and making the baroness's dark eyes dilate with terror; the baroness had learnt this long ago; both herself and Russia she consigned to perdition as victims of this fateful struggle; but she pretended to be deaf and dumb, as though she knew nothing of those songs; but Pyotr knew.

And Pyotr entered.

Here he was – in his red silk shirt: his boots creaked doughtily and his shock of ash-blond hair waved: with a twirl of his moustache Daryalsky seized the white lap-dog, laughing merrily, threw it up into the air, and then, lowering it respectfully, went boldly to kiss the baroness's hand, as though storming a fortress: 'Good morning, maman, good morning . . . Good morning, Katya: I'm sorry I'm so late . . .'

A strange business: have you never experienced, when your ailing soul is over its anguish and frenzy, a blessed calm, a strange lightness and a kind of

wild recklessness? Your soul's perdition and the horror of the dangers
threatening you suddenly seem no more than child's play, or even something that has happened to someone else and just been told to you; then it
will seem to you that somewhere you have heard the song of chaos that
unhinges the soul, but where – you would never be able to say; the dream
of life will embrace you and your memory will be taken away; and you will
be borne lightly on the waves of life, plucking nought but the flowers of
pleasure – the blessed gifts of being; and no, no – your joy will not hold: the
past that threatened and that has not ceased to be will rise then in the
twinkling of an eye; and you will curse the hour of your lightness – that
hour when, as you watched the merry round-dance on the meadow or
looked into the eyes of the girl you loved, you said to yourself: no, those
disasters were all in my imagination, no, there is nothing threatening
me . . . Then know: it will be too late.

'It is late,' the old lady drawled out nasally, making a haughty but gracious gesture over Daryalsky's head with her trembling hand, but she did
touch his ash-blond hair with her lips as he kissed her hand.

'Yes, it's late,' Katya flashed a frightened, reproachful emerald glance at
him, and her voice trembled lifelessly.

'Tee-hee-hee, sir,' Yevseich responded from his dark corner.

Daryalsky did not notice then either the chuckle, or the reproach, or
even the fateful graciousness of the seventy-year-old grandmother, just as
it did not strike him as strange that the old lady had exchanged her regular
morning anger with him for an inexplicable benevolence: condemned men
in the last minutes of their lives encounter a benevolence from those who
in a moment's time will be leading them to execution. Strange it was
indeed that for all her carping at Daryalsky, for all her plaguing the life out
of Katya on his account, in the depths of her muffled soul the old lady had
already fairly and squarely taken pity on this – in her view – unpresentable
fiancé of her granddaughter's.

A strange business: Katya saw that there wasn't a storm brewing, that
mere caprice or a sudden change in the barometer had melted her grandmama's heart, but she was not glad; the extraneous anxiety dispersed and
in its place her own came flooding over her; she glanced plaintively at her
fiancé: 'Maybe he, too, like the others, goes to . . .'

But Daryalsky noticed nothing of all this: Katya's plaint hung in the air
like a faintly throbbing string; for after all she loved him, she might be
angry with him for an hour or two – so what, it didn't matter!

Did he know how anxiously her heart had beaten when he had gone away
to Tselebeyevo in the morning without even seeing her, or with what happiness she waited for him when the distant bell informed her that the serv-

ice was over; how she had watched the road yesterday, peering out of the green acacias, her face bathed in curls; in the distance red shirts cavorted and the Gugolevo girls' gold, blue and green bodices kept reappearing, and songs were struck up in the air, and the air burned with bright red shawls, and the air was full of vibrant singing.

And he had not come.

Did he know what strings were sobbing in the golden air – the strands of her soul?

Lunch had been served and still he had not come; as she snapped a sharp retort to grandmama, its barb stung her like the rose-thorn of love; and here he was sitting there now – not even noticing her, not seeing how she had blossomed; not asking her, his Princess Katya, for forgiveness; there Katya sat, shedding the petals of her love; the wind toyed with the petals, the wind dried them out; poor Katya's bloom was fading . . .

Was there a single human feeling in him?

And as for him – he had really let himself go; he felt an extraordinary lightness in his heart, and oh, how he chuckled at the absurd events of yesterday! The heat, the oppressive air, the flies, his intense preoccupation with the classics in spite of everything – in spite of his engagement and Katya's kisses – they were what had produced such a strange emotion in his soul that from a single glance and the shameless smile of a wanton peasant woman he had been thrown into confusion and distress, the deep recesses of his soul had opened up absurdly, and his soul's innermost secrets had emerged to haunt him; but he would not let those secrets grow – he would crush those recesses; and here he was, laughing loudly, with raucous gaiety, with a lightness in his being and his heart fluttering.

'Certain philologists, maman, say that the seventh eclogue of Theocritus is *regina eclogorum*, which means "the queen of eclogues". And others say that it is sweeter than honey, the seventh eclogue. To mark this I shall today drink seven cups of tea . . .'

'Tee-hee-hee!' was heard from the corner . . .

'*Regina eclogorum.*'

But Katya thought: he was drinking yesterday – maybe he got drunk, perhaps he's like the others; perhaps before meeting her, Princess Katya, he had made visits to women with no shame.

'I once read in Theocritus, my betrothed, that a certain man was locked in a cedar chest, and a debate goes on about this among philologists; when I marry you, my betrothed, I shall lock you away, too.'

'Tee-hee-hee, sir!' was heard from the corner . . .

'Theocritus tells us further that Pan was beaten with nettles, after which he lay in a ditch and scratched himself; some philologists assert that he

scratched himself because he was lying in the nettles; however, another
philological school accounts for his itching by reference to the beating . . .
All this is told in the seventh eclogue, which is *regina eclogorum* . . .'

'Oh, stop it!' Katenka stood up and her eyes even filled with tears.

'It's a good thing, sir – er-er, that her ladyship had already got up and left
. . . for she would not have been – er-er, at all pleased,' Yevseich observed
reproachfully, but Daryalsky did not even see him, just as he had not seen
that the baroness had retired to her room, tapping with her oak walking-
stick across the carpets; he turned and gazed with rapture at Katya, standing there, while Yevseich pottered about at the table, sniffed his aromatic
snuff and muttered: 'Beat him with an onion . . . Some Polish *pan* . . . Did
you ever! Who ever heard of beating someone with an onion?.. And one of
the masters, too . . . I mean nettles, of course . . .'

. . . How she stood there, his bride, who yesterday had all but flown away
from him and now was once again restored to him, his bride, how she stood
there, wreathed in green fronds of the vine, while raindrops fell about her!

Oh, moment filled with exultation!

Two women

Katya! In the world there is only one Katya; travel the whole world, you
will not meet her again: you will pass the fields and spaces of our far-flung
land and further: you will be in thrall to dark-eyed beauties in foreign
parts, but they are not Katya; you will go to the west from Gugolevo –
straight, straight on; and you will return to Gugolevo from the east, from
the steppes of Asia: only then will you see Katya. This is what she is like –
take a good look at her: she just stands there with her arching blue-black
eyelashes, soft as silk, lowered; under those lashes shine the lights of her
distant eyes, between grey and green, sometimes velvet, sometimes cobalt;
you will think that her gaze is full of meaning, that she tells you with her
gaze things that cannot be said in words; but when she raises her gaze to
you, you will see that that is an illusion; she will tell you nothing with her
eyes; just eyes like any others; probe them with your gaze – and it will
bounce off from her simply beautiful, glassy gaze, without penetrating
into her girlish soul; however you interpet the gleam of these eyes, you will
be wrong: and you will realize that in every estate like Gugolevo there are
such eyes to be found; but when she turns and glances sideways at you, as
though by chance, slightly screwing up her eyes, with a slight blush and a
smile: then, against all the evidence, you will believe in the depth of her
gaze, so full of meaning; when she turns again, and starts to speak: what

she says is trivial; another turn – just eyes, big, bright, almond eyes; and nothing more.

And her pink, her pale-pink, slightly opened mouth, like an unfurling petal, her pale-pink lips, created for kissing; if you smile at them with a smile full of secret meaning – her lips will not quiver, they may open half-way in surprise, or tighten in irritation; and how enchantingly those lips can smile at quite empty words, at flowers, expensive dogs, and most of all at children; her pale, oval, somewhat slender face turns slightly pink, like apple blossom, when a swallow passes her with its shrill cry, slicing the air with its black wings; Katya quickly turns towards it this face with its blush of apple-blossom; and an ash-blond curl flies up into the blue air; her oval, egg-shell face is framed in thick, translucent ash-blond curls; curls fall on to her breast – and she laughs out loud at the black swallow's tricks: she knows that the Gugolevo swallows have their reasons for bustling about around her; if Katya should get lost in thought, a passing swallow would snatch a silken hair and carry it off to make a nest for its young; Katya knows this and narrows her eyes impishly, and tosses her head; but the swallow flies past; and her thick, maybe all too thick, curls fall on to her shoulders, lap over her swan-like neck, and with their wispish strands faintly tickle her slightly opened breast: then her face turns white again – and look: this outstretched neck, this upturned face in ash-blond curls, ruffled by the wind, with its pale pink-mouth, slightly opened, like a posy, and with its calm, elongated eyes of intolerable brightness – all this expresses the weariness maybe of a child, or maybe of a young woman with much experience behind her.

Suddenly Daryalsky heard the patter of bare feet on the terrace, and, as though a ray of light were singing, he heard a melodious voice:

'Sweet young lady, won't you buy my lilies-of-the-valley? I picked them for you myself in the forest . . .'

He went out onto the terrace – and saw: in green vine-fronds, in a golden, airy ray of light that sang like a dream, stood the pock-marked peasant woman of yesterday; she glanced, the pock-marked peasant woman, at Katya, cajoled the young lady, the wind trifled with her russet hair – a passing breeze; a break appeared in the clouds; the gold-edged streaks of rain withdrew, and from the rain emerged a seven-hued rainbow.

'Aha!' Daryalsky smiled to himself and assumed a dignified air. 'The mountain wouldn't come to Mahomet, so Mahomet has come to the mountain!' and he scrutinized, through narrowed eyes, the pock-marked peasant woman: not bad at all, plenty to console you there, a lusty woman: her mature, full breasts moved under her red bodice; her healthy, sunburnt legs were caked in mud, and what a trail her feet had left on the terrace; she was snub-nosed, her face was pale with large blotches of a fiery red: an ugly face but a pleasant one, only sweaty; she held out a bunch of flowers to Katya. 'That's all there was to it, and I . . . I . . . ' – thought Daryalsky – 'she's a fine woman, but I'm sure she isn't any better than she should be – look at that dimple by her lips'; he tried to convince himself of something, to exorcize, stifle, trample down a feeling that was kindled for a moment; but his heart was light: 'No, that was a dream.'

'Oh, what lovely white lilies-of-the-valley!' Katya, blushing slightly, pressed the flowers to her face.

'What's your name?' Daryalsky spoke to the woman roughly and sternly.

'Matryona, I'm from nearby' – and her blue, blue gaze flitted over him: at that moment a searing cry passed by very close: something brushed against him with its black wing: a swallow, like a bat, sliced the terrace with its wings, fluttering hither and thither, this way and that, and then flew off.

'It isn't a swallow at all, it's a house-martin,' exclaimed Katya in surprise.

'One of ours, from Tselebeyevo; will you buy them then, young mistress, I picked them for you . . .'

The snub-nosed woman smiled at Katya, grinned: and, like an innocent angel, the silly girl handed her a twenty-kopeck piece.

'Dear young lady, give me another five!'

But Pyotr put his arm round Katya; let the whole world see that she, Katya, was his betrothed; the woman was just stepping down from the terrace, still leaving a trail of muddy footprints, when Yevseich appeared in the doorway and shuffled after her: 'Good Lord above, what are you infidels doing traipsing round the mistress's garden? Where's the gardener looking, I'd like to know? . . . Now, Matryona, just you watch it! . . .'

'Or what?' Matryona turned on Yevseich, or maybe on Daryalsky, and her red bodice vanished into the greenery.

Oh, the golden sunlight, oh, the passing breeze: the flowers were blooming, the merry foliage was dancing in the sun, and Daryalsky, overjoyed at something, laughed in the sunlight; gently he drew Katya away from the terrace, and suddenly, in an access of merriment, suddenly started – not to sing – but rather to bellow.

But Katya's brow furrowed for a moment, as she freed herself from his embrace, and with a graceful toss of her head threw over her shoulder the film of translucent ashen curls that formed a smoke-haze down her back, while her lip still quivered and twitched, no matter how she bit it, and the broad pink nostrils of her slender nose dilated with impatience and restrained anxiety: all this lasted a moment, but Daryalsky saw it all. As he finished his tea, he went on with a joyfully palpitating heart:

'And there's another very funny thing Theocritus says about bees: however you translate it, it always comes out – snub-nosed bees; well, when did you ever see bees with snub noses?'

When Daryalsky was in good spirits he did not like to have conversations about deep matters; deep matters, with whatever feeling he touched upon them, aroused in him the torment of such complex, nameless experiences, experiences so fatal to him in their consequences, that he would cover those experiences with ponderous piles of Greek dictionaries; there was a permanent weight in his soul, and that was why the sunny life of blessed Greece in years long past, with its wars, its games, its sparkling thought and its always dangerous love, no less than the life of the common Russian people, called to the surface of his soul pictures of the blessed life of paradise, shady foliage and breeze-ruffled, honey-scented meadows with games and round-dances on them, which was all quite incomprehensible to his worthless girl who sat there in the corner frowning about something – picking at the tablecloth, scattering her petals.

Oh, those songs, and oh, those dances! Do you cast a veil over the abysses of his soul, or do you lay them yet more bare? No doubt they are sulphurous abysses, which spew forth evil locusts, that the heart may be pierced by the locust's sting and be bathed in blood: he did battle with his own inner darkness as Heracles once battled with the hydra, embellishing his speech with the magic and honey of garnered words, which people did not understand, like Katenka, who at that moment sat miserably sharpened to a point, like a rose-thorn. Or was it that he had assumed a look that she, poor child, was unable to bear?

Whoever is Daryalsky?

In his speech, his laughter, his mannerisms, his swagger – in everything except the alternating fire and ice that flashed from his eyes and pierced the darkness – my hero was reminiscent not of a scholar, nor of a poet, but of some dashing stranger. That is why he had created, or rather experienced, or better still constructed, with his life, a strange truth; it was highly absurd, highly improbable: it consisted in the following: he dreamed that deep within his native people pulsed an immemorial antiquity, indigenous but not yet realized in life – ancient Greece.

He saw a new light even in the everyday performance of the rituals of the Graeco-Russian church. In Orthodoxy, and particularly in the outdated notions of the Orthodox (that is, in his view, pagan) peasant he saw the torch-bearer of the new Greek who was about to appear in the world.

But if the truth be told, then, I dare say, neither his exchange of winks with village priests, nor his blood-red shirt, of silk, but worn with a swagger, nor yet the hours he spent in all-night bars and cafés in the city, and the devil knows where else, with Theocritus for his boon companion, none of this served in the least to improve my hero's appearance; from the creak of his blacked peasant boots and the strong peasant words that peppered his speech to his sudden demonstration of knowledge and his evident leaning for earnest and abstruse discussion – everything about Daryalsky grated on people, just as everything around him grated on him, repelled him; for many people Daryalsky was a mixture of smells: cheap spirits, musk and blood . . . mixed, no more, no less, with the scent of a tender lily; while to Daryalsky all those people were like nothing but discarded rags.

'Oh, what a rascal!' a lady once said of him, a lady drowning in lace, willing to try anything once with anybody at any time of day or night. To start with, his speech: Daryalsky's words rang in people's ears as a totally needless play-acting, a pantomime, and above all play-acting that wasn't in the least clever, and people were particularly angered by the way he laughed – more even than by all his playing at being a simpleton, because that simpleton coexisted with a simplicity beyond comprehension, a deafness and blindness to absolutely everything; any thought of paying attention to the opinions others formed about him made him shudder, just as his behaviour brought others to a state of convulsion. So it turned out that he was play-acting for himself and for himself alone: for who else's benefit could he be doing it?

But, as God's my witness, he wasn't play-acting: he thought he was working on himself; a cruel battle was taking place within him between the excessive caution of impotence and the anticipated behaviour of a way of life yet to be discovered, a battle was taking place between the ancient animal image and a new sanity, similar to the animal, a sanity beyond the human; and he knew that once he stepped upon the path of this battle, there was no going back, and that therefore in this struggle for the future countenance of life everything was permitted to him and above him there was nothing, no one, ever; he was afraid at times, and sometimes merry; in his oscillations of feeling, in which he anticipated his contemporaries maybe by more than one generation, he was at times more helpless than they, at times infinitely stronger; all their decrepit legacy had decayed entirely in him: but the filth of decay had not yet rotted down into good earth: and that was why the frail seeds of the future germinated in him only weakly; and that was why he so prostrated himself on the earth of his people and bowed down to the people's prayers about the earth; but he regarded himself as the people's future: and into the manure, the chaos, the ugliness of the people's life he sent a secret call – that call had gone out like a wolf's into the forest thickets of the people: and from the forest had come an answering howl.

Still he waited, still he hesitated: but already he could feel the soft, muddy earth clinging to him and tugging at him: he knew that among the people, too, new souls had been born, that the fruits were filled with juice and it was time to shake the fig-tree; out there in the dense forests, far away, yet before his eyes, Russia was composing herself, collecting herself, to burst upon the world in roaring thunder.

As it took possession of Daryalsky's soul, this struggle called forth from his soul's earthy depths a host of hidden forces as a protective wall around the sanctum, so that the evil eye, the eye that hated Russia, should not overcome him, and in secret he raised a protective wall of the spirit – the edifice of his strange fate: but that edifice was still in scaffolding, and who could understand the brilliance of this structure's plan – the building of his flesh and blood? Others saw merely heaps of rubbish with a tile from Byzantium the Magnificent carelessly thrown down amongst it; they saw fragments of Greek statues, rudely toppled in the native dust; but the secret enemy did not slumber: he had penetrated into the heart of the people and from there, from the people's poor heart, he threatened Daryalsky; and so, as he went to meet the people, he shielded himself from it with love, and this love, blessing him for battle, Katya had become. An unaccountable premonition told him that if he came to love a peasant woman – he was done for; then the secret enemy would overcome him; and all the while he waited for the enemy's arrow from the darkness: and he defended himself as he could.

Katya understood Daryalsky intuitively; she had sensed with her ardent, prescient heart that there was something great in him and quite unknowable – and she had thrown herself without reserve upon his breast, protecting him from blows: that a blow would come, Daryalsky knew; he had a dim presentiment that Katya would fall with him.

His poems rang with a wild beauty, conjuring the darkness with an incomprehensible incantation in a surge of storms, struggles, raptures. And in subduing those storms, struggles, raptures – he snapped them violently with that swagger of his – and more: he conquered the false, necessarily feigned bravado with the spirit of Byzantium and the smell of musk: but . . . oh, oh . . . the smell of blood wafted over the smell of musk.

And for him this path was Russia's path – Russia, in whom the great transformation of the world had commenced, or perhaps the world's perdition, and Daryalsky . . .

But to hell with him, Daryalsky: let the devil take him: here he is in front of us: don't be surprised at his actions: they can't be fully understood – it doesn't matter: to hell with him!

Passions are brewing: we shall describe them, not him: can you hear, there is thunder rumbling somewhere.

A rumpus

The old lady was sitting in her room by the window with her spectacles on; the old lady was frowning, bent over her embroidery frame and attacking it, so it seemed, with her needle, from which stretched a thread of crimson silk; she had been embroidering a crown of green leaves; and now she was finishing that crown off with a cherry; the wind gusted outside the window; dogs barked in the distance and a tumult swelled up; a din was coming from the barn, and voices were approaching.

The patter of bare feet passed hurriedly through the dark corridor; more and more bare feet pattered by; the approaching tumult was met by a shuffling and a whispering from the kitchen; the heavy door, with a block on a pulley, opened; the patter of feet was heard first in one place in the corridor, then in another; a woman's face kept peeping out of the kitchen; the opened door squealed and the heavy block fell with a thud; now a din, a squealing, a barking and drunken clamour welled up in the yard: outside the window a pink pig crossed the yard from the direction of the household office with a squeal.

She stood up; she stuck the needle into the crown of silken leaves, and the crimson ball rolled off her lap; she took off her thimble, and calmly sprayed her lace from her eau-de-Cologne flask; she was listening closely, however, to the noise.

Yevseich's face appeared fearfully in the doorway; it whispered, barely audibly:

'Your ladyship! The peasants are revolting.'

'What?'

'Tee-hee-hee . . .'

'What nonsense is this?'

'I couldn't say, ma'am . . . Rowdies . . . Mashka, the cross-eyed one, was saying . . . And your ladyship, it's all about the manager . . . He's held up the payment coupons, and they say he's mown some hay in Yefrem's field, and he's ruined one of the girls . . . They say it's . . .' Suddenly his voice faltered.

'They're out there with sticks, your ladyship, ma'am, they're all . . . And it's . . . If I may say so.'

The old lady's plump lips pouted and anxiously chewed at emptiness. 'Palashka, my cape!'

Katya and Daryalsky stood at the window; the view opened out from there on to the yard; the yard was big and green and surrounded by outbuildings, forming a rectangle: there were stables there, built of boards, with red tin roofs, and on a whitewashed foundation stood a thatched ice-house, mildewed from the damp, a hut that served as a bath-house and was drowning in a hemp-field, where all day long a cheerful 'chi-chi-chi' resounded, and another ice-house, and a half-built chicken-coop, and a white clay-daubed shed for some purpose or other; there were barns standing there deep in thought, like rotund old men, bursting with grain and supported by staves, sheltered by a maple-tree and sprinkled with the pink flowers of the dogroses; there was a proud regiment of crimson hollyhocks; hens scrabbled about there; and the household office was there; in one half the housekeeper was lodged; the other was occupied by the 'bloodsucker' himself, Yakov Yevstigneyev, with his ample wife, who produced a litter nearly twice a year, and their flaxen-haired offspring, the 'baby-bloodsuckers', whose freshness, youth and blood belonged, to tell the truth, to humble, unlined coffins, which would be carried from Gugolevo to the Tselebeyevo graveyard: it wasn't for nothing that Yakov Yevstigneyev had been fastened like a leech to the people here for five full years – drinking their blood with his caked lips, and had gained the reputation of a sorcerer; although he was a drunkard, he was a well-organized drunkard: he organized other people's property as if it were his own.

He stood on the steps in a leather jacket and tall hunting boots, clutching his rusty Bulldog in his hand, outshouting with his sonorous voice the clamour of the brown homespun coats that pressed in upon him from all sides, and wagging over them his dirty-white beard, like unravelled hempen rope; the homespun coats surrounded him; they clambered onto the rails of the porch; they pressed and pressed towards the office; some of them carried staves; others merely spat into their fists: all were bellowing.

Suddenly the baroness appeared on the vine-festooned porch; strands of grey hair, touched with yellow, came loose and fluttered in the wind, in the rain, towards the crowd of homespun coats; her hand gave an imperious wave; and the forest of staves bristled in her direction, as the rabble flowed away from the office, across the yard and up to the manor-house: the peasants surged forwards.

'Your ladyship! Begging your pardon, ma'am, I'm resigning!' The Bloodsucker outflanked the clamouring throng and stood before the baroness with his evil blue eyes lowered. 'It's impossible for a respectable man to work with such troublemakers: fancy saying I cut some of Yefrem's hay ... Why I ...'

'You're lying, you son of a witch!' A colossus of a man with a colossal stick in his hand pushed through to him, and stuck his colossal fist right under the Bloodsucker's nose, with the thumb protruding between two fingers, making the Bloodsucker screw up his nose unpleasantly ...

'He's a thief, ma'am: when he ought to be in the fields he's off to the priest's to lose a game of crib.'

'He's a thief; son of a witch, what business has he got to go robbing us?'

'He ruins the girls: he's ruined Malashka, he's ruined Agashka, he's ruined my Stepanida!' A sallow, puny peasant with watering eyes and an almost benign expression counted them off on his fingers.

'And what did you do with that wheel of the mistress's?'

'Never you mind!'

'Never you mind, never you mind! What he does, bless you, ma'am, son of a witch, he drives away from here with good new wheels on, and comes back with lousy ones.'

'Only one word for it – he's a swindler: he's swindling us and he's swindling you too!' voices rang out all around. 'He's a thief, he is, a snake in the grass!' Noses were pointed upwards, unkempt beards were fingered, colossal fists gesticulated in the air, throats were cleared, noses blown; suddenly a heavy, acrid smell wafted over from the peasants.

'Hats off, you blockheads! – can't you see it's the mistress!' the Bloodsucker snapped; and, strange to say, heads were bared obediently, sullenly; red, black and brown locks were moistened by the rain and a bald pate grinned; and five young lads, standing a little way off, cracking sunflower seeds, started giggling and made no move to take off their caps.

'What's the point: soon it'll all be ours anyway!'

'Listen, men: be quiet, Yevstigneyev.'

The peasants at the front stuck their beards out attentively, preparing to get their minds round the matter; an old man with a dishevelled beard stuck an ear over someone's shoulder; he listened with his mouth half-open; and a seventy-year-old squinting eye blinked craftily at the baroness; and while she explained how she would sort everything out fairly, a white louse crawled across the old man's cheek; this was Yefrem, a bit of whose hay had been stolen; he was supposed to be a rabble-rouser, a firebrand, a Slocialist – was he? Looking at his attentive face, on which time itself, eternal and immutable, was printed, all that could be read on it was submissiveness, tranquillity; someone hiccupped; someone scratched; and someone, passing from one man to the next, quietly discussed the baroness's words, his fingers splayed out under his nose. All listened.

The profound silence was suddenly broken by the jingle of carriage-bells; a troika of black horses shot out from the willow-trees; the driver, in a sleeveless velvet jacket, brandished the reins, and the rain-soaked sleeves of his lemon-yellow shirt fluttered about in the wind; his hat with peacock feathers floated by under the willows; and the bells jingled merrily as they approached the house; from a distance someone sitting in the troika first waved a red uniform cap of the gentry, then started waving a handkerchief.

'Well, we'll sort it out later: I'll stand you a gallon, men, and off home with you!' the baroness hustled, peering unwelcomingly from the porch into the distance over the crowd of grubby peasants: who could these uninvited guests be?

'Thank you kindly, your ladyship, ma'am! We'll sort it out, of course we will! Count on it . . .' came a hum of words from all sides. Only the grey-haired Yefrem, stuffing snuff up his nose, scratched the back of his head angrily and growled in a rather unfriendly way:

'We'll drink it all right, don't you worry, only . . . that hay was mine . . . and it's gone, a bit of it . . .'

'I'll say it again: he's ruined Malashka, he's ruined Agashka, he's ruined my Stepanida – and what for? Just like that . . .'

The peasants talked among themselves as they walked away; but out of the blue a foul-looking peasant sprang up to the steps, stuck up a finger and grinned all over his face:

'Now if we're all friends, and you're all right and we're all right . . . So you give me a dozen withies for my fence – nice thin ones . . .'

'Very well, very well – go along now . . .'

The troika, like a big black bush with bells for flowers, swept madly out of the foliage, rushed into the yard and halted at the steps.

'Tho glad, tho glad – been meaning to for tho long, at latht!' cried General Chizhikov, springing out of the troika.

General Chizhikov

It was five and a half years since General Chizhikov had arrived in our parts: he arrived with a bang, with drumrolls and gossip; and triumphant scandal dogged his tracks; but in the course of five years General Chizhikov succeeded, if you will pardon the expression, in shoving aside all the scandals, surrounded as he was by money, wine, women and fame.

It was said that General Chizhikov lived here on a false passport; one thing was beyond doubt: General Chizhikov was, it goes without saying, a general and moreover a man of the very highest rank; he was also Chizhikov. That this agreeable person occupied the august rank of general and wore a red ribbon was confirmed by those who were in the habit of residing in the metropolitan city of St Petersburg; they had met Chizhikov at the houses of people in high society, people of lofty rank, and who but generals and the sons of the aristocracy visit places of such *bon ton*, where generals themselves stand to attention without a touch of *chic*, and where even His Excellency the Minister may joke with them in an offhand way? Those were the spheres in which General Chizhikov used to circulate, but then he stopped circulating in them: he became an out-and-out radical and all but took the gospel of red terror to the provinces; they say that the Criminal Investigation Department was terribly cut up about it; anyway, General Chizhikov turned up in our parts, circulating all round the district: from landowner to merchant, from merchant to priest, from priest to doctor, from doctor to student, from student to policeman – and so on and so forth.

And as for him being the genuine Chizhikov – you needn't worry about that: they'll sort it out at the police-station, who's genuine and who's a fake! It was for no other reason than modesty that under this plebeian name there concealed himself – for the time being – a count of the most noble lineage, of a family famous beyond all others – yes, yes: it was Count Gudi-Gudai-Zatrubinsky! And Gudi-Gudai-Zatrubinsky peeped out of the general, you might say, in all sorts of ways – what a rascal! He comes to visit, and he's not been sitting there half an hour like a Chizhikov before the aristocrat starts bursting out of him all over until the air's thick with aristocratism: he shows off his blue blood in every way he can – pulls out a handkerchief reeking of Coeur-de-Jeanette, Oubigand, or even Fleur-qui-meurt, straight from Paris! He can chatter away with a drawing-room *sans-façon* like any popinjay, if only because of his lisp; and his expansive lordly ways show up in everything, he's so *charmant* with the ladies; you can't get past him for '*Merci, madame*', and I can tell you, you'll want to kiss the tips of your fingers: he's not like a general, he's such a sweetie, a real *crême-de-vanille* (you wouldn't notice that he's past fifty, that he's lost his teeth, and that his sideburns aren't a very agreeable colour – like phlegm). He's a count with counts and a clerk with clerks: he'll get drunk in the inn and even suck a herring-tail; and it's of no consequence that for five years he's been kicking his heels, preaching red terror and living off the charity of rich people in Likhov. Well, what of it? Doesn't mean a thing! 'Incognito' – that's a nice one! Everyone has to do something; so he runs errands for merchants in return for the legions of white-capped bottles he's emptied. Now you're frowning! Well, you might as well know, dirt won't stick to anyone with blood as blue as Gudi-Gudai-Zatrubinsky anyway.

All kinds of rumour surrounded the general: about his free and easy way with money, about awkward situations with greedily amorous ladies, peccadillos with schoolgirls, an insalubrious episode with an alluring chambermaid – and they forgave him, because who's to cast the first stone; everyone knew he was a spendthrift and a womanizer; and no one was surprised any more by anything he said! Three times already he'd been on the point of putting our whole district to fire and the sword; but so far he'd spared it. Come to that, even the peasants knew the general! It must have been something to do with the rumour to the effect that the great white general Skobelev, Mikhailo Dmitrych, had never died, but was living secretly in our district in the guise of the robber Churkin. It was just the railway workers who spread some balderdash about this civilian general getting assistance from the Criminal Investigation Department in his most gallant activity, churning out one tall story about him after another: to the effect that he wasn't Skobelev, nor was he the robber Churkin, he wasn't even Count Gudi-Gudai-Zatrubinsky, but simply – Matvei Chizhov, an agent of the Third Department.

Visitors

'There are agrarian dithorderth everywhere in the neighbourhood: ith everything thipthape on your ethtate?' General Chizhikov inquired, kissing the baroness's hand and exuding from his sideburns the aroma of tuberose, with which he had just sprayed them in the troika . . . 'Luka Thilych and I, baroneth, have come to thee you on buthineth,' the enchanter continued, pointing impishly with his red uniform cap in the direction of the troika; from the troika there emerged silently, with dignity, a tall, lean, emaciated man with a short grey beard, raising his plain cap over grey hair, cut even all round; this was the millionaire Yeropegin; then the baroness realized that the troika, the horses, the driver and all the gear were not Chizhikov's (Chizhikov did not own anything of the sort) but Yeropegin's.

The baroness, heaven alone knows why, stared intently at the merchant, and in her gaze, heaven alone knows why, was an involuntary question; an involuntary fear and irritation flitted across her face; it was even almost with anger that she thought: 'How thin he's grown, how thin: nothing but a living relic . . .' Yeropegin, for his part, glanced timidly at her over his glasses and his eyes expressed nothing at all; nothing was reflected in them

but stolid dignity; but still there was a sense that this stolid dignity was
everywhere and at all times aware of its own power: yes, yes, yes – the
longed-for time had come, when the blue blood of the baron's noble line
would have to bow down in submission before his, Yeropegin's, obstinacy:
'Bow down, bow down,' he thought, 'bow right down at my feet: if I
choose, I'll destroy you; if I choose, you'll keep half the baron's estates.'
But these thoughts were not reflected in his face, as he put his lifeless lips
to the old lady's puffy hand; white as death, her face white from creams and
powder, her hair white from time, wearing a sleeveless white fur cloak, she
reminded him of a ghost.

Somewhere inside the house a cascade of plaintive sounds rang out: it
was Katya at the piano; the sounds tumbled in a minuet, moments chasing
after moments; and time was filled with sound; and it seemed there was
nothing that was not sound; and the old lady's past years rose up in those
chords, streams of gold and rivers of milk, and a host of loathsome grasping men, with a weakness for caresses; and among them had been this footloose merchant; but he'd been kept at bay then by the spurs of a hussar.

And here he was again before her with his deep clandestine thought:
'Now the hour of my revenge has come for all of that, and for the way you
roused my hopes when I was just a young merchant and fell in love with
your already fading beauty; and you? You used to turn up now and then
from your Londons and your Parises to mock me and make a torment of
my youth.'

For a moment these thoughts coursed through his brain on wings of
sound; he made another bow; with a gesture full of majesty she invited him
into the house.

Meanwhile the legendary general had long since pranced through into
the vestibule and there had nonchalantly tossed into Yevseich's hands his
weather-beaten cloak, from which the scent of tuberose was overwhelm-
ing; revealing himself in a checked, egg-coloured morning coat, and holding in his left hand an even more egg-coloured glove, the general, puffing
out his chest with pride, strutted into the hall and forthwith began to look
for a spittoon; in the end he found one and spat. That was how this magnificent personage's first undertaking in the house was marked.

The general was introduced to Daryalsky.

'Actual Thtate Counthellor Chizhikov.'

They exchanged handshakes.

'Ah-ha, young man! What are you, an Eth-R or an Eth-D? Here'th my
tholution of the agrarian quethtion' – he spat into the corner; 'we, thup-
porterth of red terror, underthtand perfectly well that the government
needth to introduthe a progrethive takth to thtay in power, but jutht try

proving to the peathantry that thuch a measure . . .' – catching sight of the baroness entering the hall, the incognito of ancient lineage fell silent, broke off his sanguinary speech and started purring under his breath, winking now and then at Daryalsky: 'Ta-ra-ra . . . Ta-ra-ra . . . I've got thome marvellouth Newfoundland pupth for you; my friend'th dog wath taken to court, splendid pupth they are!' the general exploded like a bomb, 'wa-wa – they were born – wa-wa – in the dithtrict court . . .' (the general emitted sounds of enthusiasm half-way between 'u' and 'a').

'I thank you, general,' the old lady muttered drily, but politely, through half-closed lips, but in her eyes a vague distrust and fear were welling up; she politely indicated a chair to the general; and the general promptly sat down and started on the blackcurrant-leaf cordial, which, in accordance with long-standing summer custom, Yevseich was serving to all the visitors, although it was pouring with rain and not hot.

Yeropegin, whom the baroness, in apparent forgetfulness, had not invited to take a seat, shifted from one foot to the other in a rather awkward pose, as his lean, unyielding fingers dithered along the long flap of his black frock-coat; finally, without waiting for an invitation, he pulled up a chair and calmly ensconced himself without uttering a word.

They all fell silent; somewhere a surge of mournful sounds rang out: as though someone had quickly run from bottom to top; it was time, running through someone's life; the miller gave a shudder: Yeropegin's life was full – he had the whole district in his clenched fist; if he squeezed, the landowners' pips would squeak: that's what the days of his life were like. And what about the nights? The nights flew by – in the nights too his head, like an image on an icon, grew grey . . . wine, fruit, the bodies of all sorts of women – all flew by, as the sounds did: and where was it all flying to? He too, Yeropegin, would fly off into the void with his fullness of life, and his chorus girls would see their teeth drop out like this old lady here, and their skin would wrinkle.

So they sat and looked at each other – an old man looking at an old woman; they both seemed like the burnt-out carcasses of their own lives; the one was already sinking into the darkness; for the other, his dream of many years was on the point of fulfilment; but the souls of both were equally far from life.

'Time to begin,' thought Yeropegin, and without speaking handed a sealed envelope to the old lady, and revelled in the sight of her trembling hand as it convulsively tore the envelope open; the old lady, putting on her glasses, tapped her way with her stick over to her writing-desk. And while the papers spilled out onto the desk Luka Silych, fingering his beard, coldly examined the porcelain knick-knacks, arranged on the shelf by

Katya's careful hand; two Tanagra statuettes evidently attracted his attention; he mentally estimated their value.

Meanwhile General Chizhikov, unable to sit still, was already pressing
Daryalsky into the opposite corner of the room; with pouting lips, he pat-
ted the heavy seal on his watch-chain and continued his torrent of words.

'A very thtrange thect, young man, hath appeared in our partth . . .
Doveth have appeared, doveth' – the general raised a schoolmasterly finger
and his exaggeratedly raised eyebrows expressed a comical condescension.
'The thect of the doveth: the conthtable wath telling me that it'th a
mythtical thect and revolutionary at the thame time – doveth! Pa-pa-pa,
what do you thay to that, old chap?'

'What sort of a sect is it?' Daryalsky inquired a moment later; his
thoughts had been elsewhere: he watched indifferently over the general's
shoulder as Yevseich appeared in the doorway with a tray in his hands; but
Yevseich, noticing that no one but the general had touched the cordial,
disappeared again.

'Here, in confidenthe,' the general pulled out a paper on which a cross
was printed: 'Let me read you thith proclamation . . .' and the general
started to read aloud:

'Brotherth, the word of the Thcripture hath been fulfilled, for the
timeth are nigh: the beathtlineth of the Antichrihht hath thet itth theal on
God'th earth; shield yourthelvth with the thign of the croth, Orthodokth
people, for the timeth are nigh: raithe your thword againtht the thervantth
of Beelthebub; the landownerth are the firtht of them: go acroth the land
of Russia ath a thcorching fire; underthtand and pray: the Holy Thpirit ith
about to be born: burn the ethtateth of the devil'th brood, for the land ith
yourth, ath the Thpirit ith yourth . . .'

'Shall I go on?' General Chizhikov looked up triumphantly, but Daryalsky said nothing; he was watching the opposite corner of the room, where
Yeropegin was standing over the baroness like a grey, emaciated corpse; at
the desk the baroness was trembling, gasping, opening wide in horror her
black eyes in their dark swollen sockets, as her fingers leafed through piles
of paper, receipts, invoices; then she leaned her whole body forwards over
the papers, shielding them in desperation, so that her hunched back,
twisted sideways, white like the rest of her, heaved above the foam of lace
surrounding her head; it was as though the old lady was about to lay down
her life on these pitiful remains of once secure securities, stocks and
shares, and all the while the darts of her eyes, still firm, but somehow intoxicated by the dark, and seeming childlike, described arcs across the cup-
boards, carpets, curtains, avoiding Luka Silych.

And conversely: a religious elder, with a face that might have stepped down from an icon, stood motionless before her, quietly, modestly, with dignity, straightening his suit; with his lean fingers he took down a book, with his lean fingers he leafed through it; only the lenses of his spectacles froze the old lady with their cruel glint – they burned with a perfectly assumed indifference; then he put the book down, gently took up his cap, adjusted the long skirt of his black frock-coat and sucked his lips:

'Well then, baroness: you will pay me twenty-five thousand on account by the first of July and the remaining hundred and fifty thousand on the promissory notes I have bought up – by August. And I deeply regret to say you will have to bid farewell to your millions . . . The shares of the Metelkin Railway Company – you can see how they've fallen, because of the war; and the shares of the Varaksin mines, since the bank collapsed, aren't worth a brass farthing either . . . Strikes and all that . . . I understand what a blow it is for you and I'm very sorry, but . . . Very well, then? I will send my manager for the twenty-five thousand: I've had a lot of expense, I need the money myself, you appreciate: and then – the economic crisis the country is in . . .'

He uttered all this so quietly it was barely audible; and quietly, modestly, with dignity, sat down in his chair; under the old lady the strong mahogany and morocco chair creaked and wobbled; only the barely perceptible smile on Luka Silych's thin, lifeless, iconic lips and the trembling of his beard betrayed his evident pleasure at the sight of the Baroness Todrabe-Graaben, who, gripping the arms of her chair with her fingers, made to stand up; her emerald flashed, the knob of her stick hit the floor with a clatter; and a misshapen shadow swept across the wall from the corner.

'You must be mad, my good man! I don't have that kind of ready money . . .'

'Well, if you don't have the cash that's bad for you, very bad,' Yeropegin continued just as gently as before . . . 'I have to have twenty-five thousand at once, and the rest . . .'

Silence.

'Luka Silych, take pity on me!' the old lady blurted out.

Silence.

'Very well, then? So, by the first I will send . . .'

He did not seem filled with majesty; but still he revelled now in his deathly dignity.

'Very well?'

Silence.

He was thinking: 'If she bowed down at my feet, I would let her off even now.' But the old lady did not bow; and the gentle Luka Silych remained implacable.

In the opposite corner of the room General Chizhikov continued to warble like a regular nightingale:

'Not bad, eh? I alwayth thaid that vulgar thectarianithm wath incompatible with revolution; I'm generally all in favour of protethtantithm: jutht look what the Orthodokth Church giveth rithe to: they thay we drink God'th blood and eat hith flesh: would we eat the one we love? And tho . . . nah, nah Count Tolthtoy . . . Ta-ra-ra . . . Ta-ra-ra . . . doveth! eh? – doveth!' and he spat into the spittoon.

'Here it is,' thought Daryalsky; 'the corruption has set in . . .' He was responding to a thought of his own: hardly had the chaos subsided that had raged the previous day in his soul, hardly had victory been attained in him over the fatal feeling that made him lose his way, and the demons left his soul – when already they began again to swarm about him, taking on absurd but completely real forms; and truly – was not this troika, and the general himself, born of the misty filth that had settled over the neighbourhood: was not the troika the sediment from the mist, cast onto the estate by someone's vengeful hand? Lord alone knew from what places the troika had brought these people; was it not with the purpose of encircling him once again in a surrounding throng with the secret monstrousness of lascivious longings?

As though in answer to his thought, someone's steps were heard from the terrace; Pyotr glanced through the window; out there stood an absurd creature in a grey felt hat, wagging its little head that seemed to be squashed down on the top of a disproportionately long and thin trunk; 'this is the last straw,' Daryalsky barely had time to think, before the absurd creature, catching sight of him through the window, hurtled gleefully up the terrace steps, with a trail of water dripping onto the steps from a waterproof coat; the absurd creature was smiling; it revealed itself as a young man with a small, owlish nose and rolled-up trousers; next he tripped on the terrace steps, as though taking a leap on his gnat-like legs; then his feet stumbled once more and a small grey bundle rolled across the floor; there was something extremely pitiful and comical in the whole figure of this new arrival, and General Chizhikov, putting his lorgnette to his eyes, scrutinized him in surprise; but, overcoming all obstacles, of which there were not a few, the absurd young man, blushing pleasantly, like a bashful girl, enfolded Pyotr in his moist embrace with evident delight, whereupon the figure of the absurd young man described a distinct question-mark and his legs folded feebly; but what was the general's astonishment when the absurd creature squealed in a thin falsetto:

'My deeply respected Pyotr Petrovich . . . I, that is, not I . . . and for the very simple reason that . . . have come to, as it were, admire your, beyond all expectations, pleasant and happy situation, occasioned by the unshakeable desire to be united in holy matrimony with an angelic creature . . .'

Pyotr, freeing himself from the embrace, and suppressing his irritation, tried to change the tactless direction of the absurd creature's thoughts:

'Welcome, Semyon . . . I'm glad to see you . . . Where are you on your way to and from?'

'As I was going by Shanks' pony to Dondyukov, where my progenitrix resides – and back again: I thought to visit on my way a fellow-student, friend . . . and poet, and incidentally, congratulate that friend on the profoundly solemn occasion of his having found a companion for life . . . and in such a tranquil setting!' At this point the young man, pushing forward one shoulder, and giving his moustache a twist, suddenly summoned the courage to rush up to the baroness, intending to pay his respects with due decorum. But again Daryalsky distracted him.

The baroness and Yeropegin, occupied with one another, appeared to pay no attention to the newcomer; but General Chizhikov for some reason glowed with interest, sensing a juicy little scandal in the making; he lost no time in desiring to be introduced, as an indication of which he stretched out two fingers to the absurd creature.

'Chukholka, Semyon Andronovich, a student of the Imperial University of Kazan.'

'Never mind, never mind,' muttered General Chizhikov in condescension, 'it'th natural for young people to get carried away: Eth-R? Eth-D?' he looked questioningly at Chukholka.

'Not at all,' the absurd creature squealed, 'I'm neither an SR nor an SD, but a Mystical Anarchist, for the very simple reason that . . .'

A waking dream

Daryalsky and Chukholka were standing in the guest wing; an idle mosquito banged against the windows. Chukholka cast admiring glances at Pyotr, thinking him a *bogatyr*, an epic hero, as he stood there flexing his muscles.

'Well, how are things, Semyon, old chap?'

'They're all pretty much the same, really, that's to say, they're not anyhow, or, rather, the other way round, however, I'm reading Du Prel, writing my candidate's dissertation about ortho-acids of the benzoic series.'

'Aha!'

'Material needs get the upper hand, so to speak, and fickle fortune prevents the correct development of my mental integument . . .'

'You pack up the theosophy. D'you need money?'

'Yes, I mean – no, no' – Chukholka bridled and bristled. 'I'm actually – hm: do you mind if I use the familiar form? Yes, well then – I'm actually, no reason really . . . so: to visit a fellow-student and a poet at the place of his poetic preoccupations – what am I saying? – in the location of his amorous exploits – that wasn't at all what I meant!' Chukholka became completely confused and bumped into the table; 'in a nest of iniqui . . . I mean, a den of the gen . . . and in the sphere of his observations on the Russian people at a time, so to speak, of the greatest concentration of his spiritual energies in the struggle for what is right, and for the very simple reason that . . .'

'Aha!' Daryalsky interrupted and fell silent, hoping to stop this incoherent torrent which threatened at any moment to turn into a veritable ocean of words, in which the names of all the world's discoveries would be mixed with the names of all the world's luminaries, theosophy with jurisprudence, revolution with chemistry; to complete the monstrosity chemistry would make a transition into Kabbalism, Lavoisier, Mendeleyev and Crookes would be explained with the help of Moshe ben Maimon, and the conclusion would always be the same: the Russian people would stand up for their rights; and these rights would be couched by Chukholka in such a modernistic form that to judge by separate extracts of his speech you might think you had to do with a decadent the like of which not even Mallarmé had seen; Chukholka was actually a student of chemistry; true, he was a chemist with a leaning towards occultism, which had irreversibly disturbed his poor nerves; and so this student from Kazan was the helpless conductor of all astral impurities; why was it that Chukholka, himself an honest, decent fellow, intelligent and extremely hard-working, allowed all manner of filth to pass through him, which then, emerging, assailed his interlocutor? Every possible confusion arose in his presence, as Pharaoh's serpents arise from a pinch of powder; his lowly birth, his thin falsetto voice, his squashed head and his owlish nose contrived to do the rest; people found Chukholka burdensome, they drove him away from everywhere he had the misfortune to appear: everywhere he brought with his arrival the vibrio of chaos.

As he led the student into his room, Daryalsky could not help frowning: he had intended to spend this day alone with Katya; he had, after all, to explain to her his absence the day before. But even more Daryalsky frowned because Chukholka's appearance on his horizon was always a harbinger of ill – as though his invisible enemies were making fun of him: for example, once Chukholka had caught Daryalsky and made him stand in a draught, giving him a cold; another time he had made Daryalsky mix up all his deadlines; the third time he had appeared on the day his mother died;

since then he had disappeared; and now he had appeared again. Daryalsky would even get a particular feeling in his stomach (nausea and a nagging pain in the pit of his stomach) after talking to the student from Kazan. 'Devil only knows,' thought our hero, 'here's that Chukholka again; he'll have brought all sorts of evil to attack me.'

And poor Chukholka was already unpacking his bundle in Daryalsky's room, and Daryalsky was astonished at how neatly everything in it was packed and wrapped: there were white paper packets tied round with pink ribbons, a few new books in new bindings; toothpicks, combs, brushes of exemplary cleanliness; there was only one change of linen, two calico shirts and one belt; but there was a bottle of eau-de-Cologne, some powder, a razor and even that notorious barber's stone of invariably mysterious provenance; but what surprised Daryalsky most of all was a fresh paperbag, out of which a large Spanish onion protruded.

'What's that you've got?'

'That's for my mother: living as she does in the country in the absence of any excess of material well-being – yes: my mother is deprived of comforts, and so I am taking her a Spanish onion as a present and for the very simple reason that . . . If that aristocratic old lady were to take a liking to my onion, I would lick her – quite the opposite: I would present her with this humble gift.'

'Stop it . . .'

Daryalsky went out of the guest wing: Chukholka definitely irritated him; he could not stay another moment alone with that gibberish.

The rain had stopped: again the sun gleamed for a moment; Gugolevo appeared before him, opened itself out, enclosed him in its blossoming embrace – and now it was looking at him, Gugolevo: looking at him with the lucent waters of its lake, Gugolevo; and the lake was rocking him with its dove-blue waters which sang with silver, and all the while the rippling lake was reaching out to the banks with its waters – but it could not reach: and whispered with the reeds – and there, in the lake, was Gugolevo: it rose from behind the trees in its entirety, then gazed with a smile of longing at the water – and escaped into the water: there it was now, in the water – over there, over there.

Look – inverted now, the image of the dancing house begins to run; the columns are strangely dancing now like white snakes, piercing the water's gleam, and under them – down there, down there: a strangely inverted dome, and a shining spire that pierces the depths is dancing strangely too, and on the spire an upside-down bird with its feet pointing upwards; how everything had now turned upside down for him! As he watched the bird it detached its feet and went away from him altogether into the depths.

'Where have you gone from me, my depths?'

Over there, over there! O Lord, the ringing water whirls and eddies: that is what is happening now in Daryalsky's soul.

'Over there, that's where my soul is – deep: it's cold there, oh, so cold; and everything that is mine is unknown to me there. Can it be that my soul is no longer with me, but has left my body and flown away, like that bird that took off from the dancing spire in the deep and flew away? There the clouds float, dipping in the water – and it is the limitless underwater expanse, but this is the surface of the water; then why did that surface show me its depths, just as my years that have flowed by on the surface were not flowing by here, but there, in the mirror's reflection . . . Listen to the lapping of the waves: gaze at the brightly puckered reflection, more beautiful than life itself; the waters are calling me there, where the martins weave and circle, slicing the underwater air with their wings; and my soul is a martin, slicing through the depths. Where is it flying to, my soul, where? It is answering the call; how should it fail to fly, when the abyss summons it?

'Oho! Where, indeed, has my soul made off to?' Daryalsky thought; a pleasant sweetness and lightness flooded through his whole body from the gentle singing and the distant call of his soul.

And he realized that his soul had long since been mislaid, that it was no more in Gugolevo than Gugolevo was in the depths of the shimmering waters; there were the house, the flowers, the birds, but dive in – and the lake-bottom ooze will envelop you and a black leech will cling to your breast. Where was it, then, his soul, if there was no sign of it in this mortal coil? Just as a winged eagle, falling upon a smaller bird, grasps it firmly in its talons and circles with it in the sky where there is nothing but the currents of the air, and in the sky, in the currents of the air, a fearful battle takes place, feathers fly and blood spurts – so someone had long since fallen upon his soul in the currents of the air, and the days had flown, and the lightning-flashes of his thoughts had played – his thoughts, induced by someone – so someone had fallen upon his soul at the fateful moment when it, his soul, was in full flight far from its earthly image; his earthly image had long been searching round in trepidation, looking over his shoulder at people, at empty corners, at flowers, at bushes – what might there be for him to notice in the bushes, apart from the twitter of birds? But the battle went on: just so the mother whose young has been snatched by the eagle gazes at the sky, her arms aloft – and in the air there is no longer anyone to be seen: no eagle, no child; both are already far away, both the eagle and the child, lost to her for ever.

He was the same: Gugolevo stared at him from the water – but say, could that be Gugolevo? A slight ripple puckered the water, and there was nothing: just white bubbles, as though someone had scattered beads over the water, and the old women's whispering of the reeds – and maybe someone else: there was his arm rising out of the water, powerfully extended, marked with age.

Daryalsky came to with a weight in his head, trying in vain to recall the visions that had appeared to him in his daydream: and he remembered nothing. Gugolevo once more appeared before him, spread itself out, enclosed him in its blossom-clad embrace; it gazed out with the lucent waters of its lake, Gugolevo. And some sweet song resounded in his soul. A pink, childlike face bent quietly over him from the reeds, and the child smiled, bent down, and raised a hand with a pink flower in it – ah! from behind his back a sprig of willowherb fell onto the surface of the pond. Pyotr turned round.

Katya was standing in front of him, her pale face buried in a bunch of pink willowherb; she was looking sideways at him, as though it was by chance that she had come across Pyotr here by the water; and she did not speak.

Sacrosanct

'Poor Katya, my poor bride! Your Pyotr is unworthy of you; know this, and think what kind of fate awaits you.'

But Katya did not hear him; oh, what a look of power he had, how red his chest was, like cloth of purple fluttering in the cold wind, and how the nettle-tendrils were pawing at his breast; what a moustache, what a shock of hair, curling like scorching ash from his head, in which the eyes, glinting now with a green fire – were coals, that burned the soul to dust!

'Poor girl, what kind of husband will you take now, and will you exchange your single state for contentment, or for happiness? My hand will fall heavily and coarsely upon your fate as a woman . . .'

Oh, how the trees rustled, how Katya's blue skirt flapped and her hair blew in the wind; how the damp grass around them whistled as it swayed; the twigs, the branches, the treetops started to rock, and the ceaseless movement of the bright pink willowherb was like the surge of Katya's youthful soul: like the singing of an anthem, the beginning of a sermon – everywhere was noise . . . Here it was – the tender flower of her young soul; and the wind was surrounded by the distant whistling of pipes and the clatter of the forest timbrels, while from the hill an age-old oak stretched its arms out to the people of the forest, like a prophet.

Here it was, the flower of her youthful soul, oh, how she reached out to him – to wind her arms around him and fall asleep on his breast, but that breast had nettles beating on it; so let the nettles sting her cheek, let them smash her life to pieces.

And she laid her quiet head upon his scorching breast: her curls mingled with his – their curls were mingled in a single weft of smoke, spun in the wind, swirling from a crimson flame: what fire had they lit in that place? Their greedy lips opened greedily; arms of steel stretched out impulsively, crushing her slender frame, the incandescent lava of his breath flowed into her breast; and lips merged with lips in one prolonged, clinging, moist breath; her dress was like the blue sky in the crimson flame, like sunset, of his clothes: and over this sunset of two lives, now merged, there hung the wafting ash, a cloud of disenchantment; the pink fingers of the willowherb danced wildly.

'Pyotr, that's enough: hush!' – Katya, his betrothed, struggled in his embrace – 'Pyotr, people might see us . . .'

But Pyotr was carried away; he glanced into her half-closed eyes and drank those eyes with his moist lips, and her dark lashes tickled his lips: he threw back his head and drank her gaze with his gaze – not with his gaze: he drank the surge of his own soul, which flew down to him in the form of a dove: the dove began to beat its wings in his empty, empty breast: tuk-tuk-tuk.

'Pyotr, stop it, how your heart's beating!'

The dove flew down, fluttered its wings, with one wing gripped her throat, and pecked at Katya's tears, which welled up like transparent grains germinating from the depths of her soul – it pecked its fill: a greedy dove; it would peck at everything and lay waste another's soul: then it would break out of that soul and fly off into the heavens. But for now let those blue almond eyes fuse with those other eyes, and let an arm of steel crush those arms bent behind her; intoxicated gaze opened wide to intoxicated gaze; soul met and flew away – but where?

'Pyotr, stop it: your heart's pounding!'

She drew away from him ashamedly; the sun broke through and caught her full in the face: in her eyes were peacock feathers, and a tracery of bright sunbeams flitted across her; but then the sun was gone.

'Listen, Pyotr' – the silly girl blushed – 'is it true that men . . . that a man,' she blushed deeply, deeply – so deeply that she covered her face with her hands – 'that men love women quite at random . . . just like that: when they don't really love them at all?'

'It is true, my love: there are such men!'

'And then they kiss them just as you were kissing me just now?' – and Katya thought to herself what prickly cheeks men have; her face was burning from contact with those prickly cheeks.

'Do you love me, Pyotr?'

'How could I help loving you, my sweet?'

'So I am the first in your life?'

'Yes!' Pyotr was about to say, but faltered, and Katya looked at him with a frightened expression, pressing her hands to his chest, and her crimson lips half-opened . . . 'Yes!' he nearly uttered, but he remembered the madness of the day before, and faltered: he remembered that unique one whom he had never met, not even met in Katya. Katya he loved, but she was not that dawn: and that dawn was not to be met with in female form.

'Come on, answer me' – Katya fixed him with her eyes and her fingers absent-mindedly broke off the bright pink plume of a flower; he frowned, and once again a portcullis came down over his eyes, and the green coals of his eyes sprayed lightning over the meadow in front of her: it was possible to meet that one, but her countenance would be sullied by the earth; suddenly there stood before him the image of the peasant woman of the previous day: she, perhaps, would be his dawn; and so, burning with a subterranean flame, he stood with folded arms and spoke:

'Listen to me, my quiet Katya! If you don't take me as my mother bore me, I shall leave you and go far away, and there I shall fall low, because my passionate blood is full of fire; and my blood is poisoning me. Katya, my betrothed, who are you marrying? If only you knew!'

'I do know, I do know!' A quiet groan sounded beside him; Katya had understood everything: yes, he was just the same as all the rest; just like the rest, he had had a shameful liaison with a woman before her; oh, how he stood there, like a red apostle among the tender flowers, disturbing her peace of mind; and there was something of the wild beast gazing out of him at her. All around was noise; the clumps of trees – aspens, oaks, elms – tossed by turns; and in the distance hung an unchanging noise that bade the past farewell. It was like listening to the sermon of red apostles about that which was not yet in existence, but would soon come to pass; and close by the trees fell silent, in anticipation of the unsung song that was winging its way towards them: the anthem of her soul was being sung and a terrible sermon begun, which would spread the surge of Katya's soul far and wide through villages, hovels and the tracks of wild beasts; and the world of the beasts was responding; maybe out there on the wild beasts' tracks a feral dog had crept, its ears flattened, to throw back its head and howl to accompany the gusting wind; or maybe it had human eyes; and the dog gazed with its human eyes at the passer-by; and he crossed himself and urged on his poor nag more forcefully as it trotted through the mud, while a werewolf chased after him in broad daylight; what fear did that hold, when her Pyotr had turned out to be a werewolf too!

He stood without speaking and looked at her with his burning coals: but Katya overcame herself: in the twinkling of an eye she experienced his stormy life; with an inner eye she foresaw his fall; but she also saw the punishment hanging over them: it seemed to her that his head was emitting an invisible flame that consumed the brain; little did she know that that hellish flame was his tomorrow. She lived through everything and forgave everything.

'I'll take you however you are . . .'

He dropped onto his knees in the damp grass, in the nettles, and she kissed his burning forehead grievingly.

And so he rose from the ground, girded round by the power of her love for the battle to come.

Scoundrels!

Palashka, her ladyship's laundry-maid, was rinsing some washing at the pond; she was soft, fair-skinned, plump and rosy-cheeked; little yellow freckles blossomed on her cheeks, and her plump, pale legs, half in the water, were revealed to the knees by her tucked-up skirt; her hair was dishevelled.

When the sun peeped out, patches of sunlight danced all over her: they danced over her bare arms and her bare legs, and over her pink skirt; and there among the delicate branches, all covered in sunlight and flowers, she was – absolutely charming! And General Chizhikov danced all round her: 'Gracious, how old he is!' Palashka thought, and chuckled.

General Chizhikov couldn't restrain himself: he jumped on her out of the branches and the flowers: 'Rothe-bud, rothe-bud, give me a kith,' and, making horns with his fingers, Count Gudi-Gudai-Zatrubinsky tickled Palashka's white breast and tried to get his hands inside her blouse; they struggled and gasped, until Palashka broke free and, with a growl, slapped him across the face with some wet washing: 'Keep your hands to yourself! You just wait, I'll complain to the mistress!'

But General Chizhikov, wiping himself with a handkerchief, blew her a kiss, 'You're tho lovely and thoft . . . don't you want a little kith?'

Then he lit upon Chukholka, who had grown weary of sitting in the guest wing; catching sight of the Spanish onion sticking out of his pocket, General Chizhikov instantly forgot the recent unpleasant incident.

'Ah, what'th that? You've got an onion, a Thpanish onion? How delightful! Ah, are you sure it'th not a bomb? . . . Give me the onion!' . . . and he snatched the onion from the Kazan student's pocket.

'When the great chemist Lavoisier was doing some experiments, the test-tube burst and a piece of eye got in his glass, I mean, quite the other way round: a piece of glass got in his eye,' Chukholka attempted to joke.

The general took fright, hastily stuffed the onion into Chukholka's pocket and beat a swift retreat.

'Thuthpiciouth, motht thuthpiciouth,' he whispered and took out his notebook.

Two hours later the guests departed.

'My dear young lady, if you're ever in Likhov, you'll be most welcome at our house; it's better there than at the hotel,' Luka Silych said to Katya in farewell, passing a voluptuous eye over her bright, winsome face.

The driver gave a flourish of his lemon-yellow sleeves; the carriage-bells tinkled and the red uniform cap could be seen bobbing up and down through the trees for a long time.

General Chizhikov snorted merrily into his spittle-flecked whiskers: 'Aha, now, Luka, old man! There'th a girl for you. I wouldn't mind giving her a . . .' – and he bent over to Yeropegin and whispered an obscenity.

An ugly incident

'It's time to serve supper: must be gone eight!' – so Yevseich decided, and left the room: the stentorian summons of the gong filled the air all around; the old lady emerged with a wheeze and took her seat at table with a face blacker than a stormcloud.

She had been locked in her room ever since the visitors had left: but she had not been weeping; an arid grief was crushing her, and the old lady transferred her displeasure to those around her: who were they all? What had things come to? Ever since that son of a priest had taken up residence there had been nothing but lateness, whispering in the corners and hanky-panky in the bushes.

Now she was poor; she would be driven out of this house; how could she pay her debts now: love was past, youth was past; everything, everything was slipping away into primordial chaos; the trees outside the window jerked about, and primordial chaos rustled in their grasping branches: there, outside the window, the bad weather was creeping away; a dark, languid, white-capped stormcloud was creeping away towards Likhov; its refulgent domes, spreading mantles of light upwards, settled over the forest. The old lady bent over her lap-dog and cooed plaintively, 'Mimochka, my little pet, you're all I have left, you silly little doggie . . .'

All of a sudden there appeared in front of the old lady an absurd, horribly ugly face, and an owlish nose swayed about above her, and a pair of nasty, sugary, slit-eyes – as it seemed to her – blinked over her, and a long arm stretched out under her very nose, proffering a Spanish onion; at that moment the white lap-dog shot ferociously out from under her skirt and immediately shot back again when the slim foot of Chukholka tripped pathetically over the lap-dog's fluffy tail:

'Ah, *pardon, merci, madame,* I'm sorry: I have offended a worthy creature, an immortal monad, so to speak, of canine age, I mean, no, in canine form, and for the very simple reason that . . . the reincarnation of earthborn creatures in their fickle revolutions . . .'

'And who might you be, sir?' the old lady flared up in indignation, rising from her chair and clutching her stick in her hand.

'I . . . I . . .I,' the absurd figure stuttered in confusion, 'I'm Chukholka . . .'

'What did you say?'

'I beg your pardon, not having been presented to you, I represent the manifestation of best friend and fellow-student of your betrothed – on the contrary, your daughter's betrothed . . . I have been strolling in the salubrious air . . .'

'No, sir, how do you come to be here?' the old lady continued to advance upon him in utter fury.

'I came from Kazan,' Chukholka retreated, holding the onion out to her in supplication.

'Then be off with you back to your Kazan!' and with an imperious gesture she pointed to the door.

But Daryalsky and Katya appeared in the doorway; Katya was the first to realize the danger threatening Chukholka; she made to rush forward; but Daryalsky, turning pale, seized her arm and pulled her back; everything in him was seething with anger at the sight of this insult inflicted on a human being; but he restrained himself, folded his arms, and, breathing heavily, watched in silence the nasty scene that unfolded.

And indeed, there was reason to be angry: the disconcerted Chukholka was swaying aimlessly back and forth in front of the enraged baroness, who had at last found a way of venting both the anxiety that had been weighing upon her all day and the tempest that had been aroused in her by Yeropegin's words; but the more the old lady advanced, the more helplessly Chukholka smiled at her: all the coordination of his nerve centres had collapsed, and automatic movements of his long arms had taken over from the movements of his conscious self . . . many selves were jostling like a whirlwind in his representations, and when he spoke, it seemed that ten tearful demons, interrupting one another, were shouting their nonsense out of him.

'Nevertheless, notwithstanding . . . taking advantage of your hospitality to present you at table with this onion . . .'

'Get out!' the old lady gurgled, rather than shouted.

'What, me?' Only now did Chukholka realize the horror of his situation and the blood rushed to his face. 'What, me? a respectable person, and on the contrary; why, I'll . . . I'll . . . I'll blow you up!' he blurted out impotently and dissolved in tears.

Like an arrow shot from the bow, Daryalsky leapt forward: he could not bear these tears of Chukholka's: it seemed that the swarm of demons sitting in this insulted frame, as though in Pandora's box, came flying out, circled invisibly and entered Pyotr's breast; and, beside himself with fury, he pushed away the old lady as she advanced on the student, grabbed her arm, snatched away her stick and threw it across the room.

'Take your words back, or I . . . I . . .,' he whispered breathlessly. All were transfixed: branches were thrusting at the windows and outside the windows was a constant noise: the wind was passing through the treetops; the distances gurgled in unceasing complaint; it was as though grain were being poured, now in a thick stream, now in a thin one; grain was being poured here and there, now here, now there. But it was the wind.

The old lady looked up at Daryalsky with her large, now child-like eyes; saliva trickled from her drooping lips . . .

'You'd do that to me?!'

Mechanically, even, it seemed, calmly, as though enacting the inevitable, her raised hand unclenched itself on Pyotr's cheek: the slap rang out in the air; five white fingermarks slowly caught fire on Pyotr's pale skin: the demons, having exploded Chukholka's consciousness, and now penetrating the bodies of these people, made defenceless by anger, raised such a whirlwind that it seemed the earth had collapsed between these people and they had all hurled themselves into a gaping abyss.

In the deep silence the clock rasped and – dong: it was half past eight.

That chime restored their memory of what had happened: the abyss slammed to, the demons vanished, and the people stood facing each other, equally horrified at what had taken place: Katya's cry rang out; like a whirlwind it flew through Daryalsky's mind: now he was insulted; there is an arithmetic of actions, and, as twice two is four, he had to appear insulted, even though he understood that it was from helplessness merely that the poor old lady had struck him; now she had burst into loud wailing, and collapsed into her chair in indescribable horror, stretching out her powerless hand to Katya.

'My child, my little granddaughter, Katenka, don't you leave me, an old woman . . . Aaa-aaa-!' and the tears flowed in torrents.

Like a whirlwind it passed through his mind that now, this minute, he would consider himself insulted and leave Gugolevo for ever, and would have to spend the night in Tselebeyevo; and while he was thinking this, he was already feeling insulted and saw that his presence here was impossible: turning away, he strode to the door, his heels clattering on the parquet; his vengeful enemy had performed his execution: fate was returning him to the places from which he had fled only the day before.

'My child, my poor little love' – the old lady, in floods of tears, had lost all her rigidity: 'We're poor . . . soon they'll come and throw-ow us out onto the street . . .' The bright gleam of the departing day came in through the window and struck these swollen cheeks; and the sun itself, like a brilliant Phoenix, hiding in the delicate tracery of the swaying branches, spread its golden tail in farewell, blessing the advent of reviving sleep.

Return

He turned round, now he was saying goodbye to a place he loved; never, never again would his foot tread this ground: over there Gugolevo revealed itself out of the sunset: only recently it had been to right and left of him, spreading out in all directions: the glitter of water here, a scatter of huts and outbuildings there, dogs barking, wisps of smoke hanging in the air; but now it was all gathered together, all in one place; gathered together, and drowning far off in the clumps of green oaks; there was no place dearer!

And now it was away over there – Gugolevo.

It rang with an approaching song: some Gugolevo people going past, no doubt; tall, lit like a folklore hero gleaming in shining armour, the ancient house shone and sparkled on the hill-top amidst a stormy sea of green leaves; straight out of the waves it raised its columns aloft, pink from the sunset, like the tall masts of a ship as it sails out to sea; the silvered dome billowed out from the columns like a spinnaker: the house was sailing away from Pyotr towards the horizon on a green sea of oak crowns; and on that ship Princess Katya was sailing out of his life.

From the irretrievable past the windows struck Daryalsky full in the eyes with cascades of ruby light amongst the oak foliage that rushed by in the wind; the forest crests were falling upon Gugolevo: a pine-tree started moving; the momentum left it and passed on to the surrounding trees; another started moving beside it – raging angrily at Gugolevo; and everywhere was a raging and a singing: the old park raged angrily, the oak crowns hurled themselves hither and thither, rose in fury and marched off in fury against the sunset.

The house-ship was motionless in the sunset and beautiful as it floated on the treetops, thinking a powerful thought; it stared from afar with its red eyes straight into Daryalsky's soul from the treetops that rushed past in the wind: 'Did I not safeguard your days, you faithless one; did I not protect you with my breast, like a shield; like a shield I stretched between you and the heavens' . . . That is how the old house talked to Daryalsky as it ran away from him; the golden spire above the house had vanished straight into the greenery and the pale, transparent sky.

Daryalsky's heart was pounding: to Gugolevo he said: 'Forgive me' . . . And he ran.

> 'Why, you wayward woman, do you
> Ruin one whose heart is yours?
> Can it be you do not love me . . .?
> No? Then darken not my doors . . .'

Chukholka was approaching; he had hastily tied his bundle, and was catching up with Daryalsky; his exclamations wafted into the evening's deepening gloom:

'I'm most saddened by the fact that your misadventure occurred through me; not by malice aforethought, but for the very simple reason that . . . a Spanish onion brought the wheel of your fortune to a halt . . .'

'Oh, stop pestering me!' Daryalsky blurted out. 'I'm sorry, Semyon, but please leave me by myself . . . Goodbye!'

Chukholka, raising his hat, stopped in bewilderment in the middle of the road, sighed, and wiped away his perspiration with a handkerchief: he had nowhere, absolutely nowhere, to go; it was a good twenty-five versts to Dondyukov.

He tossed his bundle onto his back and set off for Dondyukov: he couldn't spend the night in the forest, after all . . .

A drunken horde appeared from the bushes:

> 'Why, oh why, did you ensnare me?
> Why did you compel my love?
> Don't you know that love's betrayal
> Is a crime condemned above?'

Pyotr's red shirt quickly crossed their path.
'Ain't that the squire? What's he up to?'
'He's just a parasite!' someone spat.
And the gang jeered at Daryalsky.

'I shall not be loved by others,
I shall dream of one apart.
Pray believe me, my beloved,
Yours forever is my heart.'

All around the wind swept up the mantles of the trees, loosening them at their edges; leaves, branches, dry twigs were torn away into the lustreless murk of the east.

'That way – to the east, into darkness and dissipation: Katya, Katya, where am I to go now that I've left you?'

Sounds died away in the distance:

'At church a fine carriage was waiting,
Inside was a wedding in style,
In their finery guests celebrating,
On all of their faces a smile.'

'So there's even a carriage at church for you,' Daryalsky tried to smile, but his heart started thumping painfully.

A pile of straw that the wind had snatched off the road drew tall, idle arcs in the air, dropped impotently onto the road – and moved off again, rushing away to one side.

The song could still be heard, but the words could not be made out. 'A-a-a . . . o-o-o-ly' – and a solitary voice was raised in the damp air with complete clarity: 'Oh, what an unsavoury groom . . . the girl has been ruined for nothing' – and it finally died out behind a copse.

It was growing dark; the creak of cartwheels was heard in the twilight; someone barked out at the horse, 'Whoa!'

'Where are you from?' Daryalsky muttered absent-mindedly into the darkness, dense with tree-trunks.

'From there: from that place over there,' came a voice from the darkness.

'What have you got there?'

'We've got the steppe there . . .'

The wheels started creaking again; Daryalsky walked on into the indigo gloom.

At peace

Evening had drawn in; and still she stood on the balcony, looking out at the place where, half an hour before, Pyotr's red shirt could be glimpsed now and then until he reached the point where he bade farewell to the past he loved; and though he had long since said farewell to his past, still she stood there gazing at the spot where he had done so; and from there, from the other side of the forest, Tselebeyevo gave voice in a plaintive song and the moaning of an accordion:

> 'Dressed in white as befits the occasion,
> A rosebud bouquet as her prize,
> The bride gazed aloft at the Saviour,
> And tears of distress filled her eyes.'

Katya felt like crying; she thought of her beloved, and of her grandmother, who had now become calm again; her grandmama had just finished weeping her heart out on Katya's breast, and quickly fallen asleep in exhaustion like a hurt child who has successfully begged forgiveness: and Katya had forgiven her everything and forgotten the hurt: both for herself and for Pyotr. There they sat now, quietly embracing, somnolent grandmother and quiet Katya; tomorrow both grandmama and Katya would write to Pyotr's friend who lived in Tselebeyevo: and the quarrel would be mended.

The pond lay spread out in front of her: the sunset had settled lightly on the damp paths; and the paths were faintly purpled; and the tall meadow grass was faintly purpled; amidst moist pearls of dew the orchids bloomed their last; heavily and passionately the flowers breathed out their magnificent aroma over everything and expired; in the distance a hoarse, timid sound was heard, and it carried an air of something dear, something experienced in better times; it carried an air of what had been experienced and forgotten: it was the hoarse cry of a snipe; a white sea of mist spread slowly through the hollows. Her Pyotr was far away now; but Katya would return to him; she would have her life, she would; and that life would be untrammelled and free; Pyotr and she would be in distant, foreign parts – in such places where people's evil gossip would not catch them, however hard it tried: neither evil gossip, nor her grandmother's impotent grousing; the day would come, when, a happy couple, they would fly the old nest and find freedom; and that time was close at hand . . .

Katya sat in the morning-room, listening to the gusts of the rebellious wind: 'Somewhere there must have been a hailstorm.'

Tap-tap-tap – resounded at her door: who could that be? It is frightening at such a time, when night is already gazing in at the window, for young girls to open their doors: outside the door are corridors, passages, vaults, and the attic itself.

Tap-tap-tap – resounded at her door.

'Who's there? Yevseich?'

'It's me, miss . . .'

'What do you want?'

The door opened; Yevseich's grey head peeped round, sputtering with laughter – and Yevseich's shadow flitted blackly across the white-washed stove.

'Well, what is it?'

'Tee-hee-hee, miss. It's funny, miss . . .'

He giggled, he sputtered, he snorted; Yevseich was content now; the mistress, bless her, had deigned to fall asleep – but the old man couldn't sleep: he had come to entertain the child.

'Tee-hee-hee, miss. I've a new way of making a pig on the stove, miss. Like this, if you would just bend your ring-finger, then with your thumb – like that . . . Tee-hee-hee!' Yevseich roared with laughter, and a little black shadow-pig danced on the wall . . . And Katya was glad.

'Well, that's enough, old man: it's time to sleep . . .'

Yevseich went away; Katya watched him go: it was dark in the corridors, frightening; and up there, by the attic, there was a crackling noise at the top of the stairs: it was the old man chuckling as the darkness engulfed him.

Oh, what a noise the trees made!

Night

In the night the clouds came thronging back; Tselebeyevo was immersed in sleep; a narrow, ominous strip glowed in the west.

In the priest's garden the guitar had been twanging all day: later, when it was really night, the sexton's voice had echoed through the village: 'The lads from the seminary stood in the middle of the tavern, crying: Vodka, most blessed mother! Let thy divine essence enter into us.' And the voice died away.

When the black night bellows and the sky lights up every moment, toppling down onto the earth in stifling masses of clouds, and the marble thunder growls right here, amongst us, as if on the very earth, without rain, and in the stall there is no sound of horses contentedly snorting – only the strident cockerel venting his voice at an ungodly hour, and no one joining in – then it is stifling in Tselebeyevo, frightening. The odd house in the distance gives you a wink with the light in its window; but if you enter its patch of spilt light – the darkness surrounding you will become blacker still; no, don't peep into the window of the villager who keeps his light burning late on a night like this: he who at this hour is not afraid of light- ning flashes at his window is strange and frightening himself.

You will wander around Tselebeyevo without shelter; exposed to the lightning as it strikes, you will find no place to lay your head, and moreover, you may even lose your sight when the red woman Malanya casts her eye on you from out of a cloud, and for a moment you catch sight of her cavort- ing in the clouds; and for a moment you will see everything around, far and near – red.

And then, in the darkness, some misbegotten creature will steal up on you and crush you, throttle you in its deformed hands, and in the morning you will be found hanging on a tree; only the unrighteous go carousing on nights like this, and settle their felonious deals, just as now, in the teahouse, where all manner of riff-raff had gathered, heaven only knows who they were and heaven only knows where they'd come from, and they were downing their vodka and bellowing their songs, glancing at the windows which were black one moment and red from the lightning the next:

> 'O, my Malanya,
> My goggle-eyed Malanya!
> You lived in the village
> And worked at the sexton's.
>
> You lived like that a little while,
> Then became a chambermaid,
> Then you got all tarted up,
> And led us all a merry dance . . .'

The lads were singing the song against themselves: on nights like this the dried-up bushes creep about the village, they surround the village in a howling throng; the red woman Malanya flies through the air, and the thunder rushes after her.

Who was it, what madman, who wandered all night round the village, embracing bushes, went into the teahouse and caroused for hour after hour with all the riff-raff? And who was it who then fell drunk into the ditch? Whose was the red shirt that in the early morning was lying in wait by the sloping hollow, near Kudeyarov the carpenter's hut? Whose summoning whistle was heard, and who answered it by opening the window of the hut and gazing out into the darkness for a long, long time?

CHAPTER FOUR

Chimera

The daily round

'Come on,' the carpenter, who lived with Matryona Semyonovna, would say, 'come on,' he'd say, 'let's go for a walk round our bit of the earth: let's have a stroll . . .' – That's what he would say on high days and holidays and squeeze out from his place under the icon, turning his cup upside down with its pattern of pink roses, and without fail placing on top of it a half-chewed sugar lump, already specked by flies: and when he'd said it, Matryona Semyonovna would pin on her patterned shawl: and off they'd go . . . And so they walked along our street together, spitting out the husks of melon seeds.

The carpenter would tug his homespun coat over one shoulder on top of his coarse red shirt; and with a grunt he would pull on his squeaky boots, which had been dried out on the stove: and in a most dignified way he would point before him his distinguished nose – and off he would stride, with Matryona behind him in her laced-up shoes and her canary-yellow bodice decorated with braiding (a present from a wealthy relative). And the way they walked out, they were just like husband and wife! They cracked melon seeds; dignified, perfectly worthy people; it was as though they weren't peasants at all, but belonged to the class of city tradespeople; anyone who passed them had his cap off in a trice and made a quick bow, so that his forelock jumped up and down:

'Good day, Mitry Mironych . . . My respects to you, Matryona Semyonovna!' And if it was the sexton who went by, then straight away he'd bow, 'Greetings to you, Mr Kudeyarov, sir.'

And all around are white houses, red houses, green ones, with white-painted window-frames, decorated with fretwork and with a third window, an attic window right under the roof, from which the sun's reflection hits you in the eyes; and all around are the sweet scents of this salubrious climate: the little lake splashes coolly at your feet with its fresh blue water, it beguiles you with its refreshing air, and babbling yellow streams, which might be made of living mica, trickle down the slope into it, while a gull halts its flight at the water's edge and beats its snow-white, pointed wing on the spot, with a fish in its claws! A tree seems to be dangling its fading red foliage right from the blue of the sky itself, and from that foliage comes the sweet, autumnal twittering of blue-tits: and the couple took their walks like that every autumn, year in, year out, after all three feast days of Our Lord: carpenter and carpenter's wife; the couple used to walk as far as the forest, and then turn back: sharp ridges of a soft pink hue, with myriad other tints, stood there straining into the lofty blue, and the russet birches trembled briskly in rust and brocade, like clergy robed for the festival of their patron saint; the red nose of a squirrel poked out from a hazel-bush; and among all this the face of Mitry Mironych, if seen from the side, stood out like the image on a Suzdal icon.

Look at him, just you look at the carpenter – look at his face: there's nothing there, and yet there is something, a certain dignity, but where does it come from? He's a person of no importance, material of the basest quality; and it's an obvious fact: although Matryona is nothing to look at, she's a queen; it might seem that everything was just as you'd expect, but in their rustic life the carpenter was a little scared of his blemished woman, he bowed down before her, hummed and hawed, and it wasn't as though the carpenter's woman had subdued the carpenter, but rather that our carpenter for some reason had a deep need of his woman; and she had noticed how he needed her, and it goes without saying, it's an obvious fact . . .

But if you were to conclude that it was all to do with – you know what, well, it would turn out, my dear fellow, all different: it wasn't about that at all: but the carpenter's woman had herself entwined her life with Kudeyarov in such utter dependence of the soul that they could never be unravelled: nobody in our village could tell where the carpenter ended and Matryona Semyonovna began; so they gave up wondering – well: in those days as soon as they'd sent the workmen off home and had a bite to eat, a gruel of bread and milk or a bit of onion, or something like that, they'd lick their spoons clean and tidy the crockery away, and then they'd stand side by side and bow together to the icons; and then they'd bow to each other with some special words; Matryona would say to him: 'My Lord,' and he would say to her: 'You're my spouse in the Spirit,' only 'spouse' came out sounding like a cross between 'Countess' and 'goose': a wondrous business! Or they might sit down at table in the sunset; the yellow ray of sunlight through the window would be speckled with dust; there he'd sit at the window, the carpenter, reading a book; and he had spectacles on his nose.

When he'd been reading a while, the carpenter would lay the book aside, and put his hand on Matryona Semyonovna's breast, and from the fingers of his hand, invisibly, but it seemed almost visibly, awesome, piercing streams and threads would pour out with the warmth of paradise and pour across caressingly into her breast, to well up in her throat; and after that her eyes were even huger; without this laying on of hands she could not live.

And it transpired that it was that laying on of hands, and not carnal intercourse, that had so firmly entwined them with one another; the carpenter poured his power into her, and afterwards he himself was nourished by that transferred power of his, as though it were capital deposited in the bank; and that was why the carpenter's woman, Matryona Semyonovna, exuded such an air of sweet excitement and delight (no matter that she was far from beautiful), that set your heart aching; and that was why – if you went into the carpenter's hut: you'd be met by all sorts of rubbish: benches, pots, rags; but even this rubbish would hold your attention, honestly: even the poker would be staring right into your soul, and you might well imagine that the dark countenance on the icon was gazing at you from its gilt casing for some special reason, and that there was a special reason why the icon's finger was raised towards you in the darkness from behind the icon-lamp; and the samovar was boiling in a special way, and heaven alone knew why little patches of sunlight were dancing across the red cockerels on the tablecloth, if it was a holiday and the occupants were taking tea; as though the occupants of other houses didn't have any of those things, as though they were altogether different people and all their goods and chattels were different too.

But what goods and chattels did they have? Everything in its proper place: step into the yard and your feet will squelch on the straw, and here and there a spurt of dungwater will splash up round your feet, a horse will snort, and there will be a whiskery boar rummaging around in the corner where they throw the garbage, and from the hay-loft you'll hear just the same rustling and pattering that you would in anyone else's; but if you go into the house – you're sure to bang your head full-tilt against the lintel and only after such an entry will you find yourself in the workroom with its tables and benches; and then you will see the two barefooted workmen (one with unkempt hair, the other with no nose) amidst odds and ends of wood, planks, various chisels, big saws and little saws; on top of the bits of wood you'll see drills, files, planes of all sizes, a rigid measuring stick, and a spirit-level amongst woodshavings, sawdust, splinters; there'll be a little jar of varnish, brushes, carpentry glue ready mixed in a little pail, and nearby a blue-coloured rag; by the wall you will see window-frames, stood side by side, seats without legs and without wickerwork, further on you'll see seats with the wickerwork in place but without legs or with two legs, chair-backs, likewise with legs, legs by themselves – legs of many fashions, and brass casters; the unkempt one won't give you a glance, but the cheerful noseless one will strike up a hoarse conversation with you, and you'll discover that he smells of drink; and above everything, in the corner, is the countenance of the Saviour, blessing their loaves. And if you cross the threshold of this room – you'll bang your head again so that you see stars: and then you'll see a neat, clean-swept room with a partition, decorated with wallpaper, even if it is of a miserable colour; and in this room to your astonishment you will even see curtains on the windows, even bentwood chairs and other signs of comfort; there will be benches there too, and an icon-case with a lot of lamps attached to it; there'll be a Russian stove, and a wooden trestle-bed with a patchwork quilt; and if you come in here at night, you will hear a disconcerting rustle, and the whiskers of cockroaches will threaten you out of all the nooks and crannies and from behind the chromolithographs hanging along the wall and depicting here the brocade countenance of the Virgin 'Flower of Heaven', there the stern face of St Gregory the Theologian, standing behind a mosaic border in his mitre, holding a cross, wearing an omophorion and a blue chasuble, and with a beard as white as snow; among these chromolithographs you will notice a photographic portrait, depicting a group of alluring damsels – a present from a wealthy relative, who for a long time had kept a house of ill repute for the young men of the town of Ovchinnikov.

You will see all this, but where have you not seen it all before?

Everything that you have seen many times before will strike you afresh, and you will spend a long time musing on the way they live in this carpenter's house: and you will sigh.

Ivan Stepanov and Stepan Ivanov

What of it?

Nothing. Nothing more at all. Once upon a time Daryalsky was minding his own business in Gugolevo – and there you are: what do you think of that now, good people: he turned up in our village. Ours is a fine village: there's plenty of space there for carousing, for hitting the bottle and drinking away everything you have: your money, your boots, your soul; if you don't want to drink, then don't: it's a free country; but if you do, then do it properly: and they did: first they drank away their money, then they drank away their clothes; they drank away their tackle, their huts, their wives, and then they drank away their very souls; and once you've drunk your soul away then off you go to the four winds: without a soul a man is like an empty flask; dash it down on a stone – a tinkle, and it's gone.

Well, what about Daryalsky?

Nothing, really: he jumped up, half-awake, in a hay-loft; his stomach was churning from the stifling smell of the hay, and from a fly that had got into his mouth, and from the piglet that was squelching around in the manure below him; his head was reeling, splitting, from the drink, the hay-loft was simply spinning under him, and his swollen tongue twisted about drily in his mouth, which felt as if it had been stripped with acid: 'Oh, for a piece of lemon!' he sighed, and fell asleep once more . . .

'Where am I?' he thought, waking up again, but he must have thought it out loud, and the sun must already have been high in the sky, because out of the hay above him there bent down the grubby head of Styopka, the shopkeeper's lad; the grubby head bent down and exhaled alcoholic fumes:

'Why now, squire, don't you remember how we had a bit to drink yesterday? And I was letting you in on my ideas, so as you shouldn't be in any doubt, about how I was all for the people's cause, and how I write poetry, and all that stuff about women.'

'What of it?'

'About Matryonka . . . Then I took you to their house . . . And you whistled at her window; well, she stuck her head out of the window, like, and gave you the once-over and had a laugh . . . But you were drunk, and she got scared . . . And so I brought you away to the hay-loft . . . Don't you remember? Only don't breathe a word to my dad. He's a right bastard.'

Daryalsky remembered none of this: all he remembered was the insult, and his hand shot to his cheek; his Katya rose up before him with a quiet complaint and reproach, but the dull headache stopped the recollection from developing; and what was there to recollect: wasn't it fate itself that had brought him to Tselebeyevo? So let what would be, be!

They went out onto the street; a passing cart slowly creaked by; the puddles of Tselebeyevo were drying up in the sun's rays more slowly still; most slowly of all an old man of Tselebeyevo, sitting on a stump across the road from them, was mending his old breech-band; a scrap of cloth slowly furled and unfurled itself out of the broken window of a lop-sided hut, whose punctured roof revealed protruding beams and slats, and whose owner had disappeared without trace a year before.

Daryalsky cast a dull glance over Tselebeyevo; a purple bruise stood out vividly on his face, his shirt was stained, heaven alone knew with what, his hair was matted. 'O for a piece of lemon!' he said.

'Come on then, squire, let's go to my dad's shop,' Stepan tugged him by the sleeve, 'I bet you're ashamed to go back looking like that; anyway, you can sit in our place till you're ready.'

But Daryalsky had no thought of going back at all; he had already

decided to move in with his friend Schmidt, who rented a cottage in Tselebeyevo every summer; only just now, with his hangover, he didn't want to
be seen by his friend; true, there was one other consideration, why . . . but
never mind that!

'Styopka, old fellow, couldn't you introduce me to that woman, eh?'

'Matryonka, you mean? – Ah!' Styopka gave a wistful toss of his hair.

'Tell me about her, what you know.'

'What I know? I don't know anything, and I've nothing to tell . . . Only is
it, sort of, slap and tickle you're on about?' And he shook his head sternly.
'She doesn't go in for it, she's a weird woman: she drinks vodka all right;
now and then she really hits the bottle (she's done it with me), specially if
the carpenter's away; she has a tipple – but that's all there is to it: just for
appearances; but as for anything else – not on your life, she's not having
any! . . .

'Oh!' Stepan grunted after a lengthy silence. 'I'll bring you together, if
you want; the carpenter's away. Agreed?'

Stepan Ivanov was of an unruly temperament; his father, on the other
hand, Ivan Stepanov, was of a dour one; to east and west of Tselebeyevo he
burned, spoiled and defiled our locality with ruin: just accumulating
money; but Stepan Ivanov squandered that money on women and such-
like; in church Ivan Stepanov joined in the sexton's singing from the choir
on the left; Stepan Ivanov hiccupped loudly in church and was rude to the
priest. Ivan Stepanov had been depicted by the icon-painters, when they
were decorating the church, more or less in an omophorion; but they'd
talked Stepan Ivanov round to Slocialism: and Stepan Ivanov had become
a freethinker. In the evenings Ivan Stepanov would click away on his battered abacus! But Stepan Ivanov, if he wasn't womanizing or drinking,
would spend the evenings scribbling verses. Ivan Stepanov only left the
village at all in order to go to Likhov; Stepan Ivanov had even been to
Moscow: he'd come back from Moscow by Shanks' pony, without his cap,
his boots and his watch, and just with one dog-eared little book, which he'd
bought at the flea-market; this book turned out to be the poetic works of
Mr Heine; and Stepan Ivanov took a liking to Heine . . .

'There's a brain for you: he can come straight out with a poem in Russian or in German just the same!' he would say, preparing to regale the sexton with his own compositions; most of all the sexton had come to like
Stepan Ivanov's poem 'Petya is sad'; it began like this:

> Autumn. My heart aches –
> It just goes on aching:
> It won't tell me itself –

> It makes me do it.
> I'm always in poverty,
> Always longing!
> I'd like to hide in a cavity
> In earth and sand . . .

Stepan Ivanov also had a ballad called 'Nenila': he wrote well – he'd turned out a real wordsmith; wasn't he the one his father had pulled about by the forelock when he was little? It was true that the hair on Stepan Ivanov's head was short of a tuft or two; but inside his head everything had stayed as it was; once a fool, always a fool; so his father gave him up as a bad lot; he didn't say anything (his son snarled back): he just kept the takings hidden.

On entering the shop they bumped into Yakov Yevstigneyev, the Bloodsucker; he curtly touched his cap and went to unfasten his horse; he got into the drozhky and made himself scarce. Inside the shop the air was thick; behind the counter Ivan Stepanov, with his glasses on his nose, was clicking away at the abacus; the sexton and the constable were gulping mouthfuls of tea from the saucer and playing cards fiercely with a greasy pack; at Daryalsky's entry the sexton made a bow, but snorted, while the constable, without looking at anyone, muttered in a slow nasal drawl, full of significance, 'I see-ee! Is that how it is? So you're taking your club to my knave of hearts?'

'Clubs are trumps!' the sexton snorted again, for no particular reason; Daryalsky realized that they had just been talking about the ill-fated slap in the face, and that Yakov Yevstigneyev had told them all about it: now the slap would be all round the village; to make matters worse the bruise had come up; he blushed deeply, deeply: they settled themselves by the window and Styopka, swigging from a bottle, rattled away into his ear:

> 'Oh, the boredom, oh, the cares,
> Oh, there's nowhere joy,
> Oh, where'er I turn my gaze,
> Nothing do I see but tears.'

Daryalsky had decided to put up with anything, so long as Styopka would take him to meet her, the pock-marked peasant woman: his head was splitting and his stomach churning; he was thinking, 'I could just do with a piece of lemon.'

'Mmm, diamonds are trumps!' came a voice from one side of them, and again there was a snorting and whispering and scattered exclamations:

'Serves him right . . . Shouldn't stir the people up!' And Styopka went rattling on:

> 'Rolling on the floor now,
> Wriggling on the couch,
> Tossing on the stove-top,
> Crawling on the bed . . .'

'Do trumps exist in themselves?' the sexton muttered with a pensive sigh, holding back a yawn; Ivan Stepanov went on clicking on the abacus; a bumble-bee buzzed at the window.

> 'Amongst the forest trees the hunter rests,
> His thoughts are wandering far afield –'

Styopka went bubbling on, as he emptied the bottle.

Three peasants came in, a giant, a gingernob and one with a grating voice (in fact they all had grating voices); the giant made a coughing noise, the gingernob made a spitting noise, and the one with the grating voice made a snoring noise, and then the giant rasped out: 'Noils', the gingernob rasped out: 'Baccy', and the third peasant rasped out 'Sugar'. 'Nails, sugar, tobacco . . .' Ivan Stepanov clicked out on his abacus.

As he gathered up the nails, the giant scratched himself: 'The carpenter's gone to town.' 'He's up to something big, he is,' said the gingernob, scratching himself and picking up the tobacco. And the third one had a scratch and rasped out: 'Them's sectarians, that's what!' and grabbed the bag of sugar.

And with a cough, a spit and a snore the three peasants went out.

Daryalsky glanced out of the window: there was a path trodden down across the flax field. Steering Styopka out of the shop, he implored him, 'Styopka, let's go to her right away . . .' Lord alone knew what was going on in his head; they were both rolling from side to side from drunkenness.

'We can't, my friend,' Styopka urged him, completely drunk: 'Look at you. Look at me. We need the hair of the dog . . .'

Well? Nothing really; they drank themselves sober until the evening: what about Katya, and Theocritus, and the depths of his soul? No time for Katya, no time for Theocritus, when his head was fit to burst and in that head of his there was a whole orchestra of nightwatchmen's rattles at work!

No sooner out of the teahouse than he sat himself down in the flax field; the priest's wife went by:

'What are you doing, Pyotr Petrovich, not in Gugolevo?' She gave him a mischievous glance. 'Why don't you drop in to see us; my husband has gone to Likhov this morning . . . Oh dear, oh dear, what's that on your cheek, a bruise? It'll mend before your wedding!' And off she went.

And he didn't remember seeing the moon rise into the sky; it wasn't a moon: in his drunken state it seemed like a piece of lemon.

The little angels, the fretwork window-frames, and the roofs of the houses were bathed in a silver sheen, a silver sheen lay on the puddles, and a heavy dew had settled on the flax field; a red woman went by in the distance carrying her pails to the pond, scooped up her water, and was on her way back when she was met by a blue woman carrying her pails the other way; she scooped up her water, and was on her way back when a yellow girl with a yoke over her shoulders and her skirt hitched up came to meet her; but there was no making her out in the darkness; as though she had vanished into the pond; only the bushes on the bank went on swaying for a long time afterwards and across the dew could be heard the sounds of laughter and resounding kisses.

The things people said, and the man on the bicycle

Tongues went on wagging for a long time in Tselebeyevo about how my hero had been expelled from Gugolevo, but he had vanished from the face of the earth; true, the tracks of his muddy boots wound round and round the village; it was true, too, that Ignat had straight away brought all his stuff over to Schmidt's cottage on the little brown cow, but Pyotr hadn't shown his face there himself, he had settled in and made himself at home in the village of Kobylya Luzha, where he had gathered a pretty unsavoury company about him and was visited by riff-raff of every kind. My hero was not distinguished by the quality of his reputation on the street of Tselebeyevo.

The days passed by, one after another, and every day brought new items of gossip to the village; one blue June day a pillar of smoke thrust up above the distant fir-wood: it was a fire; and on that day they scoured the neighbourhood around Dondyukov; they arrested a student; they turned him upside down, but all they found was a paper-bag with a Spanish onion, quite a rarity in our parts; they ate the onion, and locked the student up on bread and water; and on that same memorable day Yevseich, his cap thrust down over his eyes, trudged his way from the estate to our village – with a letter; here in the village he searched and searched for someone, but went away in the end empty-handed; he had a long confab with the Schmidt gentleman: well, people kept an eye on him: one after another they dropped into the shop, because the shop – well, you might say, it's a kind of club: anyone who comes to Tselebeyevo, even if it's only for a moment, always looks in at the shop. In the shop, where Styopka had just hidden a pile of proclamations he'd received among the goods, the old crosspatch sat and munched some sausage, and, taking off his cap, wheezed about this and that happening at the estate, and about the young mistress crying her eyes out; and within the hour everyone was saying that this and that had happened at Gugolevo and that the young mistress was crying her eyes out; the priest's wife decided she hadn't been to Gugolevo for ages, and that she'd go there straight away: 'Don't you dream of it, my love'; the priest tried to make her see sense.

That was what happened on a blue June day.

Then there was a cloudy day – thundery, dappled; and on that day Yevseich's cap was glimpsed again among the cottages; on that day Styopka trotted off to Kobylya Luzha to talk business with the strange people there, and they painted him a picture of how the emancipation of the people would come through the Holy Spirit, and that there were some people who were secretly waiting for the coming of the Spirit to earth; and through the same person he learned that the whole district, without exception, was gossiping about how this and that had been happening at Gugolevo, and how the young mistress had nearly taken her own life, only kind people were advising her against such a step for the time being.

There was a day just like a roasting oven, too: on that day the priest's wife, dressed all in pink, with her hat pinned on and earrings in her ears, flounced off, skirt rustling, to Gugolevo, only she evidently wasn't received there; to rub salt into the wound the schoolmarm went there on the same day, and apparently she was received: when she came back she narrated breathlessly how she had been regaled with all sorts of delicacies, and how Katerina Vasilyevna had wept on her breast, because she had entrusted her fate to that outcast of the human race; on that day the priest spat and scratched his nose in irritation at the schoolmarm, but what good was it: it would take a nice little denunciation to keep her in her place, because it was perfectly clear that the schoolmarm was both a liar and a nasty bit of work.

There was another day like a roasting oven: on that day Tselebeyevo gasped, so much so that when the stars came out they all stood around in groups and nattered on about how Baroness Graaben had had her diamonds stolen, but they weren't getting the police in, because it was perfectly clear that the thief was Daryalsky; but others swore blind that all these occurrences had a secret meaning – it was that General Chizhikov up to his tricks; and on that day Yevseich dragged himself round the village, shaking his head, trying to track someone down; and in the end he made himself scarce with nothing for his pains.

In the meantime the green meadow had turned yellow with buttercups, sticky pinks had sprung up on the meadow with a flash of mauve, the white of daisies had appeared and pink corn-cockles had poked out from the oat-fields onto the road . . .

And that's all that happened during those days that's worth remembering – but what's this? I haven't said a word about the most important adventure of all. I do beg your pardon, I quite forgot! That's about the bicycle, of course; oh, whatever could it mean, a thing like that happening to a priest? But first of all about the bicycle (it was the priest that had a bicycle); not this priest, but the one who – well, I'm sure you can guess who I'm talking about, but the bicycle was a beauty, I can tell you: it was very clever of the priest to have a machine like that: you could really have fun with it – it was nice and new, all neat and tidy, with a brake, best quality rubber tyres and really efficient handlebars! Out the priest popped from under the lean-to without his hat and wearing nothing but his cassock, one jump and he was gone: just a swirl of dust along the road: a tiny-tiny priest, a real tiddler! His glasses slipped right down to the end of his nose (gold they were), his shock of black hair stood up like a corn-stook, his cross was all sideways, his black beard was lying flat on the handlebars, and his back was arched . . . Can you imagine! . . . People watched as the priest tore along the highway on his bike, grasping the handlebars and with his over-cassock inflated like a sail, and the ginger boot-tops on his flailing legs, with turned-up stripy gaiters, flapping to the amusement of the passers-by: the puffs of dust got into their mouths, which gaped open in astonishment, and the mileposts and the villages just kept flying past the priest: the high-road itself seemed to be on the move, rushing by under the bicycle, as though it were a big white ribbon that was being quickly unwound at one side of the horizon and wound up at the other. And the priest rushed like that on his bicycle all the way to Tselebeyevo, in a welter of miscellaneous secretions; he jumped off at Father Vukol's and went straight in to see him.

There's no need to explain this was the priest from Grachikha, Father Nikolay, who'd studied at the academy and for some reason had built his nest in Grachikha and had now been living there without setting foot outside it for two whole years; there he perched and not a peep was heard from him: the people of Grachikha themselves, seeing as they lived a bit off the main road, not many peeps were heard from them either, and since they were small and ill-favoured, that is, unenlightened, God had rewarded them with a small dark priest; Father Nikolay had jet black hair. Not a peep had been heard of him before: but just lately a dark rumour had been circulating about him, and a dark spirit had been emanating from his sermons: anyway, one fine day he upped and came rushing over to us, on his bicycle. He caught our priest at the most inopportune time: Father Vukol was sitting in nothing but his underwear, catching flies, and his wife, since she'd given the skivvy some time off, was padding around the living room in bare feet, with her food-stained skirt hitched up high, rattling her washing bowl and sloshing around with a dirty loofah; but Father Nikolay set up a squeaking right in front of her with his massive boots, as he harangued them without interruption and dropped cigarette-ash everywhere, while his kindly eyes filled with tears and his voice trembled, despite the fact that the priest's wife, caught unawares, had hurried off to change, and the sober-minded Father Vukol was mainly watching to see that the little priest from Grachikha didn't kick a roll of canvas with his great big boot, and didn't knock over the wicker basket with the consumptive palm-tree or the mahogany card-table with three legs, and the fourth lying on its knitted tablecloth; at the sight of Father Nikolay the priest's brood burst into howls. And Father Vukol answered all the Grachikha priest's excitement with silence: Father Vukol was a sober-minded man; he thought, as he looked at the small dark priest: 'Don't go to meetings with the peasantry and don't mix with the riff-raff, you live the way other people live and you won't need to come lamenting that you'll soon be both defrocked and a convict.'

The samovar had already been brought to the table, along with the boiled sweets and honey, and the flies, sated with honey, were sticking to the edges of the dish, flailing their legs and looking like sparkling, golden-coloured pebbles, and still Father Nikolay went on lamenting out loud and bewailing his lot, not listening to admonitions, and so he went away again, without relieving his soul.

The hollow tree

Styopka passed on the news about all these occurrences to my hero: and my hero wondered at the gossip and the rumours and at the sudden visit of the priest from Grachikha. If this hero's star had set in Gugolevo and Tselebeyevo, then it unheroically illuminated his days in Kobylya Luzha: people kept coming to see him to talk about freedom: his tongue was sore from all the talk, but the local freethinkers kept flooding in: the district doctor looked him up as he was passing: an old soldier from the times of Nicholas I came hobbling in on his wooden leg with four St George's crosses on his chest: he was an orator of the green woodland meetings: out there in the green of the forest he banged on a stump with his wooden leg and called for an uprising: at my hero's the old soldier sniffed his snuff and showed him the four St George's crosses; finally a student who was staying in Likhov came with the purpose of shaking his honest hand.

What more could you want?

One day Styopka ran in to tell him that he wasn't a Slocialist any more, but something much better, that he had got in with a family of Doves, and that he was a Dove too; rumours about the Doves kept crossing my hero's path at this time and he listened to the rumours avidly; but what was his astonishment when Styopka whispered in his ear that the Doves were very well informed about my hero, and that they were inviting him that very day to come to the hollow oak at sunset, and that later, in the depths of the night, he would be met there by a certain good person.

'It's something to do with Matryonka, I can tell you that for sure!' Styopka said with a wink, but when some strangers came into the hut he tossed his hair back and started bellowing out a song those ears had never heard before:

> 'Elephant-phant-phant –
> Trunkety-trunk-trunk-trunk:
> Tuskety-tusk-tusk-tusk –
> Trumpety-trump-trump-trump –
> Jumbo-jumbsky.'

And so there he was, my hero, at the old oak-tree: his heart was in his boots; he realized that all his days and nights were mixed up, but there was no way back now, and that it was sweet to live in this feverish dream; better not to think about Katya: that past was dead; he fell into a deep reverie at the edge of the forest; suddenly he had a desire to break a fir branch, tie its ends together, and put it on in place of a hat; and so he did; and, crowned with this thorny green wreath, with a frondose horn rising over his brow, with green plumage stretching the length of his back, he had a wild and proud appearance, alien even to himself; like this he clambered into the hollow trunk; whether he waited a short time or a long one, he had no recollection; nor did he know what he was waiting for.

He looked – and there she was, Matryona Semyonovna, coming out of the forest with some flowers and an empty bast basket; then he realized that it was she herself who had summoned him through Styopka; he plucked up his courage and leaped out of the hollow onto the path right in front of her; it seemed he even made her jump with his charcoal-stained face (evidently shepherds used to make a fire in the hollow trunk).

'Oh, what a fright you gave me!'

She was pock-marked, and far from beautiful: she had a big stomach; he couldn't understand what drew him to her, pulled him so; no flush came over her face: she stared at her feet; there was a lump of earth under her feet, yellowing with decaying leaves; under the leaves an ant was crawling.

'Are you looking for mushrooms? Did you send for me?'

'Me? Oh, goodness: what do I need you for?'

'So you were gathering flowers; do you like flowers?'

'Of course I do . . .'

'Give me a flower!'

'Here, take one, choose for yourself . . .'

And what a look she gave him! Blue oceans welled in those eyes behind the pock-marked face; a depthless surge was in her gaze, and he was in a cold whirlpool of passion.

'D'you mind if I walk with you a bit, Matryona Semyonovna?'

'You can if you like: it's a public path . . .'

But she was smiling to herself, her eyes were sparkling, and she had a squint: one eye looked straight at you, and the other to one side; she tripped off towards the village, the white of her heels showing in the fine dust of the cart-track; the dust from Matryona's heels got into his nose; he, though, was thinking that she was cross-eyed, and how good that was.

'I've been looking for an opportunity of talking to you for a long time.'

'Well, now you've found one . . .'

'I wanted to approach you yesterday, when I saw you . . .'

'What'd you run away for, then?'

She grinned, as though she was making fun of him: her breast heaved, she lowered her eyes, and a little dimple appeared at the corner of her lips that spoke of shamelessness; and he was thinking how good it was that she had a dimple like that; but she didn't care: she tripped away in front of him, and now they had reached the village: coming out of the village Styopka passed by on his way somewhere with his accordion, he pretended not to see them, and bawled out at the top of his voice:

'Elephant-phant-phant –
Trunkety-trunk:
Trumpety-trump
Jumbo-jumbsky . . .'

'Now then,' Matryona suddenly turned round – 'you go back to your hollow tree; the neighbours'll see and then they'll tell your Mademoiselle, they'll tell Katerina Vasilyevna,' she chuckled brazenly, 'that pretty little angel of yours.'

'What a way to talk!'

She gave a snort of laughter and hid her face in her apron, and then she was at a distance from him: at the village fence she turned round to him:

'Come and visit, if you like me . . .'

And climbed over the fence.

The five-hundred-year-old triple-crowned oak with its one hollow trunk stretched its three crowns out into the fading evening; our hero had been sitting musing in this hollow for an hour or so; many thoughts came to him; but of Matryona Semyonovna it was not thoughts that came to him, but rather a sweet singing; his thoughts were light and fleeting – about his fate, about the oak-tree . . .

Who could tell what this oak-tree knew and what past events it was murmuring of with its mass of leaves; perhaps of Ivan Vasilyevich the Terrible's splendid retinue; perhaps of a lone oprichnik who had wandered into the wilds on his way from Moscow, dismounted here and sat under the oak in his gold-braided murmolka with its brocaded flaps that bumped against his shoulders, in his red morocco boots, leaning on his halberd, while his white steed grazed peacefully, untethered, by the oak, and beside his crimson shabrack there protruded from under his saddle a broom and a dog's head, baring its teeth at the road; and that oprichnik gazed a long, long time at the velvet cloud that wafted by, and then he jumped onto his horse and disappeared for many hundred years – anything may be; and maybe, later, a fugitive unfrocked monk took refuge in this hollow, to finish his days in a stone cell at Solovki; and another hundred years will pass – and then a free race of men will visit these roots protruding from the ground; they will overhear the fugitive monk's groan, the sadness of the oprichnik who flew off on his horse into the measureless expanses of time: and that race of men will sigh about the past.

Anything may be – in his thoughts he returned to Matryona Semyonovna and caught himself not in the tree-trunk any more but very nearly in the village: somehow his feet had brought him there of their own accord; the evening was already dark, but there was still a succession of women with pails going to the pond: a red woman came up, turned to the bushes, put down her pail, and, lo and behold: she was white; sitting by the water in nothing but her petticoat; the petticoat flew up over her head, and she was in the water; a blue woman trailed along to the water, turned to the bushes, put down her pails, and out of the reeds – just look: a long-legged woman creeps towards her, in the twilight it might be a man; while in the distance . . . a glimpse is caught of a yellow girl with a yoke; there's a constant laughing and splashing at the pond; the quacking of a drake, the village horses cantering off into the night, dust, barking, and distant words, clear across the dew. And already the quiet stars were gleaming and the vibrant water rocked them palely . . .

Night settled on the forest; but in the belly of the hollow trunk a hand-ful of red-hot warmth crackled, faded with the first patina of ash, and a blue petal of fire lapped up above it; the hollow trunk had a crack in it; it grinned redly into the darkness, dense with tree-trunks; and from that grinning slit a voice was raised, and the shaggy head of Abram, inserted into the crack from outside, was nodding at my hero, who was concealed within; the beggar was holding his stick pressed against his hairy chest; and from the stick the dove tilted heavily over the flames with its leaden wing; the pale stars glanced haughtily in through the opening of the hol-low trunk; and it was on them that the beggar's eyes were fixed; only the whites, lit by the flames, were gazing into Daryalsky's soul.

So this was the good person whom Pyotr had been expecting for many an hour; he was a beggar-man – and here he was cheek-by-jowl with Pyotr; and from this beggar's breast burst forth a heavy, soul-disturbing summons; on and on he drawled his seductive, singsong words:

'And the chants we sing are sweet; our services are sweeter still; with kisses, and with beautiful laments; and our women have breasts as sweet as honey; the vestments are whiter than snow; and everyone talks to each other about the diamond gates and the realm of freedom.

'And then we're known as Doves: and we fly all over, across the whole district; and then amongst us lives the greatest Dove: the mightiest Dove of all, with wings of grey; and that's why the holy rising has started out across Russia, and the Cossack clans are rising up in freedom under the lovely blue sky.

'And then, those fine Cossacks – they're just the first; they're the first swallows, carrying the Holy Spirit across Russia; when the roar of their wings passes by, the Doves will fly out after them.

'And then . . .'

'Enough: I'm yours . . .'

'In the wake of those free Cossacks the church of the Holy Spirit itself is being built; and then, if you're with us, brother, you shall have Matryona Semyonovna; but if you're not, there's nothing but perdition waiting for you.'

'Enough: I'm with you.'

Pyotr was sitting in a corner of the hollow trunk with his face on his knees – as though he was in a trance; and his crown of fir, which had slipped to one side, like green stag's antlers, made a horned shadow in the tree-trunk that soared upwards. Flashes of red light tossed the sinking twi-light high up above the top of the trunk – and a shadow danced around like some winged denizen of hell, intent on strangling the man who had girded himself round with fire.

'Abram, what made you decide to trust me?'

'Your eyes.'

The night settled more darkly still upon the forest; many a sighted man might cry out in lament now: 'May my eyes burst – what use are they to me!' But the blind, no doubt, were chuckling at the sighted.

Happenings

By day, and in the rays of sunset, amongst the flowers, Daryalsky wandered around our village, set apart from others by the jutting branch of the fir crown he had set upon his brow and by his scarlet shirt against the green; and Abram the beggar wandered around after him: and caught my hero up.

By day, and in the rays of sunset, amongst the flowers, Matryona Semyonovna wandered idly around our village; and Daryalsky came out of the bushes to meet her – sunburnt, unshaven: he stood, moving from foot to foot, fingering his moustache, casting at first apprehensive glances at her: he spoke little – and kept shadowing her for some reason of his own; she only needed to step out, or take a stroll along the road, or go into the oak-grove to look for mushrooms, and straight away there would be a crackle in the brushwood behind her, a branch would sway, although there was no wind; Matryona wasn't the least afraid; she could make him take to his heels any time she liked; and she was already growing fond of her gentleman: an affinity of the spirit was growing up between them, but they spoke little; there was just one time she got a fright; she went off into the forest – and, of course, behind her a branch began to sway; she took it into her head to catch him in the act: so she pretended to be looking for mushrooms, and came imperceptibly closer to the branch; she lifted the hem of her dress, bent over and parted the branches of the bush, and someone shot out at a run; she thought she recognized the peeping tom – not her dear gentleman at all: this one had a full beard, high boots and a bronze watch, and straightaway Styopka too leaped out of the bushes and came up to her:

'Matryona Semyonovna! Don't you worry now, I'll throttle that father of mine if he tries anything – I won't let him hurt you, now that I've become a Dove for your sake: and if you've turned me down, I'll put up with all that, and I shan't be here with you for long, because – how can I compete with that gentleman of yours, and anyway – God's my witness – I'm fond of him too: seeing as we're both in the same brotherhood now . . . But as for that accursed father of mine, always spying out after you, why I'll pull his beard out, the old devil, and drive an aspen stake through his heart!'

Matryona Semyonovna sank deep into thought then, realizing that there were no fewer than three men prowling around after her – and it wasn't that she was afraid for herself; what grieved her about the pursuits was that Ivan Stepanovich might get wind of the most important thing of all: her prayers and the spiritual freedom of her behaviour; it wouldn't be hard for him to sniff out everything that was hidden under Kudeyarov the carpenter's peaceful roof. And at the slightest thing he'd denounce them: and the authorities would be down on them like a ton of bricks.

In the village meanwhile rumours travelled around about a slap in the face, about rebellion in a certain troubled hamlet, about Cossacks and the crimson pillars of distant conflagrations: neighbour once again set fire to neighbour; the red cockerel was at large in the district; and it was expected any day in our village too. 'This is the red squire's doing!' decent people frowned; it wasn't for nothing that the red squire had taken to prowling round the village like a wolf; the deaf-mute had seen him – in the bushes, where the heart's-ease peeped out at the road with its yellow and mauve eyes, and the priest's wife with hers: she had seen him in the rye-field: when she stretched out her hand to pick a cornflower she thought she'd glimpsed his ragged red shirt; and he was seen in the Tselebeyevo tea-house, at the time when the riff-raff gather there: not those whose good sense held the village community together, but miscreants, those who went shouting and whistling under the girls' windows, and spread foul leaflets and kept gazing out along the highroad; and at night all and sundry were abroad in the village; they might be visitors from the nether world who had long since vanished from the village, long since rotted in the Tselebeyevo churchyard, and now risen from their graves to set villages on fire and blaspheme: that was the kind of riff-raff that gathered at night in the tea-house; and with them, with that riff-raff, the gentleman with the horned fir crown on his head, who had been ejected from the baroness's estate, was now carousing too.

The summer visitor who rented a cottage in Tselebeyevo – the one who didn't believe in God, although he was an Orthodox Christian – the Schmidt gentleman, he saw him too: he'd been looking for Daryalsky everywhere: had some letters to give him, or something: but as soon as the red squire caught sight of him he ran off into the ravine: just went away like that, didn't approach his friend.

Two young fellows had made up their minds to give him a thrashing, and I don't know what might have come of that business if our village hadn't been struck by a thunderbolt: a man from Likhov who was passing through told how the priest from Grachikha, along with a crowd of peasants armed with sickles and staves, had raised the holy Christian cross in his impious hand against the powers that be, and gone on strike with the whole of Grachikha, and that there were bullets flying all over the place from the Cossacks who'd arrived – the like of it had never been seen; later the news was added that the old soldier from the time of Nicholas I had pinned on his four St George's crosses and gone hobbling off to join the shady priest in person; but that turned out to be nonsense; and by that time the Cossacks had caught the shady priest, torn the cross off him and carted him straight off to Likhov with his hands tied behind his back (that's what a bicycle does for you!); and since the whole population of Grachikha belonged to only two families – the Fokins and the Alyokhins – they just rounded up all the Fokins and Alyokhins and took them off to the town jail.

Styopka the shopkeeper's lad grinned at all the talk: clearly he knew something that was a secret from everyone else, and the good people knew what they were up to when they entrusted him with the task not only of gathering a secret militia in the highways and byways, but also of driving a wedge between that secret militia and the Slocialist strikers, so as to instil into them the rules of the new faith and form a voluntary support for the Dove-brethren; Styopka knew all right – but he kept quiet: many was the time he gazed raptly out at the dusty road: and his feet just carried him off on the road, and he yearned to wander off along it – further and further: to the place where the sky leaned its breast right down to the earth, where the world's end was, and the ancient abode of the dead: and anyone who gazes raptly at the road is sure to be summoned by the dark figure that stands over there and beckons, beckons, and makes signs to you with its arms, and as you come closer, turns out to be a bush; and the figure has been standing there for many a year, now nearer, now further away, and silently threatening the village, silently beckoning . . .

A block of granite falls to the ghastly bottom of a chasm; if that bottom is at the same time the surface of the waters, the block of granite falls even further, but in the clinging silt there is no further fall: there is the limit; but the human soul knows no such limit, for its fall can be eternal, and its fall gives rapture like the trail of soaring stars above the chasm of the world: you are already swallowed by the black maw of the world, where there are neither heights nor depths and where everything there is fixed in the centre; and whether you think of this standing still in the world as sinking or soaring, it makes no difference . . . For Daryalsky, too, his sinking turned into soaring: without a backward glance he ran to where Matryona's sarafan was glimpsed; but why was he so shy of her? And she, laughing at his childish shyness, caught him up herself, walked after him from the village, making as if to overtake him, but not catching him in fact, just laughing after him, while out in front the dark figure, lost among the fields, summoned them all into a broad, unknown and terrible expanse.

And so the days flew by – blue, hazy, dusty days; the villagers took umbrage at Daryalsky both because he'd got involved with the carpenter's woman and because Kudeyarov the carpenter still wasn't back from Likhov, whether because he had a huge amount of business there, or because he'd got in with shady, itinerant, sectarian folk.

It was no wonder people gossiped about Daryalsky; however, they stopped avoiding him: the happening was explained – he started making merry with Matryona in front of the whole world; the teahouse-owner told what a fine company he'd had carousing there just lately: the red squire with fir fronds on his head and Matryonka on his knees (the daft woman had really taken leave of her senses, it seemed); Styopka from the shop was playing the accordion for them; and Abram the beggar, in the hope of touching them for a tip, was dancing away barefoot on the floor in front of them in his torn trousers, waving his tin dove.

How about that, then?

Matryona

If you fall for a dark-eyed beauty, pretty as a picture, with lips as sweet as a luscious raspberry, and a gentle face, unrumpled by kisses, like an apple-blossom petal in May, and she becomes your love – then do not say that love is yours: even though you cannot tire of her rounded breasts, of her slender frame that melts in your embrace like wax before a flame; even though you cannot tire of gazing at her delicate white foot and pink toe-nails; even though you kiss each finger of her hands, and kiss them all over again from the beginning – let all that be so: and the way she covers your face with her little hand and through the transparent skin, against the light, you see the blood flow in a gleam of red; even though you ask your raspberry-red love for nothing more than the dimples of her laughter, the haze of hair that tumbles from her brow and the light-play of the blood in her fingers: tender will your love be, both to you and to her, and nothing more will you ask of your love; the day will come, that cruel hour will come, the fatal moment will come, when her face will fade, rumpled by kisses, her breasts will no longer quiver at your touch: all this will come to pass; and you will be alone with your own shadow amidst the sunscorched deserts and the dried-up springs, where flowers do not bloom and the sunlight plays on the dry skin of the lizard; and you might even see the hairy black tarantula's lair, all enmeshed in the threads of its web . . . And then your thirsting voice will be raised from the sands, calling longingly to your homeland.

But if your love is otherwise, if her browless face has once been touched by the black blemish of the pox, if her hair is red, her breasts sagging, her bare feet dirty, and to any extent at all her stomach protrudes, and still she is your love – then that which you have sought and found in her is the sacred homeland of your soul: and once you have gazed deep into the eyes of her, your homeland, you can no longer see your former love; it is your soul that converses with you now, and a guardian angel descends over the two of you, spreading its wings. Do not ever leave a love like that: she will still the longing of your soul and she cannot be betrayed; and in those moments when desire comes upon you, and you see her as she truly is, that pock-marked face and those red tresses will arouse in you not tenderness, but lust; your caress will be brief and rough: it will be satisfied in a moment; then she, your love, will look at you with reproach, and you will burst into tears, as though you were not a man at all, but a woman: and only then will your love caress you, and your heart will throb in a dark velvet of feelings. With the first love you are a gentle, though masterful man; but with the second? Nothing of the sort, you're not a man at all, but a child: a capricious child, all your life you will follow in the wake of this second love, and no one will ever understand you, indeed you too will never understand that what you have between you is not love, but the undeciphered immens- ity of a mystery that crushes you.

No, Matryona Semyonovna's face was not adorned by a pretty pink mouth, nor did dark arching brows endow this face with any special expression; what gave the special expression to this face were the full, red, moistly opened lips that seemed to be set once and for all in a sensual smile, on her bluish-white, pock-marked face, burnt to ashes by some secret fire; and all the time wisps of brick-red hair escaped brazenly from the carpen- ter's woman's red shawl with white dapples, which was tied around her head (she was nicknamed the carpenter's woman in our village, although she was really no more than his skivvy); it was not beauty those features expressed, not the preserved chastity of a girl; in the quivering of the snub-nosed carpenter's woman's breasts, in her plump legs with white calves and filthy heels, in her large stomach, in her sloping, predatory brow – was the stamp of unconcealed shamelessness; but then her eyes . . .

Look into her eyes, and you will say: 'What mournful pipes are sobbing there, what songs is the great sea sending, what is the sweet aroma that is spreading across the earth?' She had such deep blue eyes – blue into their depth, blue to darkness, to a sweet ache in the temples: as though there were no whites to be seen in her eye-sockets: two huge, moist sapphires rolled

languidly down there in the depths – as though the deep blue sea were tossing behind her pock-marked face, and there are no bounds to the deep blue
sea and its feckless waves: her whole face was flooded by the eyes that spilled
out into the dark rings beneath them – that's what her eyes were like.

If you once glance into them, you will forget all else: until the Second
Coming of Our Lord you will flounder, drowning, in those blue oceans,
praying to God that the archangel's plangent trumpet might quickly set
you free from the sea's captivity, if you have any memory left of God, and
do not yet believe that the trumpet of judgement has been stolen from
heaven by the devil.

And you will begin to think all kinds of things: that her blood itself is the
deep blue sea; and that her white face is tinged with blue because it is
transparent: in her veins is not the deep blue sea, but the blue sky, where
her heart is a red lamp, red as the sun; and you will imagine that her lips are
royal purple: and with those purple lips she will tear you away from your
betrothed; and her mocking grin will be a fond smile, dear . . . and sad; and
she will become for you a beloved sister from your homeland, not yet quite
forgotten in the dreams of this life – she will become for you that homeland
that haunts us sadly in the autumn – on the days when orange leaves swirl
about in the valedictory blue of cold October; and the carpenter's woman's
red hair will be for you a twisted leaf in the wind, swirling up into the sky,
the brilliance, the quiver of autumn; but then you will notice that those all-
illuminating eyes – are squinting; one eye looks past you, while the other
looks straight at you; and you will remember then how perfidious, how
deceitful is the autumn.

But if she rolls her eyes: then Matryona Semyonovna's two seeing
whites will stare at you; and then you will realize that she is quite alien to
you, and ugly as a witch; and if she lowers her eyes to the ground and fixes
her gaze on the dirt, the straw and the wood-shavings, and folds her calloused hands on her stomach – a shadow will flit across her face, the folds
beside her nose will darken, the pock-marks on her skin will deepen and
become more visible – and there are a multitiude of pock-marks – her face
will become sweaty and crumpled, and her stomach will protrude again,
and at the corners of her lips such a dimple will tremble that all shame is
thrown to the winds: and then she will be nothing to you but a lewd peasant
woman.

Matryona was in the yard: bringing the cow in; her pail was rattling; then
she was under the cow; a warm stream of steaming milk splashed against
the bottom of the pail.

There were voices in the darkness, footsteps: 'Matryona, are you there, Matryona?' – 'What is it?' – 'My love, caress me!' – 'Oh, go on with you, I'm not used to all this kissing . . .' – 'Are you on your own?' – 'Leave me alone . . .' – 'Let's go inside!' – 'Oh, what a business!' – 'Well?' – 'I bet the old man will come back today . . .'

Sighs, groans: hasty footsteps across the yard; fuss and bother; hens cackling in all directions; the hen with the biggest crest, flapping its wings, flew up to the hayloft, from where dry pigeon droppings spattered down onto someone's head.

And then they were in the living-room of the house: the only light was the green lamp illuminating the bright countenance of the Saviour, blessing their loaves; there were shavings, sawdust, splinters in their hair; all the objects in the room, every one, stared silently at Pyotr at that moment; in front of him in the faint green light was the white, sweating face of Matryona Semyonovna with sunken eyes and glinting teeth, bared by her opened lips: the white face in the faint green light was like the green corpse of a witch sitting before him; she made the first advances herself, hugged him, pressing her plump breasts against him – like a wild animal with bared teeth; now the old house was floating away from him on the green sea of treetops in the immeasurable distance – and with it Princess Katya waving her hand in farewell.

O Lord, my God, what can this be?

And he burst out sobbing in front of this wild animal, like a big, forsaken child, and his head dropped onto her lap; and a change came about her; she was no longer a wild animal; those big, familiar eyes, her tear-filled eyes swam away into his soul; and the face that bent over him was not crumpled by the rushing storm of passion, but was somehow fragrant.

'Oh, my poor darling! Oh, my brother: here's a cross for you from me . . .'

She unbuttoned the collar of her blouse and from her own warm body hung around his neck a cheap, tin cross.

'Oh, my poor darling! Oh, my brother: take your little sister just as she is . . .'

Already the night was cowering in the bushes, and my hero was leaving the carpenter's house; a dog was barking at him, and all trace of him was disappearing in the darkness, and as he turned he saw an arm holding aloft on the threshold a flickering lamp, which cast soundlessly into his darkness a beam of faint red light, and behind the light, under the shawl with white dapples, Matryona's face stood out, shining into the darkness with its sensual smile and eyes blinded by the light; so small she looked; all trace of him was disappearing, and still Matryona stood there, still she held her lamp out after him, after the trace of him as it disappeared; for a long time

yet the crimson eye blinked at that point; and finally that point of sight fell
blind; soon, from that point, a cockerel crowed across the whole of Tselebeyevo; and a barely audible singing seemed to answer from . . . but
Lord alone knows from where.

The meeting

They were still standing exchanging caresses, and an ineffable intimacy
was growing between them, when footsteps rang out just outside the door
in the entrance-hall, and they barely had time to jump apart before the
master himself, Mitry Mironovich Kudeyarov, the carpenter, stood on the
threshold, back from Likhov.

'V-v-v!' he began to stutter and came in. Matryona Semyonovna's bare
feet padded off somewhere to one side; and there she hid her deeply
flushed face in an impossibly filthy apron, from out of which she glanced
expectantly at both men: there seemed to be some kind of inquisitive cunning reflected on her face, and a slight timidity; but what did she have to
fear? Their embraces had happened with the permission of her cohab-
itant, more – at his command; but fear passed through her, and her teeth
were chattering: was it not because she was fulfilling the carpenter's secret
command not in the way he wished: his command had turned for her into
a sweet, free impulse of her soul; another second, and everything inside her
turned to stone, when the lean and lifeless half of the carpenter's face
stared lifelessly at the icon, and his lean and lifeless hand, like a fishbone,
was raised to make the sign of the cross; her heart sensed that she had com-
mitted a sin before him; with trembling hands she adjusted her face, disar-
rayed by kisses, embraces, caresses, and, unnoticed in the darkness,
buttoned up her blouse.

But it seemed the carpenter could not have noticed anything; he gave
Daryalsky a friendly glance: or, more precisely, what glanced at Daryalsky
was a nose, poised directly opposite his face; only the long yellow beard
stretched reproachfully down towards the floor:

'V-v-very' (he stopped stuttering), 'very . . . I can certainly say, it's very
pleasant to see a thinking man in this lair of ours . . . Very . . .'

And he stretched out to Daryalsky his broad, work-hardened palm.

But the carpenter had seen everything, and almost took fright himself;
whatever could it all mean, what would come of it? 'No, I can't, I can't!' he
thought and sighed, but what it was he couldn't do, he evidently hadn't yet
worked out himself; only he could hardly breathe in the stuffy cottage from
the smell of black bread.

From under sternly knitted brows, with lowered head, Daryalsky fixed the carpenter with a powerful, wildly flashing gaze, ready to give him answer and rebuff; not a trace was there to see of his recent emotion; in the twinkling of an eye my hero took his measure, in order to meet with dignity whatever might take place between them; but the carpenter's gentleness, and even more his horny hand, took Pyotr's strength away from him.

'I've . . . I'm . . . I'd like . . . actually, I came to make an order: I'd like a chair, you know, a wooden one, with a carved cockerel on it'; he said the first words that came to mind.

'We can do that . . . we can do that,' the carpenter shook back his hair, 'we can do that all right'; and in that shake of his hair there was a certain condescension, maybe an encouragement, but most of all – a vicious, barely perceptible mockery: he'd like to grab that slut of a woman by the hair and throw her on the floor, pull up the hem of her skirt and give her a good kicking; and that slut of a woman followed the carpenter with her eyes from the corner of the room; and those eyes said: 'Wasn't it you yourself, Mitry Mironych, who talked me into it, and passed your strength to me by laying your hands on my breast?'

As for talking, he'd talked her into it all right, that was true enough; but it hadn't turned out as he wished: without prayers, without meaning, without ceremony; and if it was done without the ritual of the faith, then it was done by nothing but mutual lust; he himself was sickly: he had grown thin from fasting and coughing: he couldn't be dealing with womankind now – no fear: he had dealt with it once upon a time, for sure; and it was needful that Matryona should give birth; he knew well what causes would arise from this and what matters would follow from those causes: the birth of the Spirit would follow, the descent of the Dove to earth and the liberation of the peasant folk; and so it turned out right: it was needful for Matryona to get involved with her gentleman; and yet it turned out wrong if his heart was bleeding with jealousy . . . 'How could they do it with me away!' he thought, and spat out in disgust, and scratched himself, not looking at my hero.

'About the chair, then – that's all right: we can do that . . . a nice wooden chair – and with carving: we can do all that . . . And a cockerel on the back, or a dove, yes, we can do that too . . . That's no trouble, no trouble at all: there's all sorts of styles . . .'

At the word 'dove' Daryalsky shuddered, as though the secrets of his soul had been rudely touched; and he picked up his hat:

'Actually, I've been sitting here a while, before you came . . . It's time I went.'

'What's this then, you're, sort of, insulting us: I can see, you know, you're one of us,' Kudeyarov winked, 'how's that, the moment I come in – you're leaving; we can't have that!'

And on the table in front of Pyotr Kudeyarov distinctly drew a cross three times; and everything turned upside-down in Pyotr's head; now he couldn't possibly leave the carpenter; and from his lips there almost burst the words: 'In the likeness of the Dove.'

But the carpenter was already bustling about:

'And anyway: we invite you to accept our hospitality . . . Heat up the samovar, Matryona Semyonovna . . . What is this, anyway, you stupid woman,' the carpenter broke off, 'you haven't invited our guest into the best parlour.'

Suddenly he stamped his foot, not letting her reply:

'Just look at her, keeping the guest in the dark, getting him all covered in sawdust and shavings: go at once and light the lamp!'

And Matryona padded past them, casting an anxious glance over her shoulder into the carpenter's eyes: she could not understand his behaviour; wasn't he the one, Mitry Mironych, who had told her how to act with the gentleman, her lover; and now the carpenter seemed angry with her.

'Stupid woman!' he hissed after her, but he was thinking, 'She's got hitched up with him, but what for? They got together – and she couldn't wait for me to get back!' And with reduplicated courtesy, and a nervous cough, he thrust himself upon Pyotr:

'You must forgive the silly woman, sir – look at all the shavings on you – and sawdust in your moustache and sawdust in your hair; anyway, please come into the parlour!'

Again Daryalsky was seized by anxiety, and again after a moment it subsided.

The three of them sat at table; exchanging courteous words; they sat and drank tea amongst the pictures and the chromolithographs. Daryalsky talked excitedly about the people's rights, about the faith.

The carpenter was thinking weighty thoughts: maybe the fact that all that stuff had happened without ceremony, prayers, and the brethren looking on, maybe that didn't matter; but it wasn't right: 'Why did they do it without me!' He spat. And again he felt hurt; although he was keeping himself apart from her, still he didn't mind caressing her now and then; and no doubt the gentleman had been caressing her in this very place.

But the carpenter stopped himself.

'Well, yes: that's right; the people are oppressed; there was a meeting gathered in a ravine near Likhov, with speakers and all . . .

'And a chair – we can do that . . . We can do all sorts: we make all sorts of styles . . . make it look like walnut, or mahogany . . .

'If we weren't peasants, but a free yeomanry, like, we'd show them we've got what it takes!

'Yes, it's an obvious fact, there's not enough dignity in small fry . . .'

As soon as Pyotr was out of the gates, Mitry Mironych turned on Matryonka:

'You shameless creature: well, tell me straight, have you got hitched up with him or not?'

'I have!' Matryona did not say the words, she bawled them out, as she did some job or other by the bed, and covered herself with a blanket; she looked at him with a squinting, hostile gaze.

'She has got hitched, she has!' the carpenter groaned.

Finally everything calmed down. Matryona disappeared under a blanket, while the carpenter, leaning against the table with one workworn hand, his belt removed, stood motionless over the table, and his other hand, its bony knuckles sticking out from his sweat-stained red sleeve, fingered his scrawny beard, the unbuttoned collar of his shirt, the big cross round his neck, and rose in a flourish above his head, to disappear with all five fingers into his mass of yellow hair: so the carpenter stood with half-opened mouth and half-closed eyes, gazing inwards at himself, and as a furrow morbidly took shape upon his brows, so it remained: fine wrinkles flitted and fluttered all over his face, although it seemed that a single huge thought, deep and painful, shone through from under all the transient expressions of this icon-like countenance; a drop of sweat rolled down his forehead, trembled on his eyelash, twinkled on his cheek and vanished in his moustache.

Finally this calm face turned towards Matryona, and a convulsion passed right through it.

'Aaa . . . You slut!'

And again he did not see her; he stood, pecking at the floor with his nose, muttering and shaking his head:

'Aaa . . . You slut!'

Slowly he lowered himself onto the bench; slowly he lowered his arms onto the table; slowly he lowered his head into his hands; and a fleet-footed cockroach tripped across the table towards him, stopping right beside his nose, and waggled its whiskers.

Night

Bushes, humps, gulleys; more bushes; through all this confusion of branches, shadows and sunset glimmer the twisting road wound; Pyotr strode quickly along it – into the depths of the east – into the bushes, the humps, the gulleys, between the green eyes of the glow-worms.

Yevseich caught him up.

'Pyotr Petrovich, sir – tee-hee-hee – what's going to become of us? Take pity – have a thought for the young mistress; she's crying her eyes out!'

His only answer was the crackle of the undergrowth and the plashing sound of feet running off through the swamp towards Tselebeyevo . . .

'Tee-hee-hee'; Yevseich had a coughing fit; he couldn't catch up with Pyotr Petrovich: how could an old man with infirm legs chase after a young one!

Yevseich turned off towards Gugolevo; the day was fading; dull night was falling upon it in a chaos of ash.

In the Gugolevo park all was lifeless: the old grandmother, piled around with cushions, was drowning in furs beneath the window; from outside darkness assailed her through the open window; a shaft of golden light from the lamp sprang out of the window to meet it; the breeze handed half-illuminated fingers of wild vine in through the window.

But where was Katya? . . .

That was Tselebeyevo in front of her: and Katya was afraid; she stole along, alone and palely loitering; Katya had become even thinner; like a slender, grey stalk, with a fluff of white cobweb, in a pale, ash-grey dress and with hair like ash, veiled in a pale shawl, she melted palely into the ash-blue murk, drowned in the sea of night; her thin little face only just kept afloat on the surface of that sea; that she was going there was a secret from her grandmama, from the Gugolevo servants, even from Yevseich: footsteps were coming towards her; in a pale gleam of summer lightning, there, behind a bush, Yevseich was coming towards her; Katya hid from him in the bushes; the old man, too, then, the old man, too . . . he too had taken to coming here in secret.

The old man was far behind her now; in the pale gleam of the summer lightning she caught a last glimpse of the butler's grey back as she turned:

'Yevseich, Yevseich!' the silly frightened girl called out into the darkness, but Yevseich did not hear; Katya gazed after him . . . and cried.

Katya's eyes were like scraps of the blue night sky that kept a watch on her through the black lace of leaves surrounding her: Katya stopped . . . and cried.

Her grandmama's ruin, the slap, the stupid loss of the jewels, the terrible disappearance of Pyotr, the gossip about this disappearance and that loss, and to cap it all that horrid, unsigned, completely illiterate letter, written in a clumsy scrawl, in which some yokel brazenly informed her that Pyotr was having an affair with an upstart peasant woman! Katya gazed at the stars . . . and cried, and her slender shoulders shook from the rustle of a nocturnal leaf; everyone has heard that rustle: it is a special rustle, such as does not happen in the daytime.

Schmidt would tell her everything: he would seek out Pyotr for her.

Now the houses were in sight; it was as though they were cowering in the patches of black created by the bushes, scattered here and there – and blinking malevolently at her with eyes full of cruelty and light; as though a horde of enemies were lying in wait in the bushes, disguised as patches of light, as the doorposts of the houses, as the confusion of shadows, and were raising from there the black fingers of starling-cotes – all this was now staring into the forest, it had tracked Katya down on the edge of the forest and only just revealed itself to her; but at first all that emerged from the forest was a confusion of lights; and as the silly girl approached the village, the cumbersome white bell-tower passed her on the right, with the sharp squeal of a briefly woken martin.

Her light shoes had got soaked in the rank weeds, the grasses had poured their moisture on her dress, and a shiver went down her back; Katya had lost her way, and wandered to the sloping hollow; see there – a mean cottage rose from a bush in the hollow, blew the tumbling smoke from its chimney at her, glinted with flickering lights; a bloody banner of light fell from the window onto the grass; and on top of it the black cross of the window fell onto the patch of light; and all of it together stretched out towards the bushes where Katya was standing; a feeling of slight horror and a sinister merriment came over her when she saw in that reddish light jewels of lightly trembling dew on leaves and slender stems; then suddenly she became afraid: the face of a man in a cap flashed blood-red under the window; his beard and his red nose were fixed upon the window: his eyes were fixed upon it too: and whose was the blood-red fist that shook under the window? And stealthily she crept away, away from that place: how could she find Schmidt's cottage?

Only then did she realize that the Tselebeyevo shopkeeper, Ivan Stepanov, had been standing there under the window: so what had her childish heart been so afraid of?

Had she gone up to him, he would have pointed to the window, and through the window she would have made out the dirty, hirsute face of Pyotr, the snub-nosed, pock-marked peasant woman, and a cunning, sickly face that winked at Pyotr from behind a saucer raised to his yellow moustache; all that she would have seen: it was better that she didn't.

The Tselebeyevo shopkeeper kept up his watch under the window for a long time, and under that window whispered wild threats: 'Just you wait, I'll have you singing, you old pimp!' Then his face disappeared into the shadow, his hairy fist showed blood-red in the light, and he himself went away into the shadows; the crackle of the undergrowth in the bushes died down in the distance, and disappeared completely.

Daryalsky was already leaving the cottage, his light was already dwindling in the darkness, and as he turned, he saw a hand raising a paraffin lamp, to cast soundlessly into his darkness a dull red torrent of light, in the middle of which Matryona stood, there in the distance, and her face shone voluptuously with the smile she sent into his darkness and with her eyes that were blinded by the glare: how small she was there!

Daryalsky wandered about the village, and the dogs set up a howling; the dogs prowled after him, hurled themselves into the darkness and leaped back with a yelp. He wandered aimlessly up to the priest's garden, and chanced to stroll beneath the open window. He heard the priest's wife's voice:

'I tell you, he has black whiskers, a real little cockroach; now he'd make a bridegroom for you: he's just come home on leave – and he's of noble birth.'

Daryalsky couldn't resist peeping in at the window – and what did he see there? Katya, green in the face, tiny, tucked in a corner, trying to smile, with the priest's wife bearing down upon her with her stomach, her breasts and her gossip; and the sadly silent Schmidt was pretending to listen to Vukol's perorations; Father Vukol, in his white cassock, was rolling cigarettes under the lamp; Schmidt was watching Katya closely, and a barely perceptible anxiety on her account flitted across his face.

Daryalsky rushed away . . .

Quiet voices approached in the murky dark; quiet words resounded in the murky dark across the dew:

'No, it's not a slander, it is so.'

'But he's not a thief, is he?'

'He's not a thief: that's a deliberately engineered coincidence; his enemies have hidden in the darkness and are manipulating his actions. The hour will come, and they will pay for it – for everything, for everything: for him and all those they have destroyed.'

'Pyotr, my Pyotr, with that woman!'

'Pyotr thinks he has left you for ever; but this is not a betrayal, not a flight, but a terrible hypnosis that is crushing him; he has passed beyond the range of help – and for now his enemies are triumphing over him, just as the enemy is triumphing and scoffing at our country; thousands of innocent victims, and the culprits are still hidden; and none of us ordinary mortals knows who the true culprits are of all the absurdities taking place. Be reconciled, Katerina Vasilyevna, do not fall into despair: all the powers of darkness are attacking Pyotr at this time; but Pyotr can still overcome; he has to overcome himself within himself, to renounce the individual creation of life; he must reassess his attitude to the world; and the ghosts, which have taken on flesh and blood for him, will vanish; believe me, only great and powerful souls are liable to such temptation; only giants crash down as Pyotr has; he wanted to achieve everything by himself: his story is absurd and hideous; as though it were told by an enemy who mocks at all the bright future of our country . . . For now you can only pray, pray for Pyotr!'

So Schmidt talked as he saw Katya home to Gugolevo; suddenly in front of them there was a crackle in the undergrowth; her electric torch cast a shaft of white light, and Katya saw: in the circle of white light, like the protruding head of a wild wolf, Pyotr's head protruded; his dull eyes wandered drunkenly; a moment – and all was darkness again.

Firm hands held Katya to the spot by force, when she made to rush after Pyotr:

'Stop, don't move: if you go after him now, you will not come back!'

For many an hour the damp blue murk had been drenching the fields with its transparency, shot through with an earthy green and an opalescent glint in sunset patches where the black crest of the fir-wood stood out against the unextinguished remnants of the recent splendours; the east was all damp murk except in one place, which was morbidly inflamed by the not yet risen moon; though black all round, it was transparent; the bushes were etched in black, fringed with lace and the lisp of leaves; a black scrap of that lisp, like a torn-off leaf, bustled hither and thither; then it tumbled into the lace of the bushes: it was a bat; the unbroken sea of indigo overhead was spattered here and there with the summer tears of faintly twinkling stars; Daryalsky and Katya both looked at the stars – from different places in the approach to the mournfully rustling forest. They looked at the stars and . . . wept at their memories.

CHAPTER FIVE

Demons

A refuge

Strange to say: the more intelligent Daryalsky's interlocutor, the more he had of subtle, flexible discernment, the more capricious and complex were the zigzags described by his companion's thought, the more easily Pyotr breathed in his company, and the simpler he appeared himself; through the superfluous mannerisms of this dashing stranger there shone intelligence and simplicity, born of weariness with the struggles of emotional turmoil; today he had come to visit Schmidt and was sitting at his table, flicking through letters addressed to him, sunburnt and unshaven: and a blissful smile had settled on his face; the smile seemed hewn in stone; sitting here, he was on the border of two worlds, far distant from each other: a beloved past and a new reality of terror and delight, like a fairy-tale; the deep, lofty blue, already autumnally pure, glanced into Schmidt's window with its smattering of fluffy clouds, along with Tselebeyevo; in the distance the priest could be seen, sitting on a tree-stump, angrily spitting out his objections to Ivan Stepanov; Ivan Stepanov was saying to him:

'I'm of the view that it's high time that carpenter's hussy was arrested: they're sectarians and degenerates; that wench' – he spat – 'she's got no shame: maybe it's them that are those Doves we've heard of. I've been keeping an eye on them for quite a while . . .'

'Well, Stepanych, that goes to show, I think, what a God-fearing man you are; it's true: Mitry Mironych takes a lot of interest in the sacred texts, but as for . . .'

'And the Gugolevo squire, I don't mind saying, now they've got him in their net all right, they've cast a spell on him: why else would he take a job as one of the carpenter's workmen?'

'Well, that's just a gentleman's whim!'

And Father Vukol dropped his head, with a deep draw on his pipe, and spat pleasurably into the sunscorched grass; the sky thrust itself into his eyes – pure and gentle, sprinkled with pale fluffy clouds, a lofty blue.

Soon Stepanych went off to his shop; a man who was passing brashly proffered his hand as he met him, and barked out, 'Ah!. . . Must shake Ivan Stepanov's hand!. . .'

'Clear off: I don't shake hands with strangers; you may have something wrong with your hand, for all I know . . .'

And off he went.

Daryalsky, gazing thoughtfully through the window, heard none of this; he saw the sky, the fluffy clouds, the coloured cottages and the distant figure of the priest that seemed etched upon the meadow; he and Schmidt exchanged the odd brief, fleeting word.

Schmidt was sitting immersed in papers; in front of him lay a large sheet; on the sheet a circle had been drawn with a pair of compasses, with four intersecting triangles and a cross inside; between each of the angles a line went upwards, dividing the circumference into twelve parts, designated by Roman numerals, where 'ten' stood at the top and 'one' to the right-hand side; this strange figure was surrounded by another circle and divided into thirty-six segments; in each segment stood symbols of the planets in such a way that above three such signs was a sign of the zodiac; in the twelve large fields stood small crowns and crosses and planet signs, from which fine arrows were drawn in both directions through the centre of the circle, bisecting the star; in addition there were inscriptions on the figure in red ink: 'Victim', 'Reaper', '3 Goblets', 'Blinding Light'; at the side of the sheet strange inscriptions were written, such as: 'X-10: Sphinx (X) (99 sceptres); 9, Leo, Venus; 10, Virgo, Jupiter (Mistress of the Sword); 7, Mercury. The Seventh Mystery' and so on.

Schmidt was saying to him:

'You were born in the year of Mercury, on the day of Mercury, in the hour of the Moon, at that point in the firmament which bears the name 'The Dragon's Tail': the Sun, Venus and Mercury are darkened for you by evil aspects; the Sun is darkened by its quadrature with Mars; Mercury is in opposition with Saturn; and Saturn is that part of the soul's firmament where the heart breaks, where Cancer overcomes Aquila; and further, Saturn presages failure in love for you, as it comes into the sixth house of your horoscope; it is also in Pisces. Saturn threatens you with perdition: come to your senses – it is still not too late to step aside from the terrible path you have taken . . .'

But Daryalsky made no reply: he was looking over the bookshelves; there were strange books on those shelves: the Kabbalah in an expensive binding, Merkabah, volumes of the Zohar (an open page of the Zohar always lay on Schmidt's desk, catching the golden ray of the sun: that golden page spoke of the wisdom of Simeon Ben Yochai and caught the eye of the astonished observer); there were handwritten copies of the works of Lucius Firmicus, and astrological commentaries on the *Tetrabiblion* of Ptolemy; there were the *Stromata* of Clement of Alexandria, there were the Latin tractatuses of Hammer and among them one *Baphometis Revelata*, where the link was explored between the Arabic branch of the Ophites and the Knights Templar, where the faith of the Ophites was interwoven with the wondrous legend of Titurel; there were handwritten copies of *The Pastor of the Peoples*, from the eternally mysterious *Sifra Di-Zeniuta*, from a book attributed very nearly to Abraham – that same *Sefer* to which Rabbi Ben Hananiah swore he owed his miracles; on the desk were sheets with signs drawn in a trembling hand: pentagrams, swastikas, circles with magical taus written inside them; there was a table with sacred hieroglyphs; an aged hand depicted a crown of roses, on the top of which was the head of a man, and underneath the head of a lion; at the sides were the heads of a bull and an eagle; and in the centre of the crown were drawn two intersecting triangles in the form of a six-pointed star with numbers at its angles – 1, 2, 3, 4, 5, 6 – and a number written in the centre – 21. Beneath this emblem was written in Schmidt's hand: 'The crown of the Magi – T = 400'; there were other figures too: a sun, blinding two infants, with the inscription underneath: 'Quitolath – the sacred truth: 100'; a typhon above two bound people, under which Schmidt had written: 'This is the number sixty, the number of the mystery, of fate, predestination: i.e. the fifteenth Hermetic glyph "Xiron".' Then there were the completely incomprehensible words: 'Atoim, Dinaim, Ur, Zain'. On a chair to one side lay a mystical diagram with the ten sefirot-beams written in a certain order: 'Kether – the first sefirah: the chasuble of God, the first brilliance, the first exlumination, the first effluction, the first movement, the supramundane channel, Canalis Supramundanus' and the eighth sefirah, Yod, with the subscript: 'the ancient serpent'. There were strange inscriptions on the white wood of the desk, such as: 'The straight line of the square is the source and instrument of everything pertaining to the senses', or: 'All material substance is calculated by the number four'.

Out of the books and signs and diagrams rose the bald head of Schmidt and his ageing voice went on expounding to Daryalsky:

'Jupiter in Cancer foretold elevation for you, nobility and priestly service, but Saturn has overthrown all that; when Saturn enters the constellation of Aquarius, disaster threatens you; and just now, at this very time, Saturn is in Aquarius. For the last time I say to you: take care! For Mars is in Virgo too; all that could be avoided if Jupiter in your yearly horoscope were in the house of your birth; but Jupiter is in the house of fate . . .'

And Pyotr was shaken: he recalled past years when Schmidt had guided his fate, revealing to him the blinding past of secret knowledge; he had been on the point of going abroad with him – to them, the brethren, who influenced his fate from afar; but Daryalsky looked through the window, and outside the window was Russia: white, grey, red huts, rough shirts outlined against the meadow and a song; the carpenter, trudging across the meadow in his red shirt to see the priest; the gentle, caressing sky. And Daryalsky turned his back on his past: he turned away from the window, from Russia, calling him through the window as it perished, from the new supreme master of his fate, the carpenter, and he said to Schmidt:

'I don't believe in fate: in me the creation of life will overcome everything...'

'Astrology does not teach the power of blind fate. Thoth says: thought and speech created both the world and omnipotence, and the seven spirits, the protective genii that have manifested themselves in the seven spheres; their revelation is fate; man rises through the circles: in the circle of the moon he becomes aware of immortality; in the circle of Venus he receives innocence; on the sun he bears the light; from Mars he learns humility; from Jupiter – reason; on Saturn he contemplates the truth of things.'

'You're treating me to *The Pastor of the Peoples*, which bears the imprint of the last period of Alexandrianism; we philologists love the primordial, and that still doesn't contain the primordial wisdom of the magi.'

'Have you forgotten that I am speaking not on the basis of written sources, but of oral instruction. Some of the ancient copies that are unknown to your science I have seen with my own eyes – over there, in the brotherhood...'

But Daryalsky stood up: a torrent of sunlight struck him through the window.

'Have you nothing more to say?'

'Nothing!'

'Good-bye: I am leaving you and going not to your people, but to mine; I'm going away for ever – don't bear any hard feelings against me.'

And he went out; the sun blinded him.

Schmidt remained sitting among his calculations for a long time; a tear of pity froze on his aged cheek: 'He's lost!' And if they had chanced to enter here, the villagers of Tselebeyevo would no doubt have been astonished to see Schmidt the summer visitor in floods of bitter tears.

He was the only summer visitor in the area; he used to move into our godforsaken parts as early as the end of March; and by the time he left the wind would already be carrying the roars of the first snowstorms over the village; this summer visitor was toothless, balding and grey; he would

wander round the district in the heat wearing a yellow silk jacket, support-
ing himself with a stick and holding his straw hat in his hand; the village
boys and girls clustered round him; he used to visit the priest; and he used
to bring insect-powders with him against the bed-bugs; and he didn't
believe in God, although he was baptized an Orthodox Christian; and
that's all they knew in Tselebeyevo about their summer visitor.

An ugly incident

What happened in Ivan Stepanov's shop, why there was a crash of broken
bottles, on what grounds the shopkeeper himself came hurtling out of the
house with sticky cherry jam pouring from the top of his head all over his
face – all this remained in obscurity; out he flew, and made straight for the
water-trough: and started to wash it off; he washed and washed, and once
he'd got it off – a bleeding wound was revealed across his nose, as though
someone had slashed him across the nose with a knife. The shopkeeper
only recollected himself properly when he'd had a good wash; he washed
all the jam off, and then it dawned on him that it wasn't proper for him to
go outside looking like that.

But no one dreamed of noticing him: the point is that while he was dili-
gently washing the cherry jam off his face and hair in the trough, the populace of Tselebeyevo was occupied by quite another, no less extraordinary
occurrence: along the road from Likhov a cloud of dust suddenly swirled
up – and out there, in the cloud of dust, a terrified, soul-destroying roar
was heard: the cloud of dust bore down upon our village at an inordinate
speed; and in front of it there rushed a red monster: it was as though a red
demon had come running over the horizon and straight at our village; and
hardly had the old men and women come skipping out of their huts when
the red demon already stood motionless in the middle of the green
meadow, wheezing and snorting, but without the roar, and tickling the
nose with a stink of petrol. It was a motor-car – that very motor-car which
is claimed to be able to transport people without the aid of horses; out of
the motor-car jumped a man completely covered in grey tarpaulin, with
immense black glasses over his eyes; he did a lot of fiddling around with the
wheels, took off his glasses, and nodded amicably at the villagers surrounding his motor-car; his fat, creased, slightly yellowish face winked at
the villagers with bloated, squinting eyes, but they cautiously shuffled
back from this high-cheek-boned face; even the priest peeped out from his
currant bushes, holding back one of his brood who was straining towards
the motor-car; meanwhile the gentleman with the half-Semitic, half-Tatar

face, lowering his glasses back over his eyes, settled himself once more on his red demon; the demon burst into a roar, shot into motion with a hiss, and was off and away.

It was this circumstance that distracted the villagers' attention from Ivan Stepanov, leaning over the trough and washing off the cherry juice that was flowing copiously from his head, to which a lump of jam, together with splinters of a broken jamjar, were also sticking most unpleasantly; you might have thought that someone's villainous hand had smashed a jar of jam over his worthy head; but how the folk of Tselebeyevo would have laughed if they had been told that this villainous hand belonged to none other than his very own son; an hour had passed since they had pitched into one another, gone through all the words in their vocabulary, after which the lad, abandoning all sense and propriety, had cleared his throat and spat straight in his parent's face, assailed his elderly parent with a knife, and to crown the hideous scene had smashed upon his head a weighty jar of jam. It was not without some trepidation that Ivan Stepanov now re-entered the shop; on the floor were bits of broken glass and sticky juice; suppose someone came in – what a disgrace; Ivan Stepanov closed the shop, rested his beard upon his hand and fell to thinking; it was hard to tell whether the battered parent was angry with his son or just afraid; he was just thinking: 'If only Styopka would clear off quickly; then no one will be any the wiser . . .'

The perpetrator of this outrage was not only clearing off, but was all set to leave for good; he was sitting in his tiny room in front of the greasy table; beside him on the chair lay a single rolled-up bundle. He was leaving these parts today and making for distant, forest places, free places: he had been contemplating flight from our parts for a long time; he kept pestering the brethren, the Doves, to give him some commission that would let him run away completely from our parts; he was sick and tired of this place; he was sick and tired of seeing how Matryona had preferred the squire to him, Styopka; but most of all he was sick of watching his parent spying on Matryona; he couldn't bear the sight of his parent, and, without willing it, kept an eye on his parent's snooping, and he had caught his parent in a downright villainous act; the night before, when Styopka was loitering around Kudeyarov's cottage, he had clearly seen his parent, without his cap and wearing nothing over his shirt, fiddling around outside the cottage, dragging brushwood, pouring something from a bottle over it (kerosene, probably), and trying to strike a match; another moment – and the red cockerel would have risen above the carpenter's hut; well, of course, Styopka hissed at him: and his parent made himself scarce.

And today they had settled their scores. Styopka would have liked to give him a more thorough beating; should have done it long ago; anyway, to hell with him; the Doves already knew from Styopka about the shopkeeper's intentions; they'd put a man onto him, and they'd see who got the better of whom – you never knew what might happen.

Now, without let or hindrance, Styopka was leaving the region where his stormy life had passed; and he began to reflect, and his thought bore him off (it was not for nothing that the lad had turned out a scribbler): and it occurred to this fine fellow that, by way of farewell, before he left his parental home, where, when all was said and done, his late mother had spoilt him – it occurred to him to write the opening to a story he was planning; so Styopka got his greasy notebook and with his now rusty pen scratched out the following opening: 'All was quiet; the whole village was asleep; only a cow mooed somewhere and a dog barked, and shutters squeaked on their rusty hinges, and the wind wailed under the eaves . . . So it turned out that it wasn't quiet at all, but, on the contrary, actually very noisy – if you see what I mean . . .'

As the stars began to come out Styopka's black silhouette trudged off along the starlit road, becoming smaller and smaller and finally merging with the distant black figure that since time immemorial had been threatening the village. Styopka never returned to Tselebeyevo: he must have lived out his days concealed in the forests; maybe, somewhere up in the north, a black, shaggy-maned ascetic, who would come out onto the road once in a blue moon, was the former Styopka, unless Styopka had been cut down by a wicked Cossack bullet, or been tied in a sack and hoisted to the heavens on a gibbet.

In Ovchinnikov

'What a wit! . . . A frightful wit!'
   'Well?'
'An ekthraordinary, a monthtrouth wit!'
   'Well? Come on, then.'
   'In a thertain rethpectable houthehold he dashed up to the piano and, you know, played thuch a roulade . . . "Do you play?" the hothteth athked . . . "I do." "Oh, pleathe play thomething for uth!" And can you imagine what he replied?'
   '??? . . .'
'Madam, I only play with my eyeth!'
   'Hee-hee!'
   'Ha-ha-ha-ha!'
   'Hho!'

'Waiter! Thome more whitecapth!' cried General Chizhikov with a chorus-girl on his lap.

'And where is he now, general?'

'On the bottle – burned up with drink; I thaw a little blue flame in hith mouth mythelf!'

'Fancy that!'

'He'th impregnated with thpirit, like a wick: a match would thet him on fire.'

'Hee-hee!'

'Ha-ha-ha!'

'Hho!'

'Waiter. Thome more whitecapth!' cried General Chizhikov with a chorus-girl on his lap.

'How did you come by so much money, general?'

'Eh?'

'Come on, tell me!'

'The man in the pawnshop swore that you had been so good as to pawn a wonderful diamond – hee-hee! . . .'

'I hope it wasn't stolen?'

'Hee-hee!'

'I hope not!' the general guffawed ironically.

'No, gentlemen: that's not the point – that's nothing: it's not worth telling . . . That's all very well! But let me tell you: a friend of mine – now he has the names of spirits, liqueurs and wines in alphabetical order, from A to Z inclusive . . . And that one who's "burned up", why that's nothing! Now this friend of mine: you'd go and see him, and straight away he'd offer you a cocktail called "Abracadabra", or "Leviathan". In "Abracadabra", for "a" he'd pour in some aniseed; "b" was barberry; "r" was riesling; and so on. When you'd drunk that you were done for!'

This was related with much arm-waving by a glassy-eyed magistrate from Chmar.

The private room, upholstered in pink silk, glittered with lights: a lackey kept bobbing in at the door; chorus-girls flitted in and out; the provincial tycoons and aristocrats lounged about in relaxed poses on sofas, couches, tables, and a greying Adonis without a jacket, standing with his back to the piano, just collapsed onto the keys and sighed:

'Our best years, our best years! Moscow – the Assembly of the Nobility: eh? Where is it?'

'Ah, where is it?' came an echo from the corner.

'The mazurka: tra-rara-ta-trarara! The first couple – Count Bersy de
Vgrevren with Zashelkovskaya, and the second couple . . .'

'The second couple – Colonel Saissely with Lily,' the voice from the corner interrupted.

'Yes: the second couple were Colonel Saissely and Lily. Our best years!
And now: just half a bottle a day!'

'No fear: I went over to a whole one ages ago!' came the voice from the
corner.

'Any chance you've got another diamond?' a fat man who had happened to
join this aristocratic company leaned over to the general. 'I could find a
buyer for you . . .'

'Darling, do give it to me!' a chorus-girl nestled up to Chizhikov . . .

'What an idea – never! It'th an ekthepthional inthtanth that I had to part
with family jewelth: what could I do – a temporary nethethity!' the general
mumbled in embarrassment.

And from the other side of the room resounded:

'The theatre! The operetta! Do you remember *La Mascotte* . . . Chernov,
Zorina and that unforgettable: "How I love little goslings".'

'And I love little la-a-ambs,' the voice from the corner joined in.

'The way they cry quack-quack-quack . . .'

'And how they shout baa-baa,' echoed from the corner.

'Quack-quack – baa-aa!'

'Baa-baa!'

'Baa!' The greying aristocrats all joined in the chorus, recalling their
youth, Moscow the unforgettable, and the unforgotten *La Mascotte*.

Luka Silych, sitting in a corner, was quite bathed in sweat; his eyes had no
glitter today; there was no painted chorus-girl sitting on his knees today;
his back was more obviously bent over his champagne; the bags hung more
obviously under his eyes; his grey beard trembled obviously under his lip,
and his grey checked knee trembled obviously too: he was wracked by a fit
of shivering – as he had been so many, many times before; a sweet enervation and dizziness carried him home to Dovecote Annushka; chorus-girls
meant nothing to him now! Annushka was now his one and only! It was
about a month that she had been coming to his room at night, at his insis-
tence and in secret from the mistress, to sleep with him; they drank sweet
wines together on those nights, and amused themselves together in, well,
in all sorts of ways; but after those nights the enervation overcame him

more than ever; quite in his declining years he had taken a shine to his wife's barefooted housekeeper like an utter adolescent, or worse still, like a beast in rut . . . No time for chorus-girls! It was Annushka or no one now! His knee was shaking, his beard, his spider's fingers, his glass; golden drops, cold drops of champagne splashed onto the table. He was thinking: if only I could go to Annushka! Everything here sickened him: the smug aristocrats sickened him; look at those drunken mugs; gathered in the provincial zemstvo assembly to save Russia from revolution; some hope! Luka Silych was sickened by the business people; he was sickened by the champagne; most of all he was sickened by the nasty little general, Chizhikov; the general was full of filth; he'd fished out some promissory notes of Baroness Graaben's for him, for a certain consideration; now the old lady was in his hands, he had no further use for the general; he was a drunkard and a glutton, and moreover a thief, a spy and a troublemaker.

The general meanwhile was exchanging whispers in the corner:

'Well, maybe I could show you the diamondth . . .'

'Yes, our dreams are full of meaning . . .'

'Yes –

' . . . of prophecy our dreams –

' . . . are full . . .' the drunken gentlemen roared out, as their eyes tried to jump from their sockets; one turned in song to another; the second gestured to the first; another, neck protruding, made pecking movements towards the ceiling with his nose; another had long since disappeared somewhere with a chorus-girl.

'Yes, our dreams are full of meaning . . .'

'Yes –

' . . . of prophecy our dreams –

' . . . are full . . .' roared the drunken gentlemen.

Luka Silych glanced furtively at his watch: he didn't want to miss the train that was leaving for Likhov at the most inconvenient possible time – at four in the morning; he stood up, paid his bill, gave the aristocrats the once-over, recalled how many estates had been set on fire, and left.

'Drr-drr-drr' – the carriage, with him in it, bounced over the cobblestones of Ovchinnikov; it was growing light; Luka Silych reflected on Annushka's white legs and that he would be ill again after tomorrow night: weak and sweaty, sweaty and weak – time to die!

'I shan't survive more than a year of this kind of life – kaput,' he thought, and whispered plaintively: 'Annushka!'

'Drr-drr-drr' . . . The carriage bounced on the Ovchinnikov cobbles: the Metelkin branch line was just over there, its rails gleaming.

A travelling companion

In the station it was stuffy and oppressive; although it was already daylight, the lamps were flickering irksomely; a plump officer, whose disciplinary detachment had been stationed in the villages round Likhov for the best part of a month, was putting away a veal cutlet and darting glances at a lady strolling about for no obvious purpose in a bright green hat and scarlet coat and with a face on which nothing could be discerned but white grease-paint, lips delineated in crimson and a red flush on her cheeks.

Nearby on a bench, surrounded by boxes, bags, birdcages, ribbons, umbrellas tied up with tape, was an exhausted lady, tossing in semi-sleep, with a bandaged jaw, her hat crooked, and five infants, one of whom had fallen asleep there and then with a home-made pasty in his hand; a passenger of unknown profession was walking up and down waiting for the train to Likhov; the sale of newspapers had stopped; the last cutlet had been ordered in the buffet, the last glass of beer had been drunk: people were curled up on benches, worn out; only the cruel yellow lights kept breathing out their stuffy heat.

Not so on the platform: there it was morning, there was movement, it was cool; a mass of intersecting rails; on the rails were mauve and yellow coaches, a shunting engine roared as it crawled along the rails; the engine-driver in his uniform cap leaned out from the footplate; he washed his hands with a mouthful of water; everywhere the glint of points appeared; a crossing-keeper was running by, shouting at someone; he had a lantern in his hand and a rolled-up flag tucked into his lacquered belt; and a round building gaped obliquely, many-orificed, at the platform; from each orifice peeped an engine; but a signal shot up at a sixty-degree angle and a goods train rushed by on an outside line.

Luka Silych yawned lazily, glanced lazily around, trying to decipher the inscriptions on the waggons flying by: 'Vladikavkaz', 'Zabaikalskaya', 'Rybinsk-Vologda', 'South-Western'. Inadvertently he read the inspection dates: 1910, 1908, 1915 . . . Waggons flew by, in the waggons the vacant faces of masticating bullocks flew by, a white waggon with the inscription 'Refrigerated' flew by; flat waggons flew by too; empty ones, ones laden with sand or timber; one flat waggon flew by with nothing on it but two wheels; 'Ter-Akopov' oil waggons flew by, another flat waggon; and after that the last waggon; the train had flown by; its guard flew away into the distance, beneath him, down by the rails, a red lantern flew away too.

Again the expanse of rails: an engine chugging along them; with the cry of its whistle it puffed out clouds of white into the white morning: a mad, merry cry!

A clean-shaven, grey-haired gentleman in a brown overcoat with all the buttons done up was walking slowly up and down; and he kept passing by Luka Silych; he was wearing a hat with ear-flaps; the gentleman's long nose and upper lip protruded forwards; all the rest of him receded backwards; a fine figure of a man, despite his age; he kept his hands in the pockets cut at the front of his coat; and he kept walking past the merchant; he approached him from the right, overtook him from the left, let him go ahead; a servant walked behind him, carrying a travelling-rug.

And Luka Silych took an interest in the gentleman; the gentleman moved off in front – Luka Silych followed him: approached him from the right, overtook him from the left, let him go ahead; as though by chance; and he was thinking: 'Wherever have I seen this gentleman before: no doubting he's an important person; must be around sixty; from behind he looks quite young; shoulders back, there he goes, with his servant behind him.'

If the gentleman went over to the very edge of the platform, Luka Silych trailed along behind him out of boredom and idle curiosity; and if Luka Silych himself should wander to the platform's edge – on turning round he'd find the elderly gentleman right behind him, looking at him, and behind the gentleman, the servant with the rug.

And so they walked around one after the other for more than an hour while they waited for the Likhov train; and now the train approached, the signal rose; everyone spilled out onto the platform: the lady with the bandaged jaw, five infants, boxes, bags and birdcages, and separate from the lady on the platform were the plump officer and the passenger of unknown profession, a crowd of peasants with saws and sacks, a policeman and the station-master in a red cap, bowing a deferential farewell to Luka Silych; Luka Silych watched – and what an extraordinary thing: the clean-shaven gentleman went up to the station-master, gestured towards Luka Silych with his nose, blew it loudly, scratched the bridge of it, and evidently asked: who might that person be, walking around there: Luka Silych compressed his lips and portrayed haughtiness on his face: 'Where used I to see that gentleman? Only I'm sure he was younger . . .'

But the Likhov train rolled in, and here was Luka Silych in a first-class carriage; three hours he had to suffer to Likhov; he was weak, weak and sickly was the Likhov miller!

He had just taken it into his head to settle down for some sleep, when the door of the compartment opened and the gentleman sat himself down opposite; the servant wrapped the rug around his knees; and left; they sat there opposite each other, glancing at each other; Luka Silych did it surreptitiously, while the gentleman just stared at him quite shamelessly!

Luka Silych upped and went into the second class (there were some empty carriages); not five minutes had passed when the gentleman moved into the second class as well; sitting opposite; Luka Silych couldn't stand it any longer:

'Are you going to Likhov, may I ask?'

'Yes, Mr Yeropegin,' the old gentleman drawled in a high-pitched voice: he made a sound which might be laughter, or might be crying.

'Whom do I have the honour of addressing?'

'I'm travelling from Petersburg to this district on business of my mother's – yes!'

'However old must his mother be,' thought Luka Silych.

'And I am Todrabe-Graaben . . .'

Luka Silych's stomach turned over: he was overwhelmed with confusion, a fit of shivering seized him: he had forgotten all about the baron, and he would have to talk to the baron about those business matters, he would have to; and the business wasn't clean; and the baron was a senator, 'on the legal side'.

But the baron said nothing; he smiled silently; if only he would say a word about the business; Luka Silych felt pains throughout his body; he could not stand the baron's gaze; he felt a tightness in the pit of his stomach; he stood up and went into the third class.

The air was thick and stuffy in the third class carriage; the seats 'was all took'; beside the lady with the boxes a worker was perched; opposite him her bags.

'Every citizen who has bought a ticket has the right to occupy a seat,' Luka Silych rapped out drily, but his stomach was churning: he was nauseated by the lady, nauseated by her five infants, nauseated by the worker; but still he felt better here than there, alone with his enemy the senator.

Luka Silych sat there. Outside the windows were yellow, dreary, wilting cornfields, stooks erected here and there and reddening buckwheat; the distant, dusty blue horizon rushed along the same line as the train, turning off sharply somewhere beyond the carriage window, and under the windows the same cornfields came rushing towards the train: as though the spaces outside were revolving in a circle; everything that swept by in the distance rushed past in the opposite direction beneath the windows.

The talkative worker with the humble face (evidently one of those who stand and stare), unable to bear the silence any longer, turned to Luka Silych:

'I ain't been paid; I've just got some tea and sugar with me, and a few baps. We got together and asked them to give us our money; but no, they wouldn't: so I'm off.'

This angered the merchant, he came out in a sweat; he interrupted the worker.

'You had no business to: you've been treated in full accordance with the law!'

'How's that now?'

'Just because you're short, you expect the manager to go to the stake for you!'

The worker listened to him attentively:

'A hundred-and-twenty-five men went to ask again; and again they refused – wouldn't give it us.'

'I've already explained that to you: got it?'

'I've got it.'

No one spoke . . .

Outside the window the telegraph wire bobbed up and down; the window itself was covered in dust; up and down the telegraph wire ran; a midge sitting on the window-pane looked like a bird soaring over distant fields; 'Devil take that wretched general!' thought Yeropegin; there was something about the baron that sent shivers down his spine; did he know what kind of business Yeropegin was doing with his mamma? Of course he did, he was bound to: it wouldn't be surprising if the baron made his way down here, into the third class; what was Yeropegin so afraid of anyway?

The worker kept on at him:

'I've just got tea and sugar with me, and some baps: there's nothing to sow this year . . .'

'What d'you mean, nothing?' said Luka Silych in a tone of schoolmasterly surprise, and engaged in conversation with him so as not to think about the baron and the general and Annushka any more.

'Got no grain to sow the fields with, that's what I mean . . .'

'How is it everyone else has got some, and you haven't?'

'I haven't? The others haven't either; we wrote a petition; seventy-five of us signed it; and they just refused . . .'

'Because there's a statute about that for the whole country . . .'

'I'm not saying anything about that; I'm just saying that life's got harder for us . . .'

'Well, that's not a clever thing to say, either . . .'

'But I . . .'

'You should just listen to what people say to you: don't interrupt . . . In the whole of our country people are, so to speak, engaged in agriculture, tilling the land, and our country doesn't . . . er . . . play second fiddle to anybody. And we all live, thank God . . .'

'Yes, thank God, thank God: we've got nothing to sow again this year . . .'

'There you go again with your silly talk; that's hooligan's talk, you know
... If it's a hooligan you want to be, then that's the way to talk (Luka Silych
made it a rule to enlighten uneducated folk) ... I've explained it all to you
anyway: let me finish, and then you speak; and if you want to interrupt,
then you must warn me – got it?'

'Have you finished now?'

'I've finished: you can speak ...'

But their conversation was destined to be cut short; the door opened and
the ticket-collector bent cautiously over to Luka Silych:

'There's a gentleman in the first class is asking you to come and see him:
to have a talk.'

No avoiding it: grunting, Yeropegin stood up and went to the first class;
he had no wish to evade the conversation so directly; the other passengers
laughed after him:

'There's a bossy-boots for you ...'

'Must be a Kadet!'

'Barks like a watchdog!'

'A real gent!'

Now Yeropegin was in the first class sitting in front of the baron.

'You, Mr Yeropegin, are just the person I need: so we can spend the journey talking ...'

And talk they did.

For the whole of the two hours remaining to Likhov they talked about
the shares of the Varaksin mines and the Metelkin branch railway; one
word from Yeropegin – ten words from the baron; one digression from
Yeropegin – ten digressions from the baron; he gave him such a grilling,
with paragraphs and statutes, that, business-man though he was, he beat a
retreat before the baron; and the baron kept after him – threatening him
with the courts and all so quietly, gently, with restraint; he simply wore the
merchant down, who sat there writhing with weakness, nausea, dreams of
Annushka's kisses, and fear of this senator 'on the legal side'.

They were nearly at Likhov.

'I strongly advise you to withdraw your demands voluntarily; if it comes
to court I'll pack you off to jail; they'll put a ring through your nose and
drag you off to Siberia' (the baron always expressed himself pic-
turesquely: he was a great eccentric).

Thus the baron suddenly brought matters to an end with a melancholy
sigh, fastidiously blowing a speck of dust from his travelling-bag.

They fell silent: in the blue aperture of the window their ageing silhouettes rocked to and fro: a merchant and a gentleman; one sick and green, with eyes that gleamed in the sun and a small white beard, the other pink, clean-shaven, with a long nose and smelling of eau-de-Cologne – two old men: one had a gold ring with a big ruby on his grimy hand; the other had no ruby, but his hands were in black gloves; one had a travelling-rug secured with straps and a cushion; the other had a rug without straps and a little travelling-bag; on the simple, icon-like face of one debauchery had dried out the lips completely; the sexless face of the other was a melancholy pink and irony played on his lips; one was tall, angular, desiccated, and when he changed his merchant's black attire for a lounge suit the padded shoulders protruded from his jacket; the other's shoulders were round, but his back was straight, like a young man's; one wore a cap, the other a silk hat with ear-flaps and an expensive black smock; one was white-haired; the other was still grey, although the same age as the white-haired one; one was a miller, of peasant stock; the other from the gentry and a senator.

'Do you have any children?'

'Yes.'

'What are they doing?'

'My son's at university . . .'

'Poor fellow, in that case he's finished,' the baron sighed in unfeigned horror.

'How do you mean?'

'It's very simple: intellectual work requires selection and good heredity . . .'

Yeropegin did not understand that at all; he understood only one thing: he might be an eccentric, but the baron had such a head for business that it was better not to get mixed up with him.

The coach rocked from side to side; the spire of Likhov was already sticking up from the hunch-backed plain; a mill passed by, a string of waggons; the train stopped; the two Likhov porters were standing there like lords; the passengers rushed up to them in supplication; the estate foreman with his waist-length flaxen beard was darting about there too, peeping fearfully into the windows of the coaches in search of his master; the slick manservant came running into the compartment, and the baron handed him his rug and travelling-bag: 'Be so kind, relieve me of these, would you, my friend!'

'Good-bye,' the baron modestly held out his soft hand to Yeropegin, without, however, taking off his glove – and vanished into the bustling Likhov crowd.

Suffocation

It was scorching; Luka Silych all but burned himself when the touched the
metal of the cab; he could not get the baron out of his head, any more than
he could the barefooted Annushka, who would hardly be expecting him at
such an early hour; she'd be sleeping away, no doubt: Fyokla Matveyevna
herself never got up much before eleven. A strange business: it was as
though the walls of his house were poisoned by some disease; hardly would
he have arrived home these days when an endless stupor would take possession of his consciousness; everything at home seemed to be out of joint:
Fyokla kept her eyes averted from him; the servants looked askance and
seemed to be concealing something from him. He found it hard to breathe,
and then that baron too, with his threat of legal action.

They were approaching Ganshin Street, at the end of which his
detached wooden house came into view, and all around now oppressive
clouds came tumbling from the sky onto the earth, although it was barely
eight o'clock in the morning: there was a storm brewing, for sure.

Luka Silych had to ring his own doorbell for a long time: he could not
make anyone hear; were they all asleep, or what? From the little house
opposite, where the tailor Tsizik-Aizik lived, a Jewish woman, consisting
entirely of wrinkles and rags, stared at him in sympathy; she waved her
hand at Luka Silych:

'You can ring all you like . . . you won't get an answer: your servants were
having a party last night; Sukhorukov came out about five, and Kakurinsky, and an old woman from the home.'

'Whatever's all this?' thought Luka Silych: as if it wasn't enough for fate
to torment him with weakness, and nausea, and thoughts about the barefooted Annushka; as if it wasn't enough that for three solid hours in the
train the senator from Petersburg had gone on and on at him so that even
now he'd barely regained his senses; no, on top of that, if you please, he had
to restore order when he got home (Luka Silych set great store by order).
Despairing of making anyone hear the bell, Luka Silych stepped down
from the porch and started hammering for all he was worth on the gates;
then behind the gates a wheezing and a munching were heard, the bolt
creaked, and Ivan the Fire stuck out his inflamed and sleepy face; seeing
the master he became embarrassed, and lowered his eyes malevolently.

'What are these visitors you've been having at night when I'm away?'
Luka Silych set upon him, but Ivan the Fire remained as silent as a log.

'Well?' . . . Yeropegin went on interrogating him.

But Ivan the Fire even got cross, it seemed:

'What visitors? We've not seen no visitors!'

'Don't you wave your arms about, don't you start learning such habits; put your hands down . . .'

'Well, I'm just . . . we ain't seen a trace of no visitors, cross my heart.'

'All right, but what did the Jew woman tell me?' – Luka Silych turned towards the tailor's window; but the woman was no longer sticking out of it.

'Well, the Jew woman, she's just a Jew woman; the Jew woman talks all sorts of rubbish; you don't want to go believing no Jew woman . . . Now a Jew woman . . .'

'Stop arguing with your arms, put your arms down, sew them there or something . . . Take my things!' – Luka Silych's energy was exhausted. – 'We'll sort it out later . . . Look, there's going to be a storm . . .'

'Yes,' the Fire scratched behind his ear, gazing at the sky – 'it's right on top of us . . .'

With creaking boots the master went drily and pompously into his study; the study was empty and oppressive; he sank into an armchair; soon his abacus began to click, his keys to rattle, and between his fingers papers, promissory notes and receipts rustled; he anxiously looked through the papers to do with the Graaben business and began to understand that the baron was no doubt right: with papers like that you couldn't rob the old woman, all you could do was give her a fright; hour after hour the master sat there growing ever fainter from his thoughts, from weakness, from nausea and a kind of dry sadness: now there was Ivan the caretaker too; more than once he'd had the impression that the caretaker too was spying on him for some deceitful purpose – he'd have to sack him, sack him, without delay . . .

Suddenly his attention was distracted; he noticed a cigarette-end in his ashtray; the merchant stretched out his hand, examined the cigarette-end from all sides and decided that no guests of his could have smoked that sort of cigarette; so someone had been sitting there in his study while he was away; who could that be?

He looked around: the cover on the armchair was displaced, and on the carpet there was a patch of dried mud under the chair; Fyokla Matveyevna had no reason to be there, and she wouldn't leave a patch of mud anyway. 'So visitors have taken to coming in here in my absence,' thought Yeropegin. 'Fyokla obviously knows about it, but not a word to me: no wonder she's been avoiding my eyes for a while; maybe she's found herself a lover – pah!' The very thought made Luka Silych feel sick, so that he spat, imagining the Dollop in the role of mistress.

'No, that's not it!' he decided and recalled that the Jewess had told him Sukhorukov the tinsmith and the old biddies from the home had been there in the night – what the devil! 'What do they want in my house in the middle of the night?' – Luka Silych remembered the rasping and shushing in the corners, remembered how the walls had seemed to be frowning at him for over a year now, he even came out in a sweat; 'No, I'm going to get to the bottom of this: just you wait, Fyokla Matveyevna, just you wait; I'll teach you to keep secrets from me in my own house, and throw parties without my knowledge . . .'

He rang:

'Send Fyodor in.'

Fyodor appeared, the worse for drink.

'Who was here in the house last night?'

'Couldn't say: nobody, don't think . . .'

'You've been at the alcohol again, old chap, I can tell!'

Fyodor scratched himself:

'I had a drop: I were given it . . .'

'Since you admit it, I have to tell you: you're a wretched man, if you use alcohol: it is a great evil and the man who uses alcohol is lost.'

'Quite true, I admit it – a human parasite . . .'

'Well, that was a silly thing to say: how can a parasite be human? What is a pa-ra-site? Can you work that out? . . . Off with you!'

So: evidently they get Fyodor drunk – Fyodor isn't in the plot; all right, all right, we'll sort it all out, who and how. Luka Silych sat there with flashing eyes and lips compressed, but all the while he felt sick, his temples were throbbing and the weakness overpowered him more than ever: Fyodor, the baron, acts of deception . . . Luka Silych was consumed by a dry sadness. And in the house people were getting up: the patter of feet, the clatter of crockery, the shuffling sound of Fyokla Matveyevna's slippers; they all knew by now – the master was back from Ovchinnikov.

And an inconvenient day Luka Silych had chosen to arrive back from Ovchinnikov: no one had expected him at such an early hour. The things that had been going on here! All night long with him away the Doves had been praying, and not even in the bath-house, but in the dining-room; before their prayers the Doves had had an important discussion; they'd discussed how it was time to make a temporary stop to their political talk and proclamatioms; the police were already prowling around on their tail; the leaflets with black crosses on were being handed out too openly in Likhov; any day now they could be caught; particularly since the disorders in Grachikha and Father Nikolay's rebellion all sorts of strong measures had been taken in Likhov; a squadron of soldiers had arrived; the Likhovites remembered how the Fokins and Alyokhins had been taken along Panshin Street in carts with their hands tied behind their backs – on their way to prison.

The seminarist who had been expelled from the seminary tried for a long time to defend the Likhov political platform, but Sukhorukov stood his ground; on this account an unpleasant conversation had taken place between them: about intelligence.

'I might point out I'm not a fool and I've got a great deal more political sense than many . . .'

'I'm not a fool myself: we'll see which of us is more intelligent . . .'

'What a strange way of talking you have! It's impolite, I might even say it's offensive. I've never met anyone more intelligent than me. There are some, they can be found, but rarely. I've never met one . . . I can't continue this conversation with you, I don't want to: you can talk, I shan't listen' – Sukhorukov began to sulk; but the others got them to make it up. All the same Sukhorukov insisted on having his own way, and for the time being the Doves made an end of politics.

Amidst the murmurings of the old women from the home the Dollop read out a missive from Kudeyarov the carpenter, which told that the Dove-child, in human form, was coming into being from two human spiritual natures; the Doves were passing it on to one another that in the Tselebeyevo district there was an entire Dove movement going on and that everywhere round there Doves were given shelter and attention.

Fyokla Matveyevna had received that missive on the morning before the meeting through Abram the beggar, and she at once decided to make a trip next day to Tselebeyevo, to see those places for herself, on the pretext of going to the country and checking on the mill; all that time, in the absence of her husband, Fyokla Matveyevna had spent her days and nights in prayer, so that she had grown a little feeble and begun to droop; but her eyes had thereby become even more pure and luminous: the eyes of an angel in the face of a pug-dog.

Only the master had turned up at a really inopportune time; she had intended to slip off in his absence, and then later, when he came back, she could always find some pretext for having been away; but now how could she tell him she was going? But Fyodor was already cleaning the horse's harness: it was too late to put it off.

It was with such thoughts that she met her better half: drily they put their fingers into each other's palm; he looked – and saw before him a hideous, deceitful dollop; and he thought:

'Very well, very well! You drop your eyes – I know why you turn your gaze away: you've started having secrets here while I'm away.'

She looked – and, Lord above – before her was Kashchey the Deathless; pale, emaciated, bathed in sweat, with hands that twitched and rings beneath his eyes.

Her heart in her mouth, the Dollop told her husband that she would like to breathe the fragrant country air for a day or two, and, by the way, pay a visit to the Tselebeyevo priest's wife, and have a look at the mill – the mistress's eye wouldn't do any harm.

'Oh, no, my girl, I'm not letting you off so easily,' went through Yeropegin's mind, but he thought better of it: in the first place, with her away he could better conduct inquiries as to who these visitors were who traipsed around his house at night; and secondly, in the mistress's absence it was more convenient to do a bit of spooning with Annushka.

'All right, go on then . . .'

'I'll take Dovecote Annushka along with me . . .'

'You're not taking Anka!' Luka Silych hissed at her. 'Without Anka the house will get into a mess; it's Anka here, Anka there . . . She'll never manage to get everything done . . .'

The troika was brought up to the house; in got the laced-up Dollop with trussed cushions, blankets, little tubs of this and that; the carriage trundled off.

No sooner was the house empty than Luka Silych started marching round that empty house – sniffing at everything, turning everything over, rummaging in all the drawers; he made his way into Fyokla Matveyevna's room – and what should he see: the keys to the trunk, left behind under her pillow, and her rolled-up needlework; he started to examine it: strange needlework: crosses all over the place, and in the middle of those crosses a silver dove with an aura around its head: 'Ts-ts-ts!' – Luka Silych spread his hands; he snaffled up the needlework and carried it off to his study: he locked the door and came back: he picked up the keys, crawled under the bed; under the bed was an iron-bound trunk; he pulled the trunk out; opened the lid; 'Ts-ts-ts-ts, proclamations! Ought to tell the constable . . .' That is what Luka Silych thought, and squatted down over the trunk: Luka Silych started tugging various objects out of it: vessels, floor-length vestments, a huge piece of light-blue silk with a human heart sewn onto it in red velvet and a tiny, white dove pecking at that heart (the dove in that handiwork had been given the beak of a hawk); he pulled out two tin lamps, a chalice, a red silk cloth, a communion spoon and spear; one thing after another, Luka Silych pulled all the equipment out of the trunk, and started picking it over – white, frail and prehensile in his long-tailed black frockcoat, he floundered in the silks and vestments, like a spider in its web.

'Aaa! Aaa!' he managed just to utter, and he left the room even in some fear; all he could do was stand against the wall in the dark corridor – he felt weak: the sweat was pouring from him, his breathing was constricted, he couldn't tell why: he sensed that something criminal was going on.

Dovecote Annushka was pattering along the corridor; her plaits were bobbing on her supple back; she was grinning to herself and didn't notice Yeropegin, pressed against the wall; he grabbed her by the skirt. 'Oh, what a fright you gave me!' the housekeeper chuckled, pushing him away with her bare foot: she evidently thought the master was having a joke: nothing of the sort! How Luka Silych dragged her into the Dollop's room, and thrust her face down into the 'objects': and they wrestled with each other amongst the vessels, silks and vestments: 'What's this? What's this?' The master, himself apparently afraid, squeezed her down among the vessels and vestments.

'It's . . . It's . . .' – she paled and said no more.

'Speak up!'

Wham – he slapped her in the face.

'Speak up!'

'Shan't tell!' – she turned even paler.

Wham, wham – the blows rang out.

Suddenly, with a deft manoeuvre, she broke free and ran away, and how she burst out laughing, brazenly: that was the way she laughed when the old man made up to her at night.

'What are you hitting me for? You don't know yourself why you're doing it. Can't you see, this is all the mistress's secret, and if I'm to tell you about it, then I've got to do it all properly: just you wait till this evening.' She winked at him. 'I'll tell you all about it; I'll do what you like: we'll set all these objects out in order, we'll drink wine from the goblets, and make love; I'll try really hard for you!' Then she bent over to him and, laughing, whispered something that made the old man beam all over.

Ding-ding-ding – just then the bell rang for the umpteenth time; they had to go and open it: they locked the room; it turned out to be an untimely visitor on grain business; willy-nilly Luka Silych had to closet himself with him.

And in the orchard Dovecote Annushka was whispering with Sukhorukov the tinsmith:

'We can't leave things like this, Anna Kuzminishna, no way can we do that; from this time on, if we leave things alone, we're all kaput . . .'

'Oh!'

'However much you oh and ah, we'll have to settle his hash . . .'

'Oh, no, I can't!'

'You'll have to trust my political good sense: I've never met anyone more intelligent than me . . .'

Silence.

'There's no way out, you put it in his drink.'

'I can't do that . . .'

'No, no, you put it in: I say again, I've never met anyone more political than me . . .'

Silence.

'That's it, then, is it?'

'Drink, my love, my one and only, this sweet wine.'

The sound of a kiss: again and again . . .

'Annushka, my Annushka, with your wonderful white breasts!'

The sound of a kiss: again.

'Here, my joy, here's some sweet wine for you; have some more . . . some more . . . more . . .'

The sound of a kiss: again, and again.

The old man was in nothing but his undershirt, showing his hairy, desiccated legs; on his knees was Annushka of the white breasts; on the table – sky-blue satin, flowers, communion bread, chalice; two lamps were burning at either side; the doors were locked, the blinds lowered. Ivan's rattle was clamouring madly in the distance.

'My one and only, have some more of the sweet wine: O Lord!'

'What's the matter with you?'

'A twinge in my heart; it's nothing; drink . . .'

'So my Dollop spends her nights praying in nothing but her underwear, you say? Ha-ha-ha! . . .'

'Hee-hee!' – Annushka hid her deathly pale face in his hairy chest.

'Doves they're called?'

'Doves, my love . . .'

'Ha-ha-ha!..'

'Hee-hee!' – Something between a laugh and a scream resounded on his hairy chest.

'Why are you trembling all over like that?'

'It's jabbing at my heart . . .'

She raised the chalice and held it to his now inanely drooping lips.

The rattle jabbered madly under the windows; out into the darkness.

It's right: it's wrong

The great golden sun with its great golden rays washes the dry meadow, which is turning slightly brown in the sun, the grass is roasting in the rays of the great, great sun; here a flower sways on its thin, dry stalk; there a grove of white-trunked birches summons you, and amidst the white trunks are mosses, stumps, leaves; and if you give the leaves a dig here and there, the cap of a mushroom will peep out at you; an old birch boletus will be simply begging to be popped into your lime-bark basket; the sweet autumnal twittering of the blue-tit – do you hear it? It's still July: but all of nature looks at you, and smiles at you, and whispers in its birch whisper: 'Wait for August . . .' August floats along in the noise and rustle of time: can you hear – the noise of time? Already August sends the squirrel up into the nut-tree; and the month of August soars in the lofty sky in triangles of cranes; listen, oh, listen, to the familiar farewell voice of passing summer!

Among the luxuriant flowers and birch stumps, Fyokla Matveyevna was standing in quiet bliss: her hands were folded tranquilly on her stomach; the sun was playing on her chocolate-coloured dress, her half-veil, her hat of enormous dimensions with its bunch of cherries; like the goddess Pomona Fyokla Matveyevna paraded, deeply moved, among the beneficent gifts of summer; her heart was filled with the spirit: fragrances tickled her nose; she wilted and swooned from a sweet, sweet sneezing, and Father Vukol, striding along behind her in his linen cassock, after each sneeze of hers proclaimed:

'God bless you, Fyokla Matveyevna!'

Whereupon Fyokla Matveyevna bashfully responded:

'Thank you, Father Vukol: you are a fine man.'

But other thoughts were passing through her mind: that these were fragrant parts, a land of plenty, holy places, spiritual; that here, just here and now, the joy of all Russia was being born: the Holy Spirit. Keenly the merchant's wife peeped out from behind the bushes, the hummocks, the ditches – hoping to catch sight of God's grace.

Here she was in these holy, healing parts – in Tselebeyevo; beneath her feet a stream plashed in a noisy torrent; as Fyokla Matveyevna set foot on the plank that was laid across the stream, the stream became troubled and gave a hiss with its water; the water splashed and spluttered – and made Fyokla Matveyevna's feet wet.

'Be careful, be careful now, dear lady, the plank here isn't firm: you'll lose your footing if you don't take care!' – the priest fussed about behind her. He could bear it no more, and, hoisting up his cassock, jumped the stream, his red beard bobbing up and down, and with a little laugh held out his hand to the merchant's wife: Fyokla Matveyevna laughed.

But over there, over there, beyond the stream: a narrow cutting through the birch-trees ran off into the distance; white logs lay in piles, illuminated by the sun's brocade: and in that gold brocade a white dove hovered, flapped its wings, and cooed: it settled on a woodpile and ran along the logs:

on the dry bark its claws went – tsa, tsa, tsa!

'Our parts here, Fyokla Matveyevna ma'am,' the little priest smiled, wiping his sweaty face with a red handkerchief: 'they're truly a land of God's grace!'

Of course they were: Fyokla Matveyevna remembered her journey to Tselebeyevo the day before, how she had prayed all the way; and how her heart had pounded; as soon as they came close to the holy place, every tree-stump by the road took on the image and likeness of a demon; all the way there the wind had whistled at Fyokla Matveyevna and driven dry dust all over her, and out of that dust – stumps, bushes, boughs had pulled ugly, malevolent faces at her in the sun, like demons, trying to chase her back to Likhov; it was only then that Fyokla Matveyevna had realized how many demons threaten man's nature: invisible to the eye, they hover above us; only prayer, fasting and the hope of grace, in refining the flesh, can confer on bodily vision the vision of the spirit; and in that spiritual vision every material object becomes the image and likeness of things invisible; Fyokla Matveyevna had come to understand all that the day before, approaching Tselebeyevo from Likhov; the whole way, right to the village, she had been surrounded by horrible demons; it was as though a barrier of enemies had been erected round the holy places: each stump she passed turned into a demon: as many devils entered Fyokla Matveyevna's soul on that journey as arose in the sun in the image and likeness of stumps by the wayside; but she had prayed tirelessly – and here Fyokla Matveyevna was in Tsele-beyevo.

Here everything was different: sitting at the priest's wife's table by the samovar she already noticed strange occurrences: the bushes, the huts, the tin cockerel on the roof, were staring her in the eyes and seemed to say to her with pensive sweetness:

'Look at me; I am guarding a secret.' The village, the pond, the rooftop that peeped from the sloping hollow – everything was guarding the secret of these parts; even the priest himself seemed to be a resident of another, better world.

In the evening they stood on the Tselebeyevo meadow: the round-dance began to twist and turn around the meadow, feet tapped out all manner of steps, a wave ran through the grass, and the evening wind hallooed, the tousled dust sprang up on the road, and the big yellow moon rose over Tse-lebeyevo; it looked into Fyokla Matveyevna's soul and said: 'Watch, be silent and conceal . . .'

That night Fyokla Matveyevna was granted a dream vision: the carpen-ter came to stand at the head of her bed; stretching over her his pale hand, he forbade her to speak of him or see him; wordlessly the carpenter spoke to her with his eyes: 'I,' he said, 'am now in a great secret, and you mustn't see me or hear me or think of me now in these parts.'

In the morning Fyokla Matveyevna, woken from her dream vision, changed her mind; she was not yet ready to visit Kudeyarov at his abode: for that abode was now the holy of holies; and it was not accessible to the eyes of the profane . . .

Such were Fyokla Matveyevna's thoughts as she and the priest surveyed these holy places: and what places they were! Over there the blue pond gleamed, and the noisy torrents running down to it seemed to be made of mica, over there a tree dangled its fading foliage and in that foliage was the sweet autumnal twittering of the blue-tit; a golden ray fell onto her breast, and in that golden ray there fell onto her breast a hot and powerful current and, it seemed, the command of an invisible power: 'Everything that happens from now on is good: it's right.'

'That's right,' the priest too confirmed; but it was something else he was confirming to her; the little priest was standing in front of a puddle and showing Fyokla Matveyevna how the puddle was to be crossed: but Fyokla Matveyevna, blooming with the smile of an angel, flashed her eyes sweetly and tenderly at the priest: 'That's right, that's right,' and trod in the mud.

The priest was thinking: 'What a nuisance this daft woman is, she does nothing but smile all the time, and what's she smiling at?'

And the great golden sun washed the dry grass with its great rays; and the month of August soared in the lofty sky in triangles of cranes; and listen – to the familiar farewell voice of passing summer.

They had hardly sat down at the samovar in the priest's blackcurrant patch, and the priest's wife, bowing humbly, had hardly set out in front of the Dollop boiled sweets and golden honey, above which striped wasps circled, while the samovar, cleaned with a brick, distorted the face of the merchant's wife in its bronze gleam, when a special messenger hastened up and tied his horse by the priest's garden; he ran quickly up to the table and handed over a note; the note informed Fyokla Matveyevna that her husband, Luka Silych, had fallen ill in the night, and had now lost the use of his tongue, his arms and his legs.

A strange business: Fyokla Matveyevna read the note, and in her soul there sounded an imperious command: 'Everything that happens from now on is good: it's right.'

And Fyokla Matveyevna nearly said out loud: 'That's right' . . . Her heart told her to weep and be horrified, but Fyokla Matveyevna went on rejoicing, taking the news as a dream that had long since left her . . .

And now the horses were carrying her to Likhov, back where she had come from; all those stumps and bushes that had threatened her so

recently, rocked by the nocturnal breeze, were singing a new song of unutterable joy; in the faint whistle of the branches could be heard: 'That's
right' . . . And when the horses reared up over Myortvyi Verkh – from
Myortvyi Verkh the whole neighbourhood opened out; and there was such
peace all round that it seemed the world's grief had left its earthly
dwelling-place forever, and that the earthly dwelling-place was exulting in
its triumphant gleam.

In Yeropegin's house it was empty, terrifying: in its dark chambers sin was
on the wing; it seemed that from every corner the spirit of Luka Silych
strained and complained: Luka Silych was flying about in the empty
rooms, as though in an empty, senseless, aimless world, and there was no
escape for him from his house, for he had built his house himself; and that
house had become his world; and there was no escape . . .

There, there in the bedroom lay something pale and pitiful and speechless: but that was not Luka Silych; what could it be? No doubt you'd find
dry skin and a grey beard; all that was solicitously wrapped in sheets; and
leaning over it was an old woman from the home; she quietly sucked her
lips over *all that*: but *all that* was not Luka Silych; it gazed vainly at the
world with senseless eyes, it tried in vain to move its tongue, tried in vain
to remember – it could not remember; Luka Silych had already detached
himself from *all that*; invisible, he was beating at the windows, but the windows were shut tight with shutters, and Luka Silych, incorporeal, immortal, could not, however, pass through wood, and with his physical soul
hammered idly against the walls and rustled the wallpaper the way cockroaches rustle the wallpaper; bereft of voice, Luka Silych cried out that
they had poisoned him, that afterwards they had solicitously wrapped him
up in sheets; that in *all this* it was not blood that was coursing, but poison;
in vain he begged the general, who had chanced to drop in, to expose the
villainy; the general couldn't hear him; he and the doctor bent over the
little grey beard.

'A terrible occurrenth, doctor!'

'It was to be expected: it's a stroke – you can't go on living it up with
impunity . . .'

'Not true, not true!' – Luka Silych hurled himself upon them. 'What's
going on here is murder: they've poisoned me – I want revenge,
revenge . . .'

But the voice was speechless, the soul invisible; and the doctor and the
general bent over the grey beard; the grey beard was no longer Luka
Silych.

No – where was it? Luka Silych could no longer see the grey beard sticking out from under the sheets; to right and left he saw the corners of the pillows; the doctor was bending over him, feeling his head; but where was Luka Silych? Or was it all just a dream, and he had not been flying about the rooms; or had he now returned into his body? What had happened to him?

A circle of light approached; with a candle in her hand, pale as death, Annushka stood there; Luka Silych came round from his delirium: now he remembered everything, but he could not express anything; he knew he had been poisoned, and that a terrible secret was at work in his house; he looked imploringly at the doctor; he could feel the tears pouring from his eyes.

'Does he understand?'

'But he can't say anything.'

'Won't he ever say anything again?'

'Never . . .'

'Won't he ever move?'

'Never . . .'

These words were exchanged with the doctor in a whisper: but Luka Silych's hearing had become sharper; he could hear both what they were saying about him and what Sukhorukov and Ivan the Fire were whispering in the kitchen, and a cockroach crawling on the wall of a distant room.

He heard everything, but he said nothing: he had been poisoned.

Now Fyokla Matveyevna was standing over him in her chocolate-coloured dress, drenched in the sweet fragrance of the fields, but her eyes were veiled; she had not yet taken her hat off; was she weeping there under her veil, or smiling? Luka Silych moved his lips in her direction, stretched towards her: 'They've poisoned me, they've poisoned me . . .' But she did not hear; she smiled: nothing could be made out under the veil . . . As Fyokla Matveyevna looked at her husband she saw that it wasn't her husband any more, it wasn't the master, but just *something*, wrapped in sheets; she wanted to weep over her husband and grieve; but there was no grief, just *something*: in her soul the blue pond gleamed, and the noisy torrents running down to it seemed to be made of mica; over there a tree dangled its fading foliage, and in the foliage was the sweet autumnal twittering of blue-tits; it was not grief in Fyokla Matveyevna's soul, but recollection, and the sweet autumnal twittering of blue-tits, and she caught within herself the sound of an imperious command: 'Everything that happens from now on is good: it's right . . .'

'It's not right, it's wrong,' something attempted to shout out of Luka Silych, 'You should be weeping for me, not laughing . . .'

But Fyokla Matveyevna wasn't laughing; tears were pouring from her eyes, and yet . . . in her soul a golden ray arose, and in that ray a white dove hovered, flapped its wings and cooed.

'It's wrong!'

'It's right!'

It was empty and oppressive and terrifying in Yeropegin's house: in the dark corners a rustling was beginning. Luka Silych began flying round the rooms again.

Pavel Pavlovich

Above a high precipice, into which the pine-trees tumbled, Katya sat, and in front of her, above the tree-clad distance, lay the cold, angry fire of evening; a grey plaid covered Katya's shoulders; her childlike shoulders trembled slightly from the touch of the damp; here yesterday, poor child, she had all but thrown herself into the pond; here yesterday, poor child, she had forgiven Pyotr; here yesterday she had stretched out to him her slender arms – above the tree-clad distance, into the cold, angry fire of evening.

But the thought of her grandmama had stopped her.

And Katya took control of herself; she even laid out a game of patience, as always; and she and her grandma played *durachki* together – the old woman and the child; and they smiled at each other; and then towards evening Uncle Pavel Pavlovich arrived – he had been delayed a day in Likhov.

Her uncle had turned grey, but he remained the same as Katya had seen him two years before; clean-shaven, neat and tidy, smelling of eau-de-Cologne, he kissed the old lady's fingers with a slightly offhand gentleness and then, in the evening, sipping cream, he told them about Petersburg and his foreign travels in a lachrymose, despondently plaintive voice; and Yevseich, glued to the wall, listened with staring eyes to the stories of the newly arrived master; Pavel Pavlovich's manservant, Strigachov, dressed no worse than the baron himself, mixed casually with the gentlefolk, and when Pavel Pavlovich confused the events he was narrating, inserted his own corrections without embarrassment:

'If I may, Pavel Pavlovich, it wasn't like that: we arrived in Nice not on Thursday, but on Friday morning; on arrival you were pleased to take a bath, and after that we . . .'

'Perfectly true, my friend . . .' Pavel Pavlovich agreed, continuing his story.

So the three of them sat on the terrace: Katya took a melancholy pleasure in her uncle's arrival; her uncle, meanwhile, loudly blowing his nose, talked to her grandmama:

'Maman, it's a storm in a teacup: I thought you were on the verge of ruin, which would, by the way, have been very much in the natural order of things. But it turns out to be nothing more than blackmail; no one can ever have the right to deprive you of the estate; as far as the shares in the Varaksin mines are concerned, we'll have another little talk with Mr Yeropegin: I don't think he's as dangerous as he wants to appear.'

(His meeting in the train Pavel Pavlovich kept secret for some reason.)

Above the high precipice, into which the pine-trees tumbled, Pavel Pavlovich Todrabe-Graaben sat down; beside him on a bench sat Katya; and in front of them, above the tree-clad distance, lay the cold, angry fire of evening; there in the distance the first aspen was already turning crimson; it had been a hot summer: the red and golden season of autumn was approaching.

So they sat, uncle and niece, thinking their own thoughts. Katya was thinking that as soon as her grandmama died she, poor child, would go into a nunnery; and the long-nosed senator, her uncle, smiled sadly at Katya's youth, suppressing an involuntary sigh in his soul:

'You're young, Katenka, and don't know life: time will have its way.'

'Why did he leave me, uncle?'

'I can't explain it to you, my dear: you're young, and I sincerely wish you happiness: the fact that he's not with you any more raises him in my eyes.'

'? . . .'

'It proves that he sought your hand out of genuine attachment, and not on account of your wealth. After all, he's a poet, isn't he?'

'Yes, he's a poet . . .'

'That's to say, a member of the aesthetic riff-raff . . .'

Oh, how Katya flared up! How her brows arched, what a glance she cast at him! But her uncle's beardless face turned sad and humble:

'My dear child, I didn't mean to hurt you: I have to tell you that all people are divided into parasites and slaves; the parasites in their turn are divided into sorcerers or magicians, murderers and riff-raff; the magicians are those who invented God and use this invention to extort money; the murderers are the military caste of the whole world; the riff-raff are divided into simply riff-raff, that's to say people of substance, learned riff-raff, that is, professors, lawyers, doctors, and members of the free professions, and aesthetic riff-raff: to this last belong poets, writers, artists and prostitutes . . . I've finished, my dear' – her uncle the senator sighed plaintively as he sniffed a flower.

It was growing dark: they sat at the edge of the precipice; low, black, cold clouds scurried by.

In the distance, on a garden path, amongst branches, shadows, bats that fluttered up into the shadows, the baroness passed lifelessly, leaning on her stick: her dull, leaden eyes and her drooping mouth – all told that the old lady was collapsing, falling apart, that her days had long been numbered, and that the darkness of eternal night that clung already to her eyes was watching its reflection in her soul, and calling.

The three together walked towards the house: the uncle supported the grandmother, Katya walked in front and aimlessly chewed a grass-stalk.

The mother whispered to her ageing son:

'That wastrel robbed me into the bargain; on the day he left the house my jewels disappeared.'

'Oh, stop it, mamma: he's an eccentric, and eccentrics, as is well known, don't go in for robbery.'

'But . . . the jewels . . .'

'Who else was here on that day?'

'I don't think there was anyone . . . No, wait: that was the day that Yeropegin came . . .'

'On his own?'

'No, with General Chizhikov!'

'Well, there you are then, mamma, the things you say: it was General Chizhikov who stole the jewels.'

So Pavel Pavlovich whispered to his trembling mother, blowing his nose into the dense darkness that dropped down from the sky . . .

Baron Pavel Pavlovich Todrabe-Graaben was a great eccentric: but all the barons Todrabe-Graaben were distinguished by their eccentricity, all of them from time immemorial had shaved and gone about with long pink noses, which towards the age of sixty became covered in fine scarlet veins from the moderate use of the rarest and finest wines, which were still to be found in their grandfathers' cellars; they all had upper lips which protruded under their very noses; in all of them the chin was missing, so that the lower part of the face seemed grotesquely small in comparison with the protruding eyes that never looked women in the face, the huge noses and the sloping foreheads of immense dimensions; there would, perhaps, have been something sorry and crowlike about them all, if it hadn't been for their pale-chestnut, unusually well washed and silken hair; all the barons Todrabe-Graaben seemed to be weeping, rather than talking, if you did not listen carefully to their words, but the content of that brittle lamentation was invariably humorous.

The baronesses wept too; and the baronesses had foreheads and noses just like the male line; but the baronesses had chins as well; on the other hand many of the baronesses were as stupid as empty, jingling bottles, went about in lace and from an early age left Russia for Nice and Monte Carlo.

Pavel Pavlovich's father – Pavel Pavlovich – like all the Graabens was a great eccentric; he became so obsessed with cleanliness that he introduced a strange custom in his house; he would touch a towel or a handkerchief only once; when he had a cold, then, on feeling the need for a handkerchief, he would clap his hands three times; the door flew open and two serf page-boys ran in, each holding with two fingers the corner of a completely clean handkerchief; Pavel Pavlovich would grasp the middle of the handkerchief and loudly blow his nose (all the Graabens blew their noses extraordinarily loudly); the page-boys instantly rushed out of the room with the handkerchief; and if the need for a handkerchief arose every minute, then every minute the page-boys would run in: an infinite quantity of handkerchieves was carried in and out.

Pavel Pavlovich was moreover a musician; he was wont to play Beethoven symphonies on the cello and make his son accompany him; at the slightest mistake the symphony was recommenced from the beginning, even if ten pages had already been played through; so it went on interminably; and that was why Pavel Pavlovich the father was unable to play a single passage through to the end; his son, however, came to hate music from an early age. People ran in all directions from the music-making of Pavel Pavlovich the father, but he seated himself to play on the threshold between the two rooms others passed through most often; once he locked a friend of his in and played to him for many hours without a break, until his friend fell in a faint. Shortly after that episode Pavel Pavlovich the father died.

Pavel Pavlovich's uncle, Aleksandr Pavlovich, was an even greater eccentric; already as a young man he had consumed three-quarters of his fortune and drunk the cellar dry that had been left him by his ancestors; by the age of forty he removed to his hereditary estate, where he spent five years careering round the district, cracking jokes nineteen to the dozen; after that he spent five years without leaving his estate, driving round the arable fields and cracking jokes with the bailiff; it was then that he developed the quirk of wearing, in both winter and summer, a sable coat and a fur hat; the following five years Aleksandr Pavlovich did not leave the park: there he planted fruit trees and snared birds; every year after that he shortened his walks around the park, so that by the age of sixty he found himself restricted to the terrace, from where he fed the pigeons with crumbs; then Aleksandr Pavlovich shut himself into three rooms of the mansion, and finally spent his last three years without leaving the bedroom, where the serf-girl Sashka was brought to him and he stroked her shoulder with uncommon tenderness, but that was all: honestly, nothing more! Sashka, however, gave birth annually to babies from passing lads; what was most astonishing was that Aleksandr Pavlovich was firmly convinced that these children were his; to Sashka's children was bequeathed the richest of Aleksandr Pavlovich's estates.

Pavel Pavlovich's other uncle, Varavva Pavlovich, was a greater eccentric still; just like all the other Graabens he was disinguished by wit, honesty, and an especial striving for cleanliness: and this striving was expressed in so unlikely a peculiarity (only in one) that I'm ashamed to tell of it, and anyway you won't believe me: when he was living in the provinces and setting off on a visit, he would travel in a carriage with six horses; in front he would send another carriage, drawn by a team of four; two pages stood on the rear footboard, and on the leading horse rode a footman brandishing a whip: but what did Varavva Pavlovich take with him in that leading carriage? Well . . . I really can't say it, in case . . . a certain 'object', whose purpose I am ashamed to define more precisely; the front carriage would drive up; the two pages would rush to open the doors and the wrapped up 'object' would be ceremoniously carried into a specially prepared room; then Varavva Pavlovich drove up to the house himself; and only then did the hosts appear to welcome him on the threshold and take his arm to lead the old gentleman to the drawing-room. The striving for cleanliness also disfigured the life of Pavel Pavlovich's aunt, Baroness Agnia Pavlovna; in her old age she washed everything that came to hand, and disdained the use of towels: she dried her hands by waving them in the air, as a result of which her hands were always covered in hard scales. Finally, one morning she washed with her own hands a dark brown fox-fur coat of vast proportions, from which a little spot broke out on her finger; the spot turned out to be anthrax, from which the old lady duly died.

Such was the family of eccentrics in which Pavel Pavlovich Todrabe-Graaben, the baron, grew up with his sister Natalya, who was set apart from the rest of the female line by her beauty and intelligence; at the time when their mother left her husband for a hussar, Pavel Pavlovich became deeply attached to his sister; this attachment later developed into a more tender feeling; at that time Pavel Pavlovich entered the Faculty of Jurisprudence; he was a young man of refinement and wore a tricorn hat; his sister, however, married a nobleman called Gugolev; the news of her marriage so shook Pavel Pavlovich that he decided to marry too, as soon as he finished the course, and so he did; in his choice of wife Pavel Pavlovich was guided by two considerations; in the first place his wife had at all times to remain silent; secondly, her hair had to be as fine as flax; Pavel Pavlovich married his wife's silence and her hair.

The baron soon gained swift advancement in the service on account of his intelligence, his eloquence, and his ability to unravel the most delicate legal matters with perfect honesty; moreover, at that time he was a moderate liberal; and somehow imperceptibly he served his way up to the white trousers of a senator, but then suddenly he abandoned all professional activity; by that time he had undergone a transformation: Pavel Pavlovich had become a fervent disciple of Proudhon; in the salons of Petersburg he was feared for his merciless wit; in the Senate his foibles were treated with forbearance, but he was given to understand that he had no further professional role to play, to which he responded with indifference, and repaired to his grandfather's estate; he used to appear in Petersburg for three-month sojourns, so as not to lose his friends from view.

In the country the eccentricities of the Graabens rose swiftly and vividly to the surface: the cellar was laid waste, the money was consumed; the library grew at a monstrous rate; while remaining a serious person, Pavel Pavlovich found time for all manner of whims: first he festooned the house with antique porcelain; on tables, dressers, shelves there appeared noseless, headless and armless figurines, cups with their handles missing, angular lamps and other miscellaneous junk; then Pavel Pavlovich travelled the length and breadth of Europe in search of some quite worthless engraving; after that Pavel Pavlovich sent for half a dozen bicycles; he mounted one bicycle himself, and sat his wife, his manservant, the nurse and his very small son on others; after six months he gave all the bicycles away and started on the domestic education of his children; he sent for a French governess, a German governess, an English governess, and a negro; he studied treatises on education; finally Pavel Pavlovich settled on the system of Jean-Jacques Rousseau: books were taken away from the child; the Englishwoman, the Frenchwoman, the German woman and the negro were despatched from whence they had come; and the fair-haired lad swung in the trees in imitation of the apes; then Pavel Pavlovich became calm and surrendered himself entirely to his books: in his library could be found absolutely everything that bibliophiles sought in vain; on the other hand the most essential books were missing; rare books he bound in moiré bindings of delicate blue, pale-pink and other pastel shades; only to close friends did Pavel Pavlovich allow access to his library; but woebetide that friend who in his ignorance made even a faintly discernible mark upon a page; the damaged book could not remain in the library, and with skilfully concealed contempt was given to the person who had spoilt it; close friends trembled at the prospect of receiving the gift of a book from Pavel Pavlovich: it could only mean that they had forever fallen in his esteem.

In the country Pavel Pavlovich rose at cock-crow; for three hours, while the rest of the house still slept, his manservant Strigachov rubbed him and doused him with water according to a custom he had established in perpetuity, after which Pavel Pavlovich retired to his study and wrote – what he wrote remained a secret from all: most likely it was some unlikely treatise, in which new revelations on anthropology, philosophy, history and the social sciences were proffered to mankind; it was also said that it was just drivel, but Pavel Pavlovich was not deterred, and sometimes entered into correspondence with scholars; true, it was more about the niceties of bibliography than those of science that he corresponded – but correspond he did.

Before lunch Pavel Pavlovich ran through the newspapers and cut the journals; later, before dinner, brisk and athletic, with a towel over his shoulders and a tea-rose in his hand, he ran through the park to the swimming-pond.

Pavel Pavlovich treated the members of his household with humility; it was contrary to his principles to lay down the law; and Pavel Pavlovich allowed everyone complete freedom of action; but this freedom was worse than constraint; without watching anyone, he saw everything; and since his notions of cleanliness were unbearable to anyone else, deviations from those notions provoked his instant flight from the house, to the horror of the household and for an utterly indeterminate period; the whole house trembled and stood on tiptoes when his voice resounded even in the distance, lachrymose and sorrowfully humble; one day, for instance, passing through the house, he noticed a number of cigarette-butts stuck into a plant-pot; this shook him so that he could only cast a sad glance, full of reproach, at all his household and depart quickly to his study; two hours later Strigachov carried out the baron's suitcases, and two weeks later his inconsolable wife received the news that Pavel Pavlovich was safe and well, and sailing to the island of Madeira aboard the packet-boat *Victoria*.

In Petersburg the baron's friends looked forward to his visits; in his absence they felt indignant, calling him an eccentric – and worse: a harmful man, an anarchist; but on his appearance the salon doors were flung hospitably open to receive that 'eccentric'; and Pavel Pavlovich, presiding on a plush ottoman with a glass of cream in his hand (the baron refrained from drinking tea), spoke much and long about the fate of Russia, about the Mongol invasion, about the harmfulness of Christianity, its contribution to the spread of alcoholic beverages, and about the political order of the future. He spoke sadly and slowly, closing his eyes, spoke with disarming conviction, but said such strange things that a circle gathered around him; afterwards this circle commented ironically on Pavel Pavlovich's views. But while Pavel Pavlovich was talking, no one contradicted him;

indeed, it was hard to contradict him; the baron's logical premises seemed absurd in the extreme; but he defended and developed them with iron logic, brilliantly, almost with inspiration: he had a number of favourite themes, but his variations on these themes were multifarious and frequent; any conversation, as soon as Pavel Pavlovich took part in it, seemed quite to lose all independent meaning and become a canvas on which the baron would embroider his themes.

And so the remorseless Pavel Pavlovich sharpened his wit in the salons of St Petersburg; all this time he made the rounds of bookshops and accumulated books; there were occasions when Pavel Pavlovich remembered his practice as a lawyer (and he was, indeed, a remarkable lawyer – cool, well-balanced, firm); then, in passing, he would unravel some nefarious business or other; and having proved the villains guilty, would depart for the country.

When he learned that villains and rogues were threatening his mother, Pavel Pavlovich set out for Gugolevo; he made a preliminary request for certain of the documents, made some inquiries in writing and hastily set out to expose this vulgar villainy; his conversation with Yeropegin calmed the baron: he realized that the merchant represented no further threat.

However, it was not only out of concern for his mother's fortune that Pavel Pavlovich had made his swift departure for Gugolevo; more than by the thought of his mother he was troubled by the thought of his niece Katenka, who reminded him of his own untimely and extinguished love – for his sister; Katenka occupied Pavel Pavlovich's thoughts very much indeed; for her he nourished a particularly tender feeling, perhaps too tender for a relative; but as a decent man he built nothing upon this feeling; all the same, the thought that his niece was engaged to a bumpkin, and, it was said, an eccentric, disturbed him; however, that her fiancé was a bumpkin worried Pavel Pavlovich only emotionally, not in principle: in principle Pavel Pavlovich was a democrat; the fact that this bumpkin was an eccentric and a poet rather reconciled him to the marriage than the contrary (as is well known, eccentrics have a certain respect and mutual understanding for one another). Now that he had learnt about that 'bumpkin's' flight from the Gugolevo estate, and his passion for some peasant woman, a sectarian, and about the baroness's humiliating suspicions of Katya's fiancé, Baron Pavel Pavlovich Todraabe-Graaben had, for reasons known only to himself, suddenly formed the conclusion that that 'bumpkin' was a decent man, entirely suitable for Katya.

Katya: how she had occupied the baron's thoughts this last year! He had suddenly started a languorous and melancholy correspondence with her; he wrote her gloomy letters over the signature 'Uncle'; he tried to guide her reading from a distance; he wrote to her on azure-tinted paper that he kept in a special pouch, and he applied to the sealing-wax an antique seal depicting two trees, with a quatrain engraved upon it:

> Two trees divided by a brook
> May grow with boughs entwined;
> Two hearts that fate asunder holds
> Share thoughts as of one mind . . .

In recent years Pavel Pavlovich had become thinner and greyer; his nose had grown ever more pointed, as had his judgements, sharpened beyond endurance; he shone with the gloomy brilliance of his wit like the blade of a finely honed dagger; but he exercised his wit in solitude; young people were drawn to him most of all; but young people Pavel Pavlovich drove away; old people ran away from him of their own accord. Pavel Pavlovich's redundant wit, straddling two epochs, lit with its solitary light the remainder of the path he was destined to traverse in this world.

It is understandable that the ageing gentleman clung to Katya's friendship; it is understandable that, abandoning his own affairs, he appeared in our parts; and now, in the darkness, to the accompanying gurgles of the senescent baroness, Pavel Pavlovich cast melancholy glances at Katya: in his mind a plan was maturing to bring Katya's fiancé back to her; how the old gentleman proposed to execute the plan remained an enigma even to himself; but of the success of his undertaking he was entirely confident.

Such was Pavel Pavlovich.

CHAPTER SIX

The Flames of Rapture

God's servants

Mitry Mironych had paid off the hoarse and noseless workman; the carpenter's other workman, the unkempt one, was a Dove. In place of the noseless one our hero had already entered the carpenter's employment more than two weeks ago.

Daryalsky's life at the carpenter's flowed with milk and honey, and with a spot of fear; in his breast a bright light began to shine; love for Matryona burst from his breast like a torrent of fire; like a torrent of fire Matryona's glance strained to meet him; like a torrent of fire the carpenter poured his spirit over them; and both of them, bright with the light, luminous with its brilliance, were protected by the carpenter's ardent prayer; like a white-hot stove, with jaws opened wide, scorching them beyond endurance – his prayer raised them up, bore them off – where, though, did it bear them? But in the current of their days the banks of workaday life could still be seen; all three would meet of a morning, without looking at one another, without mentioning the flame that was consuming them; they would shake hands with sullen faces, melted only by nocturnal prayer or by the lightning-flashes of the night's caresses; quenched fires, they met at work, and went about their carpentry in the even glare of noonday; it was as though between the three of them, unspoken, a pact had been concluded; as though the carpenter even blessed Pyotr's love for Matryona Semyonovna, and as though in that blessing the flames of love were transmuted into flames of the Spirit. But among themselves they never spoke of this at all: a strange life it was, an eerie life; and the trees turned yellow, red, and pink; and from the pink and violet dry foliage a sound arose, the leaves drifted down, a squirrel's little red muzzle peeped out and the voice of paradise piped away, the voice of the birds; and all the while rumours flew about concerning the spiritual dalliance of these people: Father Vukol himself took to appearing beneath the carpenter's windows. Someone must have maliciously put him up to it; he even started dropping into the cottage; he would drop in on any pretext, and try to sniff things out: but off he'd go with nothing for his pains; and in the evenings Pyotr and Matryona would kiss and caress and make love in the fields and in the woods, gazing at the flame of the receding dusk and weeping for the flame; unsteady stars rocked in the indigo sky, plummeting down to this vale of tears, tumbling, burning up. So the days passed, and they passed from days to nights; from nights they passed to days.

Like this:

In the daytime, in his red shirt with sweat marks down the back, Pyotr planed planks of wood to the merry whine of saws both large and small, to the unremitting showers of sawdust that fell like snow, to the unremitting hum of flies in the carpenter's hut.

In the gentle sunlight pressing through the window a pillar of dust would swirl, bright sawdust sprinkled from the saw, like light-dust; in that bright light, in that bright dust, the worthy master's stern iconic countenance was bent over a plank; he spoke little while at work:

'Give me the spirit-level, please, squire.'

'Here it is.'

'Now we've got to get the arms of this chair level – is that right? . . .'

And he would fall silent.

Mitry Mironych at work: he would put his chisel to the wood and strike it with his hammer, which rose high above his head into the sun's brilliance, or with his bony hand he would grasp the saw and then, breathless with sweat, saw through the remnant of a plank – but everything the carpenter did acquired a special dignity, a meaning: he was able to satisfy customers of every kind; that was how he worked: and he always had work in hand; and he was paid well, very well indeed. All around was a bright heat, or a pale gleam, and over everything hung the Saviour's Countenance, blessing their loaves; beneath the Countenance a small green icon-lamp, filled with oil, sparkled, glinted, flickered; the noble labour of these dignified people could bring a lump to your throat; labour without vanity: – you might gaze on it and say: 'Lord, bless the labour of these thy servants!'

And lo, by evening six new chairs are standing by the wall, dismantled: people will sit down on those chairs with sullen thoughts, but the prayer implanted in the wood during their making will pass invisibly, in a steady flame, from the chairs into those who sit upon those completed chairs, deep in thought: all manner of people will buy those chairs: they will take them off to Moscow, to Saratov, Penza, Samara and to all the other splendid Russian cities, people will bring them there, and set them up, and sit down on them: and for a long time those folk will think, as they sit on those chairs, about the path of life, and about what that which is, is; and things will split off from their random names; and he who sits upon the chair will say: why is a chair called a 'chair' and not a 'spoon', and why am I 'Ivan' instead of 'Mary'?

So work then, workmen, on new objects: Lord, bless the labour of these thy servants!

Sometimes, amidst the tap of hammer and the hum of flies, these solemn people, bathed in sweat, would strike up their solemn songs; the unkempt workman would start them off; leaning his hammer dourly on a plank, he would begin:

> 'In my youth's still vernal hour
> I'm fading, like a tender flower,
> Lord, have mercy!'

It seemed as though some dream of yesteryear that had not come to pass had now returned to tap at the windows with its entrancing light and illuminate these servants of God, who, concealing their joy in solemnity, were crafting a new life by the sweat of their brows; something beyond description arose; a rainbow-hued veil of light fell from the veil of light: in the light everything fell away, laying bare that which was beyond description, when the carpenter joined in in his nasal voice:

> 'As soon as on the earth I trod
> I was visited by God,
> Lord, have mercy!'

And from the parlour the dulcet voice of Matryona, who was sitting there peeling potatoes, rose and fell in welcome:

> 'In God's holy walls confined,
> Kith and kin we leave behind,
> Lord, have mercy!'

And they all joined in:

> 'Lord, have mercy!'

There in the parlour Lord alone knew what was being enacted: neither the unkempt workman nor Pyotr dared to look in that direction: there, there, O Lord, Matryona Semyonovna's red skirt might be seen: there, beneath that red skirt her naked leg under the table captured any glance through the half-opened door; and that leg was severed by a ray of the light of life; the light severed their hearts; and in their breasts beat severed fragments of heart: at their carpentry they sang in muted voices:

> 'And for all eternity
> We are promised heavenly joy.
> Lord, have mercy!'

The air in the room was warmed by the light, a smell of sweat hung in the air: the solemn song welled up and died away; died away and welled up again. It was as though a new world, all their own, was being formed here, in this space of just a few square sazhens, cut off from the rest of the world by wooden walls. During the singing it began to seem to Daryalsky that the descent of the Holy Spirit was taking place in these four square sazhens; the Spirit poured from one knew not where; sounds of cracking rang out from the corners: and then a piece of wood that was laid on the table leaped up, moved by the Spirit, and rolled off into the wood-shavings. But neither he, nor the unkempt workman, nor the carpenter interrupted their work; as though none of what was happening had happened. And then a patch of light that was resting on the carpenter's breast darted off on two bright wings, and, turning pink, flew across the walls to land on Daryalsky's breast: crimson, it illumined for him his remnant of plank with its crimson light; but it was the sun's reflection; it moved quickly: the sun was sinking; it was evening.

Close by, outside the window, one of the Tselebeyevo lads was bellowing out at the top of his voice a fashionable song that someone had introduced round the village:

> 'Elephant-phant-phant –
> Trunkety-trunk;
> Trumpety-trump-trump-trump –
> Jumbo-jumbsky.'

In the evening, with work-hardened fingers, Daryalsky swept away the shavings, yellowish pink from the sunset; the unkempt workman, puffing, collected some nails and put them in his mouth; picking them from his mouth he quickly hammered them into a board; Matryona Semyonovna went by, rustling in the wood-shavings; her brow was creased in a stern frown; silly woman – why so secretive – it was evening, after all, and the stars were beginning to shine; the cool of evening spread its glistening, lambent turquoise over the distant copses, and everything grew sombre – darkness settled and the shadows multiplied – and in the opposite direction the weary sun spilled out the last of its fire: Mitry put away the planes and files and drills, dangling over them the thin bast of his beard, leaned thoughtfully upon his saw, and then shuffled quietly out of the cottage in his worn bast shoes; there he went across the meadow, and the children ran away from him; the evening grew sombre: soon all those who walk about by day with eyes that are dim will have eyes bright with longing, like blue icon-lamps filled with oil; and the words that pass between them will be hushed, and sweet as honey.

The bright light borne by morning gleams blindingly at eventide from the eyes of these servants of God, who by labour, as though by fasting, are transfiguring themselves.

A catch

A ripple of pearl ran through the moist air; and in that moist green air for over an hour Daryalsky had been a hunched patch of red; his line was far out in front of him in the water – where moist fragments of pearl were dancing on the water, to break against the bank in watery bubbles, plashing plaintively; the line stretched brightly down from the rod – the float rocked, a melancholy duck swam by – and ripples stretched behind it; fragments of pearl danced and dragon-flies above them; a mosquito that had survived from spring, Lord alone knew how, hummed at his ear; red worms wriggled in a paper-bag on the black earth by his feet; to one side the village was ruby-red from the sunset, its roofs, its windows, its beams all gleaming; in front a patch of sky was gleaming wildly, also ruby-red.

Aleksandr Nikolaevich, the sexton, who had settled himself nearby, suddenly sprang to life; his float danced, his rod swung up; and a flailing fish, sketching bright patterns with its scaly body, fell into the sexton's rough fingers, where its mouth was torn open, and – plop – into the bucket with it.

'What a catch!'

'Yes!' Pyotr responded from the moist, warm air.

'May the Lord smile on you too!' the sexton called.

'Yes, they're not biting for me.'

Silence: and in the silence the sunset faded.

'Just look at you now, Pyotr Petrovich, honest to God, if you'll forgive my bluntness: it's a funny thing you've gone and done: a real gentleman, you might say, and the good Lord didn't forget you when he was doling out the looks, and as for learning, why, you're stuffed full of it, and after all that, Lord forgive me, what's come over you: to go and be a simple work-man – and who for?! For Mitry the carpenter!'

Daryalsky's feet were hurting, his back was aching, his hands were throbbing from the work, but in his soul was joy and sweetness, bliss beyond words; he chuckled at the sexton's words; he gazed away, over the village: rhymes were forming in his head, the words were taking shape harmoniously:

> Lucently the luminous ruby
> Tumbled into fluid coolness . . .

All *u*'s and *oo*'s: what about a rhyme for 'ruby'? There was no rhyme – what the devil! But his float was dancing up and down: a big fish must have taken the worm.

'Why shouldn't I be a carpenter, Aleksandr Nikolaevich? All those books and that learning have driven me out of my mind: so I'm just doing some carpentry . . .'

'To keep fit, sort of' – the sexton grinned – 'I see what you mean; it isn't everyone that's got a head for books; there's many a one as goes quite potty from books. Take me, for instance: the minute I open a book my mind gets all full of garbage and gobbledegook.'

'It's a lousy business, studying!'

'Ha-ha: balderdash!'

Vzz-vzz-vzz – a swallow flew by.

Silence: the twilight faded.

'The last swallow!'

'They don't get to fly around here for long before they're off – and where to?'

'To Africa, Aleksandr Nikolaevich – to Africa, to the Cape of Good Hope.'

'Really, now? To Africa?' the sexton answered in surprise.

'They'll fly away all right.'

'How they fly!'

'How they fly,' Pyotr was moved to repeat.

They both followed the swallow with their eyes, watching its white breast circling, soaring, calling, squealing, hither and thither, hither and thither – 'Ivivi'; it swooped, its breast on the pond, it soared to the very cross on the bell-tower and in ethereal rapture the dancing swallow cavorted above that symbol, ruby-red now from the sunset: 'Ivivi-ivivi . . .'

'Look how it dances!'

'Like King David before the Ark of the Covenant.'

And Pyotr took to thinking: 'Dear, dear swallow, sweet swallow with your white breast'; the swallow swooped and swirled . . . And it piped away about Katya. 'Ivivi! Ivivi!' – the swallow flew off in the direction of Gugolevo: 'Ivivi' – died away above the trees; it was quiet: rings spreading across the water's surface – a soul-tormenting thought – the mournful sound of water being drawn from the well – all was still, and smooth, and somnolent, and dark.

Where had Pyotr got to? What was happening to him? Nothing like this had ever happened to him before, anywhere. You'd never dream of anything like this anywhere except in Russia; but here among these simple people, these unlearned people, here you dreamed of it for sure; the Russian fields know secrets, as the Russian forests do; in those fields and in those forests live bearded peasants and a multitude of peasant women; they haven't many words; but silence they have in plenty; if you come to them they will share that plenty with you; if you come to them you will learn to be silent; you will drink the sunsets, like precious wines; you will feed on the smells of the pine-trees' resin; Russian souls are sunsets; Russian words are strong and resinous: if you are a Russian, you will have a bonny secret in your soul, and your spirit-strewing word will be like sticky resin; it is nothing in appearance, but it clings, and from it comes a pleasant, beatific fragrance; and if you say that simple word – it seems there's nothing in that simple word at all; those who live in cities, crushed by stones, know nothing of those words: when they come to the villages, they see before them dirt and darkness, a pile of straw and, frowning sullenly out of that straw, the face of a grubby peasant; and they can never know or understand that it is not a peasant, but Kudeyarov the carpenter, the secret bearer of good tidings; they see before them dirt and darkness, a pile of straw, and in that straw they hear the silly prattle of a peasant woman; the fact that it is the comely Matryona Semyonovna, with sugared lips and kisses sweet as honey – all that is hidden from them.

Poor people, poor people! Pyotr was lost in thought: the entire dream of the West had passed before him and had gone; he thought: many a multitude of words, and sounds, and signs the West had scattered to the wonderment of the world; but those words, those sounds, those signs, as they lose their fragrance, are like werewolves, drawing people after them – but where? The Russian word, however, the silent Russian word, as it leaves you, still stays with you: it is a prayer, that word; the words taught by the West are like a cup of golden wine hurled in the air, so that its drops glint in the sun like precious stones, falling at your feet into the dirt and leaving your thirst unquenched, though gathering round you sundry folk to marvel briefly at the rain of golden drops; in the West they dissipate their

words, into books, into all manner of scholarship and science; and therefore theirs are effable words, their manner of life is a spoken one: that's
what the West is like. But the soul is not a word: it grieves for the ineffable,
it yearns for the unspoken. And it is otherwise in Russia: the people of the
fields, the forests, do not array themselves in words, and do not delight the
gaze with their way of life; their words may be foul obscenity; their way of
life is drunken, quarrelsome: slovenliness, famine, dumbness, darkness.
But look deeper: before each of them on the table stands the wine of the
spirit; and each of them drinks by himself the wine of words unspoken and
of feelings ineffable. When the peasant speaks he seems to stutter, and all
about such simple things; but when he is silent – what a wondrous silence
it is! His lips may curse you with the basest words, while his eyes drown in
the brilliant sunset; his lips may revile you while his eyes bless; he starts to
speak, and it's like the planing of a plank; but when he sings . . . – those
Russian songs are known the length and breadth of this wide world; and
who is it who sings them, who composed them? None other than that very
bumpkin who is just as likely to fill your ears with filth.

   Oh, to live in the fields, to die in the fields, repeating to yourself the one
spirit-strewing word, which no one knows but he who receives that word;
and it is received in silence. Here amongst themselves they all drink the
wine of life, the wine of new joy – thought Pyotr: the sunset here cannot be
compressed into a book: and here the sunset is a mystery; in the West there
are many books; in Russia there are many unspoken words. Russia is that
on which the book is smashed, knowledge dissipated, and life itself burns
up; on the day when the West is grafted onto Russia, a world-wide confla-
gration will engulf it: everything will burn that can burn, for only from the
ashes of death will rise the soul of paradise, the Fire-bird.

   Daryalsky remembered his past: Moscow, and the prim gatherings of
affected ladies and their sycophants, the poets; he remembered their cra-
vats, their cuff-links, scarves and tiepins, all imported, French, and all the
fashionable glitter of the latest ideas; one such damsel shrugged her shoulders when the talk turned to Russia; afterwards she made off on foot to
Sarov on a pilgrimage; a social democrat chuckled at the superstition of
the people; and what became of him? He went and fled the party, and
turned up among the sect of flagellants in the far north-east. A certain
decadent papered his room entirely in black, displaying one eccentricity
after another; then he disappeared for many years; later he declared himself a wanderer of the fields. How many, how many are secretly seared by
that dream of the fields; O fields of Russia, fields of Russia! Your breath is
resin, grasses, sunsets: there's room enough in your expanses, Russian
fields, to suffocate and die.

How many sons you have raised, Russian fields; and your thoughts have burgeoned like flowers in the heads of your restless sons: your sons run from you, Russia, they forget your broad expanses in foreign parts; and when they then return, who can recognize them? Their words are foreign, their eyes are foreign; they twirl their moustaches in another, Western way; the twinkling of their eyes is not like that of other Russians; but in their souls they're yours, O fields: it is you, familiar meadow path, that consumes their dreams, that burgeons in their thoughts with flowers of paradise. Before a year has gone, they will set off to wander through the fields and forests, on the tracks of the wild animals, to die in a grass-choked ditch.

The numbers of those who flee into the fields will grow and grow!

The chapels in the drowsy forests of Siberia will grow in number too! Does any of us know how he will finish? Maybe in his declining years he will no longer sit quietly in his armchair in the city, reading erudite books and smoking fragrant tobacco, but will swing in the open field on a gibbet of two uprights and a crossbar; in a wayside ditch, maybe, or in a monk's cell in the forests of Vologda he will end his days – who knows, who can say? Young men, you know nothing about yourselves! Wives – listen, wives, to the bells that ring unchecked: those bells have rung forever in the broad, untrammelled fields; he who has heard those bells can never find peace in the cities; the cities will grind him down; half-alive, he will flee abroad; but he will never find peace there either. His soul will sob till it can sob no more; his mind will turn arid, his tongue will stick in his throat: he will take the waters for this yearning sickness, he will spend time in lunatic asylums and in jail; and in the end he will return to you, O Russian fields!

'I'm like that too!' – Daryalsky shuddered: he looked – above his head an indigo blueness was descending; the fields, the forests, the cottages – all were indigo, nocturnal: the yellow moon was about to rise, and with it – shadows.

'As though I were in spaces new and times uncharted' – Daryalsky remembered the words of a poet he had once loved: he had been ground down, too: if he stayed in the city, he would die; in his soul, too, the thought of the fields had taken a firm hold. And involuntarily the words of his beloved poet reminded him of other words, precious and frightening:

> 'And for all eternity
> We are promised heavenly joy,
> Lord, have mercy!

> In the empty fields confined,
> Kith and kin we leave behind,
> Lord, have mercy! . . .'

Hark, from the other side of the pond came a familiar response:

> 'I was visited by God,
> As soon as on the earth I trod . . .
> Lord, have mercy!'

It was the bad-tempered unkempt workman who had finished his carpentry and was on his way home.

'I'm not a philologist any more now, not a member of the gentry, not a poet: I'm a Dove; I'm not Katya's fiancé, I'm Matryona's lover' – Daryalsky chuckled, and this sweet reality made him feel afraid; a soul-tormenting anxiety came upon him, and to silence it he sang:

> 'As though I were in spaces new
> For all eternity . . .'

'Why am I mixing things up?' he thought; and felt afraid.

'What's that you're singing, young man?' – a lachrymose and plaintive voice rang out behind his back.

Daryalsky shuddered and turned round.

A melancholy, clean-shaven elderly man with a protruding nose was standing before him, smelling a flower; his hands were in gloves; over one arm he had a travelling-rug, and in the other hand a stick.

'Nothing in particular: I'm just singing. And who might you be?'

'I'm from around here,' said the elderly man, sighing languidly.

'Where have I seen him in the distant past?' Pyotr thought; there was some strange resemblance to something dear, familiar, but long departed in these aged features – but to what, to whom? He looked – everything the old man was wearing was brand-new; he thought: 'he's a Westernizer! that's what it is!' And the old man in the image and likeness of the West carefully unfolded his rug, spread it out on the grass and sat down on it with Daryalsky; the moon was already quietly illuminating them, and the thought came to Daryalsky that it was time to go and meet Matryona at the agreed spot, but the clean-shaven gentleman had cast a spell on him; the clean-shaven gentleman's voice was as mournful as a marsh bird's cry; that cry reminds us in the autumn of the beloved past, and, bewitched, we stand for hours of an evening by the putrid chasms of the marsh, and listen in terror to the voice of that familiar bird as it weeps.

'All is past, all is past,' the water lisps, but we smile and do not believe it: 'Nothing is past,' we argue; but we will never tell what is past, and why . . . but hark – just then in the distance the voice of the bird, as it weeps . . .

'Young man: are you an eccentric?'

'???'

'Because you're a Russian: all Russians are eccentrics . . .'

'Haven't I heard all this before somewhere?' was Pyotr's response (hark – once more the voice of the marsh bird in the distance).

'You heard it inside yourself' – Pyotr was taken aback: he imagined he had only thought those words, not spoken them.

'No, wait: just a moment: where have I seen you? You remind me of . . .'

'Well, what an imagination: we all remind each other of one another, and keep on meeting.'

'What exactly are you talking about?'

'I'm not exactly talking about anything at all . . .' the gentleman wailed, calmer now, and stroked his knee.

'How nervous you are: you are an eccentric, my dear fellow; mind your nervousness doesn't cost you dear . . .'

'How do you know?'

'You're a young man; and young men are all degenerating; it's sad, but it's a fact: Russians are degenerating; Europeans are degenerating too; only Mongols and negroes are multiplying.'

'Russia has a future before her,' Pyotr rejoined, and gazed intently at the clean-shaven gentleman: quite impressive – calm, quiet; he must be a Westernizer. 'Where have I seen him?' Pyotr thought, and out loud he said: 'Russia is the bearer of an ineffable mystery.'

But Pavel Pavlovich (for it was he) had arrived at his favourite theme, and coolly set about embroidering it on Pyotr's words.

'Russia is a Mongol country; we all have Mongol blood, and it cannot withstand the invasion: we shall all prostrate ourselves before the Mongol potentate.'

'Russia – ' Pyotr started to object.

'Russia is an unfortunate country; you, for instance, talk of the ineffable; that must mean you have something on your mind that you cannot express: so you, young man, are not merely an eccentric but moreover you are an inarticulate eccentric; you are an unfortunate dumb young man, just as all young men nowadays are dumb; they talk of the fecund silence because they are unable to express themselves coherently. When they speak of the ineffable it is a dangerous symptom; it merely proves that humanity is falling into a beast-like state; unfortunately, all are now beast-like, not only the Russians!' – Baron Pavel Pavlovich sighed mournfully and loudly blew his nose.

Hark! Once more the distant, familiar voice of the marsh: 'All is past, all is past!' – and Daryalsky, as though struggling against it, exclaimed:

'No, no – it's not true, it's not true!'

'Unfortunately it is true: you now, young man, you apparently belong to the intelligentsia, but to look at – you're a complete peasant: that is because genuine culture is beyond your strength; that's why you cultivate these eccentricities; you force yourself to dream: wake up . . .'

Again Pyotr harkened to prophetic words: was not everything that was happening to him a wondrous dream that he was dreaming while awake? With astonishment he looked at the clean-shaven gentleman, but the clean-shaven gentleman had already risen from the ground, was folding up his rug and courteously offering him his hand without taking off his gloves:

'Good-bye: I have a long journey back . . .'

And he was far away from Pyotr – the West was far away: 'Where have I seen him?' Pyotr kept on wondering; the cold breeze of approaching autumn fingered the trees: a yellow leaf fell into the shadow; a trickling stream at his feet lisped:

'I'll tell it all, I'll tell it all.'

'I know it anyway!' Daryalsky smiled and suddenly caught himself out: 'What do I know? What? What?'

But it was time: Matryona must be weary of waiting for him.

'For one moment I was not asleep, I woke up for a single moment,' Pyotr thought, 'and here I go back into my dream.'

But the nearer he came to the oak-tree the more it seemed to him that he was falling asleep again; then it seemed to him that nothing of what had happened had really taken place: the clean-shaven old gentleman, his strange speeches, all that was a dream that had long since vanished into the West; and again he had been swallowed by a fearsome waking reality: the reality of Russia.

The trickling autumnal stream lisped away at his feet: 'I'll tell it all, I'll tell it all, it all, it all . . .'

'I know it anyway!' Daryalsky smiled.

The making

'Sit yourself down here, Matryona . . . You're a fine woman, and no mistake: sit down here, Matryona . . . It's boring for you, I'll be bound, being with an old man – and all that . . .'

The carpenter's eyes flashed wildly; his lame legs carried him over to the window, he grasped Matryona with his hands, and pulled her to the window after him:

'Sit down here, Matryona . . .'

'Oh, whatever d'you want!' – her eyes flashed wildly; her unresisting legs carried her over to the window; once he'd grasped her hands the carpenter started stroking her, and whispering, and pulling her after him.

'Come here, come on!' – he sat her down beside him. 'You're a fine woman, with those eyes, and strong, too: it's just those pock-marks spoil your face a bit; but I bet your lover-boy isn't complaining . . . He'll be waiting for you, I suppose, your lover-boy . . .'

'Pff . . . Pff . . .' – Matryona snorted in embarrassment.

'Waiting, is he?'

'He's waiting . . .'

'Never mind . . . He won't mind waiting a bit longer: it'll be all the sweeter later.'

'Oh, I can't bear it!' – she hid her face from her old companion, but her old companion made her sit down on the bench – 'A fine, fine woman – not bad at all . . .'

'Oh-oh-oh!' Matryona sighed . . .

'Give me your hand, Matryona: don't you want to? Well, all right, don't bother, then, I was only – not for anything else . . . But you listen to my words . . . I haven't got anything against all this . . . Only there's one thing: my friends, you're making love too often: every day, every day it happens with you. And it's all without prayers, without devotions – and all that. And what for? You've surely not forgotten what a sacrament all this business is going to turn into: when you get heavy with child; remember what a spiritual burden you are bearing to bring people sweetness.'

'It isn't just that stuff with us, Mitry Mironych,' the woman said in embarrassment; 'we pray for the Spirit: we make love for the fields, the flowers, for all the lovely scents, we sing songs . . .'

'Let me, my love, put my hand on your breast,' said the carpenter, moved, gleaming wildly with the fire that had started burning inside him. 'How soft your breast is, Matryona!'

'Oh, leave me alone, don't you touch me!'

But a weird power locked her into silence; from the carpenter's hand a current cleaved her breast; from his clammy fingers, his clinging fingers, his current welled out in fine streams and flooded into her: she became docile, her face hung motionless in space with a bluish pallor which gradually, as the current entered it, turned pink like a ruddy winter apple. 'Are you warm, are you warm, are you warm?'

'I'm warm: warmer still – hotter and hotter . . . oh, it's burning my breast: I'm all on fire . . .'

'Pray, pray: make devotions, not for yourselves, but for the child; every evening, when you go walking in the fields, or in the forest, making love in the hollow oak or in the hayloft – who is it who prays in tears for the spiritual conception of the soul? It's Kudeyarov the carpenter . . . And all that . . . It wasn't for the sake of wanton, carnal copulation that I brought you together – not that I'd mind a bit of it myself – but for the conception of the radiant spirit . . . You're a fine woman – I wouldn't mind . . . You must pray, and make devotions . . . My love, let me lay my hand on your breast again.'

With searing power, with flash and crash the carpenter's hand scorched her: ravished by his thought, she did not resist; the shawl fell from her head, her hands covered her face, and Matryona Semyonovna wept, dissolved in tears of emotion; she felt at ease, and frightened – as though she was in the bath-house: and she felt sleepy.

And the carpenter? His face seemed to have fallen from him, like the sloughed-off skin of a cockroach; his terrible, terrible, rarefied face, with the glasses that slipped to the end of his nose, glanced in a new way from under that empty, transparent skin: the carpenter's face was terrible and uncanny; there was a terrible and uncanny atmosphere in the cottage; the air between the objects here was strangely tensed, like the fabric of some spiritual force; and that fabric shone and crackled: sparks shot about the room, dry crackling sounds, and lights, as though a spider were spinning from itself a gleaming web. The carpenter thrust his hands aloft, muttering invocations and words: and again he pressed his hands to his breast; his hands flew up and down, up and down; it was as though hair-thin threads of light sprang from his sickly breast and clung to his tenacious fingers: sweet-scented and God-given; sweet-scented, God-given threads he ripped from his breast. The carpenter's finger dropped onto Matryona Semyonovna's breast, her shoulder, her stomach, and in a trice his hands had enmeshed her in his web; she drowsily drowned, drowsily drowned, drowsily drowned in a vortex of barely visible light, torn from the carpenter's breast and wrapped around her, and above all this were the carpenter's eyes, like gaping green apertures, pouring light upon her in bucketfuls. There they sat by the window; the last ray of evening stretched humbly in through the window and then turned fierce as it ran in a crimson diagonal over the table; there was no telling what was the sun's light and what was the light of the carpenter – the carpenter's web of prayers, woven by sunlight and shadow into a single carpet of air; a weird sight beyond vision – the carpenter's soul flowing out in the threads, the lights, the flames of a spider's web; around his hands now, around his head, was a ring of crimson gold: drowsily Matryona saw all that; silly woman, in her drowsiness she was already on her knees before him; she kissed his hands and – oh – how she prayed. This was no longer the man she lived with, Mitry Mironych; it was the man of righteousness, the great prophet, who had disgorged a flame; Matryona knew that if the occasion arose he could set straw alight with this flame: he would fold his hands together, make a point with his fingers, and a terrible power would flow into those spear-shaped fingers, would accumulate, and flash in a white, incandescent fire: she had once seen at dead of night how lightning flashed out of the window and thunder crashed from the carpenter's power-laden finger.

All of this passed through Matryona as if in a dream; she was completely enclosed in a net of light and heat; and the green coals above her poured over her bucketfuls of light, the hooked fingers wove a golden thread; then the carpenter moved away and a strip of brightness stretched out from him to end on Matryona, as a great ball of light in Matryona herself; the carpenter moved one way; sleepily Matryona stumbled after him; the carpenter moved the other way: sleepily Matryona followed on behind.

Then the carpenter passed his bony hand between himself and her, dividing the net of light in two; the strip of light was torn in two; winding and fluttering in the darkness, its slender blades played over Matryona; the remnant of net that had remained with the carpenter, winding about, floated over into the carpenter; the third cluster was dispersed in the air, and she alone now rested in the light that had been given her – she slept, Matryona Semyonovna, and saw nothing: the carpenter, shining with an unbearable, blinding light, walked about and thrust his arms aloft: up and down, up and down, up and down: he was enmeshing the objects in the room in the luminous fabric that issued from him, and muttering: he placed his hand on the table and stepped away from the table; and a thread extended from the table behind him; he drew that thread over to the window, to the icon-lamp, to the icons in the corner; the spider enmeshed the whole room in his web; everywhere now was the glittering of a thousand threads, gleaming, flickering – of the finest, brightest filaments – the crackling of threads: a mass of terrifying golden strands; all those threads, spun out of the carpenter's body, now returned to the carpenter – some to his breast, some to his belly, while he, sitting in the corner, made rapid movements of his fingers like a spider assembling its web; and it seemed he was about to hang there in the waves of the night air on nets of his own making; swiftly, swiftly he muttered indistinct magical words; a surge of incantations issued from his throat in a hoarse gurgle; listen carefully, now: what are those words the carpenter is whispering, blinded by the brilliance? You will be aghast not at the ineffable meaning of that stream of words: you will be aghast at their rabid meaninglessness:

'Staridon, karion, kokire, stado, stridado: I shall pray to the Lord God and the Holy Virgin. Young crescent moon, you've got a golden horn . . . Staridon, karion, kokire – stado: stridado.'

So from his lips in horrid bliss an uncanny unction issues forth: that luminous body with swiftly working fingers, which only recently believed itself to be the carpenter – is not the carpenter: it is a legion of suppressed ravings; it is a torrent of unutterable joys; look, look; the sheaves of light emanating from the carpenter turn gold, turn pale, brighten, turn blue, spin scarlet flames from his mouth, strike the floor with a hiss and skip away out of the cottage through the half-open window; anyone lurking in the undergrowth in the sloping hollow and observing the cottage from a distance with a stern eye would doubtless think he saw the pipe of a samovar sticking from the window and spewing sheaves of tiny red sparks out into the darkness.

The carpenter's eyes were now turned inwards; only the whites gazed senselessly from their sockets: the spider's web, all invisible, having become visible for a moment, had already lost its luminosity and hung limply – as though it were not there at all; but it was hanging there; anyone coming into the cottage would trip over it, become entangled in it, and would drag it home after him out of the cottage when he left; and if he had a wife, his wife would get entangled in it too; between them and Kude-yarov's hut the malignant threads would stretch; and even objects would seem to stare at him and his wife for reasons of their own; if that person left the village, those threads would drag behind him and pull him back; any-one chancing to pass by Kudeyarov's house and drop in would find himself back there with his wife and his children more and more often, until the whole family was entangled in the carpenter's nets.

The Doves' worship was taking place today all over the district, and hymns were to be sung about the little white dove; from early morning today pungent sweetmeats had been dispatched in all directions to all the places where the huts of the Doves were to be found; and it was not for nothing that tonight there was a sweet sunset. If you are delayed in the open field, and night catches you there, and if your vision has not been ruined by reading – then remember: in the darkness you will see a golden thread descending noiselessly into the darkness; and you must not imagine that it's a shooting star falling to earth: it is a fragment of the carpenter's soul, voluptuously stinging with an arrow of light, winging its way in the darkness to a praying Dove-spouse; but the carpenter?

With drooping eyelids, with his beard drooping onto his hands, he was sitting on the bench with head bowed and grimly composed countenance, while his soul was resting far away from him; he had spun much light, he had draped in the air many nets of the sweetest and finest: he had consigned to surrounding space his sighs for the Dove-brethren; now, his soul hovering in space, he caught up with Pyotr on the road to Lashchavino; he came upon him on the road by the oak; seeking him out there, the carpenter vented his flame-words upon him: out sprang a word, plopped to the floor, turned into a gleaming cockerel and flapped its wings: with a cock-a-doodle-doo and in sheaves of blood-red sparks it hopped out of the window.

'To the Lord God I pray, to the fine swain I bow: fine swain, fine swain, in the open field beside Lashchavino; at Lashchavino there is an oak; in that oak there is a hollow: in that hollow take yourself all kinds of sweethearts: dung-mites, forest-sprites, half-seas over in the clover: in the oak there's golden gravel, golden fronds, twigs of willow for a pillow, truckle in the honeysuckle – sisters, cousins, kindred all . . . Uuu-uuu . . .'

A torrent of light gushed from his mouth and – with a hop – ran off along the road in pursuit of Daryalsky in the form of a red cockerel.

Daryalsky was walking towards the oak to his rendezvous with Matryona, he was already forgetting his conversation beside the pond; at his feet the stream whispered: 'I'll tell it all, it all, it all . . .'

How strange: a big red cockerel ran across the road in front of him in the moonlight: he crossed himself; he walked along the edge of the forest. In front of him in the distance was Lashchavino: there was the oak-tree, and Matryona.

He arrived – the hollow oak was empty : Matryona hadn't come yet.

The carpenter, meanwhile, hunched on the bench, went on raving under his breath:

'Fire that sees, fire that flies . . .'

'Drrr-drrr-drrr' – a cart rumbled right under the carpenter's window; the peasant Andron shouted hoarsely into the carpenter's window:

'Mitry Mironych, hey, Mitry Mironych!'

The carpenter's frowning face protruded from the window:

'Now what is it?'

'I'm going to town: want anything?'

'Thanks for remembering me – off you go, Andron, Godspeed . . .'

'Drrr-drrr-drrr' – the cart set off again.

'Ahh!' – Matryona woke up on the bench – 'Whoever's making all that noise?'

'Andron with his cart!' came the surly, brusque reply from the carpenter, who started to light the lamp.

Matryona remembered that her sweetheart was waiting for her; she stood up with a languid yawn and a cunning glance at the carpenter.

'I'll go out for a bit of a walk, Mitry Mironych . . .'

'All right, off you go, have a walk,' the carpenter answered meekly, with an uncontrolled cough.

'Drrr-drrr-drrr' – somewhere in the distance the sound of Andron's cart died away: Andron was merry; he was off to the town, where he was going to settle scores with all and sundry.

Andron sang out into the night in his deep bass voice.

The Trinity

How she ran! She ran along the road to Lashchavino: it was night – but oh! the strength of her, the colossal strength: at a whoop from her the bright moon itself would come rolling down from the sky, just like a mare that suddenly whinnies and bolts, while the herdsman gallops along behind; in the distance – the angry eyes of the houses, many eyes; in the distance – a marsh bird let out a cry, and then hid away for a long time; oh, how she ran – Matryona's heels flashed: the moon rolled on, like a wheel rumbling in her breast: colossal strength was beating in her, thrusting her over the hummocks; her shawl slipped sideways, her hair fell loose: she passed a fingernail across her hair – and sparks were scattered: 'Where's my darling now? Is he still waiting for me – is he tired of waiting; O to put my arms around him, O to kiss him, my lover, my gentleman.'

'My shining love, with eyes so bright – I'm sure he's waiting . . .

'Wait, my joy, don't go away, wait for me . . .

'My shining love, with eyes so bright – wait.'

She whispered as she ran; leaped over one hummock, another: with a rushing sound, roused by her passage, rooks took off from the trees; the undergrowth crackled at her feet, the moon blinded her eyes.

But there behind her someone was following from bush to bush: turn round – and you will see a dark figure behind you; Matryona did not turn round.

Aah, hummock after hummock, ditch and gully: breathlessly the carpenter lurched along after Matryona: he couldn't catch her up, kept falling behind, but hadn't the strength to go back: sitting alone in the cottage without his woman was beyond him; he couldn't bear the thought of

Matryona making love with the lad: the carpenter wanted to kiss and caress her himself.

But he knew very well: there was a need for that love of Matryona's: and he was the one who had fired that love in her with his spirit; and here he was dragging after her to her tryst, and unable to keep up: no keeping pace with her young legs: something – whether jealousy or curiosity – kept driving him to the places where they celebrated their nights of love; as he walked, he spat, puffed into his beard, raised his bony hands to those forest places: in clouds he brought the power down upon them, but was afraid to come close, to watch – at times that lad was bitterer than wormwood to him – he couldn't bear the sight of him; at others he was dear to him: dear as a fair maiden might be dear: 'He's creating the Spirit in her – and all that . . . If only they'd do their loving near me, make love where I can see: but they run away from me like wolves into the forest . . . Instead of doing it where I am, in the cottage: I would watch over them; I'd put the samovar on for them; and if anything went wrong for them, I'd show them how – and all that.'

He ran along, gasping for breath: branches struck him in the chest, bushes struck him in the chest, age-old grasses, wormwood, struck him in the chest; viscous burs clung to his beard beneath his long-nosed face: the carpenter dragged along behind Matryona, coughing, stumbling, falling back, pursuing her with threats:

'Just you hurry, just you hurry – ha-ha: you shameless pair!

'I've got what it takes – and all that, I used to . . .

'Lord God, save Thy people and bless all that is Thine . . .

'I bet he's wild with waiting: hold on, my friends, I didn't bring you together for this sort of thing . . .

'Let their love be turned to prayer.

'I'll get you, I'll get you, you trespasser, you thief!

'I've got what it takes! Staridon, karion, kokire – stado: stridado . . .'

Dry scraps of imprecations, prayers, cries and incantations made a deathly gurgle as they clogged his throat: he coughed them out; and all this motley flock the carpenter spat out set off in pursuit of Matryona, while the carpenter himself, his fit of coughing ended, sat on a hillock, shaking a dry branch in the direction of Lashchavino: as threat or blessing, who could tell?

But Matryona saw nothing and heard nothing.

'My shining love, with eyes so bright, wait for me, wait . . .

'Press your sister to your breast!

'I'll rest my head upon your breast!

'My shining love, with eyes so bright – don't go away, wait for me . . .'

Night. Empty all around, attentive; in the distance – whooping sounds; Daryalsky waited and waited for Matryona in the hollow oak; and still she did not come; the bright moon rolled across the sky; in the distance a marsh bird let out a cry, and then hid away for a long time: the minutes flowed by like eternities; as though it were not night that was being enacted in the heavens but human life itself, as long as ages, as short as a moment.

Whooping sounds in the distance, but still no Matryona; Daryalsky stood waiting for a while, then went back into the hollow trunk: he lit a fire there, and the crimson embers released their warmth as they settled; from the oak's split bark a snarling grin spread redly into the darkness, thick with tree-trunks. Someone clattered by on horseback, someone suddenly reined his horse in by the hollow oak: the ringing sound of stirrups could be heard beside the tree: what might it be there? – Daryalsky stuck his head out; – nothing, no one; it must have been a vanished oprichnik come galloping back from the depths of time; more than five hundred years ago maybe he had rested under the oak – reined in his horse there, and stopped to look – and then again the homeless oprichnik had hastened away to his desolate darkness, to visit this familiar place again in a couple of hundred years.

'My love, dear love, why don't you come?'

A groan right beside his ear – an owl perhaps? Or was it, maybe, the groan of a lost soul, the soul of an unfrocked monk on the run, who had rested here more than two hundred years ago and had ended his days in Solovki? Daryalsky stuck his head out: still no one there.

'My love, dear love, why don't you come?'

'Here I am, here I am.'

'My treasure, why so long, what kept you?'

'Oh, I'm wretched, so wretched: the old man was kissing me: kept squeezing my breast . . .'

'Stop it, don't talk to me about the old man; I have a feeling of horror every time he comes between us . . .'

'The old chap's saying prayers: he's waiting for the white dove.'

And she began to sing:

> 'Bright, oh, bright is the dove-blue air
> Bright in that air is the spirit fair!'

'Cock-a-doodle-doo' resounded by the hollow oak, and a raucous cockerel peeped from the darkness into the hollow.

'My love, my love – I'm afraid, where did that rooster come from?'

'Yes, it's strange . . .'

'My love, I'm frightened!'

'Now, you stop that, Matryona, stop it; but it is strange: as though it wasn't "cock-a-doodle-doo" – but "I've got what it takes", but we're not afraid; don't you think, though, that it's the old man who casts the madness on us at night?'

'Leave the old man alone: he's expecting the white dove!'

'I don't know whether it's the white dove he's expecting, or the black raven: I only know that you and I and certain other people are caught in his net.'

'Leave the old man alone: he's expecting the white dove.'

'And I tell you: he's expecting the black raven . . .'

'Leave the old man alone: he hears everything . . .'

And they fell to thinking, watching the warm crackle of the crimson embers.

Pyotr looked at Matryona and wept: she had such fragrant, cornflower eyes; was it with the sweetness of paradise, or with the bottomless pit of hell, that she had entranced him, his she-dove.

'My love, my brother: let me unbutton your collar and kiss your white chest: a white chest it is. Why, he's got a birthmark on his chest, just like a little mouse: mousey, mousey, go away from his strong white body . . .

'Why, he's wearing my bronze cross against his body!'

'My sweet, oh, leave me! I can't look at you, my sweet, without weeping.'

'What is it, why are you crying, my dear infant?'

'O Lord, my God! Whatever is this!'

She embraced him; she rocked him like a child; she pressed his head against her breast. They drifted away into a dark crevice; she said, turning as though to address someone:

'Look at us, old man – come here, old man, is our love without prayers, without joy of the soul?'

Their shadows, waxing, danced in the hollow tree, lit by an orange flame.

Was it a dream, or was it not a dream? A body woven of fine gold threads separated itself from Matryona and leaped across to Pyotr: their bodies disappeared, were burnt up: just a cloud of golden-threaded smoke hung in the hollow tree. Was it a dream, or was it not a dream?

It lasted one short moment: but in that moment there was nothing: no world, no space, no time. And then again their bodies took on shape; as though from above, from the aperture that led into the sky, from the dark sky bright crimson threads had been poured down, sparkling, like merry Christmas streamers for the joy of children.

And from these glittering filaments a human likeness once again emerged; woven from mist, light, speechless, they drifted in the air, then settled in their former places.

How weird: Matryona looked at her beloved: Pyotr's body was still transparent, she could see the purple blood coursing in his veins, and on the left side of his chest, where his heart was, a claw-shaped flame was dancing – this way and that: tap-tap-tap, tap-tap-tap.

How weird: Pyotr looked at his Matryona: Matryona's body was transparent: he could see the black blood coursing in her veins, and on the left side, where her heart was, a blue snake writhed.

But between them were bright threads that formed their bodies; between them was a single patch of light: an instant and that patch between them trembled, like something living: and ah, it was an ethereal dove fluttering there, flapping its wings on their bared breasts: they embraced – and the light-born dove, spreadeagled on their breasts, fluttered more than ever: tu-tu-tu-u-u . . .

'My sweet, how your heart is beating: where have we been, you and me?'

'My love, is that your heart that's beating?'

The dove pecked at their hearts.

'Oh darling, there's a pricking in my heart!'

But Matryona heard nothing any longer: she could not tear her red lips from his red lips . . . And when she did, her shawl fell off – and the dove hopped away over them . . .

'Look at us, old man, come here, old man: is our love without prayers, without joy of the soul?'

'I'm here anyway: I can see everything you're doing' – a hoarse laugh rang out above their heads.

Pyotr and Matryona raised their heads in fright and looked up to the top of the hollow trunk: a patch of sky and stars ought to be visible there: but there was no sky there, someone had blocked the aperture.

'It's the carpenter . . .'

They both lowered their eyes: for a moment they imagined they heard someone climbing down from the trunk and running off at full-tilt: Pyotr glanced abruptly upwards again: from up above them now the indigo sky gazed down and the edge of the golden moon.

Pyotr quickly ran out of the hollow trunk: for a moment in the moonlight a peasant stood before him, with a shaggy beard and wearing blacked boots and a watch, but no cap: he stood there, and bounded off into the bushes: Pyotr recognized Ivan Stepanov, the shopkeeper: he seized a stone, and furiously flung the stone after him.

The stars were growing dim, a pale strip of dawning day was lighting in the east: the undergrowth rustled in the ravine and there was no telling whether it was a bear stealing away from the village, or sleepy Doves returning home, dispersing from their prayers, or simple folk creeping back from meetings in the forest. All that could be heard was a nasal voice singing a song – there, where the branches of the hazel-tree were shaking:

> 'A wonderful sea is the sacred Baikal,
> A wonderful sail is my ragged caftan.
> Hey, Barguzin, stir the waves in a squall,
> The crash of the storm is approaching . . .'

No doubt a convict creeping through the bushes.

The eve of the sabbath

That was how Matryona and he whiled away their summer nights as autumn approached: night tumbled after day, day was abducted by night. The days passed by. Overcast mornings greeted them after those nights; the sun scorched them; glistening cobwebs stretched through the air; everything was permeated by a fragrant light; the pale faces of the solemn servants of God at their work did not betray their inner turmoil; woodshavings fell; a white covering of sawdust dropped on to the feet of the men at their carpentry. The cottages of Tselebeyevo clamoured for admittance through the narrow windows; a pig rooted about below the windows; a red cockerel strode importantly through the straw, or else, with neck bent forward and crest erect, chased all round the dry meadow in pursuit of a hen . . . And a distant wisp of smoke rose over the trees from Lashchavino: there the blue of the sky was veiled with grey; at the forest's edge some shepherds lit a fire; on the meadow the horned herd was grazing; in the hollow oak a silly shepherd sat whittling at a switch and smoking a pipe; in front of him a small fire danced.

On the morning after the night just described Yevseich approached Ivan Stepanov's shop, bought supplies of paraffin, various teas, and pounds of this and that, took out his red foulard handkerchief and gossiped about matters at the estate:

'Her ladyship's son the baron turned up on the patron saint's day to give us the once-over, see what was going on, like . . . four or five days ago it'll be, ye-es . . . he's a real bigwig – Senator-General, and wha-a-at a load of fuss: just the water he gets through – five or six buckets every morning; and no one's fit to clean his trousers except his manservant: a real smarty-pants he is, name of Strigachov . . . and the things he tells about French women, he says they . . .'

Ivan Stepanov gave a spiteful frown at all this, clicked away brusquely on the abacus, and, glancing over his glasses, mumbled:

'There's rumours around you're going broke . . . Right, then, that's five roubles fifty' – he suddenly broke off his speculations.

'And who was it told you that, might I ask?' Yevseich took umbrage, and frowned as he put on his cap.

But the shopkeeper just shrugged his shoulders and started clicking on the abacus again; after a silence he offhandedly muttered:

'Nobody told me anything: what's it to do with me; there's just rumours around. Here, you've run up an account . . .'

Yevseich didn't stay in the shop any longer: it used not to be like that; he used to receive all manner of marks of respect: a spot of baccy, or some mushrooms, or maybe just some trifling remark, but now he couldn't even have a conversation there. As he was leaving the shop he noticed that Ivan Stepanov had a limp; he couldn't resist getting a dig at him:

'Hurt your leg, have you?'

'Gave it a knock, it's nothing' – the shopkeeper growled with a show of complete indifference, but in fact he went quite pale with anger.

'A pretty pickle he's got into!' Yevseich thought and walked off, seizing his bottle of paraffin in one hand and his packets in the other. This was on a Saturday; work finished earlier at the carpenter's on that day; by four o'clock the saws and files and everything else had all been put away: the red cloth with cockerels on it was laid on the table; on this day the carpenter had tea at an unusual time with all his household: with Daryalsky and the unkempt workman; Matryona had put on her bodice with the braiding: the carpenter had pulled his boots on, the unkempt workman had changed his shirt; Pyotr had smartened himself up too. From four o'clock onwards the carpenter had begun to turn white (on ordinary days he was green and sickly); you might think, looking at his face scrubbed clean, and his hair plastered down with lamp-oil, that long before evening he would be poring over the holy book: they whispered that by midnight on this day a visitor would come, but what kind of visitor Pyotr could not yet know.

'An important visitor' – the unkempt workman gave him a sly wink.

A strange business: Pyotr's recent anxieties had dissolved in his soul, like drifting smoke; even Matryona's charm had turned paler in his soul today: no, Matryona was still Matryona – only he had begun to realize something else as well, which hadn't struck him before; Matryona wasn't independent, but, as it were, the creature of the carpenter: that with which she enticed him to her did not belong to her alone, and it had nothing to do with inquisitiveness; it was not her female nature that drew him, it was her soul; but that whole soul of hers turned out to be maybe half the carpenter's; evidently the carpenter breathed his soul into Matryona and she, imbued with the Spirit, was able to captivate with the languour of her eyes, her smile, the eager flaring of her nostrils.

An extraordinary thing: for a while now Pyotr had had no sensation, no awareness, of his own soul either; his soul, clearly, had become dormant, and made no utterance to its master: the whole of his innermost self turned out to be empty and void; but there came moments when it seemed that this vacant space inside him surged and splashed to the brim with the fluid of life, with a nameless power, with warmth and the joys of paradise: 'What might this be within me, what is it that passes through me in such a rapturous flame?' Pyotr wondered anxiously; what might it be that sauntered through his breast, creating there a trembling and a weeping; as though an electric motor had been switched on there, and was beginning to work in his breast; such a feeling of compassion welled up in his throat; and when it rose to his throat – then the village was no longer the village, the peasants were not peasants, and the familiar spaces were not familiar at all, but new: as though in these new spaces everything was adorned in bright magnificence and only for appearance's sake was cluttered up with huts and peasants and straw, and out of every object, if you only turned your back, creatures of another world, bright angels, would nod their heads at you, and the long-awaited bride herself, in her brilliance, would say: 'Wait for me – I shall come.' And you would give no credence to the straw, the dirt, the ugliness before your eyes: and it would exist no more.

'What's this then, Pyotr Petrovich? You look as though it's your birthday,' the skittish schoolmarm called mockingly from her cart.

'Such a glorious day,' Pyotr enthused, 'I've finished work and that's it!'

'As though anyone's forcing you.'

And off she drove.

It was true – it might be his birthday: ever since the morning, once his head had cleared after the night – his heart had been pounding, ringing, and he didn't know what to do in his joy: whether to grasp a chisel and chip out some doodle or other, or whether to go down to the pond and do some fishing. He sat down to fish, chuckling to himself: attached the worm – out flew his line: light-ensnaring nets of water sprang into the moist air: a golden snake slid by, another, then a third: between them were wrinkles of blue, and waters rippling to lap against the bank, a merry splash of waters; nearby a duck quacked as it swam past; his float began to dance, his line grew taut and a flailing fish fell into Daryalsky's fingers, where its mouth was torn open, and – plop – into the bucket with it.

'What a catch!'

'Yes!' Aleksandr Nikolaevich, the sexton, responded from the moist warm air.

'Will you take part in the service this evening, Aleksandr Nikolaevich?'

'I will indeed: I've prepared a new chasuble for the priest to wear today, gold with bundles of blue flowers on . . .'

'I love that,' the object of Pyotr's enthusiasm was not clear: 'I love the service . . .'

'It's all right for you to love it, but what about those of us who have to take it: you sweat all over . . .'

'Ivivi,' went a martin as it flew by, 'Ivivi'.

Daryalsky looked, and saw that an autumnal thread of gossamer was stretching up towards the blue of the sky; a bright thread ran to the carpenter's cottage; and from there, out of the sloping hollow, a window flashed a rainbow brilliance; and that too seemed made not of flashes, but of gossamer: everything around was covered in gossamer; in the sweet blue day gossamer settled on the grasses, stretched taut in the air; a wisp of smoke floated out of a hut; and settled on the grass; it, too, seemed to be of gossamer.

Daryalsky looked, and he saw that there was gossamer between his fingers, attached to his chest; he tried to take it off, but it would not move: the eye could see it, but the fingers could not grasp it, as though it had grown into his chest in a glittering confusion; he unfastened his shirt collar and looked – red, blue, golden, green threads were stretching into his white chest, and unwinding out from it again – there was no breaking them, they would sooner be torn from his chest along with his throbbing heart, like a reed-stalk with its bulb; he looked, and on the branches, between the branches, he saw a glittering confusion, on the blue pond – a glittering confusion; if you squeezed your eyes tight, still the same glitter; and the same glitter in the soul: as though the whole world were nothing but luminescence.

And Pyotr in pious fear wondered whether the world's transfiguration was at hand. Or was it a sweet and poisonous sorcery – the world's perdition? But one thing was clear to Pyotr: Tselebeyevo had now become the new earth; here was not air, but a sweet, honeyed potion; to breathe it was to be intoxicated; what would happen when the time came to be sober again? Or would there never again be any sobering? Just drinking, beyond reason and restraint, and afterwards – death?

'What is this I am thinking?' – Pyotr tried to make sense of his thoughts, but realized that it was not him thinking, but something thinking itself inside him: as though someone had extracted his soul – but where was it then, his soul? Where was everything that used to be? As he watched, the threads stretched, twitched, wound together in the clear air: and Pyotr thought: 'Those are not threads, but souls: they stream through empty space in a mesh of gossamer – the souls of the Doves, separated by space ... the souls stretch out to meet each other and wind together in the blue.' Daryalsky swung his rod up.

'What is it – caught a roach?'

It was Aleksandr Nikolaevich, the sexton, calling to him through the moist air; sticking his dishevelled head out into the blue autumnal day.

'Aleksandr Nikolaevich – it's wonderful!'

'Hee-hee: it's a nice sunny day!'

'And it's going to be even better, we'll see even more of God's grace!'

'Hee-hee: it's very close, quite humid!'

'That's not it: there's no knowing what will happen ...'

'What will happen? Not an uprising, I hope?'

'That's not it: there will be days in paradise ...'

'Hee-hee: there'll be great drunkenness! It's quite a while since Father Vukol danced the Persian March: the guitar will be twanging away tomorrow, I'll be bound ...'

'So let it twang!'

'The reverend will pretend he's a Turk, on the Balkan campaign.'

'Let him, let him!' Pyotr cried out in holy rapture, wagging his finger; he saw a fine thread shoot out from his extended finger and become enmeshed in the sexton's beard.

'Me too, I'm emitting light too,' Pyotr thought joyfully, but the sexton did not see anything.

'Let him, my good fellow, let the priest have his fun and games: the Spirit will rejoice in him and he'll pick up his guitar.'

'Hee-hee: it's the spirits that does it, Pyotr Petrovich, it's the spirits, not the Spirit ...'

But Pyotr was not listening: he was in holy rapture.

'And I'm telling you, Aleksandr Nikolaevich, that the priest will start dancing to the glory of God ...'

'Christ be with you, Pyotr Petrovich, what's that got to do with the glory of God? If that's the case, then any drunkard who comes bellowing out of the tavern is a herald: it's the flagellants who think like that and no one else; they take their shameless carousing for spiritual enlightenment ...'

And the sexton broke into song:

> 'Mine's all spent
> On the green ser-pent ...'

But Pyotr was not listening: in holy rapture he gathered up his fishing-rod.

'Where are you going?'

'I'm going to the priest's!'

Aleksandr Nikolaevich the sexton didn't understand at all: 'Must be drunk,' he thought, and drew his line in with his fingers, singing under his breath:

> 'Vodka in the teapot, vodka in the cup,
> Here's a toast to vodka – we'll drink the vodka up.'

Pyotr walked across the meadow, stumbling from rapture, or maybe from the toxic exhalations of these parts; there was now a great dichotomy in his soul: it seemed to him that now he had come to understand everything, and was able now to say everything, tell everything, point everything out; but another voice kept whispering to him: 'Nothing of this is real, or ever has been', and he caught himself thinking that this other voice was his real self; but no sooner did he catch himself thinking that he was crazy than it began to seem to him that this other voice that had caught him was the voice of a devil that was tempting him . . . He was thinking like this as he walked across the meadow; suddenly a bright strand of gossamer stretched out to him from behind his back; he turned, and saw, some twenty paces from him, a peasant from the village of Kozhukhanets, who was a member of the Doves; a whole network of threads was dancing around him, emanating from his head, spattering rays of light; 'It's our souls communicating,' Daryalsky rejoiced, and bowed to the Dove; they gave each other a delicate smile of understanding, and went their separate ways.

'Let me perish,' thought Daryalsky, 'if I ever betray the Doves' cause.'

'Are you sure?' came a mocking voice: did he know that with these words he was enticing death? No, he did not know; had he known, he would have howled with horror, would have seized his cap and run from the village to the farthest corner of the earth . . .

He had hardly gone a hundred paces from the pond on the way to the road when a smart pony and trap came careering along the dusty road; a young lady, evidently, was driving the thoroughbred trotter herself; her hands in white gloves, her light-pink dress billowing in the warm air, and all along those light pink billows, like little white clouds, muslin and lace; a white ribbon swirled in the air, fluttering from her straw hat; and under her hat delicate curls danced in all directions.

Pyotr stared – his heart missed a beat: his heart pounded, but he could not tell why; he stood in the middle of the road and shouted in rapture:

'Stop, miss, stop!'

The trap stopped: from behind the pony an oval face peeped out, drowning in ash-blond curls: it was an altogether child-like face, but stern, with dark rings under the eyes, with velvet-black eyelashes over glistening eyes; the young lady stared wildly at Pyotr with terrified eyes, her pale-pink lips trembled, her dainty hand grasped her riding-crop convulsively: the young lady gazed at Pyotr . . .

Wait, why – it was Katya.

It seemed to Pyotr that nothing of what had happened between them had taken place and all was as before: the quarrel, the betrayal, the engagement – surely none of that could change what existed between them: there had never been any quarrel, and if there had been, then who remembered it now, in these new spaces? Pyotr had a feeling of joy and warmth.

'It's a lovely day, Katya!'

Silence: the pony snorted and pawed the ground.

'My love beyond compare, it's so long since I've seen you . . .'

At the words 'love beyond compare' the pale-pink lips trembled, and the eyes became thoughtful for a moment, wondering, it seemed, whether to flash a greeting; but then Katya compressed her lips in contempt; dark-blue horror shone from under her lashes: the riding-crop cracked, and the pony all but knocked Pyotr off his feet.

Daryalsky turned and called after her:

'How's your grandma! Please give her my regards too . . .'

There was nothing but a swirl of dust on the road, as though there had never been any Katya. Intoxicated by the air, Pyotr did not understand the grotesqueness of what had just occurred.

'It's the same with Katya,' he thought and strode quickly to the priest's house.

The priest already had visitors: the constable, Ivan Stepanov the shopkeeper, and one of the young Utkin ladies.

'Good day to you, Father Vukol: peace to your table!'

But the priest offered his hand only coolly.

'Such sunshine and brilliance, makes your heart flutter! Good day to you, Stepanida Yermolaevna . . .'

'Pff, pff, pff,' the young Utkin lady turned her face, narrowing her eyes towards him, not without a certain slyness.

But in the twinkling of an eye the shopkeeper had disappeared from their midst: there he was outside the window, limping off towards his shop.

'Why has he gone lame in his left leg?'

The event of the previous night did not occur to him.

The constable coolly held out a couple of fingers to Pyotr: the interrupted conversation was resumed; as though on purpose, they paid no attention to Pyotr; a feeling of hostility towards him was in evidence. But Pyotr was as if blind: he bestowed his meek benevolence on these people.

They were talking about Yeropegin: 'Who would have thought it – such a pillar of society and all of a sudden – paralysed!'

'It can happen to anyone: to a poor man just as well as to a moneybags,' the constable put in.

'Poor Fyokla Matveyevna,' the Utkin damsel sighed.

'What's poor about her? I bet she's delighted: who will his millions go to if it isn't her?'

'Doesn't matter what you are, before death and sickness and the law – we're all the same: merchant or nobleman, general or chemist . . .'

'I feel sorry for Yeropegin . . .' – the priest glanced round at the others with a kind of guilty grimace; he was thinking: 'If I go on drinking, it might catch up with me in the same way . . .'

'Never mind: all's well that ends well!' Daryalsky leaped up from his seat in rapture, but everyone seemed embarrassed, they lowered their eyes, turned their backs.

'It's nothing: you just have to understand that it's all nothing: just look round – the brilliance, the gossamer, the sun; you have golden honey on your table, Father Vukol; outside the window the aspens have turned red already . . . Ha-ha: everything is as it should be – the first Saviour's Day, the honey-day, has gone already. We're coming up to the third Saviour's Day – aha! . . . And you talk about death; there is no death – ha-ha! Where do you see death?' They all turned away: a fly with horrid yellow fluff on its back flew soundlessly in through the window and settled near the Utkin damsel's muslin blouse.

'Ah!' the young lady cried out: the fly soundlessly described a lifeless circle and settled in the same place.

'That's a strange fly!'

'It's a carrion fly . . .'

'There'll be an epidemic . . .'

'The fly too, the fly is good too!' Daryalsky went on. – 'What are you worried about: I am calm; the third Saviour's Day is nearly here, surely we have no reason to grieve: if God wills it, we shall live to see the Feast of the Beheading of John the Baptist – then there will be such a radiant day . . . And you talk about a fly!'

'Tell me, Mr Daryalsky, is it true what they say, that you have written a little book about young goddesses?'

'Tee-hee-hee,' snorted the Utkin damsel and for some reason lowered her eyes.

'There you are, you see,' the priest winked at Daryalsky, 'you go on about the Book of Revelation, and on the quiet you're putting out books with fig-leaves on them – pfa, pfa . . . Now Father Bukharev used to keep on and on reading Revelation; and what did he go and do in his old age, he got married . . . You don't want to play games with Revelation . . .'

'It doesn't matter,' Daryalsky went on, 'none of it matters: everything is permitted: let us be joyful; you ought to give your guitar a strum, father, take pleasure in its sweet strings, till your chest swells with joy. Praise the Lord God on pipes and tambourines . . . You fetch the guitar, ma'am, and we shall dance.'

At this point something quite unimaginable happened: the Utkin damsel rushed out of the room, snorting and tripping over the floorboards; the constable's face became wild and fierce, while his lips trembled with laughter; and the priest's wife, looking at this moment all red and absurd, threw herself breathlessly upon Daryalsky like a mother pig protecting her litter from a wolf.

'Your words are very strange indeed: there's neither rhyme nor reason in them: so what if Father Vukol asks me to play the guitar? You notice the motes in other people's eyes all right, but you've got a beam and a half in your own: it can be seen right across the district; we're not that sort of people, thank the Lord: we don't go filching diamonds and peeping out of the bushes at barelegged peasant women . . .'

'Oh, ma'am, there was no such thought in my head: I never meant to say anything bad about Father Vukol.'

'Pff-pff-pff!' A spluttering sound came from the next room, from which one of the priest's dribbling offspring poked his head out with staring eyes.

'Kho!' choked the constable, red as a lobster, and turned even fiercer as he tried to restrain his mirth.

'I shall ask you,' the priest's wife went on relentlessly, 'not to visit our house . . .'

'They do not see, they do not comprehend, they're blind!' thought Pyotr as he went out of the priest's garden; the priest's wife followed him with words of insult from the window:

'Maybe you really are the thief who . . .' – he didn't hear: he reached out to the sun with his eyes: in its rays a bright web of gossamer stretched and stretched; a fly was caught in it – 'buzz-zz!'

On the hill in the distance, surrounded by children, Schmidt was coming back from the forest with a basket full of mushrooms; Pyotr waved to him, but Schmidt did not notice him, did not wish to see him.

'What have I done to them? They're all sulking, they don't understand, they don't see, don't want to see!' He thought about the carpenter's cottage, where on five square sazhens the advent of the Spirit was to be fulfilled.

'Are you sure?' came a mocking voice.

'Are you sure?' Pyotr mocked it in return.

'Good day, young man!' A voice resounded from behind his back, as though in answer to him.

He turned: before him stood the clean-shaven gentleman, laughing; his hands were in gloves; over one arm he had a rug; behind his back was the West; and in the West was the sun.

'You're out for a stroll: and whispering to yourself!'

'No, I'm counting the days on my fingers.'

'I no longer count the days now: don't you count them either.'

'It's so good, the warmth – the light!'

'Nothing of the sort, what light, where have you seen light? Now the sky of Italy shines and warms; but that is in the West . . .'

'He can't see the light,' thought Pyotr 'and his hands!' – He looked at his hands, they did not shine: cold hands, white ones.

'Or have I imagined all this, perhaps?' he suddenly said out loud to his own surprise.

'Yes, yes,' Baron Todrabe-Graaben whispered to him, 'You have imagined it: it is all images, images.'

There was a strange authority in his words; and the baron went on whispering:

'Wake up, turn back' – and he pointed in the direction of Gugolevo.

'Where to?' Pyotr started up in fright.

'Where to? To the West: it's the West there. You are a man of the West; why dress yourself up in a peasant's shirt? Turn back . . .'

In an instant his life passed before him, and – Katya: not a trace now of his rapture. Good God, what had he done: he had crushed her young life; Katya was calling him – listen: somewhere a white dove was cooing: somewhere a swallow shot through the air; 'Ivivi,' went its plaintive cry. There, over there, behind the green grove – was the unchanging noise of time: it was the currents of the wind, its gusts in the trees; and that was why the noise from the trees was unchanging. The shadow of Pavel Pavlovich was spreadeagled on the meadow; the tip of the Gugolevo spire gleamed from beyond the grove: there, over there, the old house was waiting for Pyotr: if only . . . to the West.

'Get thee behind me, Satan: I am going to the East.'

Evening falls

In the priest's house meanwhile a ceaseless chattering and whispering went on.

'Ye-es, there's some funny things happening in the district: this one's done himself in, that one's run off to the Slocialists, and another's been gored by a mad bull . . . well, it might have been someone else – diamonds are trumps' – and the constable dealt the cards.

But the priest did not answer: he sat brooding in the corner, resting his chin on his fists and deep in quiet thought: 'It must be my fate to be accused of drunkenness by everyone, what more can you say?' The priest sat brooding: and rubbing his eyes with his fists.

'There was a wolf cub running around the district not long ago; some one got a close look right into its peepers: all meek and mild they were, just like human eyes; but I don't think it was a wolf at all; anyway, the peasant couldn't raise his stick to it; and the wolf cub ran off into the bushes, and as it peeped out its eyes were flashing like mad!'

And again the priest made no answer; he hunched himself up more than ever: squeezed himself into a ball; two tears trickled from his eyes: 'What a life – it's a dog's life: you're dependent on everybody, and everybody's cleverer than you, don't you see!' – the golden red sun struck his golden red hair and the priest's hair turned fluffy.

'The other day a detachment of Cossacks was seen riding by; they all had rifles and great fur hats, and they rode off to the east; the people stood there arguing about what it meant: riots all over the place; and everyone's so fed up with riots . . . Your card, young lady, is beaten, isn't it?'

'Ye-es!'

The priest filled himself a pipe; not long to the service now; he'd do his share of sweating, and then? O, for some rowanberry vodka!

'One of the village women was out looking for mushrooms; and she heard a peasant howling away in the copse – a deep bass voice: she felt really scared; so she hid behind some bushes and, lo and behold, a woman comes striding along the path, with her skirt tucked up and wopping great boots on; and bellowing away at the top of her voice: "Christ is arisen from the dead." Now who could that be but a werewolf?'

'That's a werewolf all right!' – the constable grinned at the priest's wife's words. – 'I know that werewolf: that's Mikhailo the watchman . . .'

'O Lord above!' she sighed. 'Where was it ever seen that a man turned into a woman?'

'He's looking for a convict' – the constable winked: 'there's a convict creeping around the bushes in your village, but I must ask you not to breathe a word about it for the time being . . .'

'But it's time to go to vespers; after vespers – well, tomorrow I'll observe the fast!' The priest smoothed down his red hair, adjusted his grey cassock; he went out onto the meadow – to wave his straw hat for the church care-taker. The dew-damp meadow had already turned yellow, like the sun's rays; and both were now just tinged with red: the priest screwed up his eyes in the sunlight, and in the sunset his freckles turned pink; he scowled.

In the distance someone struck up a song:

> 'Transvaal, Transvaal, my country fair,
> You're all aflame, I see,
> There sits a dignified old Boer
> Beneath the spreading tree.'

The priest made a sign with his hand and the caretaker plodded along to the bell-tower; Ivan Stepanov's shop was closing: soon he too would be plodding along to the church.

> 'The boy came to the battery
> A cartridge in his hand . . .'

resounded from far away.

And again, and again, the Tselebeyevo bell-tower jangled into the red abyss of the sunset; its ringing throbbed into the distance; and far from Tselebeyevo that ringing found an echo: peasants removed their hats.

The priest looked up at the cross, bedecked with sparks of red, and crossed himself too; and he set off to perform his vesperal vigil.

Far away the hollering continued:

> 'And now, you women, you must pray
> For all your distant sons.'

Suddenly the tinkling of a triangle was heard in the distance. A company of drunken louts was wandering around. But the decent people were stringing along to the church: bearded peasants in home-spun coats and blacked boots; women in red calico, girls, and Matryona Semyonovna in her braided bodice, and hobbling behind her the lame carpenter.

In the window of the priest's house the conversation continued:

'You keep a close eye on that gent there, Lukich.'

'Don't you worry!' the constable chuckled . . .

All of a sudden a wind arose in the open spaces, and everything surged:

thousands of trees swayed and nodded from afar; a sturdy, triple-crowned oak began to move, ominously tossing its foliage towards the village; its green sackcloth began to move; clumps of green brocade rustled; when the tocsin of the aspens had died down, a whole red family gave vent to its feelings towards the village; and again it fell silent, awaiting fresh gusts, and only the golden leaves fluttered lisping in the air, and the tin cockerel on a smart cottage jangled; and on the dilapidated roof of an impoverished hut a tuft of straw rose up and dropped back again. There was a large amount of chicken-down in the air.

The making

In Kudeyarov's cottage the shutters were closed tight, and even the yard gates were tightly locked; all that could be heard beside the tumbledown gateway was the snuffling of a young pig and the inane snorting of the mare. It seemed that not a single soul was breathing here at this hour; but that was not true: four souls were breathing ardently and avidly, sealed off from the outside world; the lips of the Doves were avidly and ardently silent; and that silence permeated a space of five square sazhens; and the rooms were filled with grace like a cup that overflows: the descent of the Spirit had been accomplished here on these five square sazhens; the dome of heaven, fallen down to earth, was held up by the pillars of four human bodies; and those four pillars were the white-breasted spouse in the Spirit, Matryona Semyonovna herself, and the lame carpenter, and Pyotr, and the unkempt workman. All those threads that through nights and long, long days the carpenter had spun from himself – all those threads, hitherto invisible, now gleamed in a thousand splendours; it was as though the yellow wood of the walls had been covered in golden paper, and the room shone brighter than the sun in the dim light of four smoking candles. Brighter than the sun the face of Mitry Mironych Kudeyarov, the carpenter, was illuminated, and reflected in the other three.

They were already sitting at the table; they had not donned the white tunics; they had no reason to appear in white, no one to conceal themselves from in disguise; whatever they had been wearing when the evening found them, that was what they wore at the table; Matryona Semyonovna sat ponderously on a bentwood chair in her bodice with the braiding; in front of her on a plate lay a white loaf – for breaking; across from her sat Pyotr, glancing at her from time to time. A weird thing: he understood now that the weird mystery came flowing into Matryona from the carpenter, and that Matryona herself had nothing to do with it, she herself was like a wild animal; he glanced sideways at Matryona and her pock-marked, sweat-covered, seemingly crumpled face, white as white could be, the rings beneath her eyes, of an unnerving blue, as though the azure sky shone through, her dirty-red hair of a dusty hue, and the swellings on her blood-baked lips aroused him wildly; he remembered the gentleness of her caresses and their fury; he wondered: 'Are you a wild animal or a witch?' But the witch sat motionless in her braided bodice, which hung on her as though on a clothes-hanger; her calloused hands were folded on her stomach; her gaze was fixed upon the white loaf, which she was to break and distribute; but when, with a sensuous lick of her lips, the witch fixed her gaze on him, heavy blue waves began to roll in her eyes, and out of her eyes there gazed the intemperate ocean; then it seemed to him that he would flounder until the Second Coming of Christ, drowning in those blue seas, until the archangel's stentorian trump he would crave for those lips, if there was to be a Second Coming at all, and the devil had not stolen the trumpet of judgement from heaven. But he was already beginning to realize that this was terror, the snare, and the pit: this was not Russia, but some dark abyss of the East assailing Russia from these bodies, emaciated by their rites. 'Terror!' he thought, and remembered the clean-shaven gentleman and his strange-sounding words, like the cry of a frightened nocturnal bird, warning the traveller that he had lost his way in the night, words which invited him to turn back, return to his homeland: 'Turn back.'

For an instant Gugolevo flashed before him, and he thought: 'Everything is pure and unsullied there; there at least there is no secret summons, which seems sweet at a distance, but close to is dirty.'

The carpenter sat solemnly in front of him with his white countenance gleaming like the sun and with a candle in his hands; he was wearing his tall tar-blacked boots on the occasion of the sabbath, his watch, and his Sunday suit; a current of green light issued from his head in an iridescent ring; but what was most awful about him was that on top of his suit, like an ecclesiastical stole, there cascaded from his neck an immensely broad ribbon of scarlet satin, rustling and folding in creases, while above it waggled his paltry beard.

'What a strange business,' thought Pyotr, 'here he is shining all over with sweetness; but why is his face unpleasant and frightening?' As Pyotr looked he saw there was just a long-snouted weevil sitting in front of him, shining all over: a very radiant weevil, though.

They all sat in silence, crossing themselves, sighing, waiting for the longed-for visitor: hadn't the longed-for visitor already knocked? Tuk-tuk-tuk; that was their hearts knocking; four small red flames licked at their faces from the four wax candles; a tin bowl on the table frothed with wine that had just been poured into it; today was a day of silent prayer; from the carpenter's lips hoarse groans and sighs erupted; at times it seemed these sounds were threats; at others they seemed to be the dull roar of the approaching flood; now and then a cockroach ran across the table and stopped stock-still in front of the loaf, twitching its whiskers; then it quickly crawled across to the edge of the table; Daryalsky reflected that he had been neither tempted by the rich wisdom of the age, nor restrained from flight by a girl's pure love; but he had been lured into the abyss by a wild animal and a weevil; but the weevil was looking sternly at Pyotr. Pyotr shuddered.

It occurred to him that he was already in the abyss; and these four walls were the hell in which he was to be tortured; but why did the soul light up in that abyss, and why did light issue from his fingers; was it the abyss, or the lofty empyrean? And if it was the empyrean, why was the carpenter just a weevil? The weevil cast a stern glance at Pyotr. Pyotr shuddered.

He looked – a ring of light, crackling, spread out over the carpenter, and the carpenter seemed not to be the carpenter, but something altogether different, a manifestation of light; sharp rays beat, pricked, cut and burned Pyotr's body, boring into his thoughts; there seemed to be something quite ominous in the carpenter: but no, it was a momentary vision.

The bowl of foaming wine went round them all; the wine dried on the carpenter's yellow moustache like frothing black blood: the white loaf was broken; they greedily swallowed the soft bread, moistened with wine; and already the walls were dissolving, the doubts were dissolving, the yellow wax of the candles was dissolving; the wax dripped onto the scarlet ribbon of satin: everything was dissolving and what was left was lightness and joy.

They flashed their eyes at one another; drunk with happiness they laughed, and spittle sprayed from their lips; the unkempt workman rumbled in his deep bass; they all clapped; Matryona began to dance: as his woman danced, the carpenter chanted: 'Jesus frees us, drives us, shrives us . . . Lord, have mercy.' They revelled in their stamping and droning and trilling, and laughed; their teeth gleamed; their eyes gleamed; Matryona tucked up her skirt and danced, heels on buttocks; their eyes were blinded by the brightness of their prayer-illumined bodies; on the table glinted a knife, left there for some reason; suddenly its blade squealed out: 'White flesh – a fine swain's!' The unkempt workman dropped to his haunches in front of Matryona to dance in a squatting position. And then – everything began to move: the four walls, which sealed this space hermetically from the world, seemed to take off; all the signs showed that this was now a ship, flying off into the blue sky; step over the threshold now, my friend – and beyond that threshold you will find the void; only far below, deep down beneath your feet, in the darkness of the night, far away the lights of Tse-lebeyevo twinkle like distant stars, or like the moon's glint in the puddles at your feet; sundered from all dwelling by the sweetest vapours, all four were flying into emptiness.

Everything began to move: the walls cracked; the cottage-ship tipped to starboard, the table tilted onto Pyotr; the empty wine-bowl tumbled to the floor, the carpenter himself rose over Pyotr . . . The walls cracked – every-thing began to move; the cottage-ship listed to port, the table fell away from Pyotr: the carpenter, too, fell away, and Pyotr was tossed up: was this hell's visitation on the abyss, or the blessed recreation of paradise – who knew, who could tell?

Matryona danced, the hem of her skirt hoisted high; but her face was blue, and her eyes could not be seen; only the whites, pouring out blueness beneath her eyes; her white teeth bit her lip; she stamped a rhythm with her ankle-boots, the unkempt workman somersaulted into the corner and breathed heavily. Pyotr danced; how indecent it turned out when he did it! Suddenly Matryona started throwing off her clothes but thought better of it: half-undressed, giggling, she looked at the carpenter, and tapped out a goading rhythm. The carpenter himself joined in the dance: away with the ribbon from his head, and hands to his hips: when he did it it turned out solemn. And Matryona urged them on with clapping, accom-panying them harmoniously with gentle singing: a fine, amusing, merry little song:

> 'Old man – old stick –
> Tartarara tartararik . . .'

And the unkempt workman joined in from the corner:

> 'Tartarara tartarara! . . .
> Tartarara tartararik . . .
> Oh, the priest
> Went coughin'
> Head first
> Into his coffin!
> Tartarara tartarara –
> Tartarara tartararik!'

It turned out jaunty: all four danced, but there seemed to be five of them . . .

Who was the fifth?

'Yes, brother – here everything is possible' – the carpenter chuckled; above and below was an invisible bounty of air; within this aerial fortress the world was invisible to them, and they were invisible to the world.

Matryona jumped up and ran from the room with a laugh, for no clear reason Pyotr ran out after her; they ran across that blessed place where the yard used to be, littered with dung, only it wasn't the yard – nothing of the sort, and it was not dung beneath their feet, but soft, cool velvet; they opened the gate, and outside the gate was – nothing at all: there was no Tselebeyevo there, nor any other place: cold black velvet whistled in their ears: the cottage was standing in the air.

All transgressions were left down there, below; here – everything was possible, was sinless, for all is God's grace; they went back into the room.

But the carpenter was now on his feet, and raised his shining hand over them; it seemed to be him – and it seemed not to be; he seemed to be talking – and he seemed not to be: just like that, the words occurred of their own accord in the air: 'What you see now, children, therein I abide forever, for I am sent to you into the world from there, where I abide forever, to perform that which is meet. Be merry, sing and dance, for all are saved by grace . . .' That was what Pyotr heard, but they were not the carpenter's words; they arose of their own accord in the air.

Here came the carpenter's words: he quietly stepped up to them, and with his sickly hand stroked first Pyotr, then Matryona: 'A strapping woman – isn't she? And all that . . . Come on, Matryona, give your gentleman a hug . . . Come on, children.' He grinned with the side of his face that said: 'I've got what it takes.'

And a burning flame joined Pyotr with Matryona; there was a pillar of smoke between their breasts; they went off to the bed. And from there they came back to the carpenter. See, everything was already different; coming back into the parlour, they saw the unkempt workman on his knees before the carpenter, bowing his forehead to the ground, and the carpenter sprawled on the bench – shining brilliantly; he was groaning, oh so sweetly, with his belt undone; his chest was bared and transparent, like a bluish jelly, and throbbing gently, and out of his chest, as though out of an egg, a small white bird's head was pecking its way; and see – from his gashed and bleeding chest, oozing purple blood, out hopped a dove, woven, it seemed, from mist – and up it flew!

'Gul-gul-gul' – Pyotr called the dove; he crumbled white bread in front of the bird, and the dove swooped onto his chest; with its claws it tore the shirt on him, and with its beak bored into his chest, and his chest was pecked apart like a white jelly and purple blood was spilt; and Pyotr saw that its head was not the head of a dove – but of a hawk.

'Ah!' – Pyotr fell to the floor; the bleeding orifice of his gashed chest let out a fountain of blood.

Then the dove swooped on Matryona: and four bodies, pecked to pieces, lay speechless – on the floor, the table and the bench – with bloodless, lifeless, but effulgent faces, while the dove with the head of a hawk nuzzled up to them and hopped about and cooed; it settled on the table – and rushed, with a pa-pa-pa of its claws, to peck up the breadcrumbs.

Then their dead bodies dissolved, frothing with a foam, it seemed, of mist, as though dispersing in smoke, and fusing together in a glistening mist: and it was not a mist – that mist collected into a single luminous body: a single white body, woven from radiance, took distinct form in the middle of the room; and in that body eyes took form, as though torn open: distant, melancholy eyes: a beardless and miraculously youthful countenance, attired in clothes as white as snow, and on those clothes were golden stars; like streams of golden wine the locks upon his head frothed and curled and billowed down his shoulders; his hands outstretched, between his fingers, tender as the petals of the lily, the distant stars seemed close: quietly the stars gleamed around this radiant youth; the Dove-child, born of rapture and arisen from four dead bodies, as the oneness that bound their souls – meekly the Dove-child nuzzled up to things; the child took a drink of red wine: his purple lips smiled with a great love. And the walls vanished: on all four sides the pale-blue sky of dawn; below, the dark abyss where clouds were floating; on the clouds, in snow-white raiment and stretching out their hands towards the child, were Doves already saved, and far away, in the depths, in the great darkness, was a red ball bathed in flame with smoke cascading from it: that was the earth; the righteous were flying from the earth, and a new song resounded:

> 'Bright, oh, bright, is the dove-blue air,
> Bright in that air is the spirit dear!'

But everything melted, like someone's fleeting dream, like a transient vision, and there was no longer any child, nor any red ball bathed in flame: above – the pale-blue sky; and in the distance – the rosy dawn; in the west the dark of night and haze; and in that haze the faint sphere of the moon, so lately crimson, and now fading ominously. Down below, a village clung secretively to the sloping land; the white bell-tower was still in the darkness of night, but its cross already gleamed golden: why – that's Tselebeyevo: raucous cockerels were crowing, here and there a puff of smoke rose from a cottage, and the lowing of a cow was to be heard. Soon the dust would rise and the horned herd would amble lazily onto the yellow-brown stubble-field.

A cart rumbled on its way from Likhov: it was Andron the peasant coming back from his jaunt; in his cart he had bags, a flagon of government vodka, and a bundle of rolls. And he was happy.

Suddenly the cart bumped into someone's body.

'Whoa! . . . Isn't that the gent from Gugolevo?' – Andron bent over the body.

'Sir, hey, sir!'

'Oh, where are you, radiant Dove-child?' Pyotr mumbled sleepily . . .

'Well I never, he's on about some child,' Andron muttered in sympathy: 'Why, I do believe he's drunk . . . He's got a skinful all right . . .

'Sir!'

'Oh, isn't my chest pecked to pieces by the dove?'

'Get up, sir . . .'

Pyotr raised himself dully and started dancing:

> 'Old man – old stick –
> Tartarara tartararik.'

Andron grasped him round the midriff and laid him on the cart: 'A fine one you are, jolly good clobbering, that's what you need . . .'

'Matryona, you witch: get away from me, weevil,' Pyotr went on muttering; but Andron took no more notice of him; he smacked his lips; 'drr-drr-drr', the cart bounced along and there was Tselebeyevo in front of him.

At this point Pyotr came round: he jumped up on the cart and looked; in front was a ditch; from it a wormwood bush whistled into the turquoise morning.

'Where am I?'

'You've had a bit to drink, sir: you'd still be lying on the road there, if it wasn't for me.'

'However did I get here?'

'It's no wonder; there's many a worse place people get to when they're drunk.'

Pyotr remembered it all: 'Was it a dream or not?' he thought, and was seized by a fit of trembling.

'Terror, the snare, and the pit,' his lips whispered involuntarily; he thanked Andron and jumped down from the cart; swaying from his drunkenness, he meandered towards the carpenter's cottage.

All was still: the pig, left to its own devices, was grunting by Kudeyarov's cottage: the door into the yard was partly open: 'So I must have gone out through the yard,' thought Pyotr, but he had no recollection of it, he only remembered the dance, and Matryonka with her skirt hoisted up, and the bird of prey that swooped upon his chest, Lord only knew from where . . . And he remembered some kind of radiant vision; and – he remembered nothing.

He went into the cottage: in the cottage was a snoring and a wheezing and a smell of stale air: on the table was an overturned tin bowl; on the table and on the floor was spilt wine, like patches of blood.

The clock ticked evenly.

Threats

After a long disappearance Abram the beggar, who had been away somewhere, turned up in the morning beneath the windows of the cottages; he chanted psalms in his cracked bass voice, beating the rhythm with his staff: soundless lightning flashes shot crisply from his tin dove; his white felt toadstool poked into a window here or there, in quest of an egg, a crust, a kopeck; and out of the windows stretched hands with an egg, or a crust, or a kopeck – a propitiatory offering; but the beggar's hoarse bass was not to be propitiated: it became harsher, more threatening; the beggar's voice threatened unknown woes, just as woes were presaged by the harsh August day: on this harsh August day Abram beat time with his staff, and his toadstool poked in through the window, and soundless lightning flashed from his tin dove.

There were only three beggars in the Tselebeyevo district: Prokl, Demyan and Abram; the fourth, nicknamed Bottomless Pit, rarely showed himself in our parts; Prokl was an old soak with a benign smile, Demyan stole chickens: and the fourth beggar nicknamed Bottomless Pit used to have fits.

Anyway, the beggars were indulged and accepted; the beggars belonged: and Abram, as he went from hut to hut, demanded his due; and hands stretched out with hunks of bread, kopecks, eggs, and the beggar's bag swelled mightily.

And so Abram appeared at the door of the shop, tapping away with his cudgel, and it wasn't a psalm he struck up this time, but an ancient song:

> 'Brethren, do you harken,
> All of you my friends,
> And in rapt attention
> Lend me now your ears.

Brethren, do you manifest
All your kindnesses,
Be yourselves not tempted,
As nothing are my sins.'

But this pleasant singing, with its lightly concealed threat, produced an uproar; Ivan Stepanov the shopkeeper leaped out of the shop with his spectacles on his nose, hobbling on his damaged leg, and raised his fist, with the thumb between the first two fingers, right under Abram's nose.

'I'll give you what you're asking for, you parasite, you stinker, you sectarian cur, you wait, just you wait till they catch up with you!'

And then the constable came out of the shop and mumbled into his beard.

Abram gave a bow and quietly set off along the road to Gugolevo.

Over the window at Gugolevo the red leaves of a fading vine hung limply; Katya stood at the open window, with her hands on her grandmother's shoulders; grandmama was winding wool into a ball; Pavel Pavlovich, the baron, was standing over the old lady and, with respectful condescension, holding the skein of wool on his fingers.

Suddenly a song was heard beneath the window:

'In the east bright paradise,
Joys in never-ending throng,
Land without a taint of vice,
To the virgins you belong.
Chambers finer than the Tsar's,
Gardens, arbours, verdant bowers,
Gilded halls and soaring towers,
Wondrous fruits beneath the stars.'

Under the window Abram the beggar was standing, beating time with his staff and sticking his toadstool hat in at the window; leaden lightning flashed crisply from his soundless dove; already a silver coin had tumbled into his hat, but still he went on:

'Smoothly there the rivers roll,
Their waters purer still than tears, –
You shall settle there forever,
My beloved daughter . . .

In your soul all passions perish,
Nothing there but calm and joy . . .'

' – A-aa!' Katya's sobs rang out; she collapsed into an armchair, covering her face with her slender fingers . . .

'Be off with you, you scoundrel!' – grandmama struck the floor with her heavy stick; but outside the window Abram had already disappeared; a hubbub was raised . . .

Puffing away at his home-rolled cigarette in deep silence, Abram was sitting under the icons in the corner; in front of him the carpenter was stalking on lame legs from one corner to the other, scratching at his finger; a powerful anger glared out from his frenzied eyes; they complained to one another:

'That shopkeeper ought to be flayed alive and sprinkled with salt: the dirty rascal; always snooping!'

'Well, there's punishment in store for him!'

'Is everything ready?'

'Everything: dry straw, and tow, and paraffin: he's done enough fire-raising round here – now it's his turn to go up in smoke!'

'Has anyone been given the job of lighting it?'

'No one's been given the job – and all that . . . I'll set him alight with my eyes.'

Silence.

'Then there's the lad: I don't like the lad; he might get scared of the making.'

'Been doing some, have you?'

'We have.'

'Did something go wrong with it?'

'It was all right: only it wasn't enough – the lad's scared of the making. There's not enough strength in him; we did some making; and a bodily child did take form from our prayers; but it wasn't firm – it dissolved into thin air, didn't last more than an hour, and all because of the lad's weakness . . . And haven't I been pumping out my strength into him! And hasn't Matryona . . . And still the fellow's scared . . .'

'You ought to tell him,' and Abram whispered something to the carpenter.

'Not likely: he'd take fright – might even run away.'

'And what if he does run away?'

'Then I'll catch him . . .'

'But if he really runs away?'

'That'd be a hopeless business: we can't have him running away now.'

'But if he did though?'

'Th-th-then I-I-I . . .' the carpenter started stuttering, 'then I'll . . .' – and with his powerful eyes he indicated the knife.

'Ah-ha! So he won't get away then?'

'There's nowhere he can escape from me; if he tries, I'll cut his throat.'

Silence . . .

On that day, in among the priest's currant bushes, a guitar began to strum: its strings twanged out across the whole village; glasses were emptied, the priest's wife's tears were shed, and the guitar twanged away so wildly, so smoothly: Father Vukol meanwhile made a fortress out of chairs, and then, armed with a poker, captured that fortress with the sexton's help; as luck would have it, one of the priestly offspring was discovered in the fortress: the priest took his offspring prisoner; but here the priest's irate wife intervened; and her guitar began marching up and down the priest's back: thump-thump-thump; the guitar was smashed to pieces; and in the bushes there was giggling; the priest took flight from his wife down the well; he grabbed hold of the rope, splayed his feet against its wooden sides, and slid down to the very bottom of the well; there he sat, knee-deep in water, gazing up above him at the blue slit of the sky; he saw his wife there beside herself with grief: poor hapless woman, tearfully she begged the priest to come back up; but he just sat knee-deep in water, and to all her nagging simply said – 'Don't want to, I just don't want to: I'm nice and cool down here.' They were on the point of climbing down after him; but finally the priest, in an access of magnanimity, gave the good people his consent to being extracted from the aqueous aperture; they dropped a rope with a bucket on the end of it, and out they pulled the priest; his feet were crammed into the bucket, he was numb with cold, and water was pouring from his cassock – like a drowned chicken he was . . . The lads laughed in an ugly way, and in the distance the schoolmarm laughed in an ugly way too.

It turned out a menacing day: beyond the trees the thunder could already be heard chattering away; and the trees were dully whispering back; and where the dusty road ran off to Likhov, the little dark figure that for years had kept an eye on the village from afar waved its arms at the village in desperation, and dry floods of dust rose up, rushed at the village and licked the feet of passers-by, hurled themselves into the sky and swirled about in yellow clouds; and the menacing sun itself, red through the dust, foretold a lengthy drought for the inhabitants of our village, faint already from the heat.

CHAPTER SEVEN

The Fourth

Talk at eventide

The angry red sun hurled itself upon Tselebeyevo from behind the crowns of the yellow forest in a five-fingered wreath of rays; above was the tender blue of the sky; and it seemed to be cold panes of glass; in the sunset stood clouds like heavy blocks of golden ice; summer lightning flickered there; all this brilliance was staring into the little window of the carpenter's cottage.

By the window were Pyotr and Matryona.

'Do you know that the carpenter is planning to do away with me?'

'Be quiet: here he is.'

Matryona was leaning out of the window as she said this; Pyotr leaned out too: between the bushes and tussocks of grass, covered in red strips of sunset like patches of patterned carpet, the carpenter was slowly approaching, spitting out sunflower husks; he was wearing his new boots; his blood-red shirt showed scarlet amongst the bushes, and his homespun coat was thrown over his shoulder; behind the carpenter walked a visitor: an anaemic tradesman with dull eyes and thick lips, around which there bristled coarse, colourless whiskers; he had an altogether wasted look, but bore himself with dignity.

'Who might that be, Matryona?'

'God alone knows: how should I know?'

The visitor meanwhile was standing at the threshold of the cottage; 'The fourth,' Pyotr thought in fear (he was responding to a thought of his own); and he could already feel his own strength waning, his determination to resist the chimera of all these recent days dissolving; 'The fourth!' he thought, and weakened manifestly: just so a strong, transparent ice-block melts away, exposed to the baking heat of a July day . . .

'Heat up the samovar, Matryona: make our dear guest welcome . . . And all that.'

And the visitor entered, crossed himself with dignity before the icons, and then, pointing a finger in the direction of Daryalsky, condescended to remark:

'He's the one, is he, Mitry Mironych, you were talking about: the object of her affections, like?'

'That's him' – the carpenter started to bustle and fuss around the dear guest, darting glances at Daryalsky and making signs at him not to contradict.

By now the sun had set behind the yellow crowns of the forest: the five-fingered wreath ascended majestically into the tender blue of the sky; the evening was crimson, the colour of porphyry.

'Ye-es . . .' the guest muttered, fiddling with his bronze watch-chain, and then without waiting to be invited sat down in the icon corner, lit red by the setting sun.

'How do you do!' Pyotr said at last, offering his hand to the wasted-looking tradesman . . .

'Hello, hello' – the tradesman condescendingly proffered two fingers. – 'I know you . . . You're doing the Spirit's work . . .'

'He's doing a bit for it,' the carpenter put in, and wrinkles of abasement clouded his face, while the half of his face that was turned to Pyotr threatened disaster.

'You keep up the Spirit's work, my good fellow; it's a good thing, you know: to do the work of the Spirit; I'm doing the same work myself – trying to do my bit . . .'

'Who are you, actually, yourself?' Pyotr could not resist asking . . .

'I'm actually Sukhorukov the tinsmith; you're bound to have heard of me: everybody knows the Sukhorukovs: in Chmar, and Kozliki, and Petushki.'

Pyotr remembered the sign that hung in the square in Likhov, on which fat letters traced out 'Sukhorukov'.

In the meantime the samovar was brought in, some ring-shaped rolls, and sugar, and the carpenter settled down to take tea with his guest, who, biting off a piece of a sugar lump, blew pompously with his thick lips on the scalding liquid; one thing was strange: they didn't light the lamps; just stayed there sitting in the crimson twilight as evening settled over Tselebeyevo.

'Sidor Semyonych gets important business sorted out for us, my lad – and all that' – the carpenter gave Pyotr a wink; and then he added: 'he's a proper Dove all right . . .'

And the proper Dove added:

'All the Sukhorukovs are like that: the whole Sukhorukov clan, you might say, are all birds of a feather . . . And how about things here, with you?'

'With us it's like this: we're busy too, and all that, just on the quiet, like, with the making . . .'

'How's that, he's doing it?'

'He's in on the making . . .'

'With the woman?'

'With my woman, yes . . .'

'And the woman's doing it? . . .'

'Yes, my woman too . . .'

'Now don't you worry, lad' – the carpenter turned to Pyotr with a special amiability – 'about all this, and so on: Sidor Semyonych, and all that' – the carpenter somehow wilted suddenly – 'he's a proper Dove all right, one of the best.'

And the proper Dove, sitting at the table, blew pompously with his thick lips on the scalding liquid; one thing was strange; they didn't light the lamps.

But Pyotr felt no fear of the wasted little tradesman; he saw how the three of them were sitting here at the table: Mitry, the unkempt workman and himself; and Sukhorukov was the fourth among them; but fear he did not feel at all; true, he felt a certain disgust, almost revulsion, towards this tinsmith; he quickly realized that this tradesman was capable of any villainy the human race could devise; that was clear to Pyotr from the look on the carpenter's face as he entertained his guest. Pyotr surmised that some shameful secret lay between them; the tinsmith, though, blew into his tea impassively, with prodigious arrogance, as though the carpenter, and Pyotr, and Matryona were all objects that had fallen into his, the tinsmith's, hands, in such a way that the tinsmith's hand would never release its spoils.

Pyotr felt sick; he went outside; the five-fingered crimson wreath still stood in the distance; Pyotr recollected how day had followed day imperceptibly, and how autumn was now falling in the twitter of the blue-tits and the yellow raiment of the richly rustling trees.

In front of the cottage Matryona was sitting under the cow, tugging at its teats; milk was splashing into the tin pail.

Pyotr stopped and stood pensively over Matryona:

'Do you know that the carpenter is planning to do away with me?'

'Oh, to the devil with you: that's a fine thing to dream up!'

'But he'll do away with you too.'

'Whatever for?'

'And there's harm coming to good people from him.'

'That's not possible; there's no need for it.'

'Why does he keep squinting at me then, spying on me?'

'Because he's the boss: just keeping an eye on you.'

'Haven't you noticed, Matryona, that we're the carpenter's prisoners: you and me; neither you nor I can take a step without him; straight away he's plodding after us into the forest; straight away he's leaning over from the sleeping-shelf . . .'

'It's a sin to prattle like that, Pyotr Petrovich!'

And the milk splashed into the pail and the cow's teats were tugged; purple streams of cloud burned so brightly away in the distance; in the east the ashen darkness turned into a darkness of blue-black hue, and from there, out of the blue-black darkness, the timid stars began to shine, and the cold, autumnal breeze whispered with the bushes.

Pyotr remembered, Lord alone knows why, his distant past; both Schmidt and the books that once upon a time Schmidt had lent him; he remembered, Lord alone knows why, Paracelsus's treatise *Archidoxis Magica* and the words of Paracelsus on the way in which a skilled magnetist can exploit people's erotic powers for his own ends; he also remembered the book by the physicist Kircher *De Arte Magnetica*; he remembered the words of the great Fludd; oh, if only Pyotr had told, oh, if only he had told Matryona about the carpenter and everything that was happening between them; but it was beyond Matryona's understanding; Daryalsky shuddered and watched; the splay-footed peasant woman had got lost in thought there under the cow and let the cow's slender teat slip from her hands; brick-red tufts of hair slipped out from her shawl: there she squatted, picking her teeth with a finger, her fat toes squelching in manure: a witch as ever was; only those eyes of hers – her eyes! only the cold, red rays of the sunset there above her; and the slenderest strands of evening clouds wafted into the dove-blue sky. The whole sky was strewn with streams of red – in all directions.

'And those prayers? Do we know, Matryona, what spirit it is that comes down upon us? Why, that is all a mirage of the carpenter's making; he needs you, Matryona, just as he needs me; without us the carpenter's power would be the death of him; there's a word for it, I would say it, but no, you wouldn't understand it . . .'

'What's the word then?'

'If I told you you wouldn't understand.'

'Lord bless you, some marvellous word you've invented; you leave Mitry Mironych out of it, in Christ's name I beg you: I don't like these things you're saying, there now . . .'

She took the pail of milk and went into the cottage; as she went in, the carpenter and the tinsmith were still whispering in the darkened corner,

they still hadn't lit the lamps; it was dark in the cottage; cockroaches were
rustling behind the chromolithographs; and with the rustle of a multitude
of cockroach legs merged the light rustle of human voices: 'shu-shu-
shu . . .'

When Matryona entered they didn't notice her at all: so deep were they
in whispering; Matryona Semyonovna became a little afraid; and she spoke
up:

'Mitry Mironych, hey, Mitry Mironych!'

They didn't hear; so deep were they in whispering – right into each
other's ear: 'shu-shu-shu – shu-shu-shu . . .'

'Mitry Mironych!'

'What?' the carpenter responded from the corner, startled by her call, in
a high-pitched voice; as though he wasn't Mitry Mironych at all, but some
scrawny cockerel.

'What are you doing there?'

'What?' the tinsmith squeaked from the corner, like a cart that neeeded
oiling.

'What are you whispering about over there?'

'Nothing special; we're making prayers: you go along now, God be with
you, my dove . . .'

'You go along, woman,' the tinsmith squeaked in turn; Matryona went
out to the cow.

Pyotr was standing there, thinking out his melancholy thought: 'And
she' – he turned to face Matryona – 'is my love.'

Pyotr thought about Katya (the clouds' light strands burned up in love);
no: Katya was now as unattainable as those clouds: she did not exist for
him; his heart ached.

'Oh,' Matryona sighed, 'I'm so sleepy . . .'

They had nothing to talk about.

'Shall we run away from here, Matryona? I'll take you far away; I'll hide
you from the carpenter; we shall have a life, we shall: it will be free and
unrestrained (he remembered that he had once said exactly the same words
to Katya): let's run away from here, Matryona.'

'Be quiet: he's bound to hear . . .'

'He can't hear; let's run away, Matryona!'

'Be quiet: he hears everything, and he sees everything; he'll be able to
find us anywhere; I'm not going anywhere away from him; and you're not
going anywhere away from him either.'

'I shall leave you, Matryona.'

'Going back to that Katenka of yours, that French mamselle, are you?
She'll send you packing, she will.'

'I feel so wretched, Matryona!'

'That's enough of your prattle!'

Pyotr thought about Katya – he thought a while, and stopped; Katya was now as unattainable as those clouds; Katya did not exist for him; and his heart ached.

The clouds' light wings burned through, like wings of love, turning into an ethereal ash, into dross; the whole neighbourhood with its cottages and bushes became ethereal and ashen; ominous mounds of ash rolled in from the east, so recently transparent; soon all this murk and all this fire-scarred sky would turn indigo, turn black, like a dead man's face, and bury the neighbourhood till the new morning – like a dead man's face that even yesterday was so fresh, even yesterday was so pink and smiled a greeting and a word of kindness; the day – ripe apple – had rotted by the evening, and the putrescence of the evening was clamouring at the windows, spilling out over those who stood at the threshold of the cottage, so that their faces turned indigo, turned black, like those of the dead.

'Do you know that the carpenter is planning to do away with me?'

'Be quiet: he hears everything.'

'He'll do away with you too.'

But Matryona, bowing her head, led the dun cow away, squelching in the manure.

'How many good people the carpenter has destroyed!'

Matryona went into the cottage; still the lamps were not lit: 'shu-shu-shu – shu-shu-shu' still filled the air in the darkened corner.

'Mitry Mironych, hey, Mitry Mironych?'

'Shu . . .'

'Mitry Mironych!'

Matryona dropped a ladle, as though by accident.

'What's that?' – the carpenter suddenly responded from the corner, sweetly, like a scrawny young cockerel.

'What are you mumbling about there?'

'We're making prayers . . .'

'Yes, we're making prayers,' – the cart that needed oiling responded too. They lit the lamps . . .

'He's her passion, then, is he?' – the Likhov tradesman poked his finger now at Pyotr, now at Matryona; Matryona blushed scarlet and stared at her own stomach.

'That's right, Sidor Semyonych, of course he is: they make love to each other as Doves; they entertain each other with kisses . . .'

'Ha-ha: like doves,' – the tinsmith squeaked, like a cart that needed oiling. 'So, let them make love!'

'Quite so: let them, Sidor Semyonych, let them; that's just what I say to them . . .'

'Pfff!' Matryona snorted, red with shame, and hid herself in the corner.

Pyotr had a feeling of shame and horror to the point of nausea. He went out, slamming the door; soon the visitor turned his cup over, and together with his host left the cottage.

In the distance the sky was still clear: the five-fingered pillar above the village was not extinguished.

What happened in the teahouse

Soot, smoke, fumes, din, peasants, puddles on the floor – that was what met Pyotr in the teahouse; Pyotr asked for some tea and sat down at a table covered with a tablecloth that was spattered all over with yellow stains; people turned to look at him, or gave each other a nudge, some whispered 'the red squire', while others spat and swore an oath; the drunken constable narrowed his eyes; and that was an end to the matter.

But Pyotr saw nothing of all that: he rested his elbows on the table, and sat transfixed in thought.

Deeply my hero sat immersed in reflection on his own fate; he could find no explanation for this strange love of his, these uncouth rites, nor for his servitude to the carpenter; he felt that something huge and heavy was weighing down upon him, stifling him, rising to his throat and throttling him with a sinful sensuality, or tickling him to the point of suffocation, so that at times he could not tell whether he was experiencing unheard-of ecstasies, or unending torment of both soul and spirit; one thing was strange: whenever the rites did not take place, this feeling of oppression turned into sweet delight: he who is doomed to pain and crucifixion, which can no longer be in any way avoided, endeavours yet to bless that crucifixion; so too the man who is suffering from toothache: he is ready to smash his jaw against a stone, just to increase the pain: and in that aggravation of his pain lies all the sweetness for him, and all the sensuality; and Pyotr did likewise: sweet languor overcame him as he waited for the rites; and in that sweet anticipation his imagination conjured up enigmas and mysteries in broad daylight. An extraordinary thing: in these days he began to love his Russia more than ever: sometimes it was a sensuous love, sometimes his love was cruel; and in these same days Matryona became everything to him; and together with Matryona he waited to see how Kudeyarov the carpenter would respond to his anticipation; then, more clearly yet, that new world revealed itself to him, in which the carpenter Mitry Mironych was waiting for him with a cup of sweet wine, and offering that new wine to all mankind.

But he had only to put that cup to his lips and all his perceptions changed; he did not know whether these strange adventures were happening to him in a waking state or in a dream; and after those rites he rose in the morning with a dull headache, nausea, a satiety of the soul – and all that had happened to him the night before now struck him as vile, shameful and frightening; in broad daylight he turned in fear to look at bushes, empty corners, and all the time it seemed that someone was stalking him; he felt an invisible, oppressive hand upon his breast; and feared suffocation; and from shame he lowered his eyes before people, horses and cattle; and all the time he felt that both men and beasts were pointing him out with their eyes; he sensed unprecedented gossip, and was ashamed of his own disgrace.

Now too he shuddered, and began to look around: soot, smoke, fumes, din, peasants; and amidst all that a distinct voice: 'Look now, good people: that's the red squire sitting over there.'

'So them diamonds wasn't found, then,' was heard quite distinctly at the neighbouring table and two peasants gave Daryalsky a reproachful stare: all these hints, thank goodness, he did not understand, indeed he did not even hear them: his ears were full of the words 'red squire'; but these words were not uttered by the peasants; and Daryalsky engrossed himself once more in the tablecloth.

And then Matryona: these recent days she had no longer seemed to him that love for whom his life should be surrendered, and his soul into the bargain; no, Matryona did not seem to be that love: she seemed to him a dirty slattern, stupid and, what's more, with an excessive appetite for coarse caresses; there was perhaps nothing but their mutual wantonness that held him to her; but most of all he was held by the carpenter's eyes: for if the carpenter should cast his eye upon you, then, my dear man, you will be bound to that gaze like a dog on a chain.

He had already, without noticing it, asked for some vodka, some sausage, and a packet of cigarettes (the brand called 'Leo' – five kopecks for ten); he had poured vodka from the teapot and tipped the fiery liquid into his mouth: he had a rasping sensation in his throat, the fire was spreading through his chest and in his head a pleasant ringing sound was beginning, when all at once he caught sight of a tipsy little old man with grey sideburns, dressed all in grey, who had taken off his peaked cap and was wiping his eyes with a red handkerchief.

'Yevseich!'

'Why, Mr Pyotr, sir: how thin you've become, my dear young man, how dark you've gone, and what a beard you've grown . . . My goodness gracious, well I never, sir!'

'Sit down with me, my good old fellow: let's have a drink together . . .'

And Yevseich respectfully perched at the table.

'Our young lady's gone away with her grandmama, and with Pavel Pavlovich, her son, to the city. Oh, Mr Pyotr, sir, you're a good gentleman: whatever have you done to us; the young mistress was beside herself, and such a good young lady too: one of God's children, little Katya . . . Wasn't it a sin for you to torture her like that, nothing but a child, and yourself too; why, she's just a child, the little mistress, Katya . . . Oh, Mr Pyotr, sir!'

'Let's drink, old man.'

'To your health . . .'

'Let's not recall the past: what's past is done . . .'

'Come back to us, my dear young man, sir; all the servants remember you: they don't like that officer.'

'What officer?'

'Cornet Lavrovsky, sir . . .'

'What cornet might that be? . . .'

'A relation of the mistress's: been staying with us now, let's see: since the third Saviour's Day, he came either from Petersburg or from Saran, their country estate.'

'Come on, old man, let's drink!'

'To your health, sir . . .'

'Do you remember, sir, how I ran after you, and you made yourself scarce, off you went skipping away from the old man, sir: why, every day, more or less, the young mistress, Katenka, sent me off to the village – with letters: we thought you'd stay at that gentleman's, Mr Schmidt's: but this is how it is' – the old man sank into thought, peeping up at Pyotr now and then from under lowered brows – 'but this is how it's turned out: it's a bad business, a bad business . . .'

Those words ate into Pyotr like a knife into his heart.

'And you've become so thin: and I'll say it again, you've gone so dark, and grown such a beard, what's more . . .'

But Pyotr was not listening: his attention had been distracted: he saw the carpenter and the tinsmith making their way between the tables, saw them sit down at one, and, catching sight of Pyotr, moreover in the company of

Yevseich, for some reason pretended not to notice their meeting at all; anyway, Yevseich was drunk too: his speech was quite incoherent, interspersed with little sobs; but Pyotr could no longer tear his gaze from that distant table, at which the carpenter and the tinsmith had sat down to have a few drinks: he saw how they were brought vodka: 'What could have brought them here?' Pyotr wondered. 'Only that horrid business,' he concluded for some reason; and a familiar tremor shot up his spine; but the carpenter and the tinsmith were busy with their own concerns: they leaned their faces towards each other and stared with their dull eyes at one another with such tenderness even, with such languor, as though they could not bear to spend a single minute without each other's company.

'So you've given it him, the merchant, then, have you?'

'It wasn't me, it was Anka . . .'

'You brought Anka the powder, then?'

'I brought Anka the powder, just a wee bit . . .'

'And the merchant . . .?'

'The merchant's got really poorly.'

'Lost the power of speech?'

'Lost the power of speech.'

'And everything else?'

'And everything else . . .'

'What a one you are, Sidor Semyonych!'

'We Sukhorukovs are all in the same mould . . .'

'No shilly-shallying!'

'What did you think?'

'Oh, Mr Pyotr, sir: who have you got involved with: with riff-raff, you might say, with a loose woman; you ought to be ashamed; so many sleepless nights I've had, tossing and turning for worry about the little mistress: I felt so sorry for her!'

'You've slipped up a bit there, haven't you, Sidor Semyonych: you should have given him a bit more . . .'

'Don't you go teaching me my business: I've never met anyone cleverer than me – politically speaking; if I'd given him any more, it'd have been obvious that he'd been, like, pois . . .'

'I'm not saying anything, only you listen . . .'

'No, you wait now: you're an odd sort; let me inform you – the merchant won't last more than a month . . .'

'Tili-tili-bim-bom,' tinkled a triangle in the corner; three peasants were gulping tea from saucers, and a crowd was huddled around them; they were autumn arrivals: threshers, men of learning; every autumn they turned up in our parts; one kept explaining which star was a *planid*, and which wasn't; the second peasant had invented a kind of machine which could go on revolving endlessly all by itself*; the third peasant tinkled away vigorously on the triangle; it was autumn: and with it the three autumn peasants appeared in the village: one peasant said he would show his machine, the second explained which star was a *planid* and which wasn't; the third peasant tinkled vigorously on his triangle; there was no fourth peasant.

'Tili-tili-bim-bom.'

Just as a wolf, run to earth by the hounds, fangs bared and hackles raised, prepares for one last battle with the hateful dogs, so now Daryalsky: propped on one elbow, he strained eagerly to catch amidst the noise, the clamour, the din, what that couple could be so intent on whispering; but all he could hear was the tinkling of the triangle, and a schoolmasterly voice:

'The earth, good brothers, is a sphere: and so we reside upon that sphere . . .'

'But I'm thinking,' a feeble voice piped up, 'that we live inside a sphere . . .'

'Strange notions you have, how'd we manage in a sphere with no air: what d'you think, they open a window in the sphere so's the spirit can pass freely through?'

That was all Daryalsky could hear: once again thoughts arose in his soul: he recalled that on the days following the prayers it seemed to him, quite manifestly, that there was someone else among the people who chatted with him, someone who could not be discerned with ear or eye or sense of smell; whether he was in the cottage at his carpentry, or taking his midday meal with his employers – always it seemed to him: here were the three of them planing; but no: as soon as you lowered your eyes, there seemed to be four: who was the *fourth*? If you raised your eyes – again they were three; lower them again – and always it seemed that the carpenter had started whispering with that one, the *fourth*; and the *fourth* would point his finger at Pyotr and smirk, and goad the carpenter on against Pyotr: 'Why don't you settle his hash, I'd like to myself, we'll get them all!' And the carpenter would lay his plane aside, and blow his nose, as though overcome with embarrassment, he'd give his beak-like nose a wipe, and make fun of the

* I presume some *perpetuum mobile* is meant. – *Author's footnote.*

fourth's words, but still keep listening to him:

'I do so much anyway, how can I, we're all in it – you should do it yourself . . .'

'No, no, no: you do it without me, you're not babies' – the *fourth* kept goading the carpenter and they all laughed together, and even Matryona would poke her head round the door to see what this *fourth* looked like; then Pyotr could bear it no more: he would throw aside his saw and stare at the *fourth*, but there was no *fourth*: he would be staring into an empty corner and could see that just as there had been three of them, so three of them there remained. As he remembered all this, like a wolf run to earth by the hounds, fangs bared, preparing for battle, Pyotr drew himself up towards the tinsmith.

'So you think the earth's a ball, do you, hanging on a string from the heavens?'

'I'm just telling you: the earth is round . . .'

'I do so much anyway, how can I, we're all in it – you should do it yourself,' whispered the carpenter, drawing back from the tinsmith.

'No, no, no: you do it without me, you're not babies . . .'

'So that means we're flying around in space . . .'

'Of course!'

'Oh, no, if the earth's a sphere, like a ball, say, then we're sitting in that ball, sort of, and the devils are chucking us around from one to another; and that, you say, explains the way the *planids* revolve.'

'The earth is the devil's football,' thought Daryalsky and again sank into reverie . . .

Or again, when they started to leave the cottage: you could see there were three of them in the room; but once they were outside and walking through the village, you could swear there weren't three, but *four*; Pyotr would stop and start counting: and once again – there were only three: as though there never had been a *fourth*.

That was how it seemed to him all these days, but to the carpenter he breathed not a word about his state of mind: it was Matryona he talked to . . .

'Matryona, my love, how many are there of us altogether in the cottage?'

'What d'you mean, how many: there's this many – me, you and Mironych.'

'And who else is there, the *fourth*?'

And the silly woman went and told the carpenter about it, but the carpenter didn't give any answer: he just grinned into his moustache.

All of this passed swiftly in front of Pyotr, as he scrutinized the tinsmith from afar; so that was the one he'd been waiting for: that was who he was, this *fourth*; only what kind of adventures could happen to him with that tinsmith? And moreover, he didn't look at all like the *fourth*: he seemed altogether a nobody, number *zero*.

With wild laughter Pyotr raised the teapot:

'Let's drink, Yevseich!'

'Your good health! . . .'

'God's my witness, what you've done to the merchant is pleasing to our church.'

'You can't pull the wool over my eyes: what church!'

A yellow fly flew in and settled on the carpenter's nose.

'But otherwise, without the church, it's a sin . . .'

'Well, if it's a sin without the church, then it's a sin whichever way you look at it . . .'

The carpenter chased the fly away: it described a circle and settled malignantly upon the tablecloth, rubbing its feet on its foul yellow belly.

'Well now, you've found a fine thing to compare it with: murder.'

'Did you think it wasn't murder? Now don't you go sighing: there's no sin, you know.'

'How's that?'

'Just like that: it's all nothing but old wives' tales; but kill that fly, it's a carrion-fly . . .'

'But what is there, if there's no sin?'

The carrion-fly took off and flew away.

'There's nothing . . .'

'But what about Him, who judges righteously in heaven?'

'Beg pardon?'

The fly settled on Daryalsky's finger.

'Don't you start teaching me: I've never met anyone cleverer than me; you can take my word for it: if there is such a thing as sin, then as regards the poisoning of Luka Silych you're the devil's minion; I'm just revealing that to you out of friendship; only – there is no sin: there isn't anything – no church, no righteous judge in heaven.'

'But wait!'

'What should I wait for: it was when I gave it him that I realized that there was nothing; just a void; nothing but emptiness; poultry meat or human being – it's all one flesh, beyond dispute . . .'

'So that means we're all walking about upside down?'

'No, it's not us, it's the Americans.'

'I wouldn't go to that there America for anything!'

Soot, smoke, fumes, din, peasants; a row broke out at the other end of the teahouse:

'And I say: you, Mityukha, I say, yes, I say: you should have, I say, an aspen stake, I say, stuck in you . . . for that disgusting fly-sheet of yours . . .'

'That's right, that's right . . .'

'Stirring the people up!'

'The scoundrels!'

'Stew-dents!'

'What's he saying, then?' the constable went on asking.

'He says: we're standing up, he says, for a just cause . . . But I say, it's the yids what caused it; ruining the people, I say, a curse upon you.'

And so the peasants vied with each other in their spitting, trying for all they were worth to get in the constable's good books; the drunken constable was carousing in a company of snub-nosed lads that day, since it was the eve of the festival; and a plump floozy was drinking with him.

Soot, smoke, fumes, din, peasants: Pyotr opened the window – a draught of cool air wafted in; Yevseich, now completely drunk, was stumbling around at the next table.

'Don't you try taking us for a ride, old fellow; don't go on about the diamonds; them diamonds vanished . . .'

'I swear on the cross – the diamonds have been found!'

'Tell us another one!'

'D'you want to go and ask the constable?'

Immersed in his thoughts, Pyotr heard nothing; he was thinking only that for some time now he had felt upon him the carpenter's sullen gaze – that selfsame gaze from which, as they say among the people, chickens drop dead; the carpenter frowned at Pyotr more and more sullenly, keeping a tireless watch upon him; and Pyotr kept a watch on the carpenter, noticing all the latter's gestures that were new to him; and so they spied on one another.

The carpenter had come to hate Pyotr both because he had done his bid-ding towards Matryona not in the way he wished, and because Pyotr had not had the powers that the carpenter had counted on; and in reliance on those powers, as though on interest from trusty capital invested in the bank, the carpenter had elaborated his words about the *child*; but it turned out that he had elaborated them in vain; and if Pyotr had not come to love Matryona from the bottom of his soul, then what had transpired was a fact of no importance: an ordinary everyday affair; and that was why the foul events had happened with the *spectral child* that had arisen from four human exhalations.

But most of all the carpenter had come to hate Pyotr because Matryona had grown so deeply attached to him: there was no tearing the silly woman away from him now; but she would have to be torn away, and no mistake!

And while they followed one another, peeping round corners, out of bushes, leaning over the edge of the sleeping-bench, Pyotr guessed that the *fourth* was walking among them too, that he was whispering his terrible words, spying, inciting, threatening, but still holding them all firmly together with a single fateful, shameful and terrible secret.

Pyotr remembered how he had recently been on the point of falling asleep, stretched out on the bench (Matryona had left him already and crawled back into her own bed) – he remembered feeling as though someone had tied a rope firmly round his neck, and, pressing with one foot on his chest, had given it a mighty tug, crushing his chest with a boot and squeezing his neck; Pyotr had gasped and opened his eyes; and he had seen the carpenter standing over him in thought and picking at his beard, attentively examining his bared chest; and Pyotr had leapt up from the bench. Mironych, though, seeing his fright, had turned away from him and reached out his hand for the jug, as though for a drink of water: he drank, coughed long and plaintively, and went off to bed without a kind or unkind word. But Pyotr was unable to settle for a long time; he sat there on the bench, squashing cockroaches, until the yellow eye of dawn peeped in at the cottage window, seeking out the dust and breadcrumbs on the floor; from then on Pyotr went to the hayloft to sleep at night; it was too stuffy for him in the cottage from the breathing of four human bodies, glowing with heat; and he began having palpitations of the heart.

All of this, Lord alone knows why, passed through his head as he watched the tinsmith from afar. 'There they are, sitting there now,' he thought, 'the carpenter, and the *fourth*; but is he the *fourth*? Perhaps he's a nothing, number *zero*? They sit there, goading each other on, and if you said to anyone here: good people, have you no eyes for *all this*? – they'd laugh you to scorn, they'd not believe you.'

And as he thought these thoughts, in the opposite corner they went on whispering, casting sideways glances at Pyotr: but the smoke, the tea, the learned peasants and the constable drowned out that whispering . . .

'And I saw a dream, my brothers; I saw that I had three heads, and each head was of a separate kind: one was a dog's, another was a pike's; and only one was my own; and those heads were quarrelling among themselves; and it made my brains rattle, that it did . . .'

'Well, you aren't half a ninny!'

'What d'you mean?'

'You want a bull up your backside . . .'

'The devil take him: we've got to make a decision about it; you think it out yourself, Sidor Semyonych: we can't just let him go to the four winds; you can see that for yourself; and then again, why should I keep him – an extra mouth – if he's no use for anything; just feeding him for nothing.'

When Pyotr passed by them on his way to the door with a firm decision that he was not even admitting to himself, the carpenter called him gently.

'Come here, come here . . .'

'Well?' Pyotr turned on them in such a way that they both shuddered: with a challenge, with pride, with his head held high; at that moment he showed his noble birth, although it was little to be seen in his shaggy beard (it had grown this last month), or his shock of unkempt hair, or the holes in his shirtsleeve elbows.

'Listen, squire' – the carpenter humoured him sweetly, 'I've got a job for you: Sidor Semyonych here is going back in the morning; why don't you go with him: Mrs Yeropegin, the merchant's wife, will give you a furniture order for me . . .'

'Very well, if you like!'

'Only please try to be ready as early as possible; we're leaving as soon as it's light,' Sukhorukov addressed him in the polite form, for reasons best known to himself.

Something went through Pyotr's head with the speed of lightning, and he all but smiled with joy, but for certain purposes he thought it necessary to dissemble.

'Oh dear!' Pyotr scratched his head disingenuously.

'No, really, you do it for me, my friend,' and the carpenter put a hand on his shoulder; strange to tell: this worthy face with its long beard stretching downwards (a cross between an icon-painter's work and a pig's breakfast) still instilled respect and fear in Pyotr; and the fact that the carpenter was drunk (it was the first time Pyotr had seen the carpenter drunk) and agitated – all this instilled in him, through all his hatred of the carpenter, a kind of tenderness. 'How is it I never noticed before,' he wondered, 'that this face is a mixture of icon and pigsdaub?' This word had only just occurred to him, and it seemed to him a successful invention.

'Very well, I'll go.'

'To your good health' – the tinsmith handed him some vodka.

They drank.

And Pyotr went out: the dark evening fell upon him with its still glowing sunset; and the evening wrapped him round in darkness and sunset; Pyotr set off towards the sunset . . .

Noise, thunder, din, oppressive smells: sea-roach and herring were brought to the table, vodka in big teapots, other miscellaneous carrion and in little red boxes Leo cigarettes (five kopecks for ten); not everyone could afford those Leos, but they smoked them for the sake of *chic*; around the drunken constable was a dense crowd of drunken peasants:

'You catch 'em, then, and into the water with 'em.'

'But what, but I . . .'

'But we . . .'

'It's the honest-to-goodness truth, if you don't mind my saying so: that's why they make it their business.'

'That's why they're stirring up the people, you blockhead . . .'

'It's the honest-to-goodness truth, your honour, if you don't mind my saying so, and that's why . . .'

'That's why you must catch 'em, and into the water with 'em . . .'

And the constable, drawing his fingernail across the red box, pulled out a Leo cigarette with shaking fingers and lit it self-indulgently.

'So what, then?'

'I think he'll run away.'

'And what if he does run away?'

'Then, Mironych, the game's over . . .'

And the carpenter sank into thought.

'We can't let that happen, no way we can't . . .'

'You mark my word, the word of a Sukhorukov, he'll run away.'

'Would you give him some of that stuff?'

'I'd give him some . . .'

Silence.

'Only seeing as you're making the suggestion, I have to tell you that for a thing like that you'll owe me ...'

'I know I will: I'll bow down before you ...'

'Bow down with Yeropegin's thousands, will you?'

'I'll bow at your feet with a thousand of Yeropegin's.'

'All right, then, you bow down with those thousands ...'

'I will ...'

Silence.

'Only there's one thing ...'

'I've already told you; there's no sin in it at all: there's nothing – just a void, it's all rubbish ...'

'All right, then, take him into town ...'

'I will ...'

'It's not convenient here; can't do anything with him here; there's that woman of mine here, Matryona ...'

Silence ...

'When will this thing be done with him?'

'It'll be done: don't you have any doubts about it . . . At the earliest opportunity ...'

'O Lord, O Lord!'

'Whatever we take on, we Sukhorukovs, brother; you ask anyone you like what sort of people we are: we're a well-known breed ...'

'He won't run away from you?'

'I'll give you run away from me!'

'It's just that I ...'

'Run away indeed: no one's ever got away from me!'

Silence ...

'Only I tell you this, and you listen carefully: chicken or man, it's all the same flesh; and there's no sin in it at all; they're all made the same way, men and beasts and birds – all in the same fashion; and since I've told you this out of friendship, you ought to thank me for it . . . Got it? ...'

An accordion began to squeal; the yellow fly flew to the constable's table and settled; the drunken woman started dancing; she beat the dust out from under her skirts with affectation, even compressing her lips and holding her hands to her hips with dignity:

> 'Married in the
> Sight of God,
> But my husband
> Was a sod ...'

The drunken constable chuckled, and the snub-nosed lads opened their mouths wide and roared in unison:

>   'This way, that way,
>   That way, this,
>   Never mind,
>   You're sure to miss . . .'

The woman stepped out jauntily and wailed:

>   'We ate cabbage,
>   There's the rub,
>   Famine robbed us
>   Of our grub.'

And the lads took it up:

>   'This way, that way,
>   That way, this,
>   Never mind,
>   You're sure to miss . . .'

It was a new song, the height of fashion: previously they had sung *Slocialistic* songs in the district; but since Father Nikolay had been tied up and carted off to prison, the neighbourhood had lost its nerve a bit; meetings had stopped, weapons had been put aside, and denunciations had started; and people started singing new songs:

>   'Husband's brother
>   Carps and cavils:
>   Cabbage makes my
>   Belly swell . . .
>   And that's all
>   There is to tell . . .'

And the lads joined in:

>   'Silly lass,
>   Drink some kvas!'

It was a new song, the height of fashion . . .

The footloose woman would have gone on dancing for a long time, for a long time the constable would have gone on chuckling as he smoked his Leo cigarettes, all sorts of songs would have been sung – merry ones, naughty ones, sad ones – if a certain extraordinary occurrence had not taken place; amidst the fumes, the reek of smoke, the murk and the cigarette-ends someone bellowed out:

'Look, lads, a fire!'

Everything fell silent: the woman stopped dancing, the lads froze with open mouths, and the constable too, holding a lighted match in the murk, the stench, the reek of smoke; cries could be heard around the village; they glanced at the windows – and the windows were red.

'Not a fire, is it?' said the tinsmith in surprise.

'It certainly is . . .'

Before they had time to gather their wits, the Tselebeyevo bell-tower rang out; its brazen bronze pealed out unwontedly into the evening's murk: swiftly stroke followed stroke; and when the people tumbled out of the teahouse, the sky was filled with murk of crimson black, in which a bright flame crackled and darted and danced, snaking hither and thither and flashing with a multitude of sparks; as though myriads of red and golden wasps, hidden in their nest, had flown out into the darkness of the night to sting people, to cover them with fatal wounds from their red barbs – and they swarmed and swirled and gleamed, those vicious golden wasps, as they flew from their nest; and smouldering brands bobbed up and down like blood-red hornets; bright serpents flared up there, slithered like lightning from nooks and crannies, stretched out their necks, hissed, and reached out to the neighbouring cottages, lighting as they did so the Tselebeyevo meadow; grim black billows of smoke rolled slowly, with a stench, low over the meadow, breaking upon the meadow and falling on the earth in a dark-red veil, from under which two-legged shadows rushed to and fro; their faces could not be seen, their calls could not be heard: just black silhouettes waving their arms absurdly, screaming, raging; it seemed an evil flock of shades had flown in from all sides to celebrate their festival in the red gleam of the flames.

'They look more like demons than people,' some joker chuckled behind the tinsmith's back, when they stopped some distance from the flames among the flowers and grasses; but no sooner had the constable turned round at that stupid joke than darkness sealed his drunken eyes; go on, just try to find him in the blackness . . .

'Fine time for joking!' people murmured all round.

'Like to give them a thrashing!'

'They weren't ours, they were strangers, lads from Kobylya Luzha . . .'

But in the darkness some drunken voices roared in unison:

'Arise you working people . . .'

and disappeared into the night.

The bell-tower cast its brazen cries: hither and thither – hither and thither: dong-dong-dong-dong; suffocating smoke billowed, falling on the earth in a blood-red veil, from under which two-legged shadows went on rushing to and fro; there was hissing, crackling, shouting and a helpless child's crying; an old woman set up a loud wailing; frenzied owners tore out of the nearby houses, and into the smoke flew boots, sarafans, cushions, featherbeds, skirts; a large bag, cast into the night, went flying; but it wasn't the shop that was burning, it was the barn next door.

'Pull-pull-pull-pull!' – a plangent cry burst out, and from right under the crimson screen a dozen hands tugged a long hook away from the flame; with its incandescent iron tooth the hook bit from the wall a blindingly blazing beam; it crashed dully down and scorched the grass; the hose spat-tered in all directions, moistening not the flame at all, but the adjacent huts and roofs, and the grass, and the people, jostling and wailing under the very awning of the fire; shortly before they had broken the village hose in their enthusiasm and if it hadn't been for Utkin, who came galloping from the next village with hose and hooks, soon there'd have been nothing but black chimneystacks jutting out from the ashes instead of a village.

'Pull-pull-pull-pull!' – loud cries rang out, and the crimson screen, like stretched satin, tottered out of the smoke; and – crash: the roof collapsed; a torrent of sparks surged over the stinging heat, like the golden lace of a foaming, overflowing goblet; and a bright, crackling tongue stretched out to the sky with merry malice.

At that moment the meadow was suddenly lit up, as though it had burst into flames, and in such a way that even those standing far away felt the heat, while the people bustling around the fire rushed away with a cry, cov-ering their soot-stained faces with their sleeves; then by the currant bushes a frail figure, all in white, was seen; there came into view in the distance a praying figure raising high to the flames an altar-cross; it was Father Vukol with his flowing curls, engaged in single combat with the fire through Christian prayer; his eyes did not see that crimson hell; Lord alone knew what those eyes did see, raised up to the hills.

It was only for a single moment that the neighbourhood was lit up so brightly, then everything began to turn dark again; and the currant bushes were again immersed in night; the outstretched cross and the priest's frail figure were immersed in night as well; a bright tongue, tossed for a moment into the sky, began quickly to fall back; and fell; the village had been saved; the shop had been saved too.

The nifty shopkeeper strutted around: his beard like a bush, his collar unfastened, and oh! what fire in his eyes! The villagers crowded around him; the half-sober constable was drawing up a report.

Rumours circulated among the people that the arsonists were from Kobylya Luzha; they pointed out one likely lad; but the shopkeeper grinned; and, strange to say, he tried to damp down all the talk of arson.

What the sunset told him

Autumn evening!

Do you remember how quiet it can be: how everything in the soul that mourns is uncomplainingly reconciled with its misfortune on a quiet, autumn evening, when out of the ashen twilight the fields appear ethereal, reveal their humble emptiness, and a noble peace floods through your limbs, as the fields gaze at you with the lights of cottages, like tear-filled eyes, and quietly converse from afar in wordless songs, and when the fear that for days on end has suffocated your soul now gives you a harmless smile with the last light of the sunset: 'Why, I'm not there at all . . .'

'Not there at all.'

But you do not believe the emptiness; over there an unharvested strip stretches its drooping ears towards the wormwood; you gaze into the emptiness without believing it, because here and there, there are things standing, and waving their arms, from there, from here: they summon you; they all stare at you, nod, and mutter; and you do not believe the emptiness.

But respond to the summons, answer the call; you will only rub the grey wormwood fronds to dust in your palms and glimpse some tiny animal scuttling away; you will revel in the bitter, heady scent of wormwood, together with the fetid smell of earth: in the evening the autumnal field is empty; along its edges runs the delicate sunset, and across it straggles a long crocodile of crows, and from where the night spreads its dark hues across the earth the forest mumbles its ancient tale about the same old thing: how it's time for it to shed its leaves; in the distance the forest sheds its leaves like waters falling, as though the night, as it engulfs the earth, were striking at it with a melancholy rumble of dreams.

In him who, at such moments, has not felt illumination in his soul, the soul is dead, because all people – all – have wept at times like this for their past lives; who has not watered the empty fields with a single tear, who has not gazed at the yellow pearls that disappear with the sunset beyond the fields, who does not know the touch of tender fingers on his breast, or the kiss of gently trembling lips upon his lips – he must be shunned – run from him, man and beast, and you, grasses, wither, if his coarse footfall as much as touches your slender stalks: on such nights it is right to weep and take pride in your obedient sobbing, which yields itself up to the fields: these are sacred tears, crime is washed away in them, and in them the soul stands bared before itself.

And Pyotr's soul was bathed in tears: he walked after the sunset across the empty field, crushing the bitter-scented, heady grasses, gazing at the yellow-tinted pearls that were disappearing with the sunset beyond the fields; on his breast was the touch of unseen fingers, on his lips the kiss of gently trembling lips; further and further he went across the empty field; in yellow-tinted pearls the evening twilight ran away across the field; at times he fancied he was on the point of catching up with the evening twilight, there was just the stubble stretching out beneath his feet, just wordless songs that sounded quietly in his ears, and all the while the one, same voice – familiar immemorially, but long forgotten, that now rang out again: 'Come to me – come, come.'

And he went:

'I hear you, I am coming back – don't go, wait . . .' He felt the touch of tender fingers on his breast, reached out to grasp beloved hands: but in his cold embrace the breeze whistled; and the voice, familiar immemorially, long forgotten, that had now rung out again, spilled forth without an answer in quiet, wordless song: no, it did have words, that song; here they were – the words that ran off into the distance through the dew:

'Carry my grie-ief awa-ay with you-ou, swift river . . .' resounded from the crossroads, then silence: the rumble of a cart was heard, the glimmer of a cigarette was seen and . . . nothing more.

'I'll carry it all away: all of it, all of it,' babbled the stream at his feet.

'I'll do it myself . . .'

The echoing tocsin chased anxiously after Pyotr across the empty fields; Pyotr turned; over Tselebeyevo stood a pillar of fire.

How they went to Likhov

The sun had not yet peeped out, the first chill of morning still stretched crisp films of ice over the ruts, and the road seemed made of stone in its deathly, frosty pallor, when a cart stopped under the windows of Schmidt's cottage; hooking his whip over his arm, down jumped the girded tinsmith and knocked quite resolutely on the window with his whipstock.

'Come on out, then!'

He put his ear to the window as he waited for Daryalsky; it was a funny business, to be sure; Daryalsky had not returned from the fields to the carpenter's cottage; he had gone straight from the fire to Schmidt's; what this summer visitor and Pyotr had been blethering on about, what sort of business they had going between them, neither the tinsmith nor the carpenter had any idea; only they had both seen how all through the long September night the lights in Schmidt's cottage had not gone out; that was why they were both anxious, and why the tinsmith had hurried along with his cart before the agreed time.

That was what he thought of as he puffed at his home-rolled cigarette, rearranged the bales of hay and flagons in the cart, and stuffed a grey bag into the front; he got it all sorted out, and thought for a moment; then again he hammered on the window with his whipstock.

'Come on out, then!'

The door opened – and devil take the lot of them! Sukhorukov's vicious eyes blinked and darted about, his fat fingers were seized by trembling; he was about to doff his cap, but thought better of it in time: to the devil with them all!

The main reason for such extraordinary agitation was that the tinsmith did not recognize in Pyotr the ragamuffin of yesterday, because he was wearing a somewhat crumpled, but still well-fitting jacket, and a starched collar sat high on his unshaven neck; a grey-coloured overcoat flapped in the wind, a wide-brimmed hat was tilted over his forehead, and – what most of all alarmed the tinsmith – his gloved hand clutched a stick with an ivory knob; his vicious, bewildered eyes blinked and darted about when Pyotr, shaking the grey-haired summer visitor's hand, rapped out to the tinsmith with more than a touch of haughtiness:

'Well, bring it round!'

'Get in, squire!' The tinsmith could not maintain his tone and to his own surprise dropped his Sukhorukov arrogance in the face of so miraculous a transformation of ragged bumpkin into gentleman.

'You can send my things on to me,' Pyotr was addressing the summer visitor, 'if I need them.'

They got in: the cart trundled off, the films of ice crunched, the sun was emerging over the broad expanses; the day promised to be cold, lofty, and pale-blue.

Pyotr turned sharply round; he waved a handkerchief in farewell to his friend; he sent his final thanks to him who had not only proved able to turn Pyotr's decision into action and give him the strength for the hard struggle to come, but in a single night had turned his shameful behaviour itself and his perdition into no more than a necessary temptation, sent to try him; there would be days – when the weird adventures of these weeks would seem to him from afar to be a mere episode, albeit a hard one, a long-forgotten dream; no, he would waste no further thought upon the absurd pattern of his fate, which he had himself unwittingly embroidered with such diligence.

And he turned once more to his past: but he must have seen there something it would have been better never to see; for a sigh of regret, like a groan of remorse, suddenly escaped from his breast; and at once he suppressed it.

What did he see?

There she was standing, beside the pond, with the yoke on her shoulders, and gazing after him from under that selfsame red kerchief with white dapples on it; did she know that they were exchanging their last glance? Had she known, she would have fallen in the grass with her yoke and torn the kerchief from her head; and for a long, long time she would have writhed on the ground, forgetting her honour and her woman's shame; no, she did not fall; no, she did not know; there she stood beside the pond, the yoke across her shoulders, and gazed after him almost merrily, it seemed, shielding her eyes with her hand; and her red kerchief fluttered in the wind. The carpenter, however, Pyotr could not see at all. And as soon as they climbed up out of the village, and the village lay spread out far off below, so that in the morning smoke the cottages and vegetable gardens disappeared, and only the great carved cross of Tselebeyevo gleamed – Daryalsky was seized by a tempestuous joy; as though all the chimeras that had overwhelmed him these last months – engagement, Gugolevo, Tselebeyevo, Kudeyarov, Matryona – were now being borne away from him in the mist, just as he and the tinsmith were being borne away from Tselebeyevo; and the world, which only yesterday had been immeasurable to him, was now gathered together there in the distance in one fibrous wisp of smoke; and the cross of the Tselebeyevo bell-tower caught his eye with its penetrating glint; he thought about the city, and thought about the friends he had left there; and he thought about Katya, how from there, from the new world, he would come back to his Katya, smiling – and freed from all his former fantasies.

The touch of the tinsmith's hand upon his neck made him twitch his shoulders in repugnance:

'What are you doing?'

'Feeling the cloth: it's all right, it's good cloth . . .'

'What?'

'I said your coat is made of good cloth, how much did you pay for it?'

'What were you feeling it for?'

'Your coat collar was turned up: and I was saying I suppose the cloth is English . . .'

Daryalsky put a hand in his pocket: he had his Bulldog with him.

'You mustn't take it unkindly, sir, if I didn't treat you right last night; who's to tell who you are? I saw you were working for the carpenter, so I thought you were an ordinary person . . . Who are you actually?'

'A writer.'

Silence . . . The cart rumbled on; empty fields all round . . .

'Don't you get the idea that I've got designs on you: I haven't got any particular ideas at all: I don't hold the same opinion as the carpenter; don't mix me up with him: I'm a perfectly respectable person; ask anyone you like – we're tinsmiths . . .'

Daryalsky was beginning to find the company of such a fellow-traveller distasteful; he moved to the very edge of the cart; but his unpleasant companion revealed a remarkable propensity for pressing up against him imperceptibly.

'Well, what about the furniture order, then?'

'The order? I'll take the order, and then I'll come back: you needn't worry about my being from the gentry; I've only been working for the carpenter because I needed to get to know the ordinary people better.'

'A snooper!' the tinsmith thought to himself, becoming even more anxious than before; his hands were shaking: 'The carpenter's really bungled this time, now what measures do we take with one like this? Because measures are needed: can't just leave it – or everyone will come to grief and all for nothing!'

'So you're not going to Moscow?'

'No, I haven't the slightest intention of leaving; I shall come back . . .' – and to himself he thought: 'why's he interrogating me about Moscow like that and how does he know?'

Not without a touch of fear welling up in the pit of his stomach Pyotr kept glancing at the tinsmith's hands and his wandering eyes; for some time they sat panting side by side. Suddenly Daryalsky was seized by a fit of trembling; and, grasping from the side pocket of his coat a little book with a fig-leaf on the cover, he poked it under the tinsmith's nose and almost shouted in his ear:

'This is my work; I'm a writer; everybody knows me; if anyone touches me it'll be all over the papers.'

But the tinsmith must have noticed something awkward about that shout: he immediately stopped breathing heavily, straightened himself up, and gradually resumed his previous tone:

'We Sukhorukovs have been in the tinware business since the year dot; of course, I'm not talking about the gentry, but I can tell you: there's no one cleverer than us in Likhov . . .'

And so they drove across the empty fields, both red, both agitated, and, Lord alone knows why, both shouting loudly, interrupting each other, boasting to one another about their own accomplishments . . .

They had already travelled some fifteen versts from the village when Pyotr began to notice that all the way from Tselebeyevo, at quite a substantial distance in front of them, someone was driving a little dark-bay horse at full-tilt; it was a light racing trap, and perched upon it sideways was a little dark figure; it kept whipping the horse on, and seemed to be silently luring them after it, as though it was talking to them without words.

Soon my hero began to notice that that little dark figure sitting in the trap seemed to be deliberately keeping at the same distance from them; if they went more slowly, the trap went more slowly too, if they went faster, so did the trap; sometimes the trap disappeared in the ravines and was nowhere to be seen in the fields; and there was no one in the fields; and then the trap shot out of the sloping hollow again and, with a surge, rushed at full-tilt across the next hill. Soon an idle curiosity got the better of Daryalsky.

'Make her go a bit faster' – snatching the reins from the tradesman's hands, he started to urge the horse on as hard as he could, thinking to overtake the racing trap; but the little dark figure drove its horse on more briskly than before; and they rushed across the fields at full speed and there was no one else in the fields at all; a certain secret intention gained strength in Pyotr; and he kept glancing surreptitiously at his watch, thinking he could still catch the train for Moscow: 'Just to get into the carriage!' he thought; and he already pictured to himself how he would settle down in the carriage and casually puff away at his Leo cigarettes, rocking to the iron rumble of the wheels: that marvellous song that would carry him away from these parts.

But the Likhov tradesman had somehow started puffing and panting again behind Pyotr's back and Pyotr half-turned to squint at him: he saw clearly the vile gaze, fixed straight on his back, and the vile hand, with trembling fingers, reaching directly for his stick; then with an imperceptible movement he switched the reins into the other hand, and with his free hand seized hold of the protruding end of the stick; now the stick was in his hands, but in such a way that the tinsmith could not notice; Pyotr waited with pounding heart to see what would happen, but nothing happened; they were already approaching Myortvyi Verkh, the spire of

Grachikha had long since pierced the blue of the sky; the little dark figure with the trap had dropped down into the gully; for some reason Pyotr began to hold the reins back, expecting the trap to re-emerge; but, once it had plunged, the trap did not rise up again; the little dark figure must have got stuck in the ravine and had no wish to come out again; Pyotr could distinctly feel the tinsmith's hot breath at his back; it burned his neck as it crept inside his collar.

Above Myortvyi Verkh Pyotr reined in the horse: there was no one down below; turning round, he saw how anxiously the tinsmith scoured the slopes of the ravine and the road that ran along the gully bottom to Grachikha; he realized that they were both thinking about the same thing; for a single moment their eyes met and then took refuge again behind their lashes.

'Does this road lead to the village?'

'That's right . . .'

For a single moment he met the tinsmith's eyes, but that was enough for him to read in those eyes an agitation, even, it seemed, vexation at something or other.

Pyotr gave the horse its head down the hill, and when they were right at the bottom of the gully, the tinsmith's hot breath once more singed the back of his head:

'Stop the horse, squire, would you . . .'

'What is it?'

'The collar's come loose, I think . . .'

The horse stopped: the end of the stick was in Pyotr's hand; who was going to get out of the cart?

But the tinsmith did not get out; Pyotr gave the stick a barely perceptible tug; the stick did not move: so the other end must be in the tinsmith's hands: 'In a moment he's going to get out to adjust the collar, and I shan't let the stick out of my hands again; when we get out I shall see that this nonsense was all a figment of my imagination.'

But the tinsmith had no intention of getting out.

'What about the collar?'

An awkward silence ensued; Pyotr turned round; their eyes met.

At that very moment he felt the tinsmith's hand palpably pull the stick towards him, but Pyotr did not let the stick go; and at once the stick stopped moving; then Pyotr in his turn pulled it towards himself: but the tinsmith's hand palpably would not let go of the stick.

All this happened in a single brief moment, but in that moment Pyotr's firm gaze, for the merest second, tried to swim away into those colourlessly blinking eyes that evaded him.

'Let's go on: it was my imagination; the collar's all right . . .'

Pyotr realized that the tinsmith would not get out of the cart and would not let go of the stick: 'What does he want my stick for?' He tried to ask himself this question and tried to convince himself that it really was a question: but in the unconscious depths of his soul *all that* had for some time now ceased to be a question at all.

Then with his free hand Pyotr gave the horse as sharp a lash as he could; they shot off uphill; he turned round to the tinsmith; straight in front of him he saw the tinsmith's hand, holding the knob of the stick, and his whole sallow little figure, bouncing up and down in the cart; but on noticing how Pyotr's eyes were questioningly following his movements, the Likhov tradesman assumed an innocent air, as though he were attentively examining the carving of the bone handle.

'It's a good stick, isn't it?' – Pyotr gave a crooked smile.

'It's not a bad stick' – the tinsmith smiled crookedly too. – 'I'm just looking to see what kind of bone it's made of.'

'Give it here, I'll show you . . .'

'Here, look, hang on – there's a stamp.'

'No, no – it's here.'

And after a slight, barely perceptible struggle, Pyotr forcibly wrenched the stick from the tinsmith's hands . . .

They were on the other side of the gully now; and rushing on across the fields.

But when they were again a long way from the gully, Pyotr turned round and saw the racing trap come flying out of the gully and the selfsame little dark figure waving its arm soundlessly, as though it was beckoning enticingly, as though it was talking without words; but the episode in the ravine had instilled courage into Pyotr: 'No, no, no, *all that* is a figment of my imagination' – he tried to reassure himself; 'Yes, yes, yes – *all that* is real' – his heart pounded in reply . . . And Pyotr did not let the stick out of his hands.

The tinsmith, however, sitting now on the edge of the cart, was neither huffing nor puffing: he seemed not to be agitated at all; but his pouting lips were pouting even more and he had pretty palpably turned his back to Pyotr.

'Do you know these merchants, the Yeropegins?' Pyotr asked him with apparent casualness.

'Everyone knows them round our way: ask any little urchin in Likhov . . .'

'No, I mean: do you mend pots and pans for them?' (Inadvertently Pyotr reverted to the polite form of address, when it seemed to him that his suspicions were soothed.)

'No, I haven't mended any pots for them yet; they have a different tin-smith; and I don't even know that tinsmith . . .'

So there: his suspicions were subsiding.

Pyotr fell to thinking; his cheerfulness of the early morning had disap-peared without trace; they were approaching Likhov. 'Now I just need to get rid of this one; and then – off to the station; I daresay the tinsmith will stick with me, even offer to see me to the Yeropegins'!'

As soon as they came into Likhov, they started bouncing up and down, as though the most ill-fitting cobblestones imaginable had been deliber-ately scattered under the cart.

Pyotr drove the cart along the soft edge of the road; they rounded the high fence of the jail, beside which buttercups were growing in profusion; in the distance a solitary bayonet gleamed; in the barred windows of the jail he saw a shaven face in a grey overall: 'that's probably one of the Fokins, or the Alyokhins,' Pyotr thought; and while he was scrutinizing that shaven face, the tinsmith, who had jumped down from the cart, ran up to a squat little house and had an urgent whispered conversation with a man wearing a cap just like his own; the man in the cap nodded in agreement, gave Pyotr an inquisitive sideways glance, and spat out sunflower husks; all this took place unnoticed by Pyotr; and when Sukhorukov climbed back into the cart and took charge of the reins, Pyotr was still scrutinizing the shaven face that had smiled at him from the barred window; they set off again.

'Why so slowly?'

'You can see for yourself what the road's like here.'

The man in the cap followed behind them; now at the house beside which the tinsmith had been whispering the trap drew up too; if Pyotr had turned round, he would have seen a little dark figure getting down from the trap, and would have seen two other figures who gathered round him; but Pyotr was now considering how to get rid of the tinsmith; and he was astonished when the tinsmith stopped the horse at an entrance on the mar-ket-place under a sign saying 'Sukhorukov'.

'Well, squire, good-bye: I've brought you this far, and now you go on on your own two feet; it's time for me to get home.'

'I see, thank you, thank you!' Pyotr proffered payment as he climbed down.

'No, hold on: you keep the money yourself; we're Sukhorukovs: and we don't take money for things like *that*' (he bore himself with dignity again; he went back to the familiar form of address).

'Well, thank you all the same!' Instead of payment Pyotr held out his hand (albeit gloved – since the previous day Pyotr had assumed manners that were downright lordly).

He gave a sigh of relief that everything had turned out so simply with the tinsmith; he chided himself for his shameful suspicions; quickly now, freely, he strode in the direction of the station; another half-hour – and it would all be over; his squalid association with this district would be broken off forever. So he strode on, brandishing his stick, and none of the towns-folk who came his way could have said, at the sight of this city-dweller, that the day before the city-dweller had been walking round in a food-bespat-tered coarse red shirt with a hole in the elbow; townsfolk walked by – and did not turn to look; only one townsman, following Pyotr unrelentingly, did not take his eyes from Pyotr's back; the Likhov townsman neither caught him up nor dropped back, following evenly upon his heels.

The station

'Devil take the tinsmith!'
    As he approached the booking-office, Daryalsky saw that it was closed.
'When's the train?'
'O-oh, the train's gone, sir, more than an hour ago!'
'When is the next one – to Moscow?'
'Not till tomorrow.'
'Where is there a train for?'
'Lisichensk . . .'
    Out of obstinacy he all but took the train to Lisichensk, but changed his mind in time: he had nothing to do in Lisichensk, after all; and he only had enough money with him to get to Moscow.
    And he stayed.
    The evening crept up; and still Pyotr sat there, sipping beer – golden beer, that formed a froth on his moustache.
    What did he think about? But do people think at all at such moments? At such moments people count the flies flying by, at such moments the half of the soul that is mortally wounded stays utterly mute: days can pass like that, weeks, years.
    Pyotr rolled little balls of bread, sipped his beer and experienced noth-ing but a pleasant warmth and surprise that it had all come to such an easy end, and that he had extricated himself from the devil's nets without more ado; he experienced a delicious excitement; he sipped his beer; he counted and recounted the flies, and watched as a distinguished-looking officer a little way off beckoned to another:
'Cornet Lavrovsky, are you still drinking?'
'I am, sir . . .'

'Squeeze another one in?'

They squeezed: and the distinguished-looking officer graciously condescended to say:

'Rollicking good chap you are!'

'Where have I heard all that? This has all happened before – but where, but when?' thought Pyotr: – 'Cornet Lavrovsky: I've even heard that name before.'

What was, is; what is, shall be: all things recur; and all things pass.

The Likhov townsman who had been following hard on Pyotr's heels was now strolling in solitude up and down the station.

What came of this

The day had been azure when he entered the station; the day was . . . – but no: when he came to leave it, there was no day; but it seemed to him that there was no night either; there was just a dark void; and there was no darkness even: there was nothing in that place where an hour before the townspeople had been bustling about, and the trees rustling; the wretched houses stood there – a single seamless nothing was hurled upon him, or, more precisely, he was hurled into it; not a sound, not a murmur, not the tiniest ticking; it seemed to him that he had gone from an azure world into the station premises; and he came out of there – straight into a town of shadows; between the town of Likhov he had so lately driven through and this Likhov there must be at least a distance of a million versts: that one was a town of people; this one was a town of shadows.

He could still make the odd thing out. It was as though on a flat grey surface that clung to his eyes a timid hand had drawn black patches here and there, any old how, and here and there, any old how, the ink had been removed: he even started feeling at these dark and pallid patches; soon he realized that these patches were not patches, but very real objects, possessing a third dimension; now he saw even at a distance the eye of a streetlamp, a second, and lights in windows: but it was all dim and as though seen through mourning crape.

Where was he to go now?

Why hadn't he left for Lisichensk while there was time? But how could he have known that everything would change so swiftly and irreversibly?

Looking round, all he could see was an utterly dark little figure that stood out against everything else that was not utterly dark.

'What's the way? How can I get through here? Hey, listen!'

But all the little figure did was to stand out silently on the background of a pallid wall: answering questions was clearly quite beyond it: perhaps that little dark figure had been drawn in charcoal by some urchin, and it wasn't a person at all. And Pyotr moved off from it into the void.

But when Pyotr moved off, the figure moved off too.

Pyotr started going up to the streetlamps; even if dimly, still the lifeless town was silhouetted in front of him. Pyotr even saw, at an open window, in a welter of dust, a dust-covered Likhov-dweller by his samovar forlornly scraping away at a fiddle . . .

'All the rooms are taken!'

So they told him in the hotel; a void – utter nothingness: a town of shadows, the town of Likhov!

Once more Pyotr began to feel his way through the darkness; soon he lost his bearings in the market-square; and soon once more he found himself right up against a pallid wall: and on the wall, just as before in that other place, a little figure daubed; clearly some jester had darkened all the whitewashed walls with shadows: a human shadow had drawn its own shadow. And when Pyotr moved off from the little figure, then it once more moved off after him.

Suddenly right beside his nose he heard a familiar voice, hoarse, like a cart that needed oiling; suddenly right beside his ear he caught the so recently familiar smell of someone's breath: a blend of mahorka tobacco and garlic.

'So it's you, my good sir?'

He recognized the tinsmith, but could not see him: he only heard him and, moreover, as it were, caught his scent: and how overjoyed he was!

'I don't know, sir, what a ninny you are, if you'll forgive the expression: in the dark and all on your own, anything could happen, there's shady people.'

Pyotr was on the point of saying to him: 'All the people are shady round here,' but restrained himself in time.

'I just don't know where to spend the night, where is there an inn here?'

'Where? Why, you must stay at the Yeropegins'!'

Yes: that was a happy thought; and there, moreover, he would at least see some people; here there were no people, only shadows.

'Just one thing, how do I get to their house?'

'I'd take you there, but I haven't time . . . Hey, my good man – are you going along Ganshin Street?'

'Yes, I'm going along Ganshin Street!' The reply rang out very close to Pyotr.

'Take this gentleman to the Yeropegins', will you?'

Pyotr turned round and was astonished to see that from the little dark figure in front of which he had just been standing a voice now emanated.

'Come with me.'

And the little figure set off along the wall; Pyotr set off behind it: as a warning he gave a mighty swipe in the air with his stick, to assure the figure what an interesting object he had in his hands.

Later, when these moments had gone by and were already in the past, then, sitting over a cup of tea amidst the carpets, Pyotr realized how things had seemed to him as he walked through this darkness: it seemed to him that they walked for long years, overtaking the coming generations by many million years; it seemed to him that there was no end to this path, nor could there be, just as there could be no turning back: there was infinity in front; and behind – the same infinity; and there was no infinity even; and in the fact that there was no infinity, there was no simplicity; no void, no simplicity – there was nothing; just a pallid wall; and on the wall – the Likhov townsman; in vain Pyotr strove to make out the real features of this Likhov-dweller, in order to find some intelligible meaning in those features, some justification acceptable to common sense, or at least some redeeming loophole for simple human weakness; but evidently those who pass beyond the pale are mercilessly robbed of that forbearance that cloaks their gaze in everyday simplicity; hard as it is, these words have to be repeated here, because the Likhov-dweller who slipped along at Pyotr's side was neither tall nor short, but noiseless and emaciated, and furthermore had a pair of palpable horns . . .

'What's that?'

'Ahem – nothing . . .'

'I had the impression, sir, that you delivered yourself of a foul word . . .'

'Will it be long now?'

'There, that's where their residence is, where the streetlamp is still flickering.'

No, that was not the devil, for the devil was walking behind.

Release

Those pale, pale faces – do you know them? And with blue rings beneath the eyes? Pleasant in an ordinary way, not beautiful faces at all, but that is just what captivates you about them: it's as though those faces rise up out of distant dreams and pass through the whole of your life – not in reality, nor even in dreams or in the imagination, but only in anticipation; but all the same, you see them, or, at least, you wish to see them: these faces begin to appear to you (but always they only begin – they never appear entirely) in women; to women they appear only in fair-haired men, and pass by tranquilly, with a touch of mockery, and never occasion a subsequent meeting.

How astonished Pyotr was to see just such a face now – and where? In the Yeropegins' entrance hall. And in whom? In the most unprepossessing housemaid, who, with head uncovered, opened the door to him. Calm, she showed no surprise, as though she had even been expecting him, she who had hitherto been unfamiliar, but dear to him notwithstanding – at the sight of him she smiled a familiar smile, as though she could tell him something that touched upon the losing or the saving of his life; and the stearin candle in her hand bobbed up and down: 'I'll tell it all, it all, it all,' she seemed to be saying to him.

But into the entrance hall there waddled an ugly dollop in a chocolate-coloured dress and with a wart on her lip.

'Whom do I have the honour of addressing?'

'Daryalsky, a writer – I have the honour to introduce myself!'

'Delighted: what can I, actually, do for you?'

'Being personally acquainted with your husband, and having received an invitation from him in June, I decided, having missed my train, to request your hospitality; might I spend the night in your house?'

'But there's a hotel here!' – Fyokla Matveyevna evidently found Pyotr's strange, untimely appearance suspicious.

'That's the whole problem: the hotel is full.'

'But my husband, you know, has lost the power of speech . . .'

'No . . . I saw him recently in good health.'

'Where did you meet him?'

'At Baroness Todrabe-Graaben's, where I was a guest this summer!' (he uttered these last words with pride: poor fellow, he was so afraid of being returned to outer darkness, where that other one, the *fourth*, was waiting for him by the house).

This last announcement had a consequence:

'Annushka, make a bed up for the gentleman in the annexe.'

Pyotr saw the candle, dripping, tremble in the hands of her whom through some unknown presentiment he wanted to call his dearest sister, whose features reminded him of something – only what?

'You're welcome!' lisped the Dollop, folding her arms over her stomach, and padded off into the other rooms past rotund vases, armchairs, mirrors . . .

And when the moments had passed, during which he overcame infinity and with his strange companion anticipated future generations by many million years, when he was ensconced in a soft, comfortable armchair with a cup of tea and a Leo in his mouth, he thought he had left Moscow far behind and even Likhov, that town of shadows, was a thing of the past; where would he set off for now? He was comfortable, and he lavished his eloquence upon this dollop with her good-natured face and modestly lowered eyes.

Wishing to be an agreeable guest in all respects, he offered to play a game of *durachki* with her; but she declined.

There was just one ingress, or rather, one *progress*, that disturbed this idyll – a progress, because . . . But what would you say, reader, if from that dark enfilade, complete with funeral candles and surrounded by mumbling crones, death itself were dragged past you? You are accustomed to reading about such adventures in novels, but this, after all, is no novel, no fantasy, but . . . – Pyotr saw the dark enfilade of rooms suddenly ablaze with candles: two old women were leading by the hand – death, in a dressing-gown and dark glasses; death tottered along, barely lifting its feet, its slippers shuffling on the floor. Behind it Annushka, a candle in her hand, smiled at Pyotr as she passed, like a dear sister, and seemed to be beckoning him to follow her, seemed to be talking to him without words.

'I'm sorry . . . my invalid husband,' the Dollop explained to Pyotr – 'It's only a week or so since he started walking . . .'

'I see . . . And his speech?'

'The doctors said he might start speaking again . . .'

'Some time?'

She lowered her eyes.

'Maybe never' . . .

Pyotr lost himself in thought; but what did Pyotr think about?

Do people think about anything at such moments? At such moments people count the flies flying by, at such moments the half of the soul that is mortally wounded stays utterly mute: it stays utterly mute for days, weeks, years – and only after such days, and weeks, and vanished years do you slowly begin to be aware of what has happened to the ruined half of your soul, and to understand whether someone whose soul is half-destroyed still has a soul at all; you cannot tell yet whether your soul has died, or is merely swooning, and is giving itself back to you; but its first beneficent return gives rise to a fierce agony, or shows itself in physical disease that brings infirmity; death manifest – have you forgotten? That half of your soul is still of the grave; and, rising from the dead, it is subject to the Day of Judgement: it lives again everything that you lived long ago, that it may turn the absurd phantoms of past days into heavenly beauty; but if your soul does not possess such strength, then its infected parts rot away, and leave no trace.

What could Pyotr think at such moments? He merely knew that he was sundered from the previous day by millions of versts traversed, millions of days elapsed . . .

'So your husband may never speak again?'

'Never . . .

'But it's time for you to have some rest: Annushka, show the gentleman the way!'

Pyotr had long since gone to his room, but still, in the blood-red gleam of the lamps, amid the feather-beds, the pillows, the eiderdowns, before the image of a dove-bird, in heavy cast silver, in nothing but her petticoat and with her hair unbraided, Fyokla Matveyevna bowed down in her stuffy bedchamber, to which no one had access save Dovecote Annushka.

She no longer feared her husband, because her husband was now quite without the power of speech; even if he had seen and understood anything, he could not have told; and, anyway, he did not understand, having lost his reason too, and was on the point of giving up his soul to God; only Luka Silych's soul, evidently, was firmly attached to his body; from week to week the process of giving up his soul to God stretched on; and strange to tell: the doctors expected his death any day, and yet a little over a week before he had regained a weak command of both arms and legs; and in the last few days he had kept working his tongue and straining out of the bed; and three days before he had actually lowered his feet from the bed; and forced them to lead him around the room; and from then on the old women led him round the rooms every day before he went to sleep; the doctor, meanwhile, insisted that these were Luka Silych's last days.

It would be a sin to say that Fyokla Matveyevna willed her husband's death, only the thought occurred to her: what if his speech returned and he upped and said to her: 'What have you got going on here, my girl, and is it true?' Only even if his speech did return, his reason surely wouldn't: Luka Silych's mind was shattered; yesterday, for instance, when Fyokla Matveyevna had visited her husband's room, he kept drawing incomprehensible signs in front of her with his trembling hand, while torrents of tears ran down his cheeks: she had to take his glasses off and wipe his eyes; and he gazed into her eyes so plaintively and wept like a child, copiously; Fyokla Matveyevna had a little cry with her husband, too; and the signs he drew with his stricken, trembling hand sank into her memory: they always seemed to start with 'p', then came the letter 'o' and an 'i': 'poi . . .', but beyond that Fyokla Matveyevna could not make anything out: she tried continuing the word and it came out: Poigin (Poigin was her maiden name); and she thought, was Luka Silych foretelling death for her, born a Poigin; these poor in spirit, with their unsound minds, sometimes divine the future as well as any sage.

'O Lord, O Lord!' the merchant's wife sighed in the red glow of the lamps.

'O Lord!'

And the heavy silver bird spread its wings over her.

Suddenly there was a tapping, and the light lisp of slippers; someone made a shuffling noise; the Dollop ran out into the corridor in nothing but her petticoat and looked into the reception room; and in the middle of the drawing-room she saw Luka Silych himself standing with a candle in his trembling hand: he had managed to get up in the night and drag his feet through the rooms, he'd even had the strength to take a candle with him (the night-nurse must have fallen asleep, and he had got up and walked); only what kind of Luka Silych was that? It was death staring at the merchant's wife through the black windows of the glasses; it saw her, reached out for her, born a Poigin; one hand swayed with the candle, the other, trembling, drew p-o-i in the air; and Luka Silych parted his lips, opened his mouth and worked his tongue impotently: was he baring his teeth at the Dollop?

The Dollop just gasped, and squatted down on her haunches, covering her breasts with her hands (undressed as she was), and looked at her husband.

And at her quiet gasp he dropped the candle, and both spouses were enveloped by darkness; Fyokla Matveyevna's weeping could be heard and the sound of slippers approaching her in the darkness, and the heavy clatter of the candlestick as it tumbled into the corner.

Home!

From her pale, pale face, framed by a black shawl, Annushka's big eyes gazed up into Pyotr's face so thoughtfully, so confidently, so calmly; she stood there sternly, holding a lantern in her raised hand, which cast a faint glow, the colour of blood, over her waxen features; her other hand held open the door into darkness; and that outstretched hand seemed to command him categorically to descend to where he could discern nothing but darkness, the rustle of leaves, and the onrushing wind in his face; dearest sister, she led the way there, and wordlessly but plainly her eyes said to his: 'I'll tell it all, it all, it all.'

'I can do it myself . . .'

'No, you must leave the telling to us . . .'

But nothing of the kind was said between them: it was their eyes that spoke thus to each other; their lips uttered quite other words.

'Is that really where I am to go?'

'That's where: your bed's made up in the annexe!'

'Where is the annexe?'

'In the orchard: this way, sir.'

For a moment Pyotr thought it wouldn't be a bad idea to take his coat; but he changed his mind: after all, it wasn't far.

He passed through the door behind her.

And strange to tell: that absence of both light and darkness, in which he had so recently floundered in the alleyways of Likhov, was now filled with darkness, but it trembled, rustled, exulted in the gusts of the cold wind, as though at the behest of his new guide; the darkness trembled with thousands of leaves; the pear-trees hurtled towards them in the circle of the lantern's light; within that circle of light the greenery flourished; and the calm night stretched unwontedly above their heads, pointing to worlds and galaxies of its own: it seemed to Pyotr that they were on their way to the stars, and he strode firmly along behind the twinkling lantern.

And here it was, the annexe, in the depths of the orchard, winking in welcome with its already lighted window.

But when Annushka opened the door Pyotr shuddered momentarily:

'Is the annexe empty, then?'

'It is.'

'And this is where I'm to be? On my own?'

'I'll stay, I'll stay with you,' she said, and smiled so straightforwardly; she stood on the threshold with the raised lantern, and with her other hand held the door wide open, and it seemed that this hand resting on the door was imperiously pointing out his new path to him.

Pyotr turned round, unable to sate his lungs with the wind that beat so forcefully upon his powerful breast, or to sate his eyes with the stars that the calm night revealed to him; how many times he had seen all that before, and yet it was as though today he saw it for the first time and he tried to commit it to memory, so as never again to forget.

She stood meanwhile and waited, directing him to the door with her lantern raised aloft.

Pyotr passed beneath her lantern: a musty smell struck him; she closed the door; they were now face to face in the stuffy vestibule.

As he went through to the room he was to sleep in, he noticed that the floors hereabouts had been washed with kvas and stuck to the soles of his shoes; the corridor turned to right and left; in the middle was a door; they went through this door; Pyotr saw a neat little room, a white bed with luxuriously fluffed-up pillows, a mahogany chest of drawers, a bedside table, a washbasin and other nocturnal appurtenances – all in perfect order: there was even writing equipment on the table, paper, envelopes, stamps; he also caught sight of a rope thrown under the bed; all this was lit by a tubby lamp:

'It's a long time since I've had the chance to sleep in luxury like this,' he thought.

And he cast another glance around the room; that was when he noticed that above the door there was an aperture from which a pane of glass had been removed and through which it would be possible to stick your head, if you wished, and provided you placed a stool in front of the door beforehand; he examined all this with no particular purpose (like all absentminded people, whose eyes instantly register unnecessary trifles, while the main thing invariably escapes their attention).

For the last time he looked round at his new friend who understood him without words: 'My dearest, sweet sister,' his heart leapt with emotion, and he felt his whole being drawn to her, to tell his story, share his secrets, give those bloodless lips a brotherly kiss and whisper, as you only whisper after a long separation: 'Well?'

And he said:

'Well?'

But she bowed to him, low and earnestly; like a young nun bowing to the ground in church, before an icon.

'Well?'

She closed the door firmly behind her; she stayed on the other side of the door. Pyotr was alone.

For a long time he sat bent over the table; he was writing to Katya, hastily, feverishly, as though he wished in this one letter to express the whole of himself, to explain to her the behaviour he had himself found incomprehensible all this time, but had now suddenly come to understand with utter clarity; and we will take it on trust that Pyotr found the words; he wrote the address, stuck on a stamp, and thrust the letter into his jacket pocket; and still he stayed sitting at the table: 'Sister, my dearest, you have opened my eyes; you have given me back myself . . .' Pyotr's soul was bathed in tears: he was already in oblivion: and it seemed to him that Likhov was left far behind his back, and he was walking across an empty field, crushing the bitter-scented, heady grasses, gazing at the yellow-tinted pearls that were disappearing with the sunset beyond the fields: on his breast was the touch of invisible fingers, on his lips the kiss of gently trembling lips; on and on he went across the empty field towards the word-less songs that quietly sounded to him; and all the while he heard the same immemorially familiar, long-forgotten sisterly voice: 'Come to me, come, come!'

'I hear you, I'm coming back . . .'

And he came back from oblivion: it must have been a rustle that awoke him, and when he looked round the door into his room was open.

'Well?'

In the doorway he saw Annushka's sad and slightly mocking face, all in white.

'Is there anything else you need?'

'What?'

She laughed in a provocative way; and it seemed she herself found it hard to say these incoherent words that grated on Pyotr's ears:

'It's just that I've never waited on young gentlemen before . . .'

'What might I need?'

'I don't know what young gentlemen need . . .'

'No, there's nothing I need,' Pyotr snapped gruffly.

Then it caught his eye that her hand was reaching out for the key, which was stuck in the door on his side.

'No, leave it: I shall lock the door overnight.'

And he made a rush for the door, but with a swift movement she slammed the door in front of his nose, laughing quietly and mocking him, but with an unearthly fervour.

Now Pyotr was locked in.

Then he understood everything: he turned out the lamp and was left in total darkness; when he ran over to the window, with its winter frame still fixed, in order to break the glass, right up against the window panes he saw an ugly visage, staring insolently back at close quarters; under the window he saw a number of lanterns running quickly past, carried by little dark figures that frantically waved their arms at him; then he rushed to the door and started listening in horror, darting glances at the windows; outside the windows little dark figures kept flitting past, but on the other side of the wall everything was still quiet, although the flame of a candle flickered in the aperture above the door; Pyotr instantly put the stool up against the door and, jumping on to it, stuck his head into the opening: he saw four dark backs pressed together and four similar caps, all huddled around the door; he could not see their faces; he jumped back to get his Bulldog; and only then did he remember that he had left it in the house along with his stick and his grey overcoat. Then he realized that it was all over.

'Lord, what is this, what is going on?'

He covered his face with his hands, turned away and burst into tears like an abandoned child.

'What for?'

But a guileless voice answered him meekly:

'What about Katya?'

Standing in the corner, he realized that resistance was pointless; with the speed of lightning a single plea shot through his brain: that they should perform on him swiftly and painlessly that which he still had no strength to give its proper name; he still believed, he still hoped:

'How is it that, in a few short moments, I shall be *that*?'

But these few short moments stretched out like millennia.

'Open the door at once, open up!' he cried in a voice that was not his, while inside him everything was trembling:

'Lord, what is this, Lord, what is happening to me? What is going on?'

By his cry and his invitation *to perform on him what they intended* he was himself, as it were, writing under his completed life: 'Death'.

Then the lock clicked, and *they* appeared; up to that moment *they* had still been wondering whether *they* should cross the fateful threshold: for *they* too were people: but now *they* appeared.

Pyotr saw the door open slowly and a large dark blob, pattering along on eight legs, edge into the room; he could see this because a candle, visible in the corridor, was lighting their way; someone's hand, holding the candle out there, was shaking. But they could not see him yet, although they were moving cautiously directly towards him; they stopped; and someone's face bent over him, an utterly ordinary face, scared rather than threatening, and from that face a whisper passed through them . . .

'Brothers, why are you doing this to me?'

Crash: a blinding blow knocked him off his feet; as he lost his balance, he was aware of being in a squatting position: crash – a blow more blinding still; and nothing; torn loose, gone —

'Come on with you!'
  'Eh?'
  'Keep pulling!'
  Tu-tu-tu – feet pattered in the dark.
  'The rope!'
  'Where is it?'
  'Give him another thump . . .'
  Tu-tu-tu – feet pattered in the dark; and stopped pattering; in the profound silence deep gasps could be heard from four backs, grown together at the shoulder and hunched over an object of some sort; then a distinct crunching sound, as of a shattered breastbone; and again silence . . .
  Tu-tu-tu – feet pattered off in the dark . . .

In the ether Pyotr lived thousands of millions of years; he saw all the splendour that is concealed from mortal eyes; and only after that did he blissfully return, blissfully half-open his eyes and blissfully see . . .
  . . . that a pale face was bending over him, framed by a dark shawl; and from that face tears dropped onto his breast, and in the raised hands of that sad face, like a crucifix held aloft, a heavy silver object was slowly lowered.
  'Dearest sister,' was uttered, somewhere far off.
  'Sleep, my brother,' came the reply from there.
  She closed his eyes while he was still alive; he departed; he did not come back . . .
  In the sullen light of barely breaking dawn the yellow flame of a candle danced on the table; in the cramped room stood sullen, unmalicious people, while on the floor – Pyotr's body breathed in spasms; without cruelty, with faces bared *they* stood over the body, examining with curiosity what they had done: the deathly blueness, and the trickle of blood that oozed from his lip, which, no doubt, he had bitten through in the heat of the struggle.
  'He's still alive . . .'
  'He's breathing!'
  'Thump him . . .'
  A woman with outstretched arms covered him with a silver dove.
  'Leave him: after all, he's our brother!'

'No, he's a traitor, he is,' Sukhorukov rejoined from the corner, rolling a cigarette.

But she turned round and said reproachfully:

'You don't know: maybe he's a brother too.'

And a whisper of sympathy went all round:

'Poor soul!'

'We haven't finished him off . . .'

'He's going!'

'He's gone!'

'God rest his soul!'

'Got the spades ready?'

'They're ready.'

'Where to?'

'The orchard.'

And once again a voice was heard clearly from the corner:

'That was his own stick I did him with, what he tried to grab away from me on the journey.'

They took his clothes off; they wrapped his body in something (bast matting, probably); and carried it away.

A woman with loosened hair walked in front with the image of a dove in her hands . . .

The morning was cool: the trees were whispering; the purple threads of feathery clouds, bright blood, passed across the sky in bright streams.

Notes

Page 33: '*Wayfarers*'. The planned sequel *Wayfarers* was never written. The only character from *The Silver Dove* to make an appearance in Bely's second novel, *Petersburg*, is the shopkeeper's son Styopka.

The extent to which the sectarians as depicted by Bely correspond to sectarians in real life has been discussed most fully in Aleksandr Etkind, *Khlyst* (The flagellant), Moscow, 1998, pp.428ff. Etkind considers that the features of various members of the sect are derived from different sectarian traditions.

Page 35: *Tselebeyevo*. The name of the village has the connotation of 'hitting the target'.

Page 35: *Whitsuntide*. The action of the novel opens at Whitsuntide, the festival that celebrates the descent of the Holy Spirit, traditionally symbolized by a dove.

Page 35: *Voronyo*. The name Voronyo is derived from *voron*, meaning 'raven', and is the first of several names in the novel incorporating bird imagery, and reflecting in a variety of ways the idea of the interpenetration of earth and heaven.

Page 37: *Likhov*. The name is derived from the adjective *likhoi*, meaning 'evil'.

Page 37: '*The yea-ears have pa-a-assed . . .*' The verse is from a popular song. The same quotation was used by Sergey Solovyov in his original draft of a short story which had considerable similarities with *The Silver Dove*.

Page 37: *Gugolevo*. This is not a 'speaking name' in the same sense as several others in the novel, but carries an obvious reference to Gogol (see Introduction).

Page 38: *Todrabe-Graaben*. The separate elements of this German name mean 'death-raven-grave'; Rabe (raven) echoes the village name Voronyo.

Page 38: *verses of that sort*. The description of Daryalsky's poetry reads as a gentle parody of the poetry of Sergey Solovyov.

Page 39: *spider*. The spider, which appears here for the first time, is a recurrent image of the hero's imprisonment, both literal, in his increasing entrapment by the Doves, and metaphysical, in his inability to escape the pull of the material world. The spider is finally embodied in the four people who create a single eight-legged creature that kills him.

Page 40: *Utkin*. The name Utkin is derived from *utka*, meaning 'duck'.

Page 41: *Kudeyarov*: The name Kudeyarov is associated with the name of the folklore robber Kudeyar (figuring in Nekrasov's poem *Komu na Rusi zhit' khorosho* [Who lives well in Russia]), and also carries echoes of the word *kudesnik*, meaning 'sorcerer'. The name also appears in Dostoevsky's eerie story about the graveyard conversations of corpses, 'Bobok' (1873). V. N. Toporov (see note 17 to Introduction) argues that an examination of the name's etymology shows it to contain meanings of 'god' and 'lover', as well as 'robber', and thus to embody every aspect of the carpenter's relationship with Matryona.

Page 41: *fist*. 'Fist' is a translation of the Russian *shesternya*, which Bely uses here in place of the usual *pyaternya*, indicating that Kudeyarov has six fingers, instead of five. Quite apart from folklore associations with evil, this might indicate a debt to Max Nordau, who included the possession of supernumerary fingers as one of the stigmata betraying degeneration, along with 'the unequal development of the two halves of the face', which is a recurrent element in the description of Kudeyarov. (Max Nordau, *Degeneration*, New York, 1895, p.17.) However, the sixth finger is not a consistent feature of his description; elsewhere the usual word is used.

Page 42: *'Save us from the devil of noonday . . .'* This is an approximation of Psalm 91, vv. 5–6: 'Thou shalt not be afraid . . . for the destruction that wasteth at noonday.'

Page 44: *the velvet sheen of his dark eyes.* The outward appearance of Daryalsky, as described here, is closely modelled on that of Sergey Solovyov.

Page 46: *Golokrestovsky.* The priest's name is derived from *golyi*, meaning 'naked', and *krest*, meaning 'cross'.

Page 47: *Kars.* The fortress of Kars in northern Turkey was the object of repeated battles between Russian and Ottoman forces during the nineteenth century. It was besieged but not taken in 1807; it was taken after heavy artillery bombardment in 1828, but returned to the Turks on the conclusion of peace; it was taken again, with heavy losses, in 1855, but once more returned to the Turks. It was finally taken in 1877 and the province of Kars was incorporated into the Russian Empire from 1878. A. Etkind considers that the priest's drunken performances symbolize Russia's hopeless struggle with the East.

Page 48: *Bishop Mikola.* This name (*svyatitel' Mikola*) is the popular form by which St Nicholas is known.

Page 49: *Ethiopian saint with the head of a dog.* This is probably St Christopher, who is sometimes depicted as cynocephalous on Orthodox icons. The image may also carry echoes of the Egyptian dog-headed god, Anubis.

Page 50: *volost.* This was an administrative district consisting of a group of villages.

Page 50: *Molokans.* The Molokans (milk-drinkers, so named because they did not observe the prohibition against the drinking of milk on fast days) were one of the many sects that flourished in Russia in the late nineteenth century.

Page 59: *Cornfield (Niva)* was a weekly illustrated magazine which published a variety of literary works, both highbrow and lowbrow, in its regular supplements.

Page 59: *Skobelev*. General Skobelev was the hero of the Russian victory over the Turks at the battle of Shipka in 1877 and of the conquest of Central Asia. 'His portrait was sold by peddlers and displayed in magic lantern shows. His death in suspicious circumstances in 1882 completed his elevation to martyrdom . . .' (G. Hosking, *Russia: People and Empire 1552–1917*, London, 1997, p.372.)

Page 61: *Boehme* . . . This eclectic reading list corresponds closely to the pre-occupations of both Sergey Solovyov and Bely himself around the time of the 1905 Revolution.

Page 61: *Diveyevo . . . Optina*. Two of the monasteries that played a crucial part in the revival of the spiritual traditions of Orthodoxy in the nineteenth century. Both are associated with the legacy of St Seraphim of Sarov (1759–1833, canonized 1903). Optina Pustyn', in particular, was a place of pilgrimage for many intellectuals and writers (Gogol, Dostoevsky, Tolstoy), and renowned for its elders (*startsy*).

Page 63: *gull*. This presents a particular problem of translation. The Russian word *rybolov* means 'fisher', but in the context clearly refers to a bird and not a person. Dal's dictionary identifies the word as denoting a gull, using as a synonym the word *chaika*, which is usually translated into English as 'seagull'. However, the action takes place at least five hundred miles from the nearest sea, and there are many different species of freshwater gulls in inland Russia, for which there appear to be no vernacular names in English. So 'gull' it has to be.

Page 64: *'Transvaa-aal, Transvaa-aal . . .'* This song is an adaptation of the poem 'The Boer and his Sons' by Glafira Galina (1899). There was much sympathy among the Russians for the Boers, with whom they identified as a people similarly fighting for freedom. A variant of the song exists in which Transvaal is replaced by Siberia. Two further couplets from it are quoted in this section.

Page 64: *Kobylya Luzha*. This name might be translated as 'Marespuddle'.

Page 65: *the Japanese stirring the people up*. The suggestion that the Japanese are responsible for fomenting discontent among the people is a confusion of the Russo-Japanese war of 1904–5 with the Revolution of 1905–6. However, the Russian defeat in that war was one of the triggers of the revolution, and the image reinforces the notion of Russia divided between West and East.

Page 67: *Serebryanyi Klyuch . . . Myortvyi Verkh*. The names mean 'Silver Spring' and 'Dead Gully'.

Page 67: *Grachikha*. The name is derived from *grach*, meaning 'rook'.

Page 70: *Solovki*. An ancient monastery on an island in the White Sea. It was the site of the earliest resistance to the religious reforms of Patriarch Nikon in 1668, and thus in a sense the birthplace of the *Raskol*, or Schism, to which, even if indirectly, Russian sectarianism can trace its source. *Kiev* was the capital of the first Russian state, and the seat of Prince Vladimir, to whom the Christianization of Russia in 988 is attributed.

Page 71: *Stundists . . . shakers.* The Stundists and shakers (*beguny*, literally 'runners') were sectarian groups.

Page 74: *Pugachov.* The leader of the most extensive peasant revolt against Catherine II in the 1770s. Kudeyarov's mention of him alongside contemporary 'Slocialists', apocalyptic portents and an obvious parody of the Annunciation, typifies the heady mixture of religion and politics that often underlay Russian revolutionary attitudes.

Page 82: *Dvoryanskaya and Tsarskaya.* These street names might be translated as County Drive and King's Avenue.

Page 83: *communion spoon and spear.* In Orthodox ritual the host is broken by the priest with a small spear-shaped instrument, symbolizing the spear that pierced Christ's side on the cross, and is then mixed with wine and offered to the communicants on a small spoon.

Page 84: *Sukhorukov.* The name has the meaning of 'withered hand'.

Page 91: *Mount Tabor.* Although not named in the New Testament account, Mount Tabor is by tradition the location of Christ's transfiguration. (See Matthew ch.17, Mark ch.9, Luke ch.9.)

Page 91: *Cana of Galilee.* According to John ch.2, the site of Christ's first miracle, turning water into wine.

Page 99: *Battle of Leipzig.* The Battle of Leipzig, in which Russian forces fought alongside Prussians and Austrians in an alliance against Napoleon, took place in 1813.

Page 100: *Eckarthausen.* German mystic (1752–1803; also known as Eckhartshausen), whose *Key to the Mysteries of Nature* was published in Russian translation (4 volumes) in 1804–21.

Page 101: *Aristophanes's beetle.* In Aristophanes's comedy *Peace* the character Trygaios flies up to heaven to visit Zeus on a huge dung-beetle, a parody of Pegasus, on whom the hero of Euripides's lost tragedy *Bellerophon* made a similar journey.

Pages 101–2: *Wilamowitz-Moellendorff . . . Brugmann.* Ulrich von Wilamowitz-Moellendorff (1848–1931) was a classical scholar, author of many books on Greek language and culture; Friedrich Karl Brugmann (1849–1919) was a comparative philologist, author of *Comparative Grammar of the Indo-European Languages* (1895).

Page 102: *priest's son.* We know already that Daryalsky is not the son of a priest, but the point of the baroness's remark is to exaggerate the modesty of his background, since the ordinary (that is to say, not monastic) clergy in Russia were by this time an economically and culturally depressed class, largely hereditary.

Page 111: *'A band of fresh warriors . . .'* In tone and metre this recalls the anonymous revolutionary song of the 1870s, '*Vy zhertvoyu pali v bor'be rokovoi*' (You fell as victims in the fateful struggle), which is referred to in the next paragraph. No version of the song has been located that actually contains this line, but, since such songs often existed in several versions, it is possible that such a variant did exist; it is equally possible that Bely invented it.

Page 113: *Theocritus*. Theocritus serves as a link between the bucolic tradition in ancient Greek poetry and Daryalsky's vision of the Russian peasantry's potential. The man locked in the cedar chest was Osiris, regarded as the Egyptian form of the god Dionysus. The god Pan was a member of the retinue of Dionysus. Yevseich's confusion of this name with the Polish title 'Pan' hints at the identification of Katya with Pani Katerina (see Introduction, page 14).

Page 116: *swallow . . . house-martin*. As competing symbols of the soul, these birds have a special prominence among the bird imagery of the novel.

Page 121: *Bulldog*. The Webley Bulldog was a revolver widely used for self-protection before the First World War. Bely possessed one himself during the period of unrest in which the novel's action is set.

Page 123: *Chizhikov*. This name closely resembles the name of Gogol's hero in *Dead Souls*, Chichikov. The resemblance is particularly noticeable in the uncertainty surrounding his real identity. The plethora of unlikely explanations with which this section ends recalls the scenes in Gogol's novel where Chichikov is imagined to be either Napoleon, escaped from St Helena, or the legless soldier turned brigand, Captain Kopeikin.

Page 125: The reference to *General Skobelev* (see above, note to page 59) returning as a robber evokes with particular clarity the traditional linkage between the pretender and the brigand, seen for instance in the person of Pugachov. The adjective 'white', applied to General Skobelev, has the connotation of 'sent by God to save' – to save the Bulgarians from the Turks, originally, but undoubtedly in popular imagination also to save the Russian people from tyranny. The robber *Churkin* is a kind of Robin Hood figure from a popular lowbrow novel. All three parts of the name *Gudi-Gudai-Zatrubinsky* have to do with blowing trumpets.

Page 125: *Third Department*. The Tsarist secret police.

Page 126: *Eth-R . . . Eth-D*. The Socialist Revolutionaries (SR) and the Social Democrats (SD) were the principal opposition parties in Russia.

Page 131: *Chukholka*. Chukholka is a parody of Georgy Chulkov (1879–1939), the author of the brochure *On Mystical Anarchism* (1906), in which he expounded a lightweight metaphysical doctrine based on Ivan Karamazov's rejection not of God, but of God's world. In subsequent polemics Bely anathematized Chulkov and everyone thought to be associated with him, including Vyacheslav Ivanov, who had written a foreword to Chulkov's volume, and Blok, who was mistakenly reported to be a member of the group of Mystical Anarchists. There were real and valid philosophical reasons for Bely's opposition to this theory, but the vehemence of his response is more easily explicable in personal terms: it was with Chulkov that Lyubov Dmitrievna Blok had sought solace after the non-realization of her relationship with Bely.

Page 131: *Du Prel.* The Du Prel that Chukholka is reading is almost certainly Carl du Prel (1839–99), the author of numerous mystical works published in German and extensively translated into Russian. This is unlikely to be a reference to Raoul du Prel (1316–82), the French translator of St Augustine, as is stated in the notes to one of the Russian editions of the novel.

Page 136: *'is it true . . . ?'* This scene seems to carry an echo of the scene in Tolstoy's *Anna Karenina* in which Levin invites his bride-to-be, Kitty, to read the diaries that record his pre-marital affairs.

Page 138: *Scoundrels!* Among the retinue of Dionysus there figured the satyrs, who were renowned, among other things, for their delight in chasing nymphs. The nymphs were associated with rivers and streams. This scene seems to have little purpose unless it is read as a parody of the Greek myth.

Pages 143–4: *'Why, you wayward woman, do you . . .'* The songs here and at the opening of the next section have not been traced to any precise source, but they clearly exemplify the genre of the *zhestokii romans*, 'cruel romance', typically a ballad of love betrayed. 'Why, you wayward woman . . .' is also quoted by Bely in a poem of 1906, which would seem to confirm its status as a real song of the time.

Page 147: *Malanya.* The red woman Malanya is a quasi-folklore figure derived from an untranslatable pun on the Russian for 'lightning', *molniya*. However, the song about goggle-eyed Malanya is a real *chastushka* (a form of urban folk poetry) which was well known at the time, and had been quoted in a story by Leonid Andreyev in 1904. The story was reviewed by Blok, and a clear line has been traced between this quotation and similar *chastushka* quotations in Blok's *The Twelve*. (See M. Petrovsky, 'U istokov "Dvenadtsati"', *Literaturnoe obozrenie*, 1980 no.11, pp.20–27.) V. N. Toporov, describing this as the 'most mythological' section of the novel, points to its connection with the primeval Balto-Slavonic myth of the sexual union of thunder and lightning, conferring fecundity upon the earth.

Page 150: *three feast days of Our Lord.* The Orthodox year includes three Saviour's days, celebrated (according to the Julian calendar, in operation in Russia until 1918, and still used for church festivals) on the 1st, 6th and 16th of August. The second of these coincides with the celebration of the Transfiguration.

Page 155: *Nenila.* A name taken from Nekrasov's poem 'The Forgotten Village' (1855) about an old peasant woman's vain hopes of redress from an absentee landlord. Styopka's other poems do not appear to have identifiable models.

Page 161: *the old oak-tree.* The complex symbolism of this passage has been well described by Maria Carlson: '. . . the scene is constructed of both pagan and Christian motifs. Sitting in the tree, crowned with a fir branch, Daryalsky is the dead Osiris in the trunk of the cedar tree; he is the horned Dionysus in the ark of wood, ready to be sacrificed in his form as Dionysus Dendritis; he is the Christ, who, knowing that crucifixion lies ahead, puts on the crown of thorns as a token of his passion. His blackened face, smeared with ashes, harks back to ancient death rituals. The ancient oak, sacred to many deities, foreshadows another sacred tree:

the Tree of Death, the Cross.' (M. Carlson, 'The Silver Dove' [cited in note 11 to Introduction], p.82.)

Page 162: *Blue oceans.* The 'blue oceans' of Matryona's eyes are a feature specifically derived from Lyubov Dmitrievna Blok.

Page 163: *oprichnik.* A member of Ivan the Terrible's private army, the *oprichnina.*

Page 163: *murmolka.* A warm winter hat which features in folktales.

Page 163: *a broom and a dog's head.* These were the symbolic appurtenances of the *oprichnina.* 'This means that first of all they bite like dogs, and then they sweep away everything superfluous out of the land.' (G. Hosking, *Russia: People and Empire*, p.54.)

Page 178: *enemies.* The idea expressed here by Schmidt that Russia is in thrall to alien forces that must be overcome by vigilance and battle is close to the tenor of Blok's poem-cycle of 1908, 'On Kulikovo Field'.

Pages 181–2: *Schmidt was sitting immersed in papers.* On the horoscope, see Introduction, page 18. The occult references in this section are derived from a variety of sources. They consist of an amalgam of different traditions – ancient Egyptian, Alexandrian, Neoplatonic, medieval European, Kabbalistic, all filtered, undoubtedly, through the theosophy of Helena Blavatsky. The *Kabbalah* is not a single book, but the name given to the Jewish mystical tradition as a whole, and it is therefore not correct to speak of it as 'in an expensive binding'. Similarly *Merkabah* is not the name of a book, but a term referring collectively to the ten Sefirot (see below). The *Zohar* is the Book of Splendour, the 'Bible' of the Kabbalah, whose putative author is the second-century AD Palestinian Jewish scholar Simeon Ben Yochai. *Sifra Di-Zeniuta* is the 'Book of Concealment', part of the Zohar. The book attributed to Abraham is the Sefer Yetzirah, the 'Book of Creation'. *Kether* – the crown – is the name of the first Sefirah, one of the ten attributes by which the unknown God has chosen to reveal himself. (I am indebted to my colleague Professor Philip Alexander for these details – translator.)

Page 182: *Lucius Firmicus* may be a reference to Julius Firmicus, fourth-century Roman mathematician and astronomer. The astronomy and astrology of *Ptolemy* were the basis of all such science until the sixteenth century. *Clement of Alexandria* (d. before 215) was believed to have recorded in his notes known as the *Stromata* extracts of ancient hermetic texts, including parts of the works of Hermes Trismegistris, the mythological originator of the doctrine, identified also with the god Thoth. *Hammer*: Joseph von Hammer-Purgstahl (1774–1856), an Austrian orientologist. The *Ophites* were a gnostic sect founded in Syria in the second century. The *Knights Templar* were an order founded in Jerusalem around 1118 to protect the Temple. The *legend of Titurel*, who, as reward for his valour and humility, was vouchsafed a sight of the Holy Grail, is to be found in such works of medieval literature as Wolfram von Eschenbach's *Parsifal*. *The Pastor of the Peoples* was one of the legendary works of Hermes Trismegistris, preserved by Clement of Alexandria.

Quitolath ... Xiron ... Atoim ... Dinaim ... Ur ... Zain. The names of some of
the arcana. In his *Histoire de la magie, du monde surnaturel, et de la fatalité à travers
les temps et les peuples* (Paris, 1870; translated by James Kirkup and Julian Shaw as
The History and Practice of Magic, Secaucus, NJ, 1972), Paul Christian describes an
initiation ceremony held by the Egyptian magi inside the temple of the Sphinx at
Gizeh. Part of this ceremony consisted of walking through a gallery of twenty-two
pairs of pictures, the twenty-two arcana, symbolic hieroglyphs, 'each of whose
attributes conceals a certain meaning and which, taken as a whole, compose an
absolute doctrine memorized by its correspondence with the Letters of the sacred
language and with the Numbers that are connected with these letters.' Thus the
'crown of the Magi – T = 400' is Thoth, the Egyptian god who was in mythology
the founder of the secret knowledge. (For these details I am indebted to Professor
Maria Carlson – translator.)

Page 183: *the brotherhood.* This is a general reference to secret theosophical
societies with which Bely had connections at the time of writing the novel, and
specifically to his relations with the self-appointed emissary of theosophy to
Russia, Anna Mintslova.

Page 184: *cherry jam.* The cherry jam which takes the place of blood in this
domestic fracas is an echo of the scene in Blok's play *The Puppet-Booth* (1906), in
which a clown, struck down with a wooden sword, bleeds cranberry juice. The
central action of Blok's play, a version of the love triangle of Harlequin, Pierrot and
Columbine, bore an unmistakable resemblance to the triangle of Blok, Bely and
Lyubov Dmitrievna.

Page 188: *La Mascotte.* A comic opera by Henri Chivot and Alfred Duru, with
music by Edmond Audran.

Page 189: *zemstvo.* An elected local government body, introduced as part of
Alexander II's reforms in 1864.

Page 194: *Kadet.* A member of the Constitutional Democrats, a liberal reformist
party in the post-1905 parliament (Duma), largely supported by property-owners.
The party was known by its initials K-D, hence 'Kadet'.

Page 199: *Kashchey the Deathless.* A folklore figure who acts as a harbinger of evil
fortune. He is emaciated (the name is probably derived from *kost'*, meaning 'bone'),
wealthy and miserly.

Page 203: *healing.* The Russian word *tselebnyi* creates an untranslatable pun on the
name of the village.

Page 208: *durachki.* A simple card-game. The name might be translated as
'simpletons'.

Page 209: *into a nunnery.* In the suggestion of entering a nunnery, and in the
description of Baron Todrabe-Graaben's upbringing, there are echoes of
Turgenev's *Home of the Gentry* (1859), a novel which similarly charts the alienation
of the educated classes from the Russia of the ordinary people. The eccentricities
of the Todrabe-Graaben family are modelled, according to Bely's memoirs, partly

upon one of his uncles and partly upon Vladimir Ivanovich Taneyev, the brother of the composer, Sergey Taneyev.

Page 219: *'In my youth's still vernal hour . . .'* The verses here and in the last section of Chapter 6 are derived from real sectarian songs that were published by V. D. Bonch-Bruevich in 1908. Bely selected and adapted the songs to give them a relevance to the plot of the novel, to the destiny of Daryalsky and the betrayal of Katya.

Page 222: *King David before the Ark of the Covenant*. See II Samuel ch. 6.

Page 224: *A certain decadent*. The decadent who papered his room in black and later disappeared was Aleksandr Dobrolyubov (see Introduction, page 16). The other characters mentioned here probably also have real prototypes in the poet Valery Bryusov's sister, Nadezhda Yakovlevna (1881–1951), and the poet Leonid Semyonov (see Introduction, page 16).

Page 225: *a poet he had once loved*. The poet is Blok; the lines are a slight misquotation from a poem of Blok's written in 1906 and dedicated in the manuscript to Bely. Blok's lines are in turn an echo of a similar passage in Bely's *Second (Dramatic) Symphony* (1902). Blok noted this sympathetic reference to their shared preoccupations in a letter to his mother of 1 April 1910 and evidently understood it as a conciliatory move on Bely's part.

Page 239: *'A wonderful sea is the sacred Baikal . . .'* This is derived from a poem by Dmitry Davydov (1811–88), written in 1858, which became popular among the left-wing intelligentsia and political exiles. It was one of the most widely heard songs during the 1905 Revolution. *Barguzin* is the name given to a north-easterly wind that blows on Lake Baikal.

Page 246: *the Beheading of John the Baptist*. The Feast of the Beheading of St John the Baptist occurs on 29 August (Old Style). It is more commonly known in the Western church as the Feast of the Decollation of St John the Baptist, but I have preferred a word that comes nearer to the Russian in its directness.

Page 250: *'Transvaal . . .'* Further lines from the song quoted in Chapter 1; see above, note to page 64.

Page 252: *terror, the snare, and the pit*. See Isaiah ch.24, v.17.

Page 262: *The Fourth*. The title of the chapter refers back to the assertion in Chapter 5 that 'all material substance is calculated by the number four' (see above, page 182). There are four participants in the 'making' in Chapter 6, indicating that this rite is in fact material, or carnal, in nature, rather than spiritual. The devil, moreover, is the fourth member of the Trinity. Four people are involved in the killing of Daryalsky.

Page 265: *Kircher . . . Fludd*. Athanasius Kircher (1601–80) was a Jesuit priest and a scholar, author of 44 books, sometimes called the last Renaissance man. Robert Fludd (1574–1637) was a British physician, author and mystical philosopher.

Page 281: *'Look, lads, a fire!'* The fire is the realization of the metaphor of the 'red cockerel', but is also associated with Dionysian imagery (see Introduction).

Page 284: *And Pyotr's soul was bathed in tears.* The sacrifice with which Dionysian rites were accompanied betokened cleansing, which is evidently represented by Daryalsky's tears.

Page 304: *A woman with outstretched arms.* The gesture of the woman who covers the dying Daryalsky with an image of the silver dove appears to be an imitation of the Pietà. Maria Carlson has pointed out how the death of Daryalsky re-enacts the sacrificial death of the god in Dionysian and other similar early religions. 'Like Dionysus, whose dismembered body was distributed among the celebrants to take home for burial in their orchards and vineyards for its fructifying powers, Daryalsky, now the "fruit of the cross", is buried in a garden in anticipation of his future "germination".' (M. Carlson, 'The Silver Dove', pp.89–90.) Other interpretations of Daryalsky's death include the suggestion that it may be likened to marriage, as perceived by certain sectarian groups, and that it is to be understood not as death at all, but as castration.

Page 305: In the 1922 edition of the novel, the text ends at 'the trees were whispering'.